Shattered by YOU

BOOK 3: TEAR ASUNDER

NASHODA ROSE

Shattered by You
Published by Nashoda Rose
Copyright © 2015 by Nashoda Rose
Toronto, Canada

ISBN: 978-1-987953-03-9

Copyright © 2015 Cover design by Kari Ayasha, Cover to Cover Designs
(http://www.covertocoverdesigns.com/)
Cover Photo by Invicta's Art Photography
Model: James Clippinger
Content Edited by Kristin Anders, The Romantic Editor
(http://www.theromanticeditor.com/)
Editing by Hot Tree Editing
(http://www.hottreeediting.com/)
Formatted by Champagne Formats
www.champagneformats.com

*Any editing issues are my own. I'm Canadian and on occasion I may use the Canadian spelling rather than U.S.

Books by Nashoda Rose

Seven Sixes (2016)

Tear Asunder Series
With You (free)
Torn from You
Overwhelmed by You
Shattered by You
Untitled (Kite's Story)

Unyielding Series
Perfect Chaos
Perfect Ruin (Fall/Winter 2015)
Perfect Rage (Date TBA)

Scars of the Wraith Series
Stygian
Take

http://www.nashodarose.com/

Dedication

To my incredible beta readers.
Your insight and feedback are invaluable.
Each of you have left your imprint
in my books, and for that I'm forever grateful.
Know that you're appreciated and loved.

Warning

Shattered by You contains dark elements and may cause triggers for drug use and references to nonconsensual sex. If you are uncomfortable with this or/and explicit sex, harsh language, and disturbing scenes, then this book might not be for you.

*Mature audiences only.

A note from Haven

When I was five years old, my brother taught me how to sing. I practiced all the time as I lay on the saggy cot in the walk-in closet with the tattered sheet pulled up to my chin.

The whistle of the cold winter air drifted through the rotting windowsills and I'd cover my ears and quietly sing to block it out. My mom once told me the wind was a monster with huge claw-like hands and no teeth. He had a black hole where his mouth was supposed to be; that's where the whistling came from. She said his arms were like elastic bands and when kids were bad, he'd slide through the cracks in the house and snatch them away.

The wind scared me.

I didn't want to be taken away from my brother, Ream.

The winter months were the worst and some nights Ream would sneak into my closet and sing with me. But we had to be quiet. Mom didn't like singing. My brother never worried about being caught, but I did because then I wouldn't see him for days.

It wasn't just the wind. It was the noises; groans of the house, shrieks from my mother and her friends, things breaking and the shouts and laughter.

Then the silence.

That scared me the most because I didn't know if Mom left us again.

Days alone in the house, no food, nothing to do but wait . . . for what I didn't know. But Ream looked after me. He never let me go hungry for long. He protected me . . . until he couldn't any longer.

We all know the definition of shattered: to break into pieces; to weaken, destroy; to damage, as by breaking or crushing.

But my story isn't about being shattered.

It's about surviving the pieces.

It's about the strength found within the damaged.

It's about love. Love found despite the jagged, tainted edges of who I'd become.

Warning: parts are ugly and dark. But there is beauty, too, and that is why we are here.

Haven

Chapter One

Haven

July 2014

MY FEET SLID in the spongey wet grass as the rain teemed. The heavy sludge of mud on the soles of my shoes bogged me down and I fell, landing hard on my hands and knees, panting.

The wind whistled through the trees, fragile branches snapped and plummeted to the ground, forgotten limbs broken under nature's fury.

The monsters lived, but they'd never catch me.

I'd survived them.

I crawled to my feet again and ran, fighting against the wind as it tried to push me back. I put my head down like a bull and fought it. Fought nature. Fought the haunting memories. Fought the pain.

Tonight unravelled me. I'd been able to keep the horrific memories hidden for months, but seeing the news about a mutilated body of a drug dealer named Olaf Gordenski, found washed up on shore, was as if a tornado slammed into me and everything surfaced at once. I didn't think. I ran. It was the only way to bury the emotions again.

He was dead.

Olaf was dead. Mutilated.

I wanted to feel relief, but my past burned in my chest like a volcano threatening to erupt.

I knew who was responsible. Deck. Or one of his ex-military men who worked for him at his not-so-legal company, Unyielding Riot. Deck was friends with my brother and after I escaped my hell, I told him about Olaf. My brother had already given Deck information on him, but what my brother didn't know was about the club, the illegal club, with girls who didn't want to be there. Girls like me who were taken there and forced to strip and keep men happy in the backrooms.

Anything I told Deck was confidential, him and his men only. 'Nothing touches me,' were his words. I didn't trust him. I didn't trust anyone, but I had no choice. Olaf had to die. Not only because he deserved it, but because he had always threatened to come after Ream.

He'd kept me prisoner for over a decade. He kept other girls too, although I was the only one who lived, or rather existed, in his house. Even at the club, I was kept separate, never allowed to talk to them.

There was an alarm on the house preventing me from escaping, although that wasn't all that stopped me. I stayed to protect my brother. But that reason detonated the moment Alexa, Olaf's psycho bitch, kidnapped my brother and his fiancée, Kat, a few months ago, which led to my escape. Alexa had been so focused on getting Ream back that she made the grave mistake of not locking me up.

I grunted as I fell again and my hands dug into the mud. The wind eased as if it were giving me a reprieve or maybe it was merely out of breath from laughing at me, knowing I was weakening.

My thighs quivered and my chest hurt as I struggled to breathe. I had to go farther. A little longer. My past would never have me again. Conquer. Destroy. Bleed the memories.

Bang.

Bang.

Bang.

I shot to my feet and ran with the memory of the vibration in my hand as I pulled the trigger. But it wasn't a gun now; it was mud clenched in my fists. I'd killed. I'd ended three lives and I had no remorse or regret.

I'd watched blood leak into their clothes, eyes widen with shock and then the light fade from them as they died. And still my hand remained steady. The satisfaction of killing them lost to the numbness in which I'd encased myself.

But that was months ago and now . . . now my pores leaked poison and tried to unlock the pain I'd kept veiled.

Strength and resolve. I had to be strong. Fight harder. Do whatever it took. No one would ever control me again. The wind was my proof. If I defeated it, it wouldn't slip through the cracks and let the monsters in.

I stumbled as the ground dipped and my ankle buckled. I crashed to my knees, and a sharp pain shot through me as my right knee landed on a rock. I remained still for a second as my chest heaved in and out while I hung my head low.

My blonde hair curtained my face in thick wet strands as the rain pounded harsh, relentless pellets into my body, over and over again. My shirt and sweatpants stuck to me like heavy cool blankets; blankets of pain and a weight of memories that refused to die.

I raked my fingers into the wet earth and crawled. I had to get the numbness back, kill the emotions, but there were so many faces, so many monsters. Gerard. Alexa. Olaf. The men, who grabbed and pulled at me, touched me, ripped me apart. Even their whistles and hollers haunted me, just like the wind.

Nature tried to defeat me, but I wouldn't break under its rage.

My knees suctioned into the earth as I continued to crawl up the hill. With each ragged breath, my chest burned as if it had been set on fire. But pain drove the body to do more than you'd think possible. I knew about pain and anguish. I knew if I pushed hard enough, the pain would fade into the darkness again.

It made you stronger.

It made you do things you never thought you could do.

It made you fight harder.

The skies lit up in a flash of forked lightning, and then a few seconds later, a thundering boom crackled. My trembling thighs buckled and I lay flat on my stomach. Blades of grass tickled my lower lip and I tasted wetness mixed with soil on the tip of my tongue.

The rhythmic drum of rain hit the surface of my body, a comfort as I lay heaving on the ground. I needed this to drive my pain back so no one would see it.

Especially Ream. I saw the way he watched me and it was with fear, afraid of what I'd suffered while we were apart for twelve years. I'd never tell him. I'd never tell anyone. That was mine to own, bury and destroy.

Ream was leaving with his band, Tear Asunder, to go on tour and he'd refuse to go if he knew what stormed inside me. Even after being separated since we were sixteen, Ream still wanted to protect me. But there was nothing of me to protect anymore. And it was my turn to protect him—from me.

The memories had tried to weed their way back into me, but running trapped them. At that moment, it was all I had. I could keep the brewing storm at bay and make my way to normal. I had to find normal.

"Jesus. What the hell?"

I jerked and my breath hitched as the voice sounded behind me. I knew who it was and leapt to my feet, but the mud gave way and I slipped as I tried to get my footing. I didn't bother to look at him as I finally gained traction and took off up the hill for the maze of the woods in the distance.

"Haven." Booted feet came after me.

Shit. No one could see me like this. Crisis was my brother's best friend, his foster brother and bandmate. He'd tell Ream.

I heard a loud thump, a grunt and then, "Fuck."

I ran faster, while putting my hand in my coat pocket and touching the familiar hard metal. Even if Olaf was dead, I needed this. My control. My safety. My protection. I gritted my teeth, fighting the urge to yank out the gun and make him stop. Make everything stop.

But I had splinters of sanity still inside me and that would lead down a path far from what I was searching for.

It was as if I ran in slow motion, the weight of the rain, the mud, my exhausted limbs, and the wind attempting to push me back down the hill. Vulnerability. It led to pain so horrific that it bled your insides into a sea of poison. Weakness killed. Weakness destroyed.

I heard his heavy breathing and a tremor of fear shot through me as the flash of men panting, eyes glazed with alcohol and lust.

God, the lust. I hated that the most.

His body hit hard as he crashed into me, sending us both to the ground. He took the brunt of the fall as he rolled at the last second, so I landed on my back on top of his chest.

Still, the wind knocked out of me and it took a second before I was able to breathe.

"What the hell are you doing out here?" he shouted above the roar of the storm.

"Let. Go." I twisted to escape him, but his muscled, tatted arms were unmoveable as they curled around my chest. I'd been in his arms once before a couple months earlier, when he grabbed me at the cottage and jumped off the cliff into the water. It had been two months after I'd escaped and I hadn't wanted to go to the cottage with the band, Kat and Emily. But the only way my brother would go was if I went with them.

I didn't know how to swim though and when Crisis snagged me around the waist laughing as we sailed through the air and submerged beneath the cool surface, I clung to him. I'd had no choice.

Now, I did.

But as I lay against his chest, both of us breathing hard, his arms like a cocoon of protective warmth . . . I wanted to stay here and forget why I carried a gun. Why I was better alone. Why I had to run to keep the memories away.

I wanted to feel protected and safe for one moment before I had to fight again. Because that was what I did every single day—fought. It was just a different fight than it was before.

"I'm not going to hurt you."

Maybe not, but he was a threat to my numbness, my cool exterior I'd taken years to build. Because when I looked at him, the brilliance of his bright blue eyes often filled with laughter, mesmerized me.

"Why did you run from me? Fuck, why the hell are you running in a goddamn thunderstorm in an open fuckin' field?"

I tried to elbow him in the ribs, but he was quick and tightened his arms so I had no momentum.

"Just stop for a sec," he growled. "Haven, seriously, what the fuck?"

My voice vibrated from the cold. "I want to be alone. Get your hands off me. Now."

"You've been alone for months." The thunder drowned out the force of his words, but I felt the deep rumble from his chest sink into my back.

The intensity of the rain picked up as we lay silent and still for a minute, as if both of us were deciding our next best move. Physically fighting against those who were stronger was pointless. All it did was weaken you. Instead, I made it an inner battle, taking my mind to another place. And that was how I won. That was how I survived.

But Crisis holding me, the wind whistling around us, horrific memories looming but unable to touch me as I lay protected in his arms . . . it made me want to stay. To be that little girl who sang to herself in the closet, her brother always near to protect her.

Yeah, well, singing didn't hack it anymore. It hadn't in a long time.

"How did you find me?" It was close to midnight, in the pouring rain, the only light offered from the lightning and . . . my reflective jacket. *Shit, that's how he saw me.*

"Saw movement out in the field as I drove up to the house. I thought one of the horses freaked in the storm and escaped the barn. If I let you go, are you going to run?"

Was I? Maybe, but I wouldn't tell him that. I also didn't lie, so I stayed silent. Few people realized what a powerful weapon silence was. I knew.

Our chests rose and fell in perfect rhythm. I parted my lips and wetness slipped into my mouth. I relished the sweet sensation of the cool rain sliding down my throat.

"Haven?" He squeezed me. "Is this what you've been doing when you disappear all the time? Running?"

I waited for the flash of light to fork across the sky, the power in its grasp able to kill, maim or set fire. I had that in me. The ability to kill without remorse, without thought. It was beauty and destruction, like me.

His fingers linked with mine on my abdomen, just above where the gun sat hidden in my jacket. "Open field. Thunderstorm. Not the smartest time to be running."

No, but the power it conveyed sunk into me with every roar of thunder, every flash of light lending me its strength to fight the memories.

He sat up, bringing me with him so I was between his bent legs, his thighs caging me in. "Don't take off," he whispered as his arms released me, but not completely. Instead, he slid his hands down my arms to my hands that now rested on my thighs. "Jesus, you're freezing. We need to get you out of the rain and dried off."

But I wasn't ready yet. I still had monsters lurking. The memories and emotions weren't shoved away in the little compartments of my mind. "Not yet."

"Yeah, yet." He shuffled back and came to his feet, then moved around to stand in front of me.

I remained sitting on the ground, watching him, assessing what he was going to do next. I'd learned to read people, guess their next move before they made it.

He reached out his hand, the ink on his tatted arm vivid from the rain.

"Take it or I'll throw you over my shoulder." His hand was steady and strong. "Not leaving you out here, Haven."

If I laughed, which I didn't, it would've been then because he'd never get me over his shoulder. Not before I had a gun in his face.

And there it was, the set jaw, the narrowed eyes, the lowering of his brows—determination. I knew when someone wasn't going to concede.

Since I'd been on the farm, I'd kept my distance from everyone, but I watched, always watched. From what I'd seen of Crisis, he was laid back, playful and flirted religiously. But with that came confidence and perseverance.

I suspected Crisis wouldn't back down from much, if anything.

And as he towered over me, a soaking wet mass of muscled strength, I knew he'd attempt to pick me up and carry me back to the house if I didn't take his hand. So, my options were take his hand, or take out my gun. Option two led to my brother finding out. And that would lead to the tour being cancelled because he found out I carried a gun and was running in a violent thunderstorm.

Ream would give up everything for me. He had. Even parts of himself he could never get back. But when I looked at him now, he'd found peace with what he'd endured as a teenager. I'd never take that away.

I'd tackle my own demons.

I reached up and Crisis' hand grabbed mine. He pulled me to my feet to stand inches away from him. My eyes slid over his face as the lightning flashed across the sky. I looked for the familiar ease in his expression that I'd found myself searching for every time I saw him. It was comforting, warm, and radiated an energy that sparked something inside me.

But it wasn't there this time. Instead, his eyes were dark to match his harsh expression. I lowered my gaze to stare at the small space between our feet. Not because I feared him or gave into him, but because acting compliant led to an advantage over your opponent; it let down their guard.

"Your brother's home." My brother and Kat had gone to Logan and Emily's farm down the road. From what I'd overheard, the girls wanted to discuss wedding plans and the guys were working on lyrics for a new song. "He'll freak if he sees you." My eyes darted to his and my breath locked in my chest. Crisis knew I wouldn't want Ream to see me like this.

"Then why make me go?" Make was a strong word, used for his benefit. The reality was he couldn't make me do anything.

"Babe, I honestly don't think anyone can *make* you do anything." My eyes narrowed because he'd read my exact thought and obviously knew me better than I'd anticipated. "Especially with that gun in your pocket." My breath locked and I put my hand on it. "Come on, we'll go to the barn to get you dried off. I think there's a raincoat in there to cover up the mud all over you."

I thought about it for a second, like five seconds, then nodded and a wet clump of hair fell in front of my eye. Crisis reached up and tucked it back behind my ear before I could react and back away. There was nothing in his expression that was the usual flirty charm he constantly displayed, although ever since he jumped off the cliff with me, he kept the flirting minimal. It may have had something to do with my knee jamming into his balls once we reached shore.

Our hands remained linked, more because I was being accommodating since he wasn't planning to tell my brother. My legs wobbled, the muscles protesting after the over-exertion of my run. He must have noticed because he let go of my hand and instead, put his arm around my waist to steady me.

I stiffened, clamped my jaw and trudged forward. Why fight a battle that would do more harm than good? I'd learned that while handcuffed to a bed, unable to get away while some stranger hovered over me with lust in his eyes. Save it for when you knew you had a chance at winning.

And I did. I fought before I was handcuffed. Unfortunately for me, they'd liked the fight.

The barn door creaked as he opened it and the horses nickered. Crisis flicked on a dim overhead light and a few horses stomped their hooves and bobbed their heads over their half-doors.

It was well after midnight, so night check had already been done by Hank, the elderly gentleman who lived in his own place at the back of the property. Crisis released me and walked down the aisle, stroking muzzles along the way. He grabbed a few flakes of hay from the end of the aisle and tossed one in each stall. When he was done, his shirt and wet jeans were covered in little pieces of alfalfa.

He peered down at himself. "Fuck. I look like I rolled in basil." He brushed himself off, green flecks falling to the cement, but most stuck to his wet denim jeans.

I stood where he left me, watching him. His hair dangled across the side of his face in wet loose curls. It wasn't long enough to sit content behind his ears, but long enough to look messy and dishevelled.

His brows pulled together and it caused a crease between his eyes. Annoyed maybe, something I'd rarely witnessed from Crisis. Despite avoiding him and everyone else, I was still aware of each of them. But Crisis was the only one who was impervious to my cold and aloof disposition. My brother treated me like a piece of glass, and maybe I was, but I liked to think it was bulletproof.

Water puddled at my feet as it dripped off my clothes and hair. I stood like a statue under the light bulb, an illuminated circle around me, bright at my feet then slowly fading out.

The protection from the wind and rain eased my shivering, but goose bumps still rose beneath my heavy wet clothes.

Crisis straightened and our eyes met.

He stood ten feet away, but it felt as if he was next to me. I expected to see desire smoldering because that was what I was used to around men. It was what I expected from every guy, not that I considered myself beautiful or irresistible, but twelve years filled with men's leering eyes on me, solidified the predictability of what to anticipate from them.

But despite the trained response in me, Crisis was different. I was beginning to realize that in the few months I'd lived on the farm with him, Kite—the drummer in the band—my brother and Kat. Still, my mind fought against it, unwilling to let anything good in because good didn't happen.

I ran my finger over the scorched words Olaf branded on my wrist. I'd been an object. A possession. Not for Olaf to use, but for others. I'd made him a lot of money.

"Come here," Crisis said. He didn't wait to see if I'd follow him as he turned and strode into an empty stall on the right.

I hesitated, not because I was scared, more because I waited for the numbness. It was what I'd been searching for on my run, the embrace of the shield of detachment.

I took several long deep breaths, the wind whistling but no longer haunting as I closed it off.

I slipped my hand into my pocket, felt the comfort of the gun and then followed him, my muddy wet shoes leaving footprints on the rough cement. Clifford, Kat's appaloosa horse, reached his neck out as far as he could, tilted his head and flapped his lips as he tried to grab hold of my shirt on my way past.

I stepped to the side, ignoring him and entered the stall. Crisis held a handful of yellow straw in his hand. He nodded to the bales in the corner. "Sit."

"Why?"

There was no grin and I didn't like that. I liked his grin. I liked how it eased some of the tension in my chest. "Do you plan on arguing with me for long? Because if you are then I'm going to sit down for it."

I sat on the straw bale.

He approached and I was unclear what he was going to do until I felt the roughness of the straw on my head. I darted to the side, my hand latching onto his wrist. "What are you doing?"

"How do you think they dry off horses?"

I frowned. "I'm not a horse."

He smirked and I saw that familiar flash of play in his eyes. I waited for his smartass remark; I'd overheard enough of what he said to know Crisis had a mouth on him. "No. But you're wet."

I had no idea if he meant that as anything but literal, but he didn't chuckle or wink. He merely stepped close enough so his calf brushed against my thigh, then began to rub straw in circular motions on my head.

I let him.

I picked my battles carefully and this was one that didn't need fighting. He was attempting to help me so if Ream saw me when I got back to the house, I'd at least appear half-decent.

An odd sensation hit my chest and there was a slight twitch at the corner of my mouth as I thought of what he was doing. It was mildly ridiculous. No, it was utterly ridiculous.

I sat in a stall, soaking wet while the bass guitarist of a hit rock band rubbed my head with horse bedding.

But I didn't smile, and laughter hadn't passed my lips since I was sixteen. Since before Gerard. Before the drugs. Before Ream and I were separated.

A few pieces of straw fell in front of my face and onto my lap and I stared at them, now damp and flimsy, having soaked up the water from my hair. Crisis' hand slowed and I noticed he barely had any straw left in his grasp; it was his hand stroking my hair.

I stiffened and his hand slipped away. I looked up and froze when I saw he was already watching me. The deep contours of his face were accentuated as he scowled, brows low, shadowing the magnetic blue in his eyes.

"Don't know what to do here." He sighed then crouched between my legs, palms on either side of me, resting on the bale of straw. I kept my eyes on him, watching for any hints of lust.

But it never appeared and my shoulders sagged, not enough for him to notice, but it was inside me, an inner relief that he wasn't helping me in order to get in my pants. He looked genuinely concerned and that worried me too because he and Ream were like brothers.

"Don't tell him," I said firmly, my voice steady, the shivering minimal.

"Can't do that." I clenched my jaw and glared. "You're his sister. He loves you and wants to help."

"I don't need help." His brows lifted. "I. Don't. Need. Help."

"You rarely talk, not even to your twin brother who you haven't seen in twelve years. You don't smile and sure as fuck don't laugh. I get that you went through some serious shit and I'm not going to pretend I know—"

"Then don't." I had to give him something to chew. Something to convince him I didn't need help because there was no way in hell I was going to sit on a couch and spill my life story to some pompous ass who probably had seen me naked at the club, then fucked me. "I'm starting university soon. I'm fine."

"Because you enrolled in school means you're fine?"

"It means I've moved on." That was what I was trying to do. Move on. Get a degree in Sociology, do what I never had a chance to do before . . . live and make something of myself. I swore if I ever escaped, I wouldn't waste my life, my freedom.

"Moving on? Do you really want to go there? Because I'm standing in a barn in the middle of the night in a fuckin' storm with a girl shivering, muddy and wet, with a gun in her pocket."

He was right. But I'd find a way back to the numb like I always did.

He reached up and picked a few pieces of straw from my hair while he spoke. "You're going to be alone for months. I don't like it. I know Ream sure as hell doesn't. We've been talking about cancelling the tour and—"

"No." I pushed on his chest and he lost his balance and fell to his ass. I stood, walked over to the back wall and leaned against it. "He needs this. He loves music. I see it in his eyes every time he talks about performing."

"Didn't think you paid attention to anything we said."

I shrugged. I did. I always paid attention; I just acted like I didn't. I avoided sitting and having meals with everyone, but on occasion I did and I listened. "He loves music."

"Yeah, he does."

When we were kids, he'd lie beside me in the closet and sing when I was scared. I felt his love for it and despite our screwed-up childhood, the music always made everything okay until it didn't anymore. Until it died in him. It was after our mom sold us to her drug dealer, Lenny, to pay off her debt and I never heard Ream sing again. Lenny was the one who made Ream go to the basement with 'clients' in order to clear my mom's debt.

When Lenny died, probably from some drug deal gone bad, Olaf moved into the house with me, my brother and Alexa, Lenny's daughter who was a couple years younger than us and obsessed with Ream.

It didn't take long before she took advantage of her father's death and concocted a plan to hurt me, so that I'd no longer be my brother's innocent angel. That was when Gerard came to my room at night. That was when he shot me up with heroin. That was when I knew my life would never be the same.

Crisis stood.

I hardened my grey eyes and curled my hands into fists at my sides. "You have no idea what he went through for me. He deserves to be free from the ugly in this world."

"Yeah, he does, but what do you deserve?" Not many met my glare head on, even Olaf. But then he'd just smack me if I ever looked at him like that. "I don't know shit about what happened to you, but I do know Ream's past was pretty fuckin' bad. I also know yours is probably worse."

Nothing was worse than what Ream had been through. We were kids and he sacrificed his own innocence in order to protect mine. Again and again. Week after week forced to go downstairs into the basement so I didn't have to.

"He's worried, Haven."

"I didn't ask him to be." It was a bitchy response, but I was struggling to find a way out of this. If Crisis told Ream, there was no way he'd leave. I crossed my arms over my chest and softened my voice as I said, "You'll do more harm than good."

"Not so sure about that," he muttered and ran his hand through his wet hair. Some of the strands were drying and were a lighter blond than the damp ones. There was no question, Crisis was good-looking and I saw why he effortlessly acquired chicks on the few occasions I'd been out with everyone socially—socially used liberally because I was far from social. He had a self-assured attitude that girls gravitated to.

He gave a single nod. "Okay."

My brows lowered, suspicious as to why he'd given in so easily. "Okay?"

He strode toward me and I braced, arms dropping to my sides and raising my chin. "Yeah." He kept coming until he was inches away, his breath wafting across my face with a hint of mint. "I won't tell him about tonight."

I tensed ready for it. My stomach churned as I realized that Crisis was like all the rest. He wanted payment for his silence.

"If we go on tour, and that's a big if, you're going to promise to call him every day. And no more running in fuckin' thunderstorms. Jesus." He ran his hand through his damp hair again and a few strands stayed back while others fell forward again and dangled in front of his eyes.

I hadn't expected that. I expected what all men wanted. Besides, who was I? I may be Ream's twin sister, but really I was just a girl who showed up in their lives several months ago who barely spoke to any one of them.

"And I'm texting you. When I do, I expect a reply."

My brows lifted. "You?"

He nodded.

"Why?"

"Because I know what you're doing here, Haven. I knew Ream after you were separated and he was seriously fucked up. He hid, just like you're doing. Music gave him an outlet and I suspect that is what you're doing with the running, but he didn't risk his life." He moved a bit closer and my chest brushed against his wet shirt. "You can't hide from me. I saw it out in the rain and I see it lingering like a shadow on your face right now. You've been pretty fuckin' good at pretending you're strong and perfectly okay with whatever fucked with you." He paused. "And maybe our leaving is what you need. I don't fuckin' know. But what I do know is that if either of us sense something's off, we're back here." He pushed away from me and the heat from his body went with him. "You will break. One day that cool exterior you're hiding behind will shatter. It has to. It has nowhere to go. And when it does happen, I intend to be there to help you pick up the pieces."

I had nothing to say, because he was right. I was a time bomb, ticking slowly and steadily, waiting for another trigger to set me off, one I couldn't run to bury again. I just didn't know which way I'd go yet—destruction of myself or destruction of others.

He walked out of the stall and I followed. He stopped to stroke Clifford, who nipped at his wet t-shirt. "You fail to answer one text, I tell Ream what went down here tonight and we're back and you're seeing someone."

"You can't force me to see someone."

"You sure about that? Because last time I checked, it was illegal to carry a handgun in Canada."

Shit.

I narrowed my eyes. "You realize this is blackmail?" Because I'd never give up my gun and Crisis appeared to know that.

The day I showed up at the farm, I had a gun in my hand and I still do. Even with Olaf dead, I wasn't giving it up. It gave me freedom and I'd never lose that again.

He chuckled. "Baby, you can call it whatever you want, extortion, threat, bribery." He shrugged. "Bottom line, I get to make sure you stay safe *if* we go." He hesitated and the cockiness in his eyes returned. "And to make sure you stay safe, one of our security guys is staying with you. He'll only report to me."

Double shit.

"Your brother will be more likely to leave if one of our guys is with you."

True. Okay, it wasn't a big deal; I could deal with those terms. "I'm not giving up my gun."

"Then follow the terms."

"I thought you were nicer."

"I am nice. I'm a sweetheart . . . most of the time. I rubbed straw in your hair, that's nice." He grinned. I frowned. "But if I asked you nicely to text me, to call Ream, to never run in an open field during a thunderstorm again . . . would you listen?"

Triple shit.

"Didn't think so." He grabbed a yellow raincoat from a hook beside the tack room and tossed it to me. "Wear this. It will hide the mud."

I caught it, the flimsy rubber material crinkling in my hand. "Crisis?"

He opened the barn door and the wind tore inside, causing the lightbulb hanging from the cord to sway back and forth. "Yeah, babe."

"If he knew . . . it would kill him." I don't really know why I said it, maybe because I needed him to get that what happened to me was bad and Ream knowing . . . it would destroy him; I saw my brother brutally kill Gerard after he found out what had been going on.

Now, Olaf was dead too.

I had a slice of peace knowing my brother was happy. I wasn't taking that away by being that little girl he tried to shield. I had my own shields.

The light illuminated his face for a second as it swung by him then bathed him in darkness again. But I caught a glimpse of that crease between his eyes.

"I know," he said.

I pulled on the coat while he shut off the light, and we ran through the storm for the house.

Chapter Two

Haven

Do cucumbers have any usefulness besides tasting like shit and looking like cock? Why the hell do they have to put them in every salad? Tomatoes, okay. Cucumbers are sliced up dicks, fuck no.

These were the texts from Crisis I was supposed to respond to.

The band, along with Emily and Kat, had been gone a month, and Crisis kept his word and texted me daily. I kept mine and responded with mundane one or two word replies, although it was becoming a little more difficult to do when he sent me random texts like this.

Ream called me daily and I think that was Crisis' doing, so I didn't have to be the one to call him. After that night in the storm, my brother told me Deck had called him. Told him Olaf was 'looked after.' Of course, Ream had no idea about the club, but Olaf being dead was probably the deciding factor on them leaving me while they went on tour.

Deck had called me too, told me they had a lead on the club's location. Since I'd been blindfolded every time we went there, I had no clue where it was.

I asked him never to call me again.

I didn't want to know. That part of my life was over.

My conversations with Ream were mostly one-sided as I had nothing to contribute or rather didn't care to contribute. But after the first few awkward silences, I looked forward to hearing his voice and the way he went on about the concerts and Kat. It cemented my deal with Crisis—I used that term loosely because I still considered it blackmail. My brother also bitched about Crisis' antics, but I was getting that was more of a habit between brothers.

I ran in the mornings, and the running was with an extra appendage—Luke. The security guy kept his distance, but I had tried to outrun him the first few days. I realized pretty fast that it was impossible. The guy didn't tire. The saving grace was that he didn't talk either, so we ignored one another and ended up getting along fine.

I carpooled to school with a girl, Dana, who I found on the internet through the university website. Luke of course checked into her, but he still followed us in his car to campus. I wanted normal and going to school with a bodyguard was not normal, but neither was carrying a gun everywhere I went.

I went to class, said little to anyone except when forced to, came home, repeat and recycle, five days a week. The weekends consisted of running and homework. It was productive. It was what I wanted and I hadn't done anything I wanted for twelve years.

But Crisis . . . he was something I hadn't been prepared for. He liked to talk and because of our deal, it was in text. And after a month of texts from him, I found myself thawing to his playfulness.

You're comparing cucumbers to dicks?

Yeah.

What about carrots?

Since when do cocks have pointy ends?

So, you don't like cucumbers in your salad because they look like cut up dicks and it gives you nightmares?

Yeah, Ice. That's what I said. But we're talking about big cucumbers, not those baby ones. And I don't fuckin' like them and they always put them in my salad. I'm here picking them out one by one and I know I'm still going to taste them after all this fuckin' work.

Picking cucumbers out of your salad is work?

He must be bored because he rambled when he was bored. I leaned over and placed my books in my knapsack then zipped it up and stood, grabbing my phone off my desk.

My fingers have been playing all night, I don't need this shit.

I was uncertain what he meant by that. It wasn't a secret that Crisis often fooled around with chicks after the concerts, maybe before them, too. I hadn't thought about it much—we texted. It was an arrangement. But after a month of talking to him every day, I started to think about it.

And from your silence, your mind is in the gutter again. Jesus, babe. I meant the guitar. We had a gig last night.

I bit my lip to keep from smiling. There was that tiny smile emerging again. It had been happening more often lately when I texted with Crisis. It was odd because he casually talked about stuff like this and I thought I'd be revolted or disgusted, and the first few times he mentioned his cock in text, I'd numbed out, but now I didn't even think about it. It was Crisis and he was just talking. It had nothing to do with sex or wanting sex with me.

Was it good?

I knew it had gone well. I checked when I got up this morning and the reviews raved about Tear Asunder, just like all the other venues they'd been to. It had become my habit to scroll the internet to keep track of the band.

Of course, Crisis dominated the pictures, the media loved him and, from his ease around the cameras, he did too. Often there were pictures with his arm around a random girl and I knew they were random because it was never the same girl twice. He soaked up the attention with his cocky grin. I found myself rolling my eyes and smiling when I saw a new girl in a picture because it was mildly absurd. I suspected each girl thought they were special to him. That they'd be 'the one.'

But Prince charming was a fucking fairy tale. No guy was going to save you. You had to save yourself.

It rocked. But Logan was off. Emily did a demo yesterday afternoon and a voter came at her. She got clear, but Logan saw it. It screwed with his head all night.

Voter?

Fuck no, horse.

Oh.

She can handle it. Logan, not so much. You in class?

Yes.

Technically, I was leaving class.

What class?

Sex Ed. We learned how to put condoms on cucumbers today.

I don't know why I said it; Crisis brought out a side of me I didn't know I had. I waited for my phone to light up, holding it in my palm as I walked from the lecture hall.

LOL . . . Shit, babe, you're really fuckin' adorable. I may have to make you mine.

Adorable? I was anything but adorable. I ate adorable. I couldn't believe he just said that. Yes, I could, it was Crisis. It was easy text chatting with him. It was safe behind the phone and he couldn't see inside me this way. I moved to the side to let students by me as I walked slowly and typed back.

And disappoint the reporters and girls?

True. But I'd be more worried about your brother's reaction. He'd slingshot my balls with a fuckin' rock.

I hadn't mentioned to Ream that I talked to Crisis and neither had Crisis.

A dart is more his style.

My balls just fucked off up into my abdomen.

A bubbling rose in my chest and I stopped in the middle of the hallway. It was an odd sensation with my insides tightening and my stomach fluttering. Laughter. I wanted to laugh, but that sound had been trapped inside me for a really long time.

Going now.

Okay, later, Ice. Be good.

I huffed at his nickname for me. I was uncertain whether it was because of that night when he found me freezing cold or because of my icy personality. I shoved my phone in my pocket and rushed to my next class.

My routine remained steady over the next month and I became accustomed to seeing Luke around. He wasn't there to protect me from anyone, rather to protect me from myself, so he didn't follow me from class to class, but I suspected he was reporting to Crisis on my emotional status.

My phone vibrated in my zippered pocket of my stretch pants and I stopped on the side of the road, fished it out and looked at the screen.

Mom saw my naked ass on Twitter. *face palm*

I plopped down on my butt on the shoulder of the road near the ditch, breathing hard after the five miles I'd just run. I glanced behind me and saw Luke stop; he didn't even look out of breath—goddamn machine. He walked over to a tree and leaned against it, his head tilted down, not looking like he was watching me, but I knew he was.

The dirt road I was on was good to run on as cars rarely passed by and it backed onto one of the horse fields I'd cut through on my way home.

I lay back and the pebbles were like tiny pin pricks as they dug into my spine. I shifted a bit until it didn't hurt, bent my knees and held my phone up in front of me as I texted back.

Was she impressed?

He'd been gone two months and I realized that whenever my phone vibrated now, a whoosh went through me. There were no filters with Crisis, and I liked that he said whatever was on his mind.

A breeze ruffled the few strands of hair that weren't drenched in sweat and glued to my forehead. The wind was calm today and warm, nothing chasing me. I'd only had a few instances where my ice cracked and the memories invaded, but I adapted just like I had before. I escaped before I let it in.

LOL, no. But what freaks me out more is that she's following me on Twitter. The bullshit I spew on there is not for a mom to read.

His mom, who was also my brother's foster mom, as Crisis' parents' took Ream in when child services had him in custody, had tried to get me to come to dinner numerous times since the boys left on tour.

I refused. The last thing I wanted was a mother figure around, telling me what to do. All I wanted was to go to school, get a degree, then a job and live without boundaries.

I'd lived like an abused animal, hit and kicked, mostly by Alexa, but Olaf was a low-life piece of shit and did his fair share when I fought the clients.

Babe, you there?

I quickly slammed down the wall blocking the memory and typed back.

How did she know it was yours?

Tattoo.

She knows you have a tattoo on your butt?

Yeah. The woman hates my tats. So, whenever I'm about to get a new one, I send her a pic of the design and ask her opinion.

Cruel.

You think? I was going more for clever. You get your license yet?

No.

Good.

Good?

Yeah, I want to teach you.

I did want to get my driver's license, but hadn't liked the idea of sitting in a car with a stranger. My phone vibrated again.

So, what are you doing?

I was running. Now, I'm lying on the side of the road texting you.

WTF. Get off the road.

No one drives down here. That dead-end dirt road behind the farm.

Calling.

NO.

I lowered my phone to my lap and closed my eyes as the morning sun beamed down on my face. He'd called me twice since he left, but both times I didn't answer then texted him that I was at school and couldn't talk. It wasn't a lie. I'd been at school, but talking to Crisis felt different than texting. Texting was . . . impersonal.

My phone sang "Part of Me" by Katy Perry.

He knew I wasn't in class and was perfectly capable of answering. Shit, I had to pick it up or knowing Crisis, he'd keep calling until I did and if I never did, he'd probably call Luke.

I answered but didn't say anything.

"Get off the road," he said. "Where the fuck is Luke?"

"Around." I sat up, curled one arm around my legs while I held the phone to my ear. The sound of his voice sent a thrum of shivers across my skin and a flutter in my belly. Crisis had a sexy voice, kind of husky with a slight deep burr that carried into his singing. Logan, aka Sculpt to the general public, was the lead singer, but often Crisis or Ream had parts of songs they sang too.

"Are you off the road? I don't hear you moving."

The gravel shifted beneath my feet as I stood and started walking. "Why are you calling?"

"You're lying on the road. Of course, I'd call. No risks, remember."

"Side of the road. Like the shoulder. And if it was a risk, I'm sure the badger you put on me would have something to say about it. He's currently"—I cranked my neck to glance in Luke's direction—"leaning against a tree not looking at me, but I'm betting he has supersonic eyes and ears and knows exactly what I'm saying and doing."

"Luke was part of the deal. And he does."

"He does what?"

"Have supersonic everything. He owns Shield Security and is the best."

"I understood Deck was the best."

He chuckled. "Deck and his men are the best, but they don't do celebrity protection. They are a whole other facet." He quieted and I heard him take a breath before he said, "You doing okay, Haven?"

"I'm fine."

"You sound pissed I called."

25

Was I? Not exactly pissed, more like defensive because I was unsettled by the fact that I liked that he called. "Out of breath."

"Bullshit. If I heard you panting in the phone, I'd be hard right now."

I couldn't believe he said that. Yes, I could. "Do you want me to pant, so your nightly chick has something to ride?"

Despite what I went through, I wasn't afraid of the sexual references. It was freeing to be able to casually text about whatever—even sex. He didn't know my past, but he knew it was ugly and yet there was no tiptoeing around me.

The band was in Vancouver and with the time difference, it was the middle of the night there, so according to the what media published, Crisis should have a chick with him after the concert.

Crisis never hid his playboy status and I was sure that was what made me feel comfortable with him because there was no pressure to pretend between us. No expectations. He flirted sometimes because that was just what he did, but that was all.

"Not doing that shit."

"Girls are shit now?"

He laughed. "Nah, you're not." The phone crackled as if he was moving and then he grunted. "Owe. Fuck."

"What happened?"

"Banged into the ice machine. Fuckin' thing is in the middle of the hallway." I huffed because I knew it wasn't and he obviously hadn't been watching where he was going. "I'm going to my suite so I can lie down and talk to you. Been one fuck of a long night."

"Was the concert good?"

"Babe, I told you, a concert to me is like an orgasm for two hours."

I smiled. Whenever he or Ream talked about music, it was as if a spark of energy came alive in them. I suspected all the guys in the band were like that, although Kite, the drummer, I had trouble reading.

"Haven?"

"Yeah?"

He sighed. "Thought you hung up on me." I heard a beep. "Fuck. Kite. Seriously, man? Use your room."

"What?" I heard Kite say.

"Haven, one sec." His voice sounded further away as he spoke to Kite.

Then Kite shouted in his faint Irish accent, "You into two guys, Missy?"

Jolted, my hand tightened around the phone.

"Sure," a faint muffled girl's voice yelled. "Is it Crisis?"

The phone crackled and I heard muted voices, but was unable to decipher what was being said. A door slammed.

"Fuck, Ice. Sorry. Kite's being an ass."

"Or generous." I hadn't expected to hear that Kite and Crisis shared chicks.

"Fuck no. We don't do that shit. He's into . . . well, we just don't." He paused and I stayed silent. "He knew I was talking to you and was fucking with me. He knows we text."

"Oh." I was uncertain how I felt about that. I didn't know Kite that well, but he was always courteous and a gentleman. He was kind of mysterious and kept his personal life out of the media. A little dark maybe, with an overabundance of confidence as if nothing could unsettle him. From what my brother told me, he handled all business aspects of the band with the manager.

"Give me ten and I'll call you back."

It was Saturday and I had no plans except homework and maybe go to the barn to groom one of the horses. But chatting on the phone with Crisis . . . it wasn't part of the deal and hearing his voice was far different than reading words. "I don't think—"

"Answer your phone."

I heard the dial tone and sighed as I shoved it back in my pocket. One thing I was getting about Crisis is he did what he said and he'd call me. Except it wouldn't be in ten minutes because I was also getting that he was characteristically late.

I climbed through the fence, picked up a light jog and made my way back to the house, hearing Luke's feet trailing behind. I grabbed a bottle of water from the fridge like I always did, tossed one to Luke like I always did, then went outside and sat on the porch swing. Twenty minutes later, Crisis called.

Chapter Three

Haven

16 years old

Take my hand. Tonight you will believe. Believe in me.
The warmth of your touch. The taste of your lips.
Keeps me coming back to you.
So believe. Believe in me and take my hand.
I'm here to love you forever.
Forever you're mine.

I ROCKED BACK AND forth on the floor as I sang quietly to myself with my arms curled tightly around my legs, cheek resting on the knobby bone of my knee. My tattered nightgown barely covered my slim thighs, but it had flimsy sleeves to keep the bruises on my arms concealed.

Chills ran through me as I quivered and trembled, while beads of sweat trickled from my hairline to slide down my face. Sleep eluded me, my stomach and limbs cramped so badly that I had trouble moving. I even bailed on going to school. My body no longer belonged to me as the uncontrollable need for the drug held me in its vicious grip.

A need I hated.

A need forced upon me.

A need that allowed me to escape and yet kept me trapped.

I swayed back and forth like a rocking chair and the rhythmic sound of the floor creaking echoed in my bedroom. A tree branch scraped against the cracked windowpane as the violent wind outside yowled, testing the fragility of the glass.

Take my hand. Tonight you will believe. Believe in me.
The warmth of your touch. The taste of your lips.
Keeps me coming back to you.
So believe. Believe in me and take my hand.
I'm here to love you forever.
Forever you're mine.

I sang quietly, the complete opposite to what was happening inside me. It gave me the vacancy, the numbness, the void I searched for in order to stay sane.

Emptiness had become my survival—my sanity.

But darkness encroached, burying me deeper and deeper and I was suffocating under the blanket of desolation. I knew I might never find my way back to the surface. I'd be lost forever in this constant cycle of anxious desperation and revulsion.

I'd managed to keep my slow decline hidden from my brother by spending less time with him, and staying in my room whenever I wasn't at school. A room where *he* came to. My savior and my hell.

He'd be here soon. He never let me get too strung out before he brought me more of my escape. And then . . .

Then I gave him what he desired. Fighting no longer existed in my world. I was a puppet, molded and played with. Limbs twisted. Body used. Abused. Ripped and torn until I no longer knew what lived inside me.

Yes, I did—nothing. But when he came to my room at night, when he held my arm, wrapped the thin band around it and flicked the syringe with his dirty fat finger . . . that was when it all stopped. I left my body behind and went somewhere else for a while. A place where no one could find me. Where I was safe. Where pain couldn't reach me.

I always watched when the needle slid into my vein. I waited breathless for his thumb to press the plunger. For my escape from what he'd do to me afterward. Disgust came later when I showered and attempted to wash away the feel of his hands. But it was more than that. I tried to wash away the hatred for myself.

To my brother, Ream, I was his innocent angel as he shielded me from the harsh life we were immersed in. He didn't know the shield had collapsed and been trampled months ago.

I discovered what he'd been doing in order to protect me. But with the sacrifice of his own innocence came the haunting guilt that ate at me. He was my brother. My twin brother and he was all I had. I knew he'd do anything to shelter me from this tainted world, but I was older and saw the truth.

I saw his gaunt pale skin when he emerged from the basement. I saw the way he gingerly walked up the stairs to his bedroom. But when he noticed me, he'd always smile. Always. As if nothing was wrong. As if he went into that basement to play video games all weekend.

I'd stayed untouched for years because of him.

It had been months since his visits to the basement stopped, our mother's debt finally paid off to Lenny. But normal didn't last long in our world. Lenny dying left us and his cruel daughter, Alexa, to Olaf. That was when my nightmare began.

Heavy footsteps strode down the hall and there was a mixture of fear, nausea and anxiety. I didn't know which was stronger. It had been three days. Three days locked in a maze of uncertainty when I would get my next hit.

When did it change? When had I given up? When did I die inside?

Motionless, I stared at the closed door, the footsteps stopped. I knew Gerard's stride, the way his left foot dragged slightly when he walked as if he'd been injured at one time. How the floorboards groaned louder under his weight than anyone else's in the run-down house.

The doorknob turned and coldness encompassed me.

I screamed for what he represented—disgust and liberation. They clashed, opposites fighting a war that neither won when it was over; instead, the war cycled over and over again.

The door pushed open and I raised my head.

I waited.

I had to be patient. He liked slow.

I sang in my head, the tune calming my mind.

But my heart disagreed as it thumped wildly. Goose bumps raised, feeling as if ice shards pelted my skin. My eyes shot to his hand and I breathed a sigh of relief as I saw the clear plastic syringe between his fingers. He twirled it back and forth watching me.

He knew after three days I'd be screaming for it. His beady brown eyes gleamed and thin lips pursed upward in a grin. He knew I was struggling to stop myself from running to him and begging for my fix.

He stepped into my room, closed the door then reached behind him and clicked the lock. A lock I'd once used to try to keep him out. I never tried again.

I stood. My legs shook so badly that I had to use the wall to steady myself. Once I had my balance, I walked to the end of the bed and sat. My stomach twisted and cramped, while the blood flowing through my veins raged.

He set the syringe on the dresser then lifted the back of his shirt, took out his gun and set it next to it. The gun was in full view, easy access to me. It was almost a dare for me to try for it. But I wouldn't. To kill him would have too many possible repercussions for my brother.

My weakness had become my strength, because keeping this from Ream meant he continued to be free of what happened in the basement. If I kept quiet, Gerard promised to help keep him away from there.

I had no misconceptions of what Gerard was capable of, or Olaf. But for months, he'd kept his word and my brother was finally losing the dark glassy look in his eyes.

Sweat trickled down my cheek and I wrung my hands together on my lap. The jingle of the metal buckle of his belt sounded so loudly that it was as if I was right next to him.

The leather slid through the loops of his jeans and it clunked as he placed it next to his gun.

He picked the syringe back up and the dryness in my mouth alleviated as I salivated like a starving dog seeing a scrap of meat. He held it up between his fingers, watching me, knowing I was that starving dog, ready to pounce.

"Do you want this?"

I nodded.

His voice squeaked, like when a car brakes suddenly. I preferred when he was quiet and, thankfully, most of the time he was. I guessed it was because he wanted to make certain no one heard us. But the only person who would care was my brother and his room was down the hall. Alexa's was beside mine and she hated me. She wanted this. She was the one who stole the drugs from her 'Uncle' Olaf for Gerard to give to me.

Gerard wouldn't waste what little money he had to buy me my fix, even if it was to help with my . . . cooperation.

He strode toward the bed, his belly hanging over his jeans. I swallowed repeatedly as the bile rose, knowing what I'd soon taste, making me gag as he shoved it to the back of my throat while his belly jiggled in my face.

The strong scent of his cologne mixed with his body odor suffocated the air and I took short breaths through my mouth to avoid the vile smell. I held out my arm as soon as the mattress sagged under his weight next to me and started singing in my head again.

But he gave me the light to my darkness. The melody to my drumming roar. The heaven to my hell. The numbness to my pain. Ironic, considering he was the cause of the darkness, the roar, the hell and the pain.

He fumbled around in his pocket for the rubber band and I wanted to shout at him to hurry up. I didn't. Of course, I didn't. But I had no control over the physical effects—the shaking, the chills, sweats and the nausea.

Ream recently noticed my withdrawal and weight loss. I played it off as the pressure of high school. But in the last few weeks, Ream had been waiting for me after classes, watching what I ate at meals. He knew something was off.

Of course he would. It was just that Ream was fucked up too and had been through worse hell than any kid should ever experience. He was intelligent and overprotective. Soon he'd find out about the drugs and Gerard, and I was terrified at what he'd do. Of what would happen to him if he went after Gerard.

We were here as a product of the very drugs I took. We'd been ten years old when we came here, bedraggled, undernourished, but we had one another. That was what kept us alive. Our bond. I'd do anything for him just as he would for me.

I stiffened as Gerard's sweaty hand wrapped around my wrist and pulled my arm toward him. He shoved my sleeve up then tied the rubber band above my elbow. I watched as the bruised vein swelled and pulsed beneath the thin surface of my skin.

"Take off your panties." My eyes shot to him and he grinned, his yellow-stained teeth flashing. Despite being in his late twenties or early thirties, his leathery skin looked ten years older.

"Please . . ." I glanced at the syringe in his hand.

He sighed and his cigarette, beer-laden breath fanned my face. "Panties first, Haven. I want to touch you at the same time."

He'd never done this. Usually, he gave me the drug then did whatever he wanted to me while I escaped into another world. Refusing wasn't an option; I was weak and pathetic, just like my mother.

I stood and shimmied out of my ripped cotton panties and sat back on the bed next to him, holding out my arm.

"Open your legs."

I did.

There were no tears. They were lost long ago to the life I was dealt. No point in feeling sorry for myself when there was nothing left of me to pity.

He flicked my vein with his finger, but he didn't really need to. It was throbbing and visible yet bruised. He slid the needle in and I held my breath waiting for the sudden rush, but it didn't come. Instead, the needle remained in my vein, the clear liquid sitting in the syringe while his dirty hand slid across my thigh to between my legs.

I tensed. My stomach cramped. My heart thumped against my ribs. I held my breath, not daring to move as he cupped me and groaned.

It happened at the same time. The pain of his rough fingers entering me and the rush of the drug raging through my veins.

I sank back onto the bed and vanished.

Chapter Four

Haven

Where are you?

School.

Doing what? I want to picture you in my head.

Gross. Are you jerking off?

God, I was beginning to sound like him now.

Answer the question, Ice.

I'm getting lunch in the cafeteria.

Something was off with him. I may not hear emotions in a text, but habits and words varied and Crisis normally would reply to my jerking off text with teasing, or humor. He didn't. I also noticed he tried to call me this morning, but I was in the car with Dana and didn't answer.

I shoved my phone in my back pocket, grabbed an orange plastic tray off the stack and plopped it down on the four aluminum bars. I waited in line while some chick prattled about her bad date to the girl next to her.

"Hey, move it." The guy behind me yelled at the girl more interested in talking about her date then getting lunch.

The chick flicked her streaked blonde hair over her slender shoulder and sneered at him before pushing her tray forward.

It took another five minutes to reach the hot counter where I took a plate of the daily special sitting under the heat lamps and placed it on my tray. A large crowd of football guys barreled into the cafeteria jostling one another being loud and obnoxious.

My cool detachment wavered as the sounds leaked through my cracks and my nerves flickered and sparked. It was worsening. My body had been conditioned to ignore the sounds, to block out what I had to. I did it so well, that when I heard the noises, any nerves sparking numbed. It was like a cool blanket fell over me and nothing could penetrate it.

But with the freedom, came a small hole in the blanket and it was ripping. My life no longer depended on being unruffled and composed, and the triggers were fucking with me.

I took several deep breaths, eyes focused on one spot and concentrated on bringing my heart rate down.

"I'm so going to enjoy watching you eat that."

My heart leapt and tore off like a horse darting out the gates. I didn't have to look to know who towered over me, chest inches from my back. I recognized his low sexy drawl with that hint of laughter on the cusp of it. Even his scent I remembered and, to my annoyance, it caused a fluttering in my stomach.

My hands tightened on the edges of the tray. "Crisis?" There was nothing good about the roar of emotions spiralling. I hadn't expected it. I hadn't been prepared for the onslaught of . . . excitement. "What are you doing here?" I avoided looking at him because I was a little— okay, a lot—stunned. He was back and standing here, and looking at Crisis after all the texts, the teasing . . . I was afraid of what I'd see.

And of what I'd not see. I just wasn't going to look at him at all.

"Got back. Thought I'd see for myself that you weren't skipping class."

He knew damn well how important school was to me, since he gave me shit for not having any fun and doing homework all the time. But this was what I wanted. To do what I should've done years ago instead of being some object for men to play with. "You weren't due back for a week."

From the corner of my eye, I saw him shrug. "Yeah, shit changed."

And that made me falter because I caught a glimpse of his face and that sent a new wave of something through me. "Why? What's wrong?"

I was getting to know Crisis enough that if there was a plan to end the tour early, he would've mentioned it before. Something happened and I wondered if Luke had said anything about my extended run the other night. Maybe that was why he called me this morning.

He reached over me and snagged my apple. Juices sprayed in a fine mist as he took a big bite and my eyes flicked away. "Next venue was in Seattle." I knew this as Ream had given me their schedule. "The publicist thought it better I make a getaway before it was announced that the Seattle show was cancelled."

"It's cancelled?"

He put the apple back on my tray on top of a napkin. "Yeah."

"You had to make a getaway?"

"Figure of speech. But yeah."

"Your publicist wanted you to leave?"

His brows rose and there was a slight twitch on the right side of his mouth. "For a chick who usually says fuck all, you've a lot of questions."

"And getting no real answers." It didn't sound very good, whatever it was. "If your publicist thought you had to sneak away, she wouldn't be happy to hear you're at a university where probably half the population knows of Tear Asunder. Plus, you're a chick magnet even without your rock star status." And my anonymity was imperative. No one knew I was Ream's sister. My brother even managed, so far, to keep it out of the media that he had a sister.

"Ah, thanks, Ice. I like it when you call me hot."

I didn't call him hot. "I didn't call you hot . . . where the hell did you get that . . ." I stopped because his blue eyes twinkled with mischief and he was grinning broadly.

"Relax, I'm in disguise." Some disguise, a baseball hat. "No one will notice me. Where's Luke?"

"He doesn't follow me around all day." He still stayed at the farm at night and came running with me every morning. "I promised him I wouldn't run into a burning building or jump off a roof."

"Funny," he said, not sounding amused.

"I was never trying to kill myself. If I wanted to do that, it would've been twelve years ago." I reached for bottled water then shuffled down the line and he slid in beside me.

"Don't say shit like that."

I remained quiet, realizing that I'd said more to him than I had anyone.

He nudged me with his shoulder. "Babe, when are you going to look at me?"

I had been, just indirectly, and that had been hard to do because Crisis was like a piece of chocolate waiting to be devoured. I didn't do devouring. "I know what you look like."

"I've been gone for months. Spent countless hours texting you and not even a hug. I'm crushed."

"Is that even possible?" I was still trying to get my emotions back into their little compartments before I met his eyes. Anyway, Crisis had an ego the size of the Pacific Ocean. And yeah, his God's-gift-to-chicks attitude was warranted—infinitesimally.

"Ice?"

Fine. I tilted my head up and looked him in the eyes, my shield ready. But it wasn't ready as my heart beat harder and faster. Then there were the little fairies dancing around in my stomach.

He was everything you'd imagine a rock star: hot, tatted skin—which bordered on an addiction to pain—muscled, and charismatic. He worked out obsessively; fucked obsessively. Played music obsessively and scrolled the internet for news about himself—obsessively.

And the entertainment gurus had a love affair with him.

Despite trying to keep my distance in the beginning, over the countless texts, he had weeded his way into my life and now . . . well, now he was in one of my little compartments with the label—care. I cared about why he was back early. And why the tour was cancelled. But caring had never led anywhere good for me. Sympathy. Kindness. Compassion. None of it belonged in my world. But I wasn't in that world now and those things were leaking back in.

"What happened?"

"What do you mean?"

I raised my brows; lips pressed together and tilted my head slightly as I scrutinized him. "Publicist sneaks you away. Last venue cancelled. What happened?"

"I wouldn't say sneak, Haven. I don't sneak. I own what I do."

"And?"

"It's not something you need to worry about. Just some pain-in-the-ass shit."

I'd run longer than usual that morning and was late so I hadn't checked the latest entertainment news. He sounded pissed and Crisis rarely did. His words were strained and his body tense. "I'd rather hear it from you than the media."

"Just some chick causing issues and I blew up at her. Didn't touch her, I'd never do that. But I lost it." He reached over and grabbed a bottle of water for himself. Without waiting until we arrived at the cash register, he cracked it open and chugged half of it back then set it down. "You know what I was like."

I wasn't sure what he was referring to, so I merely looked at him questioningly.

He sighed. "Fucking around. Lots of chicks."

Oh, yeah, I knew. I hadn't seen anything on social media lately, but what was on the internet never went away and his past was there and I'd seen it.

"Some bitch, and babe, she is a bitch, is causing problems for us. Followed us to every venue which normally is cool, but not when she's sending gifts and posting bullshit all over the internet about me and her . . . It was over a year ago. I'd fucked her. She thinks it meant something. It didn't."

"So you came home because of her?"

He shifted his weight and his hair fell across his one eye. "Kind of. No and yes, a combo thing. That's the reason I gave the guys. We only had Seattle and we'll re-schedule."

"And?" I tensed waiting to hear the combo because so far that was a single reason.

"Luke mentioned something."

Shit. Luke reported to Crisis, which meant he'd been concerned and had come back.

"What did he tell you?" But I knew what it was.

Despite telling Deck I didn't want to hear anything about the club, I received a call from Deck's man, Vic. The club was found and shut down, but they were still searching for a few girls as they'd scattered. He needed to know how many were there. I didn't know. I never met the other girls.

But after that call, I was trembling and freaked, the buried memories surfacing. I went running for three hours. Luke had not been impressed.

"He said you got a call, looked freaked-out then went running for a fuck-of-a-long time." He nudged me down the line then reached across and put his hands on the sides of the tray next to my hands. "Everything okay, Ice?"

"It's fine. I like to run. Luke doesn't."

Crisis huffed, but for some reason he didn't push the issue. "Your brother gets back tomorrow with Logan. They're making a statement today about Seattle being cancelled."

His baby finger brushed against mine and my stomach flip-flopped. I stiffened, my eyes darting to his, but he wasn't looking at me; he was eyeing the hot dishes under the heat lamps.

"Fuck, is that cream of corn? It looks like . . ."

I didn't hear the rest of what he said as the bunch of guys in line started cheering at something, pumping their arms in the air. A few

NASHODA ROSE

whistled and hooted then one of them yelled, 'I'm screwing that pussy tonight.' I didn't know why, but it was the tone of his voice that set me off.

A cold wave spread over me; the blanket ripped off.

I froze as the memories bombarded. I hated it. The glassy eyes ogling me, the dancing, the disgusting groping hands—but nothing was worse than the backrooms.

They were classy and clean just like everything in the club, even the men. But the high-quality business suits only hid the filth that was beneath.

And I lived it every Saturday night for years. After a while, I no longer knew who the men were or what they looked like. I zoned out, a mannequin used until they grunted, fell on top of me, their weight suffocating. The money I made went to Olaf who supported both Alexa and me. Although, I wouldn't call it support, more like he kept me alive to make him money while Alexa treated me like I was her pet dog . . . one she didn't like.

I shivered and tried to push the thoughts away.

"Slow, deep breaths, baby." His low voice was gentle and soothing and I felt him inch closer. I should've wanted to get away, but I didn't. He was safe. At some point, Crisis had become safe. I had no idea when it happened, or how, but it did. I just wasn't sure how I felt about it yet.

I opened my eyes, slowed my frantic inhales and looked at him.

"You okay?"

I nodded.

"This happen often?"

I shrugged. Usually, I managed to avoid the triggers, but this time, my emotions were off-kilter with Crisis showing up.

"Was it the guys?"

How much to give him? I hesitated, my eyes never leaving his, then I nodded.

"Hey, buddy. Move it."

Crisis tensed and it was like his entire body changed as he directed his gaze on the guy telling us to move. "Fuck off."

The guy backed down. Smart, considering Crisis looked and sounded scary when he wanted to be.

Crisis wore a baseball cap low over his eyes, but his playful blond curls poked out on both sides and at the back. The muscles in his arms flexed as he picked up the tray and the tats along his skin expanded and the intense black ink faded slightly.

His jeans had holes in the knees and despite the leather belt, which was more for show than anything, they hung low on his hips. But if he was trying to hide who he was, he didn't try very hard as he wore a black t-shirt with the words Tear Asunder ROCKs. Although, in his defense, I'd seen a few of these shirts around campus.

"Damn, you're the guitarist from Tear Asunder—Crisis." And anonymity botched. The guy, who a moment ago was pissed off at us for holding up the line, now grinned.

Crisis nodded. "Yeah, man. But I'm trying to keep it quiet. You know . . . have lunch with my girl."

My girl?

Crisis shifted the tray into one hand and slapped the guy on the shoulder with the other. "She hasn't seen me in months and is dying to get her lips on me."

I snorted and moved off toward the cash register. Unfortunately, they followed. I knew he was attempting to get the lightness back after what just happened with me by teasing, but I was uneasy with the fact he'd been recognized.

The guy laughed. "Sure. That's cool. Better lower the hat though. If the chicks find out you're on campus, it'll be mayhem."

Crisis tagged my arm before I had the chance to escape without my food and disappear into the crowded cafeteria. "Whoa, babe." He glanced back at the guy. "Later, bud."

He guided me with his body to the cash register where he passed the lady a twenty dollar bill and didn't bother waiting for change as he strode through the hordes of students sitting at the rectangle tables until he found one unoccupied. He slid the tray onto the surface then dipped his hat lower over his face.

I stood at the end of the table, uncertain whether I should avoid a catastrophe that was imminent as soon as that guy told his friends Crisis from Tear Asunder was in the cafeteria. I glanced over my shoulder for the door . . . I wasn't that hungry and had class in fifteen minutes.

"Don't even think of it. Do you really want me running after you, throwing you over my shoulder and bringing you back here to sit and eat?" And again with the delusion that he could really get me over his shoulder. "You've lost weight and I guarantee your brother is going to notice." I glared. He shrugged. "Come on. I need a good laugh and seeing you eat that sloppy joe will end my dry spell."

Crisis had incredible eyes, brilliant blue that sparked with tiny star-like speckles of playfulness. Nonthreatening . . . safe.

I sat on the bench and Crisis grinned then sat across from me. He snagged my water bottle and opened it for me. "You didn't tell me you wanted to move out of the farmhouse."

Ream must have told him I planned to move closer to school. "Was it a pre-requisite?" I'd been looking for a job, too, so I could afford a place of my own.

He snorted. "Fuck yeah. I don't jump off cliffs with just any chick." He leaned forward and placed his elbows on the table. "Come on, Haven. We talk every day. I'd think it would be something you'd tell me."

"We text every day," I corrected.

"Fine. We text. But I don't normally text a chick more than twice. You're an exception."

"Is that a rule?"

"Fuck yeah. You know that. We talked about it."

I did.

He'd also told me that it was perfect when they toured because they were never in a city long enough to have to see the chick more than twice. Twice was his limit, he said 'his cock had always liked variety pussy.'

"You look cute with your book bag and all . . . school-like," Crisis drawled and it drew my attention because Crisis had this husky tone to his voice that couldn't be ignored and I was betting he knew it.

"School-like?"

"Yeah. You know, studious and shit."

He watched me as I picked up my apple, took a bite next to where he had and put it down. I wasn't exactly uncomfortable under his watchful gaze. I was accustomed to being on display, but it was something else. Something undecipherable that made me . . . aware of him.

"Your brother tell you he and Kat are buying the farm from Emily?" My brother had told me weeks ago. He also told me that Kite and Crisis had bought a place together so they wouldn't be back at the farm.

Originally, Logan and Kite owned the farm under a numbered company, something about keeping anonymity at the time. Then Logan put it in Emily's name and later decided to buy another farm to build a custom house and stables.

"So, where are you looking?" he asked.

"Not looking yet. But it will be closer to school."

I took a sip of my water then picked up my sloppy joe, the meat dripped out onto the plate. Of all days, the special had to be the sloppy joe. I always went for the specials on the days I was running late and didn't bring a lunch. They were cheaper and I hated using my brother's money. He'd set up an account for me, insisting that the money was partially mine anyway. That it was left to us from Urma, the old lady who had let us live in her shed when my brother and I were sixteen and living on the streets.

I knew the cottage had been hers, but the money was no doubt Ream's.

"You good with that?"

I had no idea what he said, so I said nothing. I leaned over my plate and took a bite of my sandwich. The juices slipped from the corners of my mouth and more meat fell out of the bun and dropped onto the plate than into my mouth. I put it down and Crisis held out the napkin, a cute grin on his face.

"Never thought I'd see the day when you had juices all over your face."

I took the cheap white paper from him and wiped my mouth. "Funny."

Crisis' sexual references were usual, but it was the clench between my thighs that surprised me. I'd never had that.

Crisis showing up at my school put me off balance and, regardless of our texting, I was unsettled with him sitting in front of me. Just his legs outstretched beneath the table, inches from mine, made me hyper-aware of him and it was a hyperaware that overpowered the numbness.

"So, what do you think?"

Had he said something else? "Huh?"

"Am I that boring, Ice? Jesus, ego is taking a beating today."

"I highly doubt that."

He plucked my apple from my tray and bit into it again. A solid crunching sounded as he chewed with his perfect white teeth. His hand holding the red apple moved as he spoke. "You're right. It's not. But I'm thinking it's easier to get your attention if I act hurt." He grinned. "Is it working?"

I shook my head. "No." *Maybe.* I picked up my lunch and started eating again.

It was a few minutes before either of us said anything and finally I set my sandwich down and met his eyes. "What are you doing?"

"Watching you."

"Why? Don't you have anything better to do?"

He shrugged. "Not really. I like sitting with you. It's a hell of a lot better than staring at my phone screen waiting for it to light up." It was said casually without that flirty tone and I felt the change in my heartbeat as our eyes locked for a second longer than I liked.

I leaned over and picked up my sloppy joe again and took too big of a bite because . . . well, I was unguarded by him and I'd been so accustomed to protecting myself from everyone for years that it was unnerving. I didn't know how to take it. I was used to being cold and detached and, suddenly, I was heated and connected.

To Crisis.

My mouth overflowed with sloppy joe and I tried to chew it all, but some slipped from my mouth. I swallowed unchewed meat and it scratched my throat. My eyes watered and I wanted to cough, but couldn't unless I sprayed half-eaten meat all over the table.

Jesus. I shoved my tray aside as I finally managed to swallow and wiped my mouth with the napkin.

"You not eating anymore?"

I shook my head. He took my water bottle off the tray and set it on the table and passed me the apple. He picked up the tray and strode over to the trash and tossed the rest of my sloppy joe.

I heard the four girls at the next table start to giggle and when I looked over they were staring at Crisis. He turned around and one girl darted to her feet and pranced over to him. The flock soon followed and surrounded him, blocking his way back to the table.

"Oh, my God, you're Crisis."

" . . . so hot."

"Can you sign . . . ?"

"Why are you here?"

"Do you want to have lunch with us?"

All I could see was the top of Crisis' baseball cap as he bent his head saying something to the one girl on his right then took a pen from her hand. I couldn't see anything now as they formed a tight ring around him. I guessed he was signing some body part because they sure as hell didn't have their books with them.

I had no intention of sticking around for Crisis to work his way back to me. I hadn't even told the few friends I had at school that my twin brother was Ream from Tear Asunder. The last thing I wanted was hordes of people around me asking questions or pretending to like me because of my famous brother and the band. And, of course, there was always the lingering fear of anyone recognizing me from the club. Naked pictures of me surfacing was only the tip of what could happen. Ream was famous and my shit would lead right into his if the reporters did any digging and I'd never let that happen.

I grabbed my water, picked up my book bag and threw it over my shoulder then quietly sneaked away.

"Haven!" Crisis shouted.

I weaved through the tables, pressed my palm to the swinging door and darted out into the hallway.

Chapter Five

Haven

DANA CAUGHT ME just before I escaped into the safety of Professor Neale's Creative Writing. I stopped and glanced past her to make certain Crisis hadn't managed to follow me.

"Have, where are you going so fast? I've been screaming your name like a lunatic since the cafeteria. Who were you with? I was just coming over to your table when you took off."

"I didn't want to be late for class."

"So who was the guy?"

"An old roommate." Truth with the omittance of exactly who he was.

Dana had bouncing red curls falling all over her head as if she'd been in a wind storm, and she dressed rather . . . provocative, especially compared to me. Even at the beginning of October, it was still warm and I wore long sleeve shirts. I had no intention of being asked questions about the words burned into my wrist.

She shrugged it off. And I think that was why I was okay with Dana. She was laid back and calm, and didn't pry into my past. Of course, she asked the usual questions: where I was from, what schools I went to. None of which I answered and she didn't seem to mind that I didn't, merely proceeded to tell me about herself.

She lived with her dad and older brother on the outskirts of the city. Her dad was a mechanic and had his own shop, and her brother was currently helping out. She never mentioned her mom and I didn't ask.

"My place or yours? Just saying, my place sucks. Dad. Older brother. You know, annoying as hell."

I didn't know. I'd never had a dad, neither Lenny nor Olaf could ever be classified as a dad, even a bad dad. I had no idea who my father was, didn't care, and I suspected my druggie mom didn't know either.

My brother I'd never consider annoying. I loved him more than anyone; he was part of me, the good part. We may have been separated, but there wasn't a day that I wasn't reminded of him. Sometimes, those reminders were cruel because I missed him, but I locked my feelings for him in the compartments of my mind. But seeing him again unlocked the compartments along with other parts of me.

A girl nudged by me, giving me a dirty look beneath the rim of her glasses as she went into class. I met her glare, unflinching, and she was first to look away. I hitched my slipping book bag up on my shoulder. "What do you mean?"

Dana rolled her eyes and her long lashes, accentuated by heavy mascara, touched the light pink eye shadow below her brows. "The party?"

I was hoping she'd forget about that. But I knew better. Dana was the opposite of me in that she loved to socialize. She was also a few years younger than me since I had started university so late.

"You promised." She lowered her voice as she leaned toward me. "Dillon will be there." And Dana liked Dillon—a lot.

Dana bounced on the tips of her toes as she grinned at me. I'd avoided three parties so far and finally said yes when Dana begged about this one, insisting it was mostly friends of hers from her old school and the lacrosse team. The lacrosse team weren't like the football team and appeared sort-a-kind-a okay. But what won my yes to the party was the fact that appearing social and having friends was normal and I was trying my best to get that, despite the gun lying at the bottom of my bag right now.

"So, your place to get ready?"

"Okay," I said. At least no one would be there as Ream wasn't back yet and Crisis and Kite had bought a new place.

"Great," Dana shouted then flung her arms around me.

I stilled. The immediate reaction to her touch pushed the trained response in me and my body tightened up like a spring, hands curling into fists.

She must have felt my tension because she lowered her arms and backed off. There was only a flicker of question in her eyes before it vanished and she smiled. "Okay, and I'm bringing something for you to wear because you aren't going like that."

I looked down at my black jeans and my long sleeve baggy shirt. There was nothing sexy about my clothing and I liked it that way.

Dana spun on her heel calling over her shoulder, "See ya at seven."

I watched her flounce down the hall and then I slipped inside the large auditorium where Professor Neale cleaned the chalkboard from the previous lecture. I heard my phone vibrate against something hard in my bag.

I walked up the steps to my usual seat at the back right then unpacked my writing book and saw the bright glare of words on the screen of my phone in the bottom of my bag. I took it out and glanced at it.

You reading this?

That was all he said. I went to put my phone away when it vibrated again.

Do you realize that reading my texts and not responding is considered bad etiquette?

I sighed. I was pretty sure if he texted one of those girls in the cafeteria, she'd have texted back within milliseconds.

I'm ego-dented. You realize that, right?

I huffed and felt the corners of my mouth curve up. I dropped my phone into my bag hearing it vibrate again, but I ignored it as Professor Neale wrote on the chalkboard in big capital letters Heads-Up.

A Heads-up was where we wrote non-stop for an allotted amount of time. Our pens had to remain moving no matter what, even if we had to write 'I can't think of anything to write' over and over again.

I hated it at first and that is exactly what I wrote over a hundred times the first day. The second time, I wrote that only fifty times then my mind got sick of it and I started writing about Urma's shed.

I don't know where the memory came from because I'd been high most of the time. Ream and I huddled in the corner of the shed, between the rake and the snow shovel. He'd found an old smelly brown blanket with oil stains all over it, which he tucked around me. I tried to share it with him, but he always insisted he wasn't cold.

I closed my eyes. God, I failed him time and again. I'd been so broken and weak and scared, spiralling out of control into the escape of the drugs, needing anything to make the pain disappear. And Ream . . . Ream never gave up on me. He kept trying and I kept screwing up until Olaf finally found me in the hospital after one of my overdoses and took me away.

Pathetic. I'd been our poison, our weakness. But not anymore. Despite the minor hiccups like what happened in the cafeteria, I had control.

"You thinking about what you're going to write?"

I tensed at the male voice sitting beside me and the tiny hairs on the back of my neck stood up. My pen dropped from my grasp and rolled down the decline of the smooth surface of my desk and fell to the floor. I leaned over to grab it and so did my new neighbour and our heads hit.

"Owww," we said simultaneously.

I rubbed my head and he smiled. "I'll get it." He leaned over again and grabbed my pen, then held it out to me. But I was looking at him. I was aware of everyone around me. I made it my business to know who

51

was near me and this guy I hadn't seen before. He was nice-looking, in the clean-cut sort of way, with a sharp, angular jaw and high-cheek bones. Probably over six-foot with how far his legs stretched out into the aisle.

When my eyes reached his, I saw the curiosity in them as he waited patiently for me to take my pen back. "Thanks." I took it and glanced away. There was a building of a familiar unease in my chest as I felt the burn of his gaze on me.

I didn't bother looking back at him as I said in an abrupt tone, "You want something?"

"Your name?"

I wrote the date on the top of my page. "Why?"

He laughed quietly. "Because it's polite and I'm new—transferred to this class a few days ago. I was in the eight o'clock class, but there was a conflict."

I remained silent, but I felt his eyes still on me. I didn't like it.

"Be nice to talk to someone in this class."

I thought about it. And I really had to think about it hard because I didn't like strangers and to me everyone was pretty much a stranger. I doodled on the corner of my notebook while he shuffled through his bag beside me.

"I'm Lac," he said as he placed his laptop on his desk and opened it.

I didn't say anything and it may have been rude, but silence was my best friend. It kept people out.

Being a prisoner for endless years taught me one important lesson: life wasn't precious; it was cruel and selfish and people looked for ways to make their lives better by using others. Make themselves happy. Human nature, I guessed. But I wasn't happy and didn't pretend to be, nor would I pretend to believe that it would change. I accepted who I'd become and I didn't regret when a few months ago, I coldly stared at Alexa and pulled the trigger.

I hadn't once felt remorse for ending her life or the two men she'd hired to kidnap Ream and Kat. And I should have. I killed and I had no emotion over it. I never hesitated or thought twice about it. I merely pulled the trigger, poured gasoline all over the basement and set it on fire.

Olaf thought I died with them. Deck assisted in the investigation of the house fire I started, meaning he knew people who knew people and it was squashed and deemed an accidental fire. And to keep anyone from knowing I survived it, Deck made certain the bodies were unrecognizable. That guy was scary and had too much power.

The thing was, my jagged pieces were beginning to show through, like today in the cafeteria. It was like a paper cut that was merely an annoyance at first, but it was getting infected and I was afraid the pus would ooze out and make me fragile again like I had been in the beginning. I couldn't let that happen. I'd never let that happen.

And then there was Crisis. He was breaking through. There was a burning spark that contained my smiles, and I felt as if . . . that maybe I could trust him with parts of me. Never the secrets, but the parts of me that lingered from before all the bad.

Dr. Neale said, "Today, heads-up is fifteen minutes. Go."

I wrote. I'd planned on writing about my run this morning, but my mind took over. The purpose of the exercise; no planning and no thinking about every sentence and just write whatever was sitting on the edge of your mind. No constrictions. And that was why it was so hard for me.

Partway through, I glanced over at Lac when the clicking from his fingers on the keyboard stopped. He must have noticed because he titled his head and looked at me.

I expected him to frown because I'd been rude before, but instead, he cocked a half-grin and nodded to my notebook where my hand was paused over a half-written word. "Looks intense."

I'd written two pages with messy scribbles lining the page. "Not so much." Maybe to others it would be, but they were just sporadic ramblings about . . . I looked at my page and started reading, just what we weren't supposed to do as it was an exercise in freeing the mind from constraints of grammar and rules. But I had rules all my life and now . . . I didn't have any, so I read what I'd written then stopped. I tore it out of my notebook and crumpled it up.

"That bad, huh?" Lac chuckled and it was a nice sound, kind of soft.

Yeah, it was bad. It had been a rambling about Crisis. How he made me smile, the feeling in my stomach when my phone vibrated, knowing it was probably him texting. The way my heart raced when he showed up today and how he didn't push me when I'd had a minor glitch and froze.

"Is there a problem, Haven?" Professor Neale asked and students shifted in their seats to peer in the direction he was looking.

I raised my chin a little and clearly said, "No, sir." I hadn't realized he even knew my name.

"Heads-up are not to be judged by you or anyone else. Next time, I'd prefer if you didn't crumple up your work in the middle of the exercise."

There were a few snickers, but it didn't bother me. They had no idea what it was like to feel embarrassed or made to feel like nothing but an object.

"Yes, sir." I met the eyes of the few students who were still looking at me—each one of them turned away first. I put my head down and started writing again until he announced time was up.

I looked at my page and saw Charlie written over and over and over again. My breath hitched and my heart pounded so hard against my chest that it hurt. I quickly closed my notebook, put it in my bag and pulled out my textbook, trying desperately to swallow the lump in my throat that was crawling upwards, ready to break apart the buried memory that brought with it horrific anguish.

Why? Why did that come up now? It was gone—over. Charlie happened years ago. Why didn't it just go away?

Stop.

I closed my eyes and sang to myself. It took two verses before a wash of cold settled over me. My heart slowed and my hands uncurled from the death grip on my textbook.

I opened my eyes and stared straight ahead, listening to Professor Neale.

Lac remained quiet the rest of the class and it wasn't until class was over and I was walking out that he tugged on my sleeve outside the door. "Have a good weekend, Haven. Like the name by the way."

Most people would assume I was named after a sanctuary, a safe haven . . . ironic that there'd been nothing safe in my life. And my mom had named me after Haven Dust—cocaine.

I forced a smile because I'd been a bitch when he'd been nice. It was difficult being around people who were kind, as I searched for a deeper purpose as to why they were kind. I was accustomed to cruel and selfish, and I could handle that. I was prepared.

I wasn't prepared for nice.

Chapter Six

Crisis

"**R**EAM'S GOING TO kick your ass when he finds out," Kite said, coming down the stairs, barefoot, towel wrapped around his waist, and another in his hand as he rubbed his wet hair. "I'd load up on painkillers before he gets back tomorrow."

I shut the fridge with my foot and cracked open my beer. It hissed and fizzed, the foam spilling over the top, soaking my hand and splattering my jeans. I jumped back, holding it away from me as the cold liquid dripped to the ceramic tiles. "The fuck—" I shot my gaze to Kite who half-smirked. "Kite, fuck, man—you ass. What a waste of good beer." Half the bottle was empty.

Kite stopped drying his hair and tossed his towel over his shoulder. Fucker looked smug as hell with that silver studded brow raised. "Next time, you pick up the groceries, instead of fucking off after a chick you shouldn't be lusting after."

"Not lusting." *She did look fuckin' hot today.* But no, it wasn't lusting; it was way more than that. "We talk."

Kite huffed. "No, you text and that's because you want in her pants."

"It's different."

"Yeah, she kneed you in the balls instead of licked them."

She had, after I jumped off the cliff with her at the cottage. Maybe it was then that I knew it was different with her; well, it was because no chick had ever kneed me in the balls. But the snippets of who she was lay beneath that cold exterior and I liked the snippets—a fuck of a lot. Shit, I liked her cold exterior, too. She was strong yet vulnerable at the same time. What I didn't like was that I'd never seen her smile, but she could be playful, and that surprised me and solidified that she was different.

"Mind your own fuckin' business."

He sighed, shaking his head. "Oh, man, it's all our business when we need to find a new guitarist because you're in the ground after Ream finds out you're getting close with his sister. Especially, when you have this shit happening with some crazy chick you fucked. Seriously, not a cool move."

"Not my fault I'm so good in bed they can't forget me." Kite half-laughed. "And Haven . . . we get along. It's not sexual." That was total bullshit. I got hard when she playfully texted with me. That couldn't be helped. She was beautiful, with stunning gray eyes with a hint of green in them. Then she had this soft, flawless skin and honey blonde hair that hung past her shoulders in waves. Of course, it was sexual, but there was more to it.

"Yeah, tell Ream that," Kite said.

Kite was the type of guy you never saw coming. Quiet. Subtle. Didn't say much to strangers, but it wasn't because he was shy. He had the confidence of a bull. There was something quietly sinister about him. Known him since high school and he'd never done anything to make me think that, except Kite was aloof. He stood and watched. It was like he was getting the play on how to defeat his opponent.

Anyone looking at him would reach the conclusion that the pierced-up, tatted drummer was a rebel with an attitude.

But Kite was a gentleman, polite and kind, at least on the surface, and had one fuck of a good head on his shoulders. Which meant he was probably right. And the asshole had been riding my ass ever since he saw my phone flash Haven. Yeah, well, screw him. I liked talking to Haven, and it may have started out as lust, but now . . . well I wasn't sure what you'd call it, but I wasn't giving it up.

"And Logan . . ." Kite adjusted his towel hanging around his hips. "He's pissed and is going to fire your ass next time you cause a scene like that."

It was my turn to snort. Like hell I'd be fired. We'd been together since high school and stuck together through some serious fucked-up shit with Logan and his dad. "That chick needed a rude awakening that I'm not fuckin' interested." Who the hell let her backstage anyway? "And Logan can't fire me. Band would be nothing without me. Besides, Emily loves me."

Kite grabbed bottled water from the fridge then walked toward the stairs. "She loves Logan. You're an afterthought," he called over his shoulder.

Afterthought, my ass.

I set the beer on the counter, dried off my hand with the horse print dishtowel, courtesy of Kat, then turned on the stereo in the living room. I cranked the volume and the bass instantly broke the silence and pounded through the house. The floor vibrated under my bare feet like electricity pulsing in my blood stream.

My head bobbed to Pink Floyd's "Comfortably Numb," the music coming alive, breathing a potent energy inside me. It was as if I lived in a drab world of grey until music hit and color darted with strings of light through me in every direction.

I strummed on my naked chest, legs braced as the music blared. There was nothing in this world better than music. I'd give up chicks before I gave up music. Besides, music was timeless, chicks weren't. Who the fuck was I kidding? I'd already given up chicks.

I dropped to my knees as David Gilmour's guitar solo hit, leaned back, eyes closed, one hand holding the imaginary neck of the guitar while the other strummed the 'strings' on my abdomen. Working out had its advantages and my ripped abs were made for playing fake guitar.

I told myself a lot of bullshit.

The music died down to a soft murmur.

Fuckin' Kite. "What the—" I stopped abruptly when I opened my eyes and saw that it wasn't Kite. I straightened, sat back on my heels, then smirked.

Haven stood looking at me with raised brows and a subtle smile. Okay, it wasn't quite a smile, more like a lip twitch. It was something that was better than her usual nothing. And she obviously witnessed my rockin' display of godliness.

"Pink Floyd," I said. She didn't respond and I took great delight in the fact that her eyes flicked, albeit briefly, to my naked chest. "I'll take you to their concert next time they come to Toronto. And if you're really nice to me, I'll even get us backstage."

"I'll pass." She crossed her arms over her chest and leaned back against the entertainment wall unit.

I grinned, as this time, her eyes trailed slowly and deliberately down me. I didn't think of it as anything sexual, although I liked to pretend it was. The first few months I'd known her, Haven looked at everyone like that—it was like a quick assessment.

"So, you have a good afternoon, honey?" I hopped to my feet and strolled toward her. Her back stiffened and her slender shoulders straightened. It pissed me off that she did that. It was like I was going to attack her or something and she braced herself.

Her hard grey eyes never left me. She was confident as hell, but skittish. A snow-white lynx. That was what she reminded me of. Quiet and elusive, agile, with a sleek toned body and soft white skin that I was betting my prized guitar . . . felt like velvet beneath my fingertips. And the attitude, predatory and ready to fight, or if necessary—bolt.

But I'd managed to peel back another side to Haven these past few months. She had an elusive sense of humor, at least in text.

Instead of continuing my approach, I backed off, leaned against the back of the couch a couple feet from her and rested my hands on either side of me. I crossed my ankles because it looked casual and relaxed, despite the thread of energy shifting through me and it wasn't from the music any longer. It was her.

"Why are you here? Ream said you and Kite wouldn't be living at the farm anymore." The strap of her book bag slipped off her shoulder and fell into the crook of her arm. She let it drop to the floor. I heard a loud *thonk* and was betting my right testicle that it was that gun.

Well, at least it moved from being *on* her to in her bag. When I'd told Luke, he'd freaked, said she couldn't have it. I knew legally she couldn't, but if Luke tried to take it from her, I was betting there'd be a fight, one that didn't end well for one of them.

Luke conceded to let her keep it, but I also told him none of the guys, his or the band, could know she had it. Part of my deal with her to keep it quiet. Luke agreed with the stipulation that if she ever pointed it at anyone, it was gone.

"Slight exaggeration." And this was where my charm should have some effect, but Haven's face was locked up tightly and I was getting to know her well enough that she was shutting down on me.

I thought about our cliff jump at the cottage. She clung to me like a smooth silk blanket; unfortunately, it wasn't due to my magnetism like I first thought. It was because the girl couldn't swim. But for a brief moment—*I'm talking a lightbulb spark before it burned out*—she smiled. Then we reached shore and she kneed me in the balls once we were out of sight of the others, who were still in the water. It wasn't hard, but any hit to the jewels fuckin' hurt. She ignored me for the rest of the time at the cottage.

My gaze trailed down her body because . . . well, I couldn't help it. Haven had this natural beauty about her. It was the whole package, nothing outstanding like big breasts or hips, but subtle and gentle. She flowed with beauty and Angel, her brother's nickname for her, suited her looks. The attitude was another thing entirely.

"Do I have a disgusting pimple on my face I don't know about?"

I chuckled when I met her eyes. There was her sense of humor, although I didn't think she meant to be funny. My fingers dug into the leather back of the couch as my cock stirred. I thought maybe my desire for her would ease after all the texting, but this chick did something to me and despite my words to Kite, I wanted her.

"Nothing wrong with any part of you. And you'd still be beautiful with pimples."

"You going to tell me I have an inner beauty you can't resist?"

I laughed. Thank fuck, some of that text humor still lingered. "There you are, Ice."

"Why are you and Kite"—she nodded to the stairs where I heard Kite slam the dryer lid closed—"at the farm when you supposedly bought a place?"

"I was going to tell you at school but—"

"You mean you came to suck up to me so I wouldn't bitch to my brother that you and Kite hadn't moved out?"

Fuck, she was good, and steady as a rock. My stiff cock pushed uncomfortably against the confines of my jeans, rubbing against the coarse material like sandpaper. Commando didn't always have its benefits. "Well, yeah."

"You have a wrong impression of me. I don't bitch to my brother about anything. And what happened to the place you 'bought'?"

"It's a good story actually."

Her thin brows rose and I watched her finger slide down her temple and tuck a few stray strands that had escaped her ponytail behind her ear.

Mind-fart. It was a term that never came into play with me. I always had something to say, but my head at that moment was a big-ass fart. Seriously, nothing. Haven would see through any bullshit I fed her. Even through text, she had a bullshit radar and she wasn't afraid to call me on it.

I shrugged. "Didn't happen."

"Obviously." She glanced at my shirt thrown on the kitchen chair and my guitar case on the table, then over to the puddle of beer on the floor I had yet to clean up.

"I thought I had more time. Then the rest of the tour was canceled . . ."

"One venue."

Fuck. "Yeah."

She cocked her hip and placed her hand on it. "So you and Kite never bought a place?"

"We put in an offer. It was rejected." Because I low-balled it. The truth was I wanted to come back to the farm for a few months and decide where I wanted to live. Kite didn't give a crap where he lived; his train of thought was a house didn't deserve attachments because it didn't give anything back except problems and bills. Yeah, because it was a fuckin' house.

"The real estate agent says there isn't much out there with our wants and needs. And she's been really busy fighting with her ex who wants custody of the dog. Some little foofoo thing. I have to admit, it's kind of cute. She emailed me a picture of it in these little sneaker boots and winter jacket with a—"

"Does this story have an ending?"

Hmm, and how to answer that because my ending was certainly different than what she wanted to hear, but I'd discovered the truth was always the best with Haven. "Well sugar, I low-balled the offer so we wouldn't get the place." Fuck, I wanted to see her tuck her hair behind her ear again. "I wanted to hang here for a while longer."

"Hang?"

I shrugged. "Sure."

Oh, she didn't look impressed. Her hackles were raised as her chin hitched up a notch and her angel-like eyes weren't angel-like any- more as they darkened and narrowed. "Ream know?"

Ream and I were like brothers after my parents fostered him. He'd just turned seventeen and was in the custody of child service. A little late fostering a seventeen-year-old, but my parents said they'd seen something in Ream when they'd gone to make their quarterly donation. My mom said he'd been sitting against the wall, knees bent, arms casually hung over them. But what his body language displayed wasn't what my mom saw in his expression—anguish. Pure anguish, so deep she feared what it would do to him being locked in the system for a year.

They'd come home and discussed whether I'd be cool with them taking in a foster kid. I didn't give a shit one way or other. My par- ents had always been involved with kid charities and social services.

I was surprised it had taken them this long before there was another kid living with us. It had been a shock seeing Ream as I'd expected a younger kid. I soon found out why my parents took him in. Ream was completely fucked up.

"Nope."

"So, what will you tell him?"

Now that was the trick question, wasn't it? I tapped my fingers on my crossed arm then pushed off the couch, which landed me right in front of her. Fuck, I could smell her hair, a mixture of coconut and kiwi. Every time I smelled the stuff while on tour, I'd been reminded of her.

Yeah, there was no question Kite was right. I had one hell of a hard-on for her, but Haven was off-limits, and it wasn't because of Ream and his pussy-ass threats. Okay, not pussy, Ream would try to kick my ass, optimal word try. It was because she wasn't a chick to just fuck and walk away from. Not that you could even get close enough to get her to want to fuck you. But I was trying to penetrate, bad choice of words or good, depending on how you looked at it, her armor and I think I'd made progress.

Not that it mattered much. She wasn't interested. I was confident enough to not let it affect me—too much. After the months of texting, I realized that I enjoyed shooting the shit with her. She had a curt honesty that I liked . . . with what little she shared.

The running I knew she did it to try to bury the bad shit that messed with her, and I suspected one day it'd surface. Shit, I saw a glimpse of it today in the cafeteria.

"Don't know yet." I saw that cute little twitch above her left eye. Fuck, it was adorable. Like she was trying to keep herself from smiling. "But, I make one hell of a lasagna. Your brother's favorite."

And there it was, a soft huff and crack of a smile. And that right there made me want her more than I already did. I was so screwed.

"No, your mom does," Kite said, coming down the stairs now wearing clothes—thank fuck. "Haven, he puts the lasagna in the fridge, playing it off as his, but the pink container gives it away. And if that doesn't do it, the neat handwriting on the lid does." He chin-lifted to Haven. "How's school?"

She picked up her bag and moved away from me and into the kitchen. "It's fine."

She put her bag on the chair at the kitchen table and Kite asked her about classes. I droned out of the conversation, instead turning the music back up, though not as loud, then strolled into the kitchen, grabbed a dishrag and wiped up the beer on the floor.

Kite was telling Haven about the crazy party at one of the hotels a few weeks ago. Crazy was an understatement. Insane. Psychotic. A wild party of drugs, alcohol and lots of chicks wearing very little clothing and too much make-up. We had to pay the hotel one hell of a damage bill.

I stood and threw the wet rag into the sink. I caught Haven's eyes dart from my chest to my face. Interesting. I smirked.

" . . . and they will be back tomorrow morning." Kite finished. "Then dinner tomorrow night."

She was going to be pissed hearing what I was about to tell her. "Going to Mom's for dinner when they get back." I tagged my beer off the counter. "She expects you to be there this time, Ice. No excuses." Haven had managed to avoid my mom and dad even though she'd been invited numerous times to go over for lunch, dinner and even for tea, and my mom didn't do tea. Every time Mom called me, there was some reference to Haven and how I should convince her to come over to the house.

Ream heard it from Mom, too. But Haven was resistant to meeting our parents and as an extension, since she was Ream's sister, her parents. I chuckled to myself as I realized in an off-shoot sort of way, I was her 'brother.'

"I have studying to do. I can't go."

I grabbed my navy t-shirt from the back of one of the chairs and put my arms through, then ducked my head as I pulled it over top and let it fall into place. "Oh, baby, you really want to mess with my mom? She's a sweetheart, but she's now yours and that means she has some say. Plus she's making my favorite—spaghetti and meatballs with a shitload of spice."

Haven scooted out of the chair, grabbed her bag and headed for the stairs. "I have to get ready."

"Jesus, what's wrong? You don't like spaghetti? I can get her to make you something else. No big deal." She continued up the stairs. "What the fuck did I say? Ready? For what?" I called after her.

I knew she wasn't thrilled about meeting my parents, but we were all going. It was a welcome home dinner kind of thing. Even Logan's mom, Isabelle, was coming. The only two who couldn't make it were Georgie and Deck, but they invited everyone over for a Sunday brunch at Deck's.

Kite slapped me on the shoulder. "Good call setting up the dinner with your mom. Didn't think you were that . . . tactful." Yeah, well, Logan was already reeling about having to cancel the last venue and Ream soon would be for exaggerating the situation on the house. "Still think he's going to beat your ass."

"Never. The guy hasn't got me off my feet since we were seventeen."

"You better hope he doesn't get Logan on his side."

Logan used to be an illegal underground fighter and even though I was confident with my fighting skills, I was smart enough to know Logan was one guy who could seriously kick my ass. I was hoping a nice dinner with Mom and Dad might cool Ream off about the living arrangements and Logan about the bullshit with the chick.

"And what makes you think you're exempt? I see your ass standing here. I'm the one who hired the real estate agent. You did fuck-all."

"Because I don't talk about his sister like I want to fuck her and haven't been texting her non-stop for months." He walked over to the couch, did a half-leap so his whole body landed lounged out on the black leather. He reached for the remote and flicked on the television. I grabbed my beer and joined him.

"'Call of Duty?'" Kite asked.

"Fuck yeah." It was a Friday night and I was staying in with horses grazing outside my window. My reputation would be ruined if it got out. At least there was a hot chick in the house.

Chapter Seven

Haven

I STEPPED OUT OF the shower, dried off, then opened the door. The cooler air invaded the steam-filled bathroom and I shivered as goose bumps popped up like little gems across my skin.

Crisis and Kite being at the farm had surprised me. My brother had been pretty adamant that he and Kat were taking over the farm and Crisis and Kite were moving into their own place. I planned to move out once I found a job, but I didn't own a car. I didn't even have a driver's license. Alexa purposely used to flash her driver's licence at me, and a few years later, Olaf bought her a car with the money I made at the club.

That was when I learned how to syphon gas. I did it twice when she parked her car in the garage. She freaked when she couldn't start it. The second time, she caught on and that was when I went back to being locked in my room. Then she made my life hell for a few months. But, it was worth it.

"Kite, shoot him. Shoot him. Shoot him." There was a pause and I heard bangs and crashes on the speakers. "Where the hell are you . . .

Kite! Seriously get back . . . man, you suck."

There was a mumble and I was guessing it was Kite's reply. He didn't raise his voice; at least, I never heard him, and he was pretty calm and patient. His appearance contradicted his business-like attitude, all tatted-up and pierced.

I pulled out my long-sleeved V-neck grey shirt and a pair of jeans and threw them on my bed. I inhaled swiftly when there was a quick knock on my door before it flung open.

"Some chick is outside leaning over the fence patting Clifford."

I glared at Crisis. My hands clenched around the towel wrapped around my body. "Just because we texted a few times, doesn't mean you have access to my room."

"I knocked." He strode over to the window and parted the white pleated curtains. "And it was more than a few times texting, babe. Few hundred maybe."

His voice took on a grumbling tone and from the way his broad shoulders flexed beneath the snug t-shirt I could tell he was a little pissed at my casual reference to our texting.

I walked to window and glanced out. He stood beside me and for some reason, it was different with him than before he left on tour. He was in my bedroom, me in a towel, hair dripping wet and there was no overwhelming need to get him out of my space. Instead, there was comfort in his presence and something else . . . a whoosh in my belly that I was currently trying to ignore.

It also meant vulnerability.

A rare ambiguity compressed my constant barrier into a tight little package at my feet. If he took one step to the right and touched me, he'd step on it and crush it.

I swallowed.

There was no room for what was traipsing all over my body like some engorged fire that fed off a pile of dynamite. I didn't know if he felt it too or what, but I saw his fingers curl tightly around the curtain. I glanced at him and he was still staring out the window, but his jaw clenched.

He abruptly turned, eyes locking on mine. There was a moment of silence as we stood completely still, bodies inches apart, his one hand at his side, so close to mine that if I took a deep breath, our fingers would touch.

He was first to break. "Haven." It was a husky whisper.

That was all I needed to snap me out of it and I clamped up. I stepped away and focused my attention on the girl outside. "It's Dana. Don't worry. She isn't one of your stalkers." Although, she may soon be when she found out Crisis and Kite were here.

"Funny, Ice. That girl is a misguided chick with a fucked-up delusion of what happened between us."

I didn't say anything.

Dana stroked Clifford's white and dapple-red head. Clifford was rescued from an abusive home a few years ago. When I first came to live here, in order to avoid everyone, I'd sit in the field, under this oak tree and Clifford would always find me and nudge my leg then eat all the grass around me.

I turned around as Crisis threw himself down on my bed. He lay on his side, perched up on his elbow and looked at me. The loose-ringed blond curls hung just over the cusp of his ears, unkempt strands that couldn't decide which side to part on.

I eyed him for a second . . . maybe it was more admired . . . it was another moment of weakness, but there was no denying Crisis was attractive.

He grinned. "Want me to pick you out something to—"

"I want you to get out of my room." His muscular thighs rested on top of my clothes and he lifted slightly so I could yank them out from under him. I strode to the bathroom and the mattress creaked behind me. "Get out, Crisis."

I shut the door.

"I'll go introduce myself," he called.

There'd be no introduction needed. Dana lived on Earth; she'd know who Crisis was.

I quickly dressed, applied a small amount of mascara and lip gloss, then emerged from the bathroom. Crisis was like a leech that kept sucking the blood out of me, but it wasn't blood, it was my coldness. It was as if he was the heater turned on high and I was the block of ice that was slowly melting. And it had happened over text—text. How was that even possible? I thought it was safe. I thought I could keep my distance, but it was too late. Crisis had somehow become important.

Fifteen minutes later, after changing tops two more times—not to try and look better, but the complete opposite—I walked downstairs into the living room. Dana sat on the couch with Kite and Crisis, a game controller in her hand.

"Yes!" she screamed, leaping to her feet, pumping her fist in the air as her car crossed the finish line a millisecond before Crisis.' "I rock."

"No, sugar, we're the ones who rock." Crisis grinned and tossed his controller onto the glass coffee table.

Dana noticed me and put her hands on her hips. "Seriously? What the hell? Why didn't you tell me you lived with Tear Asunder? Like, this is huge. Huge, girl. And you kept it from me?"

I shrugged. "They just got back. They were—"

"Yeah, on tour." She leaned over and playfully punched Crisis on the shoulder. "Tickets. That's what I get for winning. To your next concert in Toronto. And I want a backstage pass." She was virtually hopping up and down with excitement. It was going to be a night of talking about the band. And this was why I'd never told anyone. Not that I had anyone to tell except Dana and a few acquaintances who were her friends, not mine.

Her grin vanished as she took in my attire. "And you're so not wearing that. You look like a nun off-duty."

Crisis burst out laughing and Kite chuckled, eyeing me, then he winked because I suspected Kite knew I was not into going out and dressing up. I liked being a mosquito on the wall, watching, ready to get out of the way of any threat or be the threat. Either way, I was a bystander until I was forced not to be a bystander anymore.

Dana picked up a classy red designer bag off the floor and climbed over Kite's long legs that were stretched out and perched on the coffee table. "Good thing I brought clothes for you."

Shit. And double shit. If they were anything like Dana was wearing now, short black skirt and skin-tight red V-neck that had slits under both arms and a thin strap for sleeves over her shoulders.

"Don't un-nun her too much. She gets . . . cold," Crisis blurted out.

I ignored him, but Dana didn't. "Oh, she won't be cold when the guys see her and can't keep their hands of her."

"Ice hates hands on her," Crisis called after us.

I walked upstairs and heard a smack come from the living room. I was uncertain if it was Crisis smacking Kite or the other way around.

Dana dumped her bag on my bed then faced me, her eyes wide, mouth gaping. "That's Crisis. Crisis from Tear Asunder. I swear I peed a little when he answered the door. And then. . . . Holy crap, Kite . . . that tatted-up pierced pack of muscles is a God. I didn't know which one to drool over first." She stomped her foot and crossed her arms. "How could you keep this from me? A month I've known you and not once did you mention you lived with Tear Asunder." Her brows lowered over her dark walnut eyes. "Wait a sec . . . why do you live with the band? And they live on a horse farm? That is so . . . well, weird. I expected some mansion downtown or a penthouse at a hotel with raving parties. What's the deal?"

I shrugged. "I don't want who my brother is to be all over school and—"

Dana screamed. "Oh. My. God. Who is your brother? Kite? There is no way Crisis is. That guy was looking you up and down like he wanted to tear off your clothes."

"He looks at all girls like that." And according to the internet, he did a hell of a lot more than tear off their clothes.

Dana snorted. "No. I've seen enough of him on social media to know his looks. Yeah, he flirts and plays them up, but the way he looked at you, even dressed like that, it was different."

Crisis had never hidden from me that he was a man-whore who didn't keep it in his pants. And why should he? But, I hadn't seen any of that. At least not on this tour. Any pictures I'd seen with him and chicks were older.

Dana unzipped her bag and threw articles of clothing on the bed. "So, is it Kite? He's kind of mysterious and quiet. I could see him as your brother. Anytime he's quoted, it's composed and polite. He reminds me of a hot businessman without the suit. I'm betting he'd look hot as hell in a suit and knows how to make a girl—"

"Dana. Stop." I walked to the bed and shifted through the clothes, or rather the small scraps of material. There wasn't a chance I was going out wearing any of this. I was showing as little skin as possible. "Ream's my twin brother."

Dana dropped the black silk item she'd been holding up to her chest like a top, although to me it looked like panties. "Holy crap. Ream's your twin?"

I nodded. It was kind of weird him being famous and having a girl freak out over him. The last time we'd been together, we were huddled in an old lady's shed, starving, dirty and probably smelling like garbage. We ate enough of it that it must have leaked from our pores.

"He is smokin' hot. Oh, my God, and Sculpt . . . Jesus, that guy is intense and gorgeous."

"And taken." Logan made it clear that Emily was his fiancée one night on stage. Supposedly, it had been all over social media within minutes, although he'd proposed to her privately in bed. I knew about it because Kat told me one of those times when I sat outside on the porch and she came and joined me to talk. I listened. "And my brother is too." From what I'd seen so far of Ream with Kat, he was over-protective and possessive. I had a good feeling he was that way because of what had happened to me. Ream always felt responsible and I knew he carried guilt for not seeing what was happening with Gerard.

But he was finally happy and that was the best gift I could ever receive.

And Gerard . . . I hated him. I wanted to kill him again and again for what he did. For the loss of more than myself. Of a part of me I'd never get back. I wish I'd been able to reach the gun before Ream smashed the statue down on his head. It should've been me who killed him, but I'd been pathetic back then.

"Are you okay? You're shak—"

A hand came down on my shoulder and the violence inside me erupted as I swung around and knocked Dana back with both my hands to her chest. She stumbled backwards, the bed stopping her momentum as she crashed into it.

"Haven?"

But her voice had become another's, one I hated . . . Alexa. One who locked me up in a cage in the dark when Olaf wasn't around. Unable to stand, sitting cramped in a metal cage that was at the end of her bed. I was her pet to let out when she felt like it. Of course, I was always released when Olaf was home. He was tolerant of Alexa's abuse of me because she 'looked after' him, but there were limits. I was the one who made them money.

"What's wrong?"

It was Alexa's voice again, weeding her way back into me. I knew she was dead, but I couldn't stop the feeling as if she was holding me down.

Alexa was leaning over me, her fingers digging into my shoulders as she yelled at the doctor . . . oh, God, the doctor. He was here.

I shook my head, trying to clear the vision. Desperate to bury it again, but it was like a movie on fast forward, playing a jittery black and white scene.

Pain. Between my legs, so much pain, but the emotional anguish was so much more.

I tried to get to the door. I tried so hard to get free, but they kept pushing me down into the mattress.

Sweat dripped down my face, my hair plastered to it and eyes blurred as I reached out crying.

"Nooooo," I screamed.

But strong hands pressed onto my shoulders as I lay screaming and crying. I heard the doctor and Alexa arguing, then the needle came toward me and I fought even harder. I hated needles ever since Gerard. I didn't want a needle. But the doctor's hand grabbed my arm and yanked. I cried out as the sharp prick punctured my shoulder.

Then I begged.

Stop. Stop.

Oh, God, I was cracking. I could feel the pieces slipping through and surfacing.

The door burst open beside me.

"Haven."

Crisis? Crisis. Not the doctor. Not Alexa.

He came straight for me and without hesitation, wrapped me in his arms, pulling me into his warm, hard chest. A soothing hand rubbed down my back. "It's okay. You're safe."

I stiffened and went to push him away when I inhaled a ragged breath and felt my starved lungs expand and take in his scent. My mind knew him. My body did too.

He quietly spoke to me, but I didn't know what he said. I just listened to the gentle tone of his voice.

I closed my eyes and sagged against him.

"What happened?" Crisis asked, but it wasn't to me; it was to Dana.

"I don't know. We were just talking about the band and then . . . she started shaking and freaked out when I touched her."

Crisis kissed the top of my head before he pulled back and tilted his head down to look at me. "You good now?"

I heard the floor creak to the right of us and saw Kite standing in the doorway scowling, but his eyes were filled with concern.

"I'm calling Ream," Kite said. "Maybe he can get a flight out tonight."

"No." I shook my head violently. "Don't. He can't know. This has nothing to do with him. Nothing." I directed my words to Crisis now. "Don't tell him." I could deal with this. It was a minor break in my armor.

Crisis had seen my pain, knew I ran to keep the demons away and he'd kept his promise and never told my brother. He understood.

Crisis' arms stiffened around me and I felt his heart beat steadily but thumping hard against my chest. "Kite, I got this," he said.

"Man, I don't think—"

"I fuckin' got this." Crisis' tone hardened, as did his grip around me. "Do not call him."

I breathed a sigh of relief when Kite lowered the phone and nodded.

"Dana, give us a sec?" Crisis asked.

"Umm, yeah, sure."

Kite and Dana silently left the room and the door clicked shut behind them.

I pulled from Crisis' arms, but our eyes remained locked, his narrowed and . . . the playfulness had vanished from earlier and in its place was a combination of determination and disquiet, meaning I was going to have to give him something.

"What happened?"

I was able to block this shit out. What the hell was wrong with me?

"It's . . . stress." Not a lie, it was a form of stress.

His brows rose and he braced himself against the dresser, arms crossed. "Stress?"

I shoved a strand of hair behind my ear. "Yeah, I freaked for a second."

"Freaked?"

I nodded and ignored him while sifting through the clothes on my bed. I hadn't realized I was holding the pseudo-panties until I looked down at them in my hand. I quickly tossed them aside.

"Haven, I get this is different now that I'm standing here, but I'm the same person you've talked to for months."

I didn't say anything because I was scrambling to find my steady. That part of me that I'd built up over the years that meant my survival.

"You're not going to tell me, are you?"

Not a chance in hell.

"Okay. What do you need?"

"Need?" I turned to face him, frowning.

He shrugged. "I get you don't want to tell me, but you need an outlet." He paused, biting the inside of his cheek. "Kat has that ugly pink clown statue in the bathroom upstairs. Fuckin' thing gives me nightmares. I can't even piss with that thing watching me from its high and mighty shelf above the toilet. We could smash it with a hammer."

Crisis knew how to take a horrible moment and make it easier because as the memories faded back, I pictured Crisis with a hammer in his hand sitting on the floor and breaking the clown into little pieces. And there was a cute grin on his face as he did it.

I shook my head and went back to looking through the clothes. "I don't need an outlet."

"Bullshit. I know you, even if you think I don't. I caught you running to the point of exhaustion. I know all you do is study and go to school. You don't go out. You dress like it's cold even in the middle of summer and you conceal that scar on your wrist, but often run your finger over your shirt where it lays." I never expected Crisis to have noticed that. When did he notice that? It had to be before he left, before all the texting. "I'm surprised about Dana. You never mentioned her. I didn't expect that. But I'm glad you're making friends." He chin-lifted to me, expression serious. "Now, are you going to keep bullshitting me? Or should I go on?"

I sat on the end of the bed, shoulders erect, unflinching as he stared back at me. "Maybe I need you to leave me alone." It was stupid remark, but what I really needed was to forget what just happened and just be normal. The problem was, I had no clue what normal felt like.

He laughed. "Look what happened when you said that last time." He pushed away from the dresser and strode toward me, one hand in his jeans pocket and the other clenched into a fist at his side. He stopped directly in front of me and I had to crank my neck up to look at him.

"What do you want from me, Crisis?" I was an out-of-control sled, sliding down a mountain and I couldn't stop the words. "We texted because it was part of the deal, that's it."

His brows lowered even further over his eyes and it made him appear hazardous. My stomach unsettled and it wasn't because I was nervous around him, but because I put that look there.

Crisis crouched like he'd done in the stables months ago, but this time, he put his hands on my thighs. I should've moved away, felt uneasy with him touching me, but I didn't. His hands weren't groping or prodding; they were steady and calming. "That's not it. And we didn't do it because of some goddamn deal. We both know that."

My breath hitched and his hands tightened on my thighs. Then I caved because it was wrong. What I said was a lie and I'd never lied to him. I'd used avoidance maybe, but never lied.

"Yeah."

He sighed, stood and gently ran his hand over the top of my head before striding toward the door. "I'll tell Dana you're staying in. We can watch a movie and order pizza."

"No. I want to go." I paused then added. "I need to do this."

"Why?"

"I just . . ."

"You have nothing to prove, Haven." Crisis had his hand on the doorknob, his back stiff. "But if you think you do, then we're coming with you. Kite can be the DD."

"No. You can't." I didn't want the attention he dragged with him.

He glanced over his shoulder at me. I did a quick scan of his face. He wasn't scowling. He wasn't smiling either. His brows were drawn together and he looked . . . pensive. Contemplative.

"I can. And we are. And don't change. Nuns are a sweet-ass fantasy of mine." He jerked open the door and shut it behind him.

I collapsed back on the bed, arms outstretched above my head, clasping the pillow and pulling it over my face. My screwed-up mind was short-circuiting.

Something had triggered the memory. A hand on my shoulder wouldn't normally set me off, but my emotions were shooting off like pellets and I needed to run again.

The wind pushed against the windowpane and I trembled. Closing my eyes, I sang to myself, the sound muffled under the protection of the pillow.

Chapter Eight

Haven

16 years old

"HAVEN?" THERE WAS a light tapping on my door and my eyelids peeled open. My eyes rolled back in my head before refocusing.

Gerard stiffened, his hands locked onto my wrists, pressing them into the mattress on either side of me. "Answer him," he spat into my ear. "Tell him you're in bed already."

I was too drugged up to refuse, my haze a spiralling spectrum of colors in my surreal dreams. Gerard's voice was wonky and deep as if he was talking in slow motion.

A sudden hard sting hit my cheek. "Tell the little fuck to go away."

"Sis? You missed classes again. I need to talk to you. Let me in."

My head twisted to the side, the pillow easing the burning in my face from Gerard's slap. There was a loud banging on the door and I stared at it, the wood appearing as if it warped and pulsed with the sound of his fist.

Cruel hands gripped my shoulders and shook me violently. My neck whipped back and forth as if it was attached to my body by a thin layer of skin. "Damn it. Answer him before he breaks down the damn door," he growled in a low whisper, the heat of his breath wafting onto the spot just below my ear lobe. It tickled and I tried to move away, not liking the feeling, knowing I didn't like what was happening to me, but being unable to do anything about it. I wanted to go back to the haze, the escape, but Gerard hovered above me, his glaring eyes furious.

I watched a bead of sweat appear at his hairline, dribble down to his right brow then drip onto his eyelash and disappear. His heavy weight lay on top of me and my nightgown was scrunched up above my breasts. The smothering heat of his revolting skin blanketed me and I had to get away, but my limbs were pathetic and weak, as if they were trapped in quicksand.

"Haven!" Ream shouted. One loud bang sounded on the door.

"Ream," I answered in a soft ragged voice.

Gerard leaned closer, grabbed a handful of my hair and pulled my head up so that his mouth was against my ear. "Tell him you'll talk to him tomorrow."

Pain ripped through my scalp, awakening some form of reality of what was happening. "Tomorrow," I managed to get out.

"No. Now. Something's wrong. Let me in."

Gerard swore under his breath. "Pull your shit together. You have two minutes to get rid of him or he's dead." He rolled off me and went into the closet.

I tried to focus, but my vision was blurry and everything was distorted, but I had to let him in before he broke down the door and Gerard came out of the closet and killed him.

"Okay," I said, but it took me a while to get to the door and I could hear the floor creaking under my brother's feet outside as he paced back and forth.

I opened the door.

Ream was my twin. We'd been through hell together and even though I tried to hide it, the second he saw my face, he knew. Our mother had the same look. He grabbed hold of my arm, yanked up the sleeve of my nightgown and ran his finger over the track marks. "Haven?" He let my arm go then cupped my head, thumbs slowly stroking back and forth. "Angel, what are you doing? Fuck."

I didn't say anything mostly because I was still fucked up and couldn't, but there was also the fear of Ream discovering Gerard in the closet. My legs buckled and Ream picked me up and carried me to the bed.

"Why? Jesus, why?" Ream was stubborn, always had been and it was probably why he survived what he did in the basement. "Who did this? Who gave you the drugs?" His voice hardened. "Damn it, what is going on with you?" He refused to stop, his voice getting louder and I heard the rage in it. "Tell. Me."

I just wanted to sleep. To curl up and go away, make Gerard go away, everything to go away.

"Who?" He came to his feet when I didn't say anything and that was when he went ballistic. It terrified me. I'd never seen him lose control like that, kicking the old wooden chair in the corner of the room so hard the two front legs busted. He tore a painting down from the wall and put his knee through it. It was one we found in the back alley that had yellow staining on it. But it was a picture of a little girl with a palomino horse nose to nose.

My eyes kept going to the gun on the dresser, Gerard's gun. Oh God, Ream was going to see it any second and when he did, he'd freak even worse. I had one choice—tell him now while Gerard didn't have a gun or an advantage.

I reached out my hand and Ream stopped pacing and came over to the side of the bed. He knelt on one knee and I urged him closer. "Please, you have to stay quiet. Please," I whispered, then said, while raising my voice so Gerard would hear me, "You used to sing to me." He scowled, but didn't say anything. I had to make sure Gerard didn't catch on to what I was saying.

"Remember where you sang to me?"

He opened his mouth to answer and I put my finger over it. His eyes darted to the closet and I nodded. My head spun and it took a second before I could focus again and continue. "For months . . ." His eyes widened and I knew he understood that whoever was in the clos-et, had been fucking with me for months. Ream and I often finished one another's sentences; he knew where I was taking this.

"Like Mom."

He put his head in his hands. He knew. Our mother would get high then have sex with whoever was at the house. Most of the time I never saw who the men were as I stayed hidden.

I nodded to the closet then to the dresser where the gun lay. "I can do it," I whispered. "You have to leave. Olaf will find you and kill you if you do it."

Olaf hated Ream. I wasn't sure why, maybe because he saw the threat in Ream. But this was our only chance. The path we were on had changed and the only way out was to kill Gerard. But I had to be the one to do it, not Ream. I'd never let him carry that with him.

But my brother dove for the closet like he was flying through the air, and there was no gravity. "You disgusting piece of filth. I'll kill you."

Gerard moved fast for his size as he ducked under Ream's fist then kicked out, sending Ream crashing into the hangers, then to the floor. Gerard's feet thudded like drums across the bedroom and I knew where he was headed.

"Ream, the gun."

"She's worthless, just like you are. Garbage." Gerard had bulk, but it was fat bulk, and Ream was lean and toned, although he was only sixteen and still lanky. I grabbed the bedpost, using it for steadiness as the dream-like euphoria mixed with the reality of what was going down. Fear churned when I saw Gerard's intent and panic slammed into my head.

"No. No." I scrambled from the bed and landed hard on my knees. The sensation was like I'd fallen right through the floor and bounced back up.

Gun.

Gun.

Gun.

I didn't know if I said the words aloud, but they were screaming inside my head over and over again.

Gerard dove for the dresser, but Ream had gained his feet and was right on top of him. His fist connected with the side of Gerard's head. His body went down like a rock and a loud thump vibrated through the room. I attempted to climb to my feet, uncertain what I was going to do, but knowing I had to move. I had to get to the gun.

"You're dead. You're fuckin' dead." Ream didn't go for the gun that had slid off the dresser onto the floor; instead, he grabbed with both hands the solid stone statue that we had found in the trash on our way home from school a few months earlier. It was heavy, too heavy for me to lift, but Ream had carried it all the way home because I said I liked it.

"Ream!" Fear skidded into me as he raised the stone gargoyle above his head. He straddled Gerard, who was laying on the floor with his hand to his head as if dazed. The consequence of killing Gerard was death. Olaf wouldn't allow my brother to live.

Ream's face was a mask of red, lips tight, brows dangerously low over his piercing dark eyes. "Ream. No." I had to be the one. This was my fault.

I crawled through the quicksand, making my way to the gun on the floor while tears streamed down my face. Ream didn't look at me. It was as if he didn't see anything except Gerard.

"You're dead, kid." Gerard tried to push to his feet.

Ream slammed the statue down on his skull. I heard a sickening crack then a thump as Gerard's body slumped back to the floor.

"Ream! No. You can't." It had to be me. I had to be the one to do it. But it was too late as I watched him raise the statue above his head again then smash it into Gerard's head.

Blood splattered the faded and torn flowered wallpaper, my mind playing havoc with me seeing the beauty in the mist of red. But somewhere inside, I knew it wasn't beauty but ugliness and this was going to be the end, not only of Gerard but of Ream and me. Yet the meaning of the end, I couldn't decipher.

My cries were lost to the crushing sound of the statue connecting with bone. I curled up on the floor, the drug and what I witnessed too much for my mind to handle as I trembled and shook. Warm tears slid down my cheeks, feeling like heated wax as they dried and stuck to my skin, then new ones glided overtop.

I had no perception of time, but eventually, the blows stopped. I squeezed my eyes shut, arms hugging my legs to my chest.

"Angel." Ream's voice was a strangled cry of despair. "Fuck. Angel." His hand stroked my head, pushing my hair back from my face. I heard the slight catch in his throat and it tore into me like a knife. "I'm sorry. I'm so sorry."

"Leave. We have to leave." I was too screwed up to say anything more, but I opened my eyes briefly and saw blood speckled across his face like spray paint. I quickly shut them again, trying to block out what was happening, what all this meant for my brother.

"I know." Ream lifted me off the floor into his arms. My head hung limply over the back of his arm, and I was too weak to pull it back up. He shifted me in his arms until I was cradled against his chest, my head resting on his shoulder.

I choked on a sob that was lodged in my tightened throat. We had nowhere to go and no money, and I was a mess. I couldn't go two days anymore without being completely strung out, needing Gerard and the drugs he brought with him.

Trapped in a vicious cycle there was no escape from.

Just like my mother.

But even in my drugged-up state, I knew the consequences of what Ream had done for me. We had no choice.

We had to run.

As he ran with me, I caught a glimpse of Alexa standing at my bedroom door.

Chapter Nine

Crisis

WHAT THE HELL was that? She'd freaked out, pale, shivering . . . like in the cafeteria but worse. The flip in my stomach wasn't a good one. It was knotted and churning with the frothy beer. I was no psychologist, but this shit she was fighting was going to blow up in her face. I knew it. I saw it coming. I told her it would months earlier, yet we texted and she appeared as if she was getting better, even joking with me.

But the moment I heard her scream, my heart jammed up into my throat and lodged there like a fuckin' rock. I hadn't moved that fast in . . . maybe ever. I flew over the back of the couch, charged up the stairs and into her room. Kite right behind me.

Haven was an ice angel, strong and untouchable. But since being back . . . her ice cracked twice and what scared me was I hadn't been around to see how often this was happening. None of us had. Luke hadn't either, which meant if shit like this was happening, she hid it well. The excessive running she couldn't hide, but Luke had seen something haunted in her face when she went for that three-hour run, and that was why he'd called me.

I yanked on a fresh pair of jeans then hopped on one foot as the end caught on my heel. It finally gave and I did up the buttons and grabbed a black t-shirt from the dresser.

Tonight was going to be fucked up. I knew it. I told Kite and he swore numerous times under his breath then suggested we call Luke back in as he'd gone home for a few days. Luke had two of his guys with Logan and Ream in Vancouver still.

I reached for my baseball cap then tossed it aside. "Fuck it." We weren't escaping notice, and in certain situations, it was better not to try to hide because that was when the shit usually hit the fan.

I chugged back the rest of my beer while Kite and I waited for the girls. We sat on the couch taking turns flicking elastic bands across the room trying to topple over the empty beer bottle I placed on the shelf under the television.

"She needs help," Kite said and shot his elastic, hitting the base of the beer bottle.

"Ream and Kat tried. She doesn't want it. Her choice." I squinted and pulled back on the rubber then let it fly. It hit the bottle and it wobbled but didn't fall over.

"Sometimes, people need a push. You flirted with Kat to push Ream into making his move on getting her back."

And it landed us in a shitload of fights with Ream hating me until he finally picked up his balls and claimed his chick like he should've done from the beginning. "This is different. Whatever went down with her for the last twelve years . . ." I ran my hand through my messy strands that I'd given up trying to tame way back in high school. Plus I discovered the chicks liked a disheveled look. "Fuck, man, that Alexa chick was a sadist from the look of Ream's back when they escaped that shit storm six months ago. That bitch was crazy."

"Yeah."

"I'm glad Haven shot her."

Kite looked at me and after a second nodded.

We were silent for a minute, neither of us shooting elastic bands.

"You want to tell me exactly what a sadist does? You know . . . in the bedroom," I asked.

Kite flicked the elastic at my head. "Don't go there. I'm not a fuckin' sadist."

I knew he didn't give a crap what I said about his sex life. Kite had his own pleasure-pain that rivalled on a little fucked-up for my tastes. But it was consensual.

"And why the fuck would you let any guy hold your dick and jab a needle through it? What the hell, man?"

Kite hit me in the chest with his fist this time. "It was a chick and I've never had any complaints about it."

"Yeah, because by the time they see it, you have them tied up with a whip in your hand."

"Don't do that at home. Ropes. That's it. All else is at the club."

I did know that. He'd told me once that his tastes involved trust and he was never with a girl long enough to get that, so instead, he went to the club. It was a safe place for those interested in that lifestyle.

I shot my elastic again. "She does need help, but she needs our trust more." Haven may never tell anyone what hell she'd been through. But regardless, it was her right to refuse.

Kite didn't say anything and he wasn't taking his turn so I looked at him. He was looking at me, eyes narrowed—assessing.

"What?" I punched him in the chest then threw my handful of elastic into the bowl on the coffee table and stood.

The floorboards at the top of the stairs creaked and stole my attention. Haven stood with her hand on the railing, her hair falling in soft blonde tresses over one shoulder and her legs . . . shit, she'd changed out of the jeans. It was the first time I'd ever seen her naked legs. Even when I jumped in the water with her, she was wearing pants and a long-sleeved shirt.

My breath locked down. My heart did the opposite and thumped wildly, which propelled my blood through my veins like a raging river right down to my cock. I went hard as a fuckin' rock. Shit, no it was harder . . . like iron. She wore shiny black pumps and even from here, I could see her toes curled in the open toe on her right foot that was tipped forward about to make the first step downstairs.

The mid-thigh length black dress gripped every curve of her body like cling wrap, sweet hips, slimming into a tight abdomen and waist. But it was her thighs I kept going back to, muscled and toned from the running, smooth silk that begged me to caress and grab and have wrapped around my waist.

Screw the nun fantasy.

I was the man-whore with every part of me at the sight of her, because sure as fuck, I wanted to drag her to my room and fuck her until she screamed my name over and over again and I didn't care if she hated me in the morning as long as I got to taste her.

Well, that was where my head was, all in my cock with no blood feeding my brain. Because I did care if she hated me and not just in the morning.

My eyes trailed to her breasts, not big, but would fit nicely cupped in my hands. Her neck was bare, no jewelry, no material to hide her collarbone that I imagined sliding my tongue across and leaving little red marks as I nipped her skin up the gentle curve of her neck.

When my eyes finally made it up to hers, she was glaring, mouth tight and brows low. Haven certainly wouldn't like being looked at like she was something to eat. But she fuckin' was. I'd lick every inch of her then taste the sweetness between her legs.

But that wasn't happening. Shit, I didn't want to ruin anything we had and she was too screwed up to be with a guy like me. My loyalty track record with chicks was zero and I lost interest as soon as I had a taste. I liked what we had and I was determined not to screw it up by thinking with my cock.

Didn't mean I couldn't look and jerk off later to that image of her standing at the top of the stairs looking like a hard-ass angel that could cut off my dick with her teeth or stroke it with the velvet touch of her tongue.

Kite punched me in the shoulder and knocked me off-balance. "Ream's sister. And your mom wants her in the family, not running for her life."

"Don't fuckin' mention my mom when I'm looking at a hot chick. Jesus." It was like a pinprick to my inflated cock. As she approached, my mouth dried up and I had trouble forming a single sane thought, because all that was raging through me was the desire to grab her, throw her down and sink into her while I crushed her mouth with mine.

"Snap out of it." Kite shoved me and I staggered sideways into the coffee table. I was seeing a face plant any second and took a large leap with one leg to the other side so I was straddling it.

Kite shook his head at me then looked at Haven. "You look good." He smiled at her, then grabbed the car keys and went outside, the screen door clanging behind him.

"Wow, Ice. You look smokin' hot." I jumped forward to get away from straddling the table. She frowned and that wasn't the reaction I was searching for. Embarrassment, a little heat in the cheeks, fuck, a smile would be good enough. A guy tells a girl she looks smokin' hot, you'd expect her to be happy. But Haven wasn't just some girl. She was . . . distinctive.

She walked up to me and looked me up and down. "You wearing that?"

I looked down at myself frowning. What the hell was wrong with . . . I glanced back at her and saw the slight upward curve of her shiny pink glossed lips. Nice. She was teasing me and teasing from Haven was fuckin' special as hell. "Oh, baby, I could wear a snow suit and the chicks would still flock to me."

She bit her lip but I saw her eyes flicker in the direction of my cock. "Flock South, you mean."

I laughed, then stepped closer to her. It kind of sucked that instead of a chick wilting and getting all mushy when I came toward her, Haven stiffened.

God, she was breathtaking. Literally, breathtaking. I reached out and cupped her chin to make sure she kept her eyes on me. "You're striking, Haven." Her grey eyes flickered and there was a hint of warmth in them. I hadn't meant to keep going, but the words tumbled out before I could stop them. "Something to treasure and never touch." And that right there was the reality. I couldn't touch. And I wanted to, because fuck, if I didn't care more for her than I probably should.

Her eyes widened and her long thick lashes lowered over her eyes and for the first time, I saw a slight pink hue on her cheeks. Suddenly, I wondered if she ever got that when we texted.

She raised her chin and met my eyes. "Thanks," she whispered.

One word and it was as if she'd handed me a piece of her that no one ever saw. Everything in that one word was her letting me in. It was Haven trusting what I said to be the truth and not some bullshit coming out of my mouth. And it was fuckin' precious.

"So, is Kite seeing anyone?" Dana pranced down the stairs and did a little hop to land next to Haven.

I thought about it for a second then slowly a smirk formed. Payback for the beer. Haven must have noticed my expression change and subtly shook her head.

"Nope," I said. "But he was talking about you earlier."

"He was?" Her pitch went up.

She blushed and excitement danced in her eyes. Well, at least the chick was pretty. I was probably doing Kite a favor more than anything, except that he was particular about his women.

"Sure. He's a little standoffish, but just keep on him and he'll come around." I turned the dig a little more. "He said you were hot." He did say she was cute, same thing.

She squealed and I chuckled, avoiding looking at Haven, but I felt her glower. "I call front seat," Dana said as she dashed out the door.

"Liar," Haven muttered as she went for her purse.

"No gun, Haven."

Her hand stilled on the black leather bag for a few seconds before she followed Dana out the door . . . without her purse, thank fuck. I didn't know why she needed it. I was told about the scumbag Olaf being 'looked after' by Vic. But for Haven, that gun was her safety and if I had it my way, I was changing that. I was making myself her safety.

A horn honked and I pressed the alarm to 'Away' and followed Haven out the door.

Even though the farm had yet to be exposed to the media, we had issues when Logan's past came back to bite him in the ass. So, we had the security system put in by Deck's team. State-of-the-art, he'd told us.

The old guy, Hank, wouldn't notice if anyone was lurking. He was responsible for the care of the horses, which Kat and Emily rescued from meat auctions.

I'd never really paid much attention to the beasts, but after seeing Emily work her horse whispering magic, it was majestic. I gained a huge respect for her ability. She could take a completely freaked-out, crazy stallion and within a half-hour, have him walk up to her and place his muzzle on her shoulder.

Respect, trust and love. That was what she always said. He couldn't love you if he couldn't respect you, and he couldn't trust for the same reason. But you gained a horse's respect, then gained his trust and you'd have a bond for life.

My step faltered as it hit me. I shoved the keys in my front jean pocket and stared at the cobblestone path. Did Haven respect me? How could I ask her to trust me if she didn't?

I ran my hand through my hair . . . I wanted her respect. I never gave a crap with other chicks, but I didn't want her seeing me as a man-whore with a guitar in his hand. Some rock star who could only stroke his guitar and a chick's pussy. Didn't help my case that I had this obsessed chick hanging over me.

The fucked-up part of it was . . . that playboy status had been in limbo for months. Fuckin' months. Logan asked me a few weeks ago if I'd caught crabs and that was why I was laying off the chicks. But the truth was I was tired of chicks who didn't even know my real name. Sure, it was easy pussy and got me off, but . . . I glanced over at Haven sliding into the back seat. I'd rather lie in bed and text Haven than fuck some random chick.

Seriously, fucked-up.

I walked to the car, yanked open the backdoor and slid in. "So, where we headed?"

Dana turned around, her elbow resting on the back of the seat. "Frat party. It's going to be wicked."

Kite groaned. "Crisis, you said a small party. We need to call in Luke."

Dana fiddled with the radio and turned up the sound when Coldplay came on. "Don't worry. The guys are pretty cool. It's mostly the lacrosse team. There won't be any trouble."

"I wasn't worried about the guys," Kite said in a deep pissed-off tone. "How about we go to a movie?"

Dana laughed. "You sound like my dad." Kite snorted. "If you really don't want to go, I *guess* you could drop us off and then come back later to get us."

"Oka—" Kite started to say, but I interrupted him. "No, we're good. Besides, I'm not leaving my hot sister alone with a bunch of frat boys."

Haven kicked my shin. "Don't call me that."

I raised my brows, attempting to pull off my most innocent expression. "What? Hot?"

"No. Sister. Well actually, both."

"Why?"

"I don't like it. Ream's my brother. You're not."

"Well, legally maybe, but—"

"Stop."

"Okay, baby. Whatever you want." And I was getting fast that I would give her whatever she wanted—for now. "What about wife? Can I call you that?"

Chapter Ten

Haven

I WAS STILL TENSE about Crisis and Kite coming with us since they were attention magnets. Being Ream's twin sister had repercussions when my past was screwed-up. I may have been kept locked away for years, but I'd been surrounded by greed and I knew how it worked. A story about me would pay a large sum because it would lead to a story about Ream, and his past would be looked into.

"The dress is too short," Crisis said as we got out of the car.

I raised my brows. "Are you really going to go there?" It wasn't too short, not even close. It had long sleeves and there was no cleavage. The dress Kat had given me, not one of Dana's which revealed more skin than material.

He scowled as he looked at my bare legs then scooted up to my eyes. His disapproving expression slipped away and he shrugged. "Just sayin,' princess. Gives the wrong idea." He chin-lifted to the three-story house that blared music and people spilled out onto the front lawn.

"And what idea is that?" I knew what idea, but I wanted to hear him say it. Compared to how I walked out on stage at the club, I was the one wearing the snowsuit tonight.

Kite and Dana were arguing because Kite was trying to convince her that bowling was a better way to spend the night than a drunken party filled with twenty-year-olds. But Dana was twenty-one and younger than us since I started college late.

"Do I have to spell it out for you?" Crisis asked.

"Yeah. Please."

He moved in on me until my back was against the car. I raised my chin and straightened my spine. He leaned forward, arms straddling me as he rested his hands on the roof. "A guy sees a chick in a little black dress, sexy heels and a hot bod like yours, it's pussy they're going for. And a party . . . a frat party . . . is filled with guys who can no longer decipher the word 'no' because the alcohol has made their brain one big swimming pool of bad decisions. So, yeah . . . dressed like that . . . you're pussy to take advantage of."

And all of this should've bothered me. It didn't. Because I was getting Crisis and he wasn't telling me because he thought I was easy pussy, he was telling me because he didn't want guys taking advantage of me. And I knew better than anyone what some guys would do to get pussy.

"Oh, shut up, Crisis." Dana grabbed my hand and pulled me out from under Crisis arm. "You just want to screw her yourself."

I slipped my hand from Dana's after a couple steps, but followed her up the path to the house. Why did I agree to this? I hated crowds and shouting, jeering and drunk men. This was exactly what I'd avoided and yet in some way, I wanted to prove to myself that I could do this. That my past had no control over me. The two episodes today were like a gauntlet to my confidence and I wanted it back.

I had to get it back.

This was normal, a party with school friends. Make a life for myself and forget what was constantly hammering at my head because there was nothing I could do about it.

It took all of five seconds before people noticed Kite and Crisis, and the whispers behind hands became a hum of excitement. I kept my distance to make certain I didn't land in any pictures. I had to hand it to Crisis, he was good with people as he grinned and shook hands with strangers. He was completely casual and relaxed about being the center of attention. Everything opposite to me.

Kite was a little more standoffish, although he half-smiled and appeared as if he was comfortable, and he probably was in that he was confident, but he didn't take to the attention like Crisis. Kite was like a jaguar cichlid fish swimming amongst the minnows, casually watching them before he devoured them with one swallow.

Dana pulled me through the kitchen farther away from Kite and Crisis, who were completely surrounded by fans. "Look for Dillon. He's tall, spikey brown hair and has a really cute smile."

"You just described half the guys here."

She laughed. "Yeah, but Dillon's smile is breathtaking."

"Don't you like Kite?"

She shrugged. "Hell yeah. But I'm not stupid. He's Kite from Tear Asunder. That isn't happening."

We found Dillon out in the backyard with a group of guys, some of who Dana knew. She introduced me to them and I hovered, spoke when I needed to and sipped on a beer Dana passed me.

There was nothing I liked about being surrounded by strangers, and strangers who were getting drunk, even less.

I finally managed to sneak away to a dark corner of the patio, sipping my beer that had too much foam at the top and smelled like skunk. I never drank . . . never had a beer before.

I leaned against the brick wall, the rough notches digging into my upper back. There was a group of girls giggling and squealing like hyenas down by the edge of the patio and I didn't have to guess why they were acting as if they were four-year olds excited to see Spiderman. It was pitiful, really.

"Here." Startled at the voice coming up beside me, some of my beer spilled over my hand.

A guy I recognized from one of my classes, although I couldn't remember his name, held out a white plastic cup with another beer.

"No foam. Fresh keg."

"Thanks. But I'm not a fan of beer."

He laughed. "Certainly not that one. Skunk, right?" I nodded. "I swear this one will taste much better. They changed the keg. Yours is all foam and probably tastes like sewer water with whip cream on top."

I half-smiled and so did he. He was kind of cute, with dark eyes that drooped in the corners giving him that puppy-dog look.

I took the cup from him and he dumped my old one into the planter a few feet in front of us. He raised his cup. "Cheers. I'm Kevin. You're in my Sociology 101 class, with the guy your friend is talking to, Dillon."

I didn't raise my cup to his or tell him my name, but instead, took a sip. He was right. This one tasted better and was colder. He leaned against the wall beside me so our shoulders touched. I shifted an inch away and took another long sip of my beer. I wasn't exactly uncomfortable. I'd been forced to be around plenty of men since I was sixteen, but coming up with meaningless conversation wasn't my thing. The men at the club paid to fuck me, not to have a conversation.

But Crisis had sent me many meaningless texts. Some of the conversations he started were ridiculous like the one about the cucumbers and, once, he went on for a dozen texts about no longer getting the tiny packages of peanuts handed out on flights.

"You hear about the Tear Asunder guys showing up?"

I didn't say anything. I had no intention of telling some guy about my association with the band.

His eyes widened and his mouth dropped as he pushed away from the wall so he could face me. "You serious? You don't know Tear Asunder? The rock band?" Obviously, he took my silence for I'd never heard of the band. I stayed quiet, no need to burst his bubble. "Sculpt is the lead singer and used to be an illegal underground fighter and Ream is the lead guitarist and had some melt down last year, but that was squashed. Probably paid off the reporters. Can't figure out why the drummer and bass guitarist are crashing our party."

I shrugged and sipped my beer. Neither did I.

He nodded to the crowd where Crisis was. "He thinks he's God's gift to women." Well, he might be right about that. "He treats chicks like trash. What an asshole."

I stiffened and the tiny invisible hairs on the back of my neck stood at attention. "You ever think the chicks are using him?" Where was my silence? But I was pissed-off and pissed-off trumped silence. "That he's the one being treated like trash? Because from what I've seen all over the internet, it's the chicks bragging about having slept with Crisis, not the other way around." Probably, a lot were false reports but, either way, those chicks he slept with . . . that was their choice. They sure as hell weren't tied down and forced to spread their legs.

"Thanks, Ice."

Crisis strolled toward us having obviously heard my speech. He didn't bother introducing himself to Kevin; instead, he moved past him, kissed the top of my head then looped his arm around my waist. "I'm flattered you'd stick up for me."

"I wasn't sticking up for you."

Kevin's eyes were on Crisis' arm around my waist. "You know one another?"

"Sort of," I said at the same time as Crisis said with a definite, "Yes."

Crisis tugged me closer. "I'm her favorite *trash.*" I choked on my beer and had to put my hand over my mouth to stop it from spraying Kevin.

Kevin looked like he swallowed a bottle of hot sauce as his eyes widened and mouth gaped looking from me to Crisis.

"You're dating him?"

"God, no," I said.

Crisis leaned into me, bowing his head so that his breath swept across my cheek. "Cupcake, really? You embarrassed to admit you're going out with a smokin' hot rock star?"

I smacked him in the chest and he grinned.

Kevin looked at us, his face with blotches of red. "Umm, well. I'll see you in class. I better go . . ." He raised his half-full cup. "Need another."

"Later," Crisis said, all the while grinning.

"Can you let go of me now?" His fingers slid from my waist to trickle across my lower back then finally fell away. I expected relief, but I was discovering that when Crisis touched me, I didn't get that anxious feeling like spiders were crawling all over me.

It was comforting. And despite his man-whore reputation and his crude mouth, I didn't feel like an object. Shit, I had words scored into my wrist to remind me of the fact.

"Let's get the hell out of here," Crisis said and linked his fingers with mine. "Where did your friend go?"

"She's with Dillon." I tugged on my hand, trying to free it from his. He merely tightened his hold and chuckled. I obviously didn't find it funny. "Crisis. I don't want to be seen with you." He certainly didn't like that as he scowled something fierce. And I didn't like it when he scowled.

"First time a chick has ever said that to me. Why not, Ice?"

"Because . . ." And that was all I had at the moment. His grip was firm, his hand a little rough as he had callouses on the tips of his fingers. But the inner part of his palm was warm and soft like velvet.

We stared at one another for a moment and I got shivers . . . good shivers. Ones that made my heart race.

He was first to break away. "Well, I want to be seen with you. But I'll let you have that . . . for now." He let my hand go, but he kept close, within arm's reach, as we made our way into the house and through the crowd.

The music was loud and thumping inside, as were the shouts. My step faltered as my mind tried to play dirty with me again.

I am not running.

I came here tonight to prove that I could do this. That I could fight the memories just like I fought my way through years of hell.

My body bumped and separated from Crisis. A hand rubbed against my ass and I spun around only to be shoved to the side and have another hand latch onto my arm as I lost my balance. I yanked away and circled around, staggering back as I tried to find my way through the crowd. From the hands pulling at me. Touching me.

Too many hands touching me. Sweaty and cold, clammy and warm.

Be a mannequin.

Be a mannequin.

I closed my eyes and pretended to be somewhere else. Anywhere else but here, like I'd done at the club night after night.

Something cold and hard pressed up against me and I froze. Unable to get away. The music blared in the background, accompanied by shouts and leers. Touching. Prodding.

Oh, God, my hands were tied. I couldn't move.

I was jostled to the side and someone grabbed my forearm to steady me. I swung around and knocked the guy's hand off me.

I fell back into someone else, lost my balance and went over on my ankle then crashed to my knees.

I was naked on the bed, except for a jewelled belt around my waist that had a thin chain down my ass and back up again between my legs. It was tight and hurt, but the men stuck their money in it when I danced.

Oh God, I hated it. I hated it so much.

The monsters were all around me and I had no escape. I couldn't get away. One shadow strode toward the bed, licking his lips as his eyes trailed the length of my body. I knew the handcuffs wouldn't give, but I pulled on them anyway.

He laughed.

"Fuck. Haven. Baby. Open your eyes. Look at me."

That voice. It was as if a blanket of heat wrapped around me and I was no longer cold and naked and alone fighting for my sanity. "Crisis?"

"Yeah. Open your eyes, honey."

I opened my eyes. Voices were all around me, but it was Crisis' I heard as he crouched in front of me. He gently cupped my chin as if to make certain I didn't lose focus on his eyes. They were calm and steady like his voice. I fed off his composed energy and took several deep breaths.

After a minute, he took my hand and squeezed. "You good to stand?"

I nodded and he helped me to my feet.

A crowd had circled around us, staring and murmuring words like crazy and drunk. I saw Kite grab a phone out of a guy's hand who had just snapped a picture of me. He tossed it on the floor and crushed it with his foot.

I should've known this would happen. I hated crowds, hated the feeling of being trapped. It was like my body was in wet cement, heavy and unable to get free.

"Haven?" Dana pushed through the hordes of people. "What happened? You okay?" Her words slurred and she had a glassy look in her eyes.

"She just tripped," Crisis said then looped his arm around my waist, his fingers solid on my hip. "Let's go."

I'd never heard his tone so hard and abrupt before.

I caught a glimpse of Kite snagging another phone out of someone's hand—Kevin's. "No pictures. Jesus. Have some respect." Kite leaned into the bathroom near the front door and I heard a splash as the phone hit water. Kevin started swearing and ran into the bathroom muttering "assholes."

Kite didn't even glance at Kevin or seem to care that he'd just ruined two phones. He went ahead of us and started the car. Dana jumped in the front with Kite, and as soon as her door shut, Crisis started talking.

Crisis didn't open the door; instead, he gently leaned me against it and ran his hand over my head until he cupped the back of my neck. "Shield back in place I see," he said as he watched me for a second. "You okay?"

I nodded.

"Good. Cause now I'm telling you that this shit fucking with your head is serious."

He had no idea. No one did. I'd found a way to live and now I was finding a way to survive the memories. I just needed ordinary. If I had that, everything else would eventually disappear. It had to.

"Don't look at me like I'm spurting bullshit."

"You don't know anything, Crisis." I pulled out of this grip on my neck.

"Yeah, because you won't talk to me. You won't talk to anyone."

He argued back. "Ream's tried to help. Emily. Kat. You refuse to see a therapist. I get that. But damn it, you need someone to trust or the shit that just went down is going to get worse."

"I don't need anyone." I hadn't meant to say it out loud, but the bubble of anger was cracking in my chest.

He shook his head and sighed. Before I could stop him, he reached out and caressed the side of my face. "Yeah, you do, Haven. I've been trying for months to get you to see that." His finger came under my chin and his thumb stroked back and forth softly. "I like you. I care about you."

I tensed but kept my voice soft as I said, "I won't have sex with you, Crisis." If that's where he was going with the liking me, I needed him to know that sleeping with him wasn't an option for me.

His arm dropped to his side. "Don't want to fuck a girl so damaged she can't breathe without hurting." He lowered his voice and it went all husky. "What I want is to help her learn to laugh again. And I want her trust." He leaned to the side and opened the car door.

Why? Why would he want to help me? Crisis was all about attention. His music. His goal in life was having something about him go viral on Twitter.

But that was the Crisis everyone saw. After texting with him for months, I knew that there was far more to him. I knew he was really proud of a song he wrote for the band and he wanted to do more of that. I knew he had a list of things he wanted to do before he died. I hadn't seen it, but he told me two of them: learn to make his mom's spaghetti meat sauce and that led into another one which was 'so he could teach his kid one day.'

And maybe that was when I truly knew that Crisis was way more than he let on, and as he looked at me, I saw the concern in his eyes. I heard it in his voice. I felt it in his arms.

Crisis had parts of him that the media never saw. But I did and that was why I said what I did to Kevin. It was just hard to trust when that piece of me was damaged. I lowered my head and for the first time, I reached out to him and placed my hand on his arm. "I know you care."

And this was the Crisis I was getting to know. He didn't take my words, my slight give in my armor, and push for more; instead, he nodded and opened the car door for me.

He waited for me to slide in, then shut the door and walked around the car to the other side. My stomach whirled as I watched him and it was a good whirl.

Kite chatted with Dana about the band that was on the radio and how they'd partied with them a number of months ago. Crisis and I remained quiet in the back, our hands next to one another on the seat. Close but not touching.

When we arrived at the farm, Kite helped Dana to the house as she stumbled and laughed, obviously having had one too many beers.

Crisis walked beside me up the path, the only sound that of our feet along the gravel and the slight rustle of the trees in the breeze. Normally, I'd shiver at the sound of the wind, but not now. Not with him next to me. He opened the screen door for me, but caught my arm before I entered.

I stopped.

"Tomorrow, nine o'clock." My eyes narrowed with confusion and he smiled, the first time since we left the party. "First driving lesson. Be ready, Ice, and if you fail to show up, I'm coming for you."

"Driving?" My heart raced and it wasn't in fear, it was with excitement. The freedom that would come with being able to drive . . . more control over my life.

He let me go. "Yep. But when you're with me, no gun." He smirked. "I don't need you shooting me when you get tired of me telling you what to do." He was trying to make light of the gun scenario, so I gave him that and nodded. Then he went inside and disappeared upstairs. I heard his bedroom door shut then his music turned on.

I was going to learn how to drive. Crisis was going to teach me. I didn't think he'd remember. I bit my lower lip to stop from smiling. There was a certain amount of exhilaration with getting my license because I'd been antagonized about it for years by Alexa, especially after the siphoning incident.

The shackles were releasing, slowly, but with each day, I came closer to having complete control over my life. I'd never belong to anyone again. I rubbed my finger over the branding on my wrist which read 'Owned.'

Never.

"Haven, get in here," Dana shouted. "Your phone's ringing."

I answered to Katy Perry after it rang through the chorus twice. That had been Crisis' doing before he went on tour and I hadn't figured out how to change it. I was technically unsavvy since Olaf never allowed me a phone or access to the internet and everything in the house had passwords.

I glanced at the screen—Ream. "Hello?"

"Where've you been? I've been calling for an hour."

I hadn't talked to him today. I talked to him every day. Saying my brother was over-protective was an understatement, but I couldn't fault him for it. He'd thought I was dead for the last twelve years. He sacrificed his innocence for me. He killed a man for me.

"I went out with friends." And this was exactly what he needed to hear.

Silence, but I could hear his footsteps and the slight jostle of the phone as he paced. "Why didn't you take your phone with you? I was about to call Luke."

"I didn't need it. Dana had hers and Crisis and Kite were with—"

"What?" I pulled the phone away from my ear. "What the hell? Where are you? Why are Crisis and Kite with you? I thought Luke was."

I'd known this was coming, and it was better he heard it from me now than walk in here tomorrow and find out.

Ream was saying something to someone and I guessed it was Kat who, I'd discovered in the few months before they left on tour, was pretty good at calming Ream down. Stubborn and determined, just like him.

"They're at the farm?"

"Yeah." And as I said the next words, I realized it was true. "Ream, it's good. It's . . . nice to have them here."

"I don't want him near you." He made a rough growl noise. "If he lays his hands on you . . ."

"Ream." Ever since Crisis jumped off the cliff with me, my brother had this idea that Crisis was interested in me. "He'd never do that and I think you know that."

Silence. Then, "I still don't like it. He has some chick he fucked following him around. I don't want that near you."

"I'm fine." And I certainly wasn't worried about some chick. "I have to go. Dana is here and we're about to start a movie."

"Shit, Haven. I'm sorry. I know it's been hard on you with us around and I didn't want them coming back to the farm. I wanted it just to be us and Kat."

I didn't say anything because as soon as I found a job and saved enough money, I'd move out. I wanted that for me just as much as I wanted it for them.

"I'll be back tomorrow late morning. Sophie and John are having a big dinner for us. I know you've avoided meeting them, but they really want you to come, sis." I closed my eyes briefly when he said sis. It was like a waterfall of warmth washing over me and yet I was afraid to feel it, to get pulled into the shelter of my big brother again. "I wouldn't make a big deal out of it, but . . . shit, they were there when I needed someone after you were gone. I was in a really bad place and I don't think I would've pulled through living that year in child services. They knew that when they saw me. Fuck, no one fosters a seventeen-year-old kid." My hand tightened on the phone as I thought of what Ream had suffered. Maybe it all stemmed from our mother, but what killed us was my weakness to let Gerard do what he did and then my addiction that ended up separating us and taking us on vastly different paths.

I'd never let Ream hurt again because of me. Not the one person who had sacrificed everything in order to protect me.

"Maybe." That was all I could give right now. I didn't want parents, but I heard the pleading in Ream's voice. He wanted this.

Crisis' music cranked louder and I quickly said goodbye before Ream started in again about the guys being here. Dana sat cross-legged on the couch, the television on and the previews playing in the background. Kite surprisingly had joined her and sat in the leather chair, his legs resting on the coffee table while he sipped what looked like steaming coffee.

It was a strange feeling. Like I was missing something as I sat and watched the movie. I looked down at my phone in my hand as if hoping it would vibrate and I'd see a text from Crisis.

It didn't and I wanted it to.

Chapter Eleven

Crisis

I WAS ACCUSTOMED TO waking with a chick sucking on my cock or nursing a hangover that required a chick to suck on my cock. I had neither. My cock was rock hard and . . . I lifted the sheet, yeah pulsing and angry as fuck from lack of use . . . I needed to jerk off before I caught some strange disease associated with my recent cock-abuse. It had a purpose and not using it was just simply—abuse.

I reached for my phone and saw the time. Eight in the morning. When was the last time I saw that time? I'd fallen asleep last night lying on my bed with my headphones on, trying to forget about the girl downstairs who had scared the shit out me three times yesterday with whatever was fucking with her head. I was pissed-off, too. Not at her, at myself because I hadn't been here for months. No one had. She'd been alone, except for Luke, and it was stupid for us to have gone on tour.

But I sure as hell was here now and I was going to do something about it. She may not respect me, shit I didn't even know if she liked me, or just tolerated me. But she'd become someone I could talk to, even if it was only over text until recently.

I liked that she talked to me, not because I was Crisis from Tear Asunder because I knew she didn't give a crap about that, but for me. I caught snippets of who she was underneath the fucked-up and I wanted more snippets. Damn it, I wanted all of them.

The smell of coffee wafted under the door and I shoved back the covers. I got up, brushed my teeth, and thought about jerking off, but the idea of Haven standing in the kitchen making coffee had me skipping the latter.

I walked down the hall, pulled the elastic band on my boxers and glanced at my hard throbbing cock. "You'll have to wait a little longer, buddy."

"Are you really talking to your cock?"

I let go of the elastic and it snapped hard on my abdomen. Haven wasn't making coffee; she was coming up the stairs with an armful of clothes. Fuck, she looked hot, long blonde hair messy as if she'd tossed and turned in her sleep, and she had sleepy eyes—adorable.

"Yeah. He's angry this morning." I stood right in the middle of the top of the stairs so if she wanted to get by, she'd need to brush up against me. It was childish, but fuck, I was a guy.

Her brows lifted. "Why is he angry?"

I smirked, loving that she was down for a little play. "Placed an 'out of order' sign on him." Her brows drew together and her eyes flicked to my tented boxers.

"Doesn't look out of order."

I laughed and couldn't help myself as I stroked the back of my hand down her cheek. It took her by surprise and she swayed backwards. I grabbed her arm before she toppled down the stairs and pulled her up onto the landing next to me.

A white piece of clothing slipped from the pile she was holding and fell at her feet. I smirked when I realized what it was, and took great pleasure in helping her out since there was no way she could bend over and get it without everything falling from her grasp.

I let her go and crouched, picking up the white lace panties. I held them out and her nose twitched like a rabbit sensing danger. "I like white. Prefer pink though, for future notice. And lace I love."

She was trapped because if she snatched them from my hand, she'd drop the clothes and if she didn't then . . . I curled them up in my palm.

"They aren't mine," she blurted.

God, she was cute. "Darlin' I know they are and I love that you're denying it. Means you care."

Now that raised a little heat in her cheeks and I liked it. Shit, I liked it a lot because when I left a few months back, that would've never happened and now that was twice. She was affected by me—good to know. "I don't care."

I shrugged. Then turned to head back to my room to hide my newly acquired treasure. I had no doubt she'd search for them the second I left the house. I looked back over my shoulder and caught her eyes staring at my butt; could've been my back, but unlikely. Really, it didn't matter which. I was just impressed she was eyeing me up.

"You can look, but don't touch," I said.

Her mouth dropped open then snapped shut. I disappeared around the corner, then heard her stomping down the hall. Haven wasn't a stomper. She was graceful, elegant and controlled. Too controlled. And that part of her was coming down.

I laughed to myself, then hid her lace underwear in my room. I went downstairs, and grabbed coffee that I knew Kite had made because he had his mug sitting beside the coffeemaker.

Dana, who had slept on the couch, must have heard me in the kitchen. I saw her arms stretch above her, then her head popped up over the back of the couch. As soon as she saw me standing half-naked in the kitchen, her eyes widened in what looked like horror.

Luckily, I was pretty confident—okay, overly confident—about my body and there was no way that was what scared her. She frantically straightened her hair and clothes, keeping her body turned away from me. My guess, she was more concerned about how she looked hung-over first thing in the morning.

"You look like hell." Girls were funny about how they looked in the morning. Most of the girls I'd been with didn't stay the night, but a few had and not one of them was confident about their appearance in the morning. "How do you feel? Want some coffee? Kite will be back down any minute." I smirked. She looked as if she idolized Kite more than me, and that got her moving faster as she darted around looking for her purse. "On the floor by the TV," I graciously offered.

"Ahhh, yeah, thanks. Tell Haven I'll talk to her later." She darted out the door.

"Sure thing, beautiful."

She was already gone.

I drank my coffee while I watched the news for a half-hour, then went and showered. I jerked off in the shower thinking about Haven in that little black number last night. I hadn't planned on it, but fuck, she was in my head and my cock was aching, balls hurting. There was no way I could hang with her today without being in physical pain unless I got myself off.

I tugged on a pair of worn-out jeans and a t-shirt, tagged my phone off the dresser, then headed downstairs to meet Haven for her first driving lesson.

Haven

I glanced at the clock on my phone—9:06 a.m. gleamed in the middle of the screen. After the panty incident I put a load of laundry in, but it was more like threw them in, taking out my frustration on the clothes. Why was I frustrated? There was no reason to be, except Crisis was getting to me. In one day. One day.

Of course, he knew the panties were mine. There was no one else currently living in the house. And why would he take them? It was silly. I was unaccustomed to silly and childish games. My entire life had been about survival right from childhood.

But Crisis was slowly showing pieces of a life that wasn't all about being productive and survival. It was about the simple joy of living. I never could equate the two together before. But even looking at a cucumber made me smile because I didn't just see its mundane function of being food. I saw it as something silly and funny. It also made me think about Crisis.

I rested my hands on top of the washer as it did the final spin and my body leaned against it as it jostled and shook.

He unhinged me. He teased, played, talked about chicks like they were playing cards, at least he had in the beginning, and then he pulled shit like he did yesterday and held me when I freaked out.

Crisis was supportive and knew what I needed even if I didn't, because I would've never let anyone hold me. But Crisis . . . he was comfort and safety. He didn't push me and yet he told me what he thought at the same time.

"Ice, are you really doing that? Jesus, even I wouldn't get off in the fuckin' hallway."

I shoved away from the washing machine so fast and hard I hit the wall on the opposite side of the hallway. Words lodged in my throat as I looked at him standing at the top of the stairs a few feet away.

"I wasn't . . . it was almost done and I was . . ." Oh. My. God. I never stuttered. Ever.

But, he saved me from any further stuttering as he winked at me and turned away saying, "Come on, babe. Let's get you driving."

Facing my sexual desire was a subject I was still tackling on the confidence scale. To me, sex was cruel and vile and I never once enjoyed it.

This . . . the clenching between my legs, the butterflies flapping madly in my belly, it was new, well, new since Crisis, and to my mortification, it started over texts. Crisis' texts. Words on a screen typed by him and they hadn't even been sexual. It was just the thought of him sitting back with his long, lean legs outstretched, hair falling haphazard over his head while he typed on his phone.

"You coming, Ice?"

"Umm, yeah." I straightened and pulled my shit together, except I couldn't do anything about the butterflies; they were out of control.

I followed him downstairs. "Are we using your car?"

He came to an abrupt halt, eyes widening. "Fuck no. Do you know what kind of car I have? Shit, it's not for learning to drive. It's not for any chick to drive."

Oh, my God, he was totally being a guy. I may have been sheltered from what most girls did growing up, but I still had ears and many conversations revolved around guys and their cars. It was like they were talking about the most precious stone in the world. My 'work' at the club had afforded Olaf a really nice Audi that he talked about all the time.

We walked past the four-car garage that housed Ream, Kite's, Kat's and Crisis' cars, but we failed to stop. Where were we going? We walked past the barn, empty of horses as they were all out in the pastures. I skidded to a halt, the gravel rolling beneath my feet as I saw exactly where we were headed.

Crisis stopped and turned. "What?"

"A lawn mower?" I choked out.

He shrugged then walked into the shed and threw his leg over the driver's seat and started it up. It took a few tries before it smoked, rattled and puttered, then crawled toward me.

I stood staring at the little ride-on mower, Crisis sitting on it wearing his baseball cap and worn-out jeans with holes in the knees. Knees bent too high on the machine because he was so tall. It was ridiculous. The hot rock star with tats and the most stunning ripped body was driving a shitty lawnmower and he still exuded hot.

It was so ridiculous that I laughed. My smile widened first, then a strange bubbling in my chest that stole my breath and locked down in the center of my core as the sound emerged.

I laughed until my stomach cramped and my eyes watered.

The mower shut down beside me.

Crisis leaned back in the green plastic seat and crossed his arms over his chest. The tightness around my mouth felt funny as I stopped laughing and smiled. It was weird, smiling and laughing. I couldn't recall the last time I'd laughed or felt the lightness hit me in the chest like it did now.

He cocked his leg and rested his foot up on the frame, appearing casual and relaxed but his eyes . . . they were intense as they drove into me. My smile faded and a tingling flared between my legs as I stared at him. We were both silent for a moment, merely watching one another, assessing maybe.

"When you laugh . . ." he paused as if thinking about it, "it's like being handed a piece of you that no one else has ever seen."

Those words held more truth than he could ever know and I didn't know how to respond, so I didn't.

He re-adjusted his hat that didn't need re-adjusting then shifted to perch up on the back of the seat. "Come on, let's get you driving."

"Okay." I slid onto the hard seat and was instantly aware of his thighs next to my shoulders and my head close to his abdomen, and therefore cock. I swallowed as the sensation in my sex intensified and I clenched, which only made it worse.

He leaned forward, his chest up against my back and my breath hitched. "You need to press down the clutch with this leg." He put his hand on my thigh to indicate which one and I nearly shot out of the seat. "Whoa, what's wrong with you? You're all jumpy and shit."

"I'm fine. Just nervous." I added, "To drive." But, I wasn't nervous about driving. I was nervous of him, because what I was feeling was more than I knew how to handle.

Crisis was taking this seriously, so I tried to ignore what my body was doing and pressed the pedal like he said.

"Now, turn the key. But don't let go of the clutch until it starts."

I looked around for the key and saw it in the ignition to the right of the steering wheel. The mower started easily and I was giddy as it vibrated underneath me.

"The gears are a little tricky for timing," he explained. His chest rubbed against me again as he showed me the three gears. "The brake is on the other side, but if you stop completely, you need to press the clutch at the same time or it will stall."

Too much information, but I learned to shoot a gun from merely watching Olaf with his, for Christ's sake. This couldn't be too hard. Clutch. Gear. Gas. That was all I had to remember.

"Okay, let's go, sweetness." His hands rested lightly on my

shoulders and, normally, I hated hands on my shoulders. But Crisis' hands were steady and calming—reassuring. I pressed the clutch, and jammed the gear into first. "Not so rough. It should slide right in."

Oh, damn. I pictured him above me, his cock sliding in and there was nothing vile about it. I abruptly let go of the clutch and the mower violently jerked.

"Fuck," Crisis shouted.

I turned around to see Crisis on his butt on the grass behind the mower, his hand to his cheek. I bit my lip to stop from laughing, but a giggle and smile did escape as I looked at the cocky rock star on his ass looking a little dazed.

I realized that the mower was getting further away from him as it continued to creep forward.

"Crisis." I cranked on the steering wheel with both hands, turning it as far as it would go as it puttered straight for the stable wall. It was a slow crawl but, slow or not, it would still crash into a wall. I looked down at the two pedals and the gear. Crap, I forgot what he said about stopping.

"Crisis? How do I stop it?" There was a loud grinding sound as the mower scrapped the side of the barn.

He appeared beside the mower and my eyes widened when I saw the big red mark on his cheekbone. "Knee to the face when I went over backwards. Anyone asks, I'm telling them you punched me," he said. I bit my lip smiling. He kept pace with the mower and grinned. "You sure know how to knock a guy off his feet."

I rolled my eyes and he laughed. He hopped up onto the mower and brushed against me as he slid in behind to perch up on the backrest again. "Okay, let's get driving this piece of junk."

His finger brushed back my hair from my neck and goose bumps played havoc along my skin. I wanted to turn around and look at him to see if he noticed, but I was afraid of him seeing what was raging through me.

"Second gear it, baby."

The muscles in my face ached by the time I drove the lawn mower back to the shed an hour later. And it was from smiling. It may have been just a lawn mower, but it was a step toward what I was searching for—control over my own life. A sense of normality. And freedom. I ran my finger over the words scorched into my wrist and I don't know if he noticed what I was doing, but he gently took my hand in his.

"You'll get there."

I was uncertain what he meant by that, if it had deeper meaning than just a reference to learning to drive. But it didn't matter; it was the right thing to say, and even better was that he didn't say anything more.

We walked out of the shed, and Crisis let my hand go and kissed the top of my head. "In a couple days, we can move up to the tractor."

"Wouldn't it be easier to start with a car?"

Crisis chuckled and threw his arm around my shoulders. "Fuck yeah."

I scrunched up my nose and subtly inched out of the embrace. I liked his arm around me and I was fast realizing that I liked a lot of things about Crisis. And becoming involved with a rock star who was constantly on social media was a hard limit. "Then why are we doing this?"

His steps were long compared to mine and I took two to his one even though he was walking slowly. I glanced up at him just as the warm breeze shifted across us and lifted a curl of his hair and caused it to dance across his face for a second. It was cute when he frowned and annoyingly pushed it behind his ear where it fell forward again.

"I'm sure Ream will let me use his car if you don't want me driving yours."

I hated when he procured that little smirk because there was always a reason behind it that revolved around his ability to make my heart pitter-patter and the temperature in my body go up two degrees.

"Do you have to have a reason to do everything? It's fun."

I frowned. "So you're teaching me to drive on a lawnmower because it's fun?"

"Sure." He shrugged then jerked his head toward the car pulling into the driveway. "Ream's back."

I looked up at the house and saw the car pulling in. I was excited to see Ream again, but a little uneasy too. The triggers had escalated and I didn't want Ream to witness them. Running helped, maybe because I exhausted my body until it had no energy left to freak out.

"Aren't you nervous about what he'll say? He was pissed that you and Kite hadn't moved out."

He laughed and nudged my shoulder with his own. "Nah. Ream can throw a punch, but he's my brother. Not much will ruin what we have." His hand lightly touched the small of my back as he slowed his step. "When he first came to live with us, he'd wake up in the night screaming your name."

I jerked to a stop as coldness washed over me, but Crisis' hand on my back gently urged me forward again.

"I confronted him about it, asked him who you were; he wouldn't say anything. Instead, the fucker hit me a good one right across the jaw. Never punched him back. Couldn't do it. Jesus, he looked so fuckin' haunted. Didn't talk about you, though, and it took him six months before he slept through the night. I think it was the music that finally helped. He connected to it, you know?"

I nodded. I did know because music helped me too. We were separated, but the ironic part was music was our one connection which helped us both. I hated to think of Ream those months after he thought I was dead, but in a way, it was probably better than him knowing I was in Alexa and Olaf's grasp. He'd have died trying to get me back, and there was no question, Olaf would've put a bullet in his head, especially with the amount of money I ended up making him.

I heard car doors shut then footsteps strode toward us.

Ream, who was approaching, chin-nodded to us. Crisis was completely relaxed and I couldn't help but feed off his energy. It was comforting and I realized that despite Crisis being the attention seeker and the player, he had composure in him that I craved. Even when he texted me, he was straight up with whatever was on his mind even if it was maybe silly to some.

"Don't tell him," I said. Crisis glanced at me, his head tilting down, a questioning look in his eyes. "About the episodes yesterday. I don't know what triggered them, but . . ." I decided to give him something, a sliver of me. "He protected me and I screwed it up." Crisis opened his mouth and I glared; he shut it again. "I don't want him living with the guilt of what happened to me. Because he will. He can't help it. It's in his make up to protect me, has been his job all his life and now it's mine to set him free from it. So, I don't want him to know. I don't want that on him."

"Shit, Haven." He sighed, the dimples in his cheeks gone, brows low over his eyes. "I'd never tell anyone, okay?" I nodded then went to ask him about Kite when he said, "Kite won't either, but I'll talk to him just in case." His hand on the small of my back shifted slightly and tingles shot up through my spine. "Do you trust me, baby?"

Did I? Yes, I thought so, but trust was easily broken.

His hand gently rubbed my back, soothing and . . . sexual. Maybe he didn't mean it to be, but it was. Goose bumps popped up all across my skin and my heart pumped madly. I didn't even want to consider what was happening between my legs because this wasn't just a clench. It was way more than that.

I knew how to lock down everything, but this . . . the desire for Crisis was intensifying and I didn't know how to stop it.

My brother's shoulders were tense and his lips pursed together as he walked across the yard. "He looks pissed."

"Yep. Don't worry about it. It's nothing compared to when I hit on Kat. That was pissed."

"You hit on Kat?" I asked.

"Fuck yeah, Ream was being a pussy and not claiming her. I helped him out."

I didn't have time to respond as my brother stopped in front of us. "What the hell, man?" Ream said. "I told you I didn't want you anywhere near my sister. One day. One fuckin' day and you're all over her."

Crisis completely ignored his outburst. "You going to say hi to your sister?"

Ream grunted then his scowl lifted and his eyes softened. "Haven, hon. You okay?" My brother's hands were curled into fists. I reached out and wrapped my hand around his, and instantly he relaxed. He dragged me into his arms and gave me a hug. "How's school?"

Despite loving my brother, I was still uneasy being held in his arms. He was my twin and there'd always been a strong connection between us. I was afraid of what he'd find if I got too close. I'd always been the little angel, until I screwed that up. "It's school."

"What are you two doing out here?" Ream asked his tone tight.

"Crisis is teaching me to drive."

"Drive?" he repeated, looking from Crisis back to me again.

I glanced over my shoulder at the garage where the lawn mower sat. "Yeah. We're starting small."

Ream was quiet.

Crisis chuckled. "Your sister is a natural with the lawnmower."

I bit my lip to stop from smiling, but Ream noticed my reaction because he got that look, like when we were kids and he would get all sweet and nudge me on the tip of my nose with his finger. He hadn't done that since we were kids. "Lawnmower?"

I nodded. "He thought it was . . ." I hesitated. Fun?

"Safety first," Crisis finished.

Ream's eyes narrowed as he looked from me to Crisis and back again. "Nothing better be happening here. I'm serious, Crisis."

Crisis put up his hands. "Bro, she's my . . . sister."

Ream snorted. "By association and a fuck of a flimsy association."

"Yeah, well, Mom might have something to say about that. Haven is part of the family now. And she is going to have a shit fit when she sees that new tat on your neck."

Ream huffed. "She won't even notice it when she's busy bitching about your hair. Fuckin' cut the locks, man."

"I like his hair." Why did I just say that? My brother's eyes widened, appearing startled by my comment. Damn it, I was startled by my comment. "I'm going to . . . the clothes need to go in the wash," I quickly added and headed for the house.

"You already did that," Crisis yelled after me. I heard his chortle trail after me.

Kat was in the kitchen when I came in the front door. She smiled and set her water on the counter then came straight for me. "Hey." She grabbed my hands and squeezed them. "You look great. How's school? And Hank? Has he been managing the horses okay? And Tear? Where is Tear?"

Tear was Logan and Emily's German Sheppard that lived on their farm, but when they traveled, he came and stayed with Hank. "I saw Hank drive out with him in his truck this morning so I assume he was taking him home." He'd been laughing and shaking his head at Crisis and I on the lawnmower as he drove by.

"Yeah, she's crazy about that dog. Do you know she had Hank send her pics every day?" Kat and I chatted. Well, it was more like she chatted and I answered when necessary. When I managed to escape to my room, I changed into my work out clothes then snuck out the side door to go running until any emotion I had was exhausted and buried.

Chapter Twelve

Crisis

I DROVE UP TO my parents' place an hour before everyone else was due to arrive. I'd searched around the house for Haven to ask her to ride with me, but she took off somewhere.

The house sat on a cul-de-sac backing onto the golf course. It was a kick-ass house with a massive deck out back, five bedrooms and a state-of-the-art kitchen; one of my mom's favorite things to do was cook. There was a pool table downstairs that Ream and I spent hours playing on, and yeah, I fucked a few chicks on it, too. I probably fucked a chick in every room in the house except my parents'—that was just gross.

"Mom." I hugged her as soon as she opened the door. She was the best, and had always supported my music. My dad did too, although, he used to grumble and complain about the noise. Admittedly, it was fuckin' noise when I first started learning the guitar. But my dad soundproofed the garage so I could play as often as I wanted.

She pulled back and clucked her tongue while smoothing back my hair like I was five years old. "Vincent! You need a haircut."

"Fuck that, Mom, chicks love the blond curls." And Haven just said this morning she liked my hair.

She rolled her eyes, but I think it was more due to my language than the chick referral.

My mom was tall, five-foot-seven, and had slim narrow hips and legs with big feet. Yeah, it was one of those things that she'd been teased about when she was in high school. "Looking good. You trying to impress some hot guy other than Dad?" Her auburn hair had been highlighted with gentle blonde streaks and hung in a stylish bob.

"Vincent Wesson." She smacked me lightly on the chest. "I didn't raise you to talk like that and I certainly didn't raise you to be a prick to women."

I threw my head back laughing. "Prick? Really, Mom?"

She huffed and strode into the kitchen, which opened into the living and dining area. "Yes. You're a prick." I followed after her, breathing in the heavenly smell of her homemade spaghetti sauce. "You think I don't see Facebook?" Facebook, too? The posts on FB were not ones a mom should ever read. "Why don't you take after your brother and find a nice girl and—"

"Mom," I groaned. Same old shit, ever since Ream and Kat hooked up last year. Now, she was on my case about settling down. I dipped my finger into the thick red sauce on the stove then stuck it in my mouth.

"Vincent," my mom shouted. "I don't even want to think where those hands have been."

I grinned. "Yeah, good idea. Don't think."

She attempted to slap my hand, but I ducked out of reach, laughing.

"Son." My dad strolled into the kitchen and shook my hand while squeezing one shoulder. "Back from the salt mines. How was the tour?"

"Great." Except for some Tammy chick, who was thinking she was going to marry me. I didn't like having to cancel Seattle. Doing that to the fans sucked big time, but with the Tammy shit, my blow up at her and Luke's phone call about Haven, it was enough. Kite was already talking to the manager about re-scheduling Seattle at least.

My dad and I were the same height, although that was where our similarities ended. He had a slight paunch, and dark thick eyebrows, which matched the stubble on his face. He spoke eloquently and had poise, fitting the status he worked hard to get to as one of the top condo developers in Toronto. Bottom-line, though, he was one hell of a good guy. Mom lived doing charity work and they had a yearly scholarship in their name at the University of Toronto's business program.

"Where's your brother?" And that made me love my parents even more. They insisted on calling Ream their son and it was fuckin' cool of them.

I thought of Haven—when wasn't I?—standoffish and keeping everyone at a distance. She was going to have a tough time doing that once my parents got their hooks into her.

"Come on, son, leave your mother to cook. I want to hear about the tour." I thought I was going to get away with it, until he added, "And why you're back early."

Fuck.

"Hon," Mom called. "A girl called here for you yesterday."

"You didn't give her my number did you?" I didn't need any chicks getting my cell number.

She rolled her eyes, tsking. "I've been filtering your calls for years, no. Of course not. She said she'd catch up with you later."

I kissed my mom on the cheek. "Cool, thanks, Mom." Then I followed Dad out onto the large deck where the patio table was already set for dinner. Mom did the balloon thing like it was a kid's birthday party and a welcome home banner strung above the sliding glass doors. Fuck, she rocked.

Dad and I chatted about what went down with this Tammy chick following me around and sending me gifts. Well, I chatted, and he listened, brows drawn low over his eyes as he nodded and took it all in. Only after I was done did he say anything and that was, "You must take after me in the looks department. Girls can't resist us."

I laughed because there was nothing further from the truth and we both knew it.

Kite showed up an hour later, then Logan and Emily with Logan's mom Isabelle. I leaned against the railing of the deck, nursing my beer while Logan and Kite told my dad about the business side of the band: the manager we fired, the security issues we encountered until six months ago when we hired Luke's Shield Security, a recommendation from Deck, after Haven came back.

I took it slowly with the beer since I was driving later, but I was on edge while constantly listening for the front door to open. Where the hell was she? No way would Ream be a no- show.

I saw her laugh today. It was brilliant—stunning. It was like strumming the guitar and hitting a few new chords that makes your chest open up and your whole body to fill with electricity. It was that magical moment when you find something fresh and knew it was going to be a hit.

The front door opened and shut, and my heart skipped a beat then tap-danced its song.

Ream's voice echoed in the large marble foyer as he called out to Mom. The girls were in the kitchen and my mom was laughing at something Emily said about Logan's shoes being chewed by Tear.

I watched the screen door, the grip on the neck of my beer bottle tight, the cold damp glass clinging to my skin. The undeniable reality was . . . Haven did it for me. I loved how she was tall, yet still fit under my chin when she was curled into me yesterday. Confident and strong but I'd seen her vulnerability and fuck, that broke me. I wanted to bust down her walls and force her to let me in. That was the exact opposite as to what she needed, so I didn't push. I waited. And waiting was hard as hell because I wanted to kiss her. I wanted to pull her into my arms and have every inch of her wrapped around me.

Ream slid across the screen door and walked out. Our dad got up, slapped him on the back and shook his hand. "Good to see you, son. Where's your other half?"

Ream gestured with a head tilt toward the kitchen. "With the moms and Emily. Something about testosterone overload for the last few months."

"Where's Haven?" Subtle wasn't my thing.

Ream opened the cooler and the ice clinked as he rooted around for a beer. Water dripped from the bottle as he lifted one out, then the lid clunked shut. He twisted the cap and the bottle hissed as the pressure released. Fucker was making me wait on purpose.

He chugged back the cool liquid before he finally said, "Not feeling well."

I stiffened. No way was she sick. She went running for fuck's sake. "You let her get away with that?" I took out my phone and quickly texted her.

You bailed. WTF.

Ream shrugged. "I'm not forcing her."

And I had no brilliant come back except, "It's just dinner."

He was right, but this wasn't about seeing a therapist. It was having dinner. I glanced at my phone, as if willing it to vibrate.

Nothing. I took a long swig of beer and set it down on the table. The screen lit up and a wave of relief shifted through me.

I'm not ready to meet your parents. Or Ream's. It's weird. They're his, but not mine. Not ready to see that.

It may be small, but with Haven it was a huge step. She told me the real reason why she didn't want to come and that was something special.

Still . . .

You'll have to at our wedding. ;)

"I'm getting really sick of hearing about my sister from your mouth." I ignored Ream as my phone vibrated.

I don't find you funny you know.

Sure you do. I saw you laugh today, Ice. I might have to start calling you fire instead.

I slid my phone in my back pocket. "You're blind, bro. You're not seeing her. You're thinking of her like she's still sixteen."

Ream took a step toward me, his temple throbbing. "You have no fuckin' clue what she went through. No clue! Shut your mouth, Crisis.

And stay the hell away from her. She doesn't need you teaching her to drive, flirting with her . . . fuck, just stay clear of her. Better yet, move out like you were supposed to do."

I knew some of his anger was because he was worried about her. I got that. That was why I didn't plow my fist into his face. I casually pulled out a chair and sat, right in front of him, stretching out my legs, ankles crossed. My toes curled in my running shoes and the muscles in my abdomen tense, ready for Ream's assault. "Not happening, bro." His lips pursed. "Haven and I are friends." And like hell was I giving that up. One step at a time, not my usual way, but she was worth it.

"Friends?" Ream ground out. "You've never had a girl "friend" in your life."

Kite coughed and Ream looked at him. Yeah, Ream couldn't deny that his fiancée Kat and I were 'friends,' had been before they got together, and Georgie and I were friends since the band started hanging out at her coffee shop when we were in high school. Never fucked either of those chicks.

"Baby?" Kat opened the screen door, a tray of cheese and crackers balanced in one hand. Ream strode over and took the tray. "Thanks. You realize it's a screen door and we can hear everything." She stepped into him, hands settling on his waist then leaned over the tray of food and kissed him. She whispered something and he took a deep breath and nodded. "Hey, Dad," Kat said then pranced over and placed a kiss on both of his cheeks. It was nice she called him dad, as Kat and her brother Matt's parents died in a drunk driving accident.

He smiled, showing off his teeth he just had whitened. "Has Mom been after you about a date yet?"

Kat's blue eyes sparkled as she nodded. "First question when I walked into the kitchen." She scrunched her nose up at Ream. "And he bolted."

Ream shrugged. "I'm not the issue here." He put the tray onto the patio table, snatched a cracker and stuck it in his mouth.

Kat raised her brows, crossed her arms and looked at Logan. "No, you are."

Logan chuckled, putting his hands up. "Hey, Mouse wants a big winter wedding, I'm giving her one."

"Yeah, next February," Ream said. "And Kitkat won't get married until after you guys. Some girl bullshit rule."

"Logan asked Emily first." Kat objected. "They get married first."

Ream took a sip of his beer. "What's the big deal? Tell Eme to pick a place and do it."

Kat smacked Ream in the arm and there was a mild twitch at the corner of his mouth.

Logan reached for the cheese knife and cut a slice of cheddar. "She wants the whole deal at our farm with Clifford pulling a sleigh and we can't do that until the place is finished. I'd marry her tomorrow at city hall if she'd let me."

I laughed. "Wouldn't that screw over the reporters? Lead singer from Tear Asunder, marries his girl at the old city hall in jeans and t-shirt." I slapped my knee.

"Logan Theodor Evans, don't you dare." Isabelle came up behind Kat and handed my dad the tin foil-wrapped garlic bread to go on the BBQ. "I want a beautiful wedding." She lowered her voice. "Emily deserves that."

Before shit could get all sappy, I jumped to my feet. "Hey, Mom." I snagged Isabelle around the waist and gave her a hug and kiss on the cheek. She loved that we all called her mom. Isabelle was majestic with long blonde hair that she kept tight in a bun most of the time and had angelic features. She was quiet and refined, but underneath, the woman had guts. She'd risked her life to get away from Logan's father, who had been some drug and sex trafficking asshole in Mexico.

Isabelle's long slender fingers cupped my cheek. "Nice to see you, Vincent. You riling up the boys?"

I raised my brows, smiling. "Damn right. They both need a kick in the ass to get their girls to the altar." I winked at her. "If it was me, I'd have thrown my girl over my shoulder and plopped her on a plane to Vegas and married her kicking and screaming." But Haven wouldn't kick or scream. Shit, I doubt I could get her over my shoulder without one hell of a fight.

"Yeah, any chick would be kicking and screaming if she had to marry your ass," Logan said and tossed a piece of cheese into his mouth.

"Not marrying my ass, she's marrying my dick."

"Crisis," my dad warned in his disappointed tone. The one where you felt like total dirt after you did something he disapproved of.

Ream huffed. "Bro, no chick is marrying that over-used diseased thing."

I snagged my beer off the table and raised it in the air. "Hey, I'm a religious wrapper."

"Good to hear, Vincent," my mom said, coming out onto the patio with Emily. "But why don't you try keeping it in your pants?"

"Fuck, Mom. I am."

"Yeah, fuckin' right," Ream said, laughing at the absurdity of the idea.

"Language, boys." My mom used 'that tone,' and no matter how old we were, that tone would never lose its effect. Just one of those things a son never outgrew.

Except for the constant niggling of wanting to jump in my car and go get Haven, the evening settled down with Ream at least accepting the fact that I wasn't moving out of the farm anytime soon. It was likely the fact that Kite stated that the closing date wasn't for six more weeks and until then, Emily still legally owned it.

Guessed I owed Kite one.

Six weeks. I wasn't thinking of how long that was to find another place. I was thinking about how long I had with Haven. Most chicks it took me six seconds to get their undivided attention. But Haven . . . I wanted more than her undivided attention. I wanted her to trust me enough to place her shattered pieces in my hand.

Chapter Thirteen

Haven

I WOKE UP TO my phone buzzing on the nightstand. I rolled over and put the pillow over my head. My leg muscles ached from my run last night, having pushed myself farther and longer than usual. The wind had been strong, trying to unhinge me with each step. I refused to give in. I'd win this fight. I'd kill the monsters. I'd watch them bleed until they no longer lived inside me.

But they did. My last few episodes proved that.

Buzz.

I sighed and tossed the pillow aside.

"Pick up your phone," Crisis called through the door.

Oh, my God. "What are you doing outside my door?"

"Pick up your phone and find out." I heard a thump on my door.

I reached over and snagged my phone.

Move it, Ice. We're taking out the big tractor.

I scrolled.

Don't ignore me, baby.

Third text.

I made coffee.

Fourth.

Okay, maybe not yet, but I will.

Fifth.

I'll just sit outside your door until you get your ass out here.

I glanced at the time on the screen. Nine. "It's Sunday. I'm going back to sleep," I called, then tossed my phone aside and rolled over, tucking the sheet under my chin.

The door burst open and quickly shut again. Crisis leaned against it, his lips pushed together with that familiar crease between his eyes. "Our brother is a fuckin' Terminator. I swear he has radar in his head that goes off every time I talk to you."

My eyes narrowed in on him; he was so full of crap. "Crisis. Get out." My brother wasn't—

A light knock sounded on the door. "Sis?"

Shit. I sat up, making certain to keep the sheets covering me because I was wearing a pink silk negligee with skimpy spaghetti straps and it barely covered my breasts. Kat had bought it for me when I first came to live with them, along with a drawer full of panties and bras. She said, 'every girl deserved to have beautiful negligee next to her skin.' At first, I balked, internally of course, wanting nothing to do with anything sexy. But after a few months feeling the soft silky material on my hands as I pushed them aside in my drawer . . . I tried one of them on.

I'd never had anything but cheap clothes, and the negligee felt nice against my skin. It made me feel . . . good about myself.

Crisis crossed his arms and I couldn't stop from glancing at his tatted biceps. Then my gaze trailed down his hard muscled body to strong thighs clothed in worn jeans hanging low on his hips.

God, where was my head? It was too early in the morning and I was wavering under the sweet clenching between my legs and the whirl in my belly. He was a rock star, a hot rock star who was always on social media. Triple hard limit.

"Haven? I just saw your door close."

I cleared my throat and gestured to Crisis to get away from the door before my brother barged in, saw him and jumped to conclusions. He pushed away and came straight for me, his eyes sparking a mischievous glow.

My brother knocked again. "We're going to brunch today at Georgie and Deck's. I'd really like you to come."

Fine. Crisis wanted to play . . . he froze halfway toward the bed when I raised my brows and smiled. He shook his head back and forth and mouthed, "Don't do it."

"Yeah, come in," I yelled.

Crisis dove for the bed, threw the duvet up in the air and landed flat on his stomach, the cover settling over him just as Ream strode in. I lay frozen beneath the covers, my heart racing, and a whoosh of blood charging through my veins. My breath hitched as warm heated air brushed across my bare thigh and goose bumps popped up along my skin.

"Listen, if you don't want to go, I won't force you, but I'd really like you to. Emily missed seeing you last night and you know Georgie and Deck."

If anyone could say they *knew* Deck.

Ream sat on the edge of the bed and I hastily bent my knees so the duvet tented and he didn't notice Crisis' breathing.

If he found him under the covers in my bed . . .

"I'd rather not. I have studying to do." Crisis' hand brushed against my calf and my heart leapt. I swallowed and shifted away, but it wasn't far enough because my body knew he was there. My mind did, too, and I had no way to control the intense sensations roaring through me.

"I want you part of my life, sis."

God, this was insanely awkward. I was completely turned on and my brother was sitting on the bed beside me.

Ream sighed and looked down at his hands. "I shouldn't have left. I guess I thought with Olaf dead that you were safe and, well, you never seem to want me around. Any of us. "

I stayed silent because I couldn't lie to him. He was right, at least that was how I had felt. Not so much anymore. After years being a prisoner, trapped within a shell of a girl I'd never had a chance to grow into, I needed time alone, to heal, repair the holes, find who I was now, not who I'd been for twelve years.

He continued, "You know, if you want, I can teach you how to drive. I didn't realize you were interested; otherwise, I would've offered before we left for the tour. I can buy you a car and—"

I stiffened. "Ream. No. I don't want you buying me anything more. I already live here and you support me and pay for school."

"You're my sister. Of course I would."

I saw the pain in his expression, the tight brows over his concerned eyes. He took so much of what happened to me onto himself. The drugs, the rape—he blamed himself for not seeing it. "It wasn't your fault."

"Jesus, Angel." He ran his hand through his hair. "It was. I should've seen what was happening. What Gerard was doing."

"I hid it from you, Ream. I didn't want you to know."

He rested his elbows on his knees and put his head into his hands. "Why Haven? Why? You know I would've stopped it."

I didn't reach for him; I wasn't in that place yet to do that with Ream. We were still so far apart even sitting next to one another. "I was scared." He looked at me and I saw the tears in his eyes. "I couldn't see you go back down in the basement again."

He swore beneath his breath.

"Maybe it was my turn to keep us safe."

"But you weren't safe." Ream's voice raised and Crisis' hand tightened around my calf.

"And neither were you," I stated.

He was quiet for a second, then, "What did Olaf and Alexa do to you?"

"What happened doesn't matter anymore." My brother could never know about the club or about Charlie; he'd never forgive himself.

"Of course it does. Jesus. You matter. And I want you to feel like you can tell me anything."

I met his eyes, refusing to waver as I said, "I can't." No, I wouldn't.

"Then talk to someone else. Please." He raised his hand as if to reach for me, but changed his mind and drew back.

He'd tried to get me to see a therapist Emily once had gone to, but there was no chance I was letting out the demons that lived lurking inside. I knew what would happen . . . I couldn't survive the pain. I raised my chin and met my brother's eyes. "I don't want to talk about it with anyone. When I escaped, it ended. Gerard, Alexa, Olaf, they're dead and so is what happened."

The muscles in his neck throbbed and there was a moment I thought he'd fight me on it. "Yeah."

I scooted up further on the bed trying to move away from Crisis, whose hand gently caressed my lower leg. I knew it was meant to be reassuring after what he'd just overheard, but I had a sweet ache between my legs and I needed to get away.

"You okay?" Ream had always been stoic and intense with this cool wash of distance to him. I'd noticed since I'd been back, he'd changed. Softer, although still overprotective.

"Yeah. I'm good." Except Crisis was in my bed, stroking my leg and I was getting turned on.

Ream's brow lowered as he looked at the bed where the duvet had settled over Crisis. *Shit.* I coughed as I shuffled the duvet. "I better get up."

"Sure. Yeah." Ream glanced once more at the duvet then rose and walked to the door. "If you change your mind about brunch, we're leaving at eleven."

I nodded.

The door quietly clicked closed and I threw back the covers hiding Crisis. He rested his chin on his hands. "Pink negligee? You know that's my favorite color, right?"

"I didn't buy it."

He grinned. "And definitely nice legs. Runner's calves."

This is what I liked about Crisis. He didn't bring up the conversation with my brother because he knew I wouldn't want to talk about it. He let it slide and was his usual self.

"You're a good guy, Crisis." I had no idea why I said it. Crisis didn't need an ego boost, but sometimes, I wondered if he really knew that he was.

He never said anything and I didn't expect him to, but his grin faded and he stared at me with those bright blue eyes. My breathing picked up to match my racing heartbeat as I imagined him grabbing me and pulling me underneath him, his mouth crashing down on mine. I pictured tasting him for the first time, feeling his weight on top of me, not suffocating but protective and warm. I wanted his hands on my body, touching every crevice while I explored his. I licked my dry lips and his eyes darted to them.

Oh, God.

I scrambled from the bed, staggering a couple steps before gaining my balance and escaping to the washroom. "I don't want to drive today."

I closed the door and leaned against it. God, what was that? Dangerous was what it was. What we had was perfect, and feeling anything more would ruin that. He was helping me get to normal and that was all I wanted. Sex wasn't part of that. Even casual sex because I was sure from his reputation that was what it would be.

After I showered and dressed, and disposed of the simmering heat inside me, I walked down the hall, smelling the sweet aroma of coffee as I entered the kitchen. Kat was sitting on the counter, Ream standing between her legs, his hands on her hips. She glanced up and smiled. "Morning. How are you feeling?"

My brother obviously played it up that I wasn't feeling well last night. "Fine." I liked Kat; she was good for my brother, and from what I'd seen, held her own against his overbearing nature. I reached for a cup and poured myself some coffee.

"What's the story with Deck and Georgie?" Kite asked as he strolled into the kitchen wearing ripped jeans and a white dress shirt, looking business chic. He was such a contradiction even in his clothing choice. "Suddenly, it's brunch at his penthouse and she's moving in."

"She is?" Kat blurted.

Kite leaned back against the counter and sipped his coffee. "That's what Logan said last night."

Crisis walked by me, his hand lightly brushing across the small of my back. I watched as he stretched and pulled down a mug from the second shelf then poured himself a coffee. Every movement was casual and with easy confidence.

"About time he tasted some of that," Crisis said. "Do you think she dyes her pussy like her hair? Fuck, Deck, going down on pink streaked pussy." He laughed.

Kat snorted. "Figures you'd think of that."

"Hey, I just say aloud what every other guy is thinking." He leaned against the counter—beside me. Right beside me so our arms touched whenever he lifted his coffee.

"I wasn't thinking that," Kite said.

Crisis chuckled. "No, man, you were thinking about tying her down then whipping her ass until it was pink streaked."

My eyes darted to Kite. The quiet, mysterious drummer with piercings and tats. It made sense, the control, the patience and calm he exuded. I bet when Kite took a girl, he took every piece of her and made her his. Jealousy wouldn't even play into him because there'd be no question she'd be his and she'd never walk away unless he told her to.

Crisis nudged me and whispered, "Stop looking at him like you want to fuck him."

"God, I wasn't," I whispered back. I had no interest in Kite. His mystery made me uneasy and I had enough pain in my life to never want to have it in the bedroom.

Ream lifted Kat off the counter, kissed her on the lips. "Let's shower, babe. We have to go soon." His gaze slipped over me to Crisis. "You need to go house hunting. Get on it."

"What about Kite? Shit, man, I'm your brother."

"Doesn't mean I want to live with you. Did it for months, now I want time alone with my girl." I tensed as I realized that maybe he wouldn't say it, but wanted me gone, too. "Not you, sis. Just the guys." Ream kissed me on the cheek then headed for the stairs, his hand in Kat's. "And until you find a place . . . no bringing chicks back here—

period. Don't need any more psycho chicks causing problems for the band and my sister. That should get your ass moving," Ream said over his shoulder. "Shit, wouldn't doubt you'll have a place by tonight."

Kite opened the fridge and grabbed the orange juice. "Penthouse downtown. Right by the water."

Crisis groaned. "Fuck. We'll need security every time we walk out the door. You should've seen Haven's school. I had an hour of signing."

Kite scowled. "You shouldn't have gone to her school."

I picked up my mug and was about to slip away when Crisis snagged my hand. "What about you?"

"What about me?"

"Are you going to stay here?" He shrugged. "Didn't you say you wanted to be downtown, closer to school? Find a job?"

My eyes narrowed. "Yeah." Where was he going with this?

"Well, we could find a place for all of us."

I balked. "Like, live with you?"

He nodded. "And Kite."

"You're kidding, right?" I looked to Kite and he shrugged. "I meant my own place."

"Why not? It makes sense. Close to school. Less traveling time."

"With you?"

"Well, yeah, me and Kite."

It would be a hell of a lot easier to get to school and I wouldn't feel like I was encroaching on Kat and Ream's space. But living with Crisis and Kite? They were famous and I didn't need famous in my life. But what I did need was a job and that would give me the opportunity to work.

"We'd buy a place big enough to have your own space," Kite said.

I bit the insides of my cheek. "I don't like all the attention you guys draw. No, it wouldn't work."

"Babe, it's not like we have reporters outside our door every day. Besides, we have security and we'd buy a place that has it as well."

I'd never be able to move out of here unless I had a job and it was impossible to find a job while living on the farm with no license or car.

But living with Crisis when I had this unmistakeable desire filtering through me . . ."It just wouldn't be a good idea."

"It's a great idea," Crisis continued. "I'll keep a low profile." Kite huffed. "If anyone finds out we live there . . . which will take months . . . then you don't leave the building at the same time as us. It's simple."

I looked to Kite and he shrugged.

"We'd hardly be there," Crisis said. "We'll be at the studio most of the time working on the album. And I can talk to Georgie about a job at her coffee shop. It's right downtown."

I'd been a marionette for twelve years and this would give me the chance to get a job and make my own money. Money I'd get to keep for myself. "Why?" I asked.

Crisis frowned. "Why what?"

"Why would you want me living with you guys?"

Kite completely threw me off guard when he walked over and cupped his hand around the back of my neck and kissed my forehead. "Why wouldn't we? Plus, it will keep this guy from parading around naked." Kite let me go. "Think about it." Kite glanced at Crisis and frowned. "What happened to your face?"

I bit my lower lip as a smile creeped up on me. There was a bruise on his cheek now from the lawnmower incident.

"Haven punched me."

Kite's brows lifted and he half-cocked a grin before he left us alone. Live with Crisis and Kite? Wasn't I doing that now? Hadn't I done that for two months before they went on tour? My brother was marrying Kat and they certainly didn't need me hanging around.

There was the possibility of a job.

To make my own money.

Close to school.

"No barging into my bedroom," I said.

Crisis held up his hands. "Done."

"And no parading around naked." My pulse rose as I thought about his naked hard body and I swallowed.

He quirked a grin. I glared. "Okay, deal, but you're missing out."

"And as soon as I get a job, I pay rent." Crisis scowled, but I stared him down and he relented with a nod. "If you have chicks over, I don't want them parading around naked either."

He threw back his head and laughed. "Yeah, Ice. Got it. But that won't be happening."

"And I get my own bathroom."

"Sweetness, you sure are asking a lot. You want a soaker tub, too? With the jets?"

I scrunched up my nose.

He pushed away from the counter. "Okay, so no nakedness. Own bathroom. And paying rent."

"And no barging into my room."

"Sure, but that goes both ways, Ice. You parade around naked once and you're out on your ass." He winked at me then strolled away.

I huffed, but I doubt he heard me. Taking my coffee, I went out to the porch and sat looking out onto the horse field. I'd miss this, the quiet and calm of the farm. But I couldn't get a job staying here and, more importantly, I needed my brother to see that I was okay. That he could stop worrying about me.

I lay back, my hand on my abdomen. This hurt the most.

The rape. The drugs. The club. They had bent pieces of me, but I was repairing them.

But one piece remained trapped and it was like fighting against a tornado. It whirled and spun inside me, damaging more and more each day. I didn't know how much longer I'd be able to stand in the eye of the storm and ignore what was churning around me.

Chapter Fourteen

Haven

Babe, we'll pick you up in five.

What?

Kite and I want to show you a place.

Don't pick me up at school.

It's fine. We won't even get out of the car.

I was walking across the parking lot with Dana to her car. "Crisis and Kite want to take me to see a place. You want to come?"

Dana smiled. "Yeah. I'll text Dillon and let him know."

She'd been dating him since the frat party.

Where are you?

St. George Street. Where we met before. You'll see my car.

Oh, shit. Crisis' car was a cranberry red muscle car. He didn't have to get out of the car to gain attention; the car did that all by itself. Crisis hadn't allowed me near the driver's seat. Although, we had moved on to the tractor a couple weeks earlier and since I passed my written exam last week, I drove Ream's Audi to the store on Sunday and that turned out to be pretty important because I'd gone to my brother and asked him. He grinned from ear-to-ear and grabbed his keys and we were out the door.

Over the last month, Crisis and I had fallen into an easy friendship. Easy wasn't really true because whenever I was near him, I fought the escalating desire. He acted like it was nothing when I jumped at the slightest graze of his hand or when I darted away from him and went for a run. Now, it was a run to smother something else entirely.

I began to join everyone for dinner, and although I remained quiet, it was nice to see the banter between Ream, Kite and Crisis. Sometimes, we'd all watch a movie together; Crisis taught me to play Bullshit, a card game where I discovered I excelled since I read peoples' expressions so well. My brother was my competition as he could easily keep a straight face.

A few times Crisis sat with me out on the porch writing lyrics while I studied. It was a comforting silence, his fingers tapping away on his laptop and the pages flipping on my text book with my highlighter skimming sentences.

Crisis was like breathing in fresh air. The beauty of him was that there were no lies. No mask. He said what everyone else was too polite or afraid to say.

And for some, it may be too much, but for me, with all the lies and shadows that lurked inside me, Crisis had become my anchor to keep me afloat.

I walked up to the driver's side. "Can I drive?" I had my G license, so I could only drive during the day and a licensed driver had to be in the car with me.

Crisis burst out laughing. "Like hell, Ice. Do you know what kind of car this is? It's a 1970 Chevrolet Chevelle SS 454 LS6." I sighed, having heard this before. "Only twenty of these suckers ever made. Twenty. Get in the back." He lifted the seat so I could crawl in the back where Dana was already sitting and laughing her ass off.

Kite was in the front and looked over his shoulder at me. "He'd give up the band before this car. That tells you something."

"What about chicks?"

Kite paused. "He already did that."

My brows drew together as I thought about it. Crisis never talked about chicks and I never saw him with any. Had the scenario with that chick changed his playboy status? I hadn't heard anything about that.

"What happened with that girl?"

Kite glanced at Crisis who was hopping in the front seat. "Ask him."

Crisis started the engine. It purred. No, it rumbled and the vibration of the power beneath me was exhilarating. I kind of got why he didn't want me driving it. I'd probably put my foot on the gas and ram it right into the car parked ahead.

"Ask me what?"

"Haven was asking about the girl," Kite said.

"What girl?"

Kite shook his head. "You know . . . Tammy."

"Who's Tammy?" Dana asked while putting on her seat belt.

That was her name. I didn't like it.

Crisis hands fisted around the steering wheel. "Nothing is happening. She posts crap on social media, trying to get attention. I'm ignoring it. Our publicist, Jolie, says not to feed into it and the lawyer says don't respond. I don't."

I was getting that social media had a lot of power. People were pretty brave behind the safety of a computer screen. I could tell Crisis was agitated by it though, and when I saw him looking at me in the rear-view mirror, I gave him a reassuring smile. His hands relaxed on the steering wheel and he started chatting about the place we were going to see.

Five minutes later, Crisis pulled up to a stunning building only a few short blocks away from the university and right on Bloor Street in Yorkville, one of the most prestigious areas of Toronto.

"You're shittin' me. This building is freakin' awesome," Dana said as Kite held the seat up and she climbed out, her gaze following the smoky glass lines of the building. "And look at all the men in suits."

"Security," Kite explained. "One of the reasons why we looked here."

Crisis lifted the seat and held out his hand. I took it and instantly my heart raced. I got out and looked up at the building, to avoid looking at Crisis. "It looks expensive." It was the first thing I thought of, considering I'd lived in run-down houses all my life. The farm was beautiful but it was an old century home, nothing like this.

"It's close to your school and Georgie's coffee shop isn't far." Crisis shut his door and kept hold of my hand as we walked inside, which I liked . . . a lot.

"Oh, my God, it has a waterfall. Do you see that, Haven? A waterfall in the lobby." She ran over and gaped, then dug in her purse and pulled out a coin. "My wish is to live here." She tossed the coin in. I was betting hers was the only one in there, because it didn't look like a building many residents had to make wishes.

"Where's the real estate agent?" I asked as Crisis pressed the button for the elevator. Kite raised his brows and looked at Crisis. "What?"

"Don't need one." The elevator doors opened and we all piled in, although piled wouldn't be the right word as it was huge and mirrored and had this little pale pink loveseat along the back wall.

"Squeee! It's like *Pretty Woman*." Dana sprawled out on the loveseat and Kite snorted like she was crazy, and she was a little, but my friendship with Dana had crept up on me. She never mentioned my few breakdowns and she never put her hand on my shoulder again. "You're no fun."

That statement was loaded because Kite probably had more fun than she did, except it was in private. Crisis used a card in a slot then pressed the PH button—penthouse. I was surprised a real estate agent would give him access to the place, but they were pretty famous, and denying Tear Asunder much of anything probably didn't happen too often.

When the doors opened, I gawked. My mouth actually fell open as we were greeted with marble floors and a wide-open space that looked right through to sixteen-foot windows overlooking the city.

"Holy mother of God," Dana whispered.

"Come on, princess," Crisis said. "Let's see your bedroom."

"Potential bedroom," I corrected. Could I do this? Live with Crisis and still keep what we had? He seemed to think so; I'd just need to run more.

He tugged on my hand and walked through the place, which had to be five-thousand square feet, and had a second floor. The terrace alone had to be six-hundred square feet with a built-in brick fireplace. It was the library that stole my breath away. Floor-to-ceiling shelves lined the walls, and although they were empty, the deep mahogany wood contrasted against the cool grey marble floors giving it a modern, yet old-world feel. One entire wall had an inlaid seat against the window with soft cream cushions.

"Private space," Crisis said, standing at the door while I walked around, sliding my finger along the wood shelves. "You can do your homework here. Kind of like your own place to hang."

I laughed and then stopped short when I saw his expression. He was locked on me, eyes watching, and there was desire smoldering. I liked it. I liked his eyes on me and I never thought I'd enjoy that after the club. I never thought I'd want a guy to touch me ever again. "Crisis, I don't need a library. All I need is a bedroom. And this place is too much. I feel like if I breathe, I'll break something."

"What, the marble floors?" He stepped away from the door chuckling and I followed after him.

"You know what's missing?" Dana called from the patio. "A pool. Where's the pool?"

"Downstairs," Kite said, then sat on one of the stools around the island in the state-of-the-art kitchen.

She rolled her eyes. "Oh. Well, isn't that a pain in the ass to have to share with other residents."

I followed Crisis up an iron spiral staircase to an open area. He pointed to a door. "That will be the gym. And the next room's mine. The one on the other side is Kite's and across the hall is a guest room.

Each of us have our own bathroom and they're pretty much exactly the same." He walked me down a hall. "And this is yours."

I stared at the enormous space with windows on two walls and a private balcony. Crisis opened a door on the left. "Bathroom with a soaker," he said grinning.

I backed out. "No. I can't afford this." It was overwhelming. Way too much. I expected a nice place, but this . . . this wasn't a place I could imagine myself in. God, all I imagined was Crisis and I in the soaker tub together, naked with his arms wrapped around me as I leaned back against him while he nuzzled the side of my neck, then licked the slight moisture clinging to my skin. Jesus, what the hell was wrong with me?

"Babe," Crisis called as I escaped and went back downstairs. "Haven." I heard him come after me and he caught my arm before I reached the elevator. "It's just four walls."

"Yeah, with marble floors, four bathrooms and a library. Crisis, it has a library." Kite and Dana joined us. "You guys can do whatever you want, but I don't want to live in a museum." And I was scared. I hated being scared. I'd been able to lock that away with everything else for so long, but what I felt for Crisis . . . it terrified me because I didn't know what to do with it.

"Christ, it's not a museum." Crisis crossed his arms, leaned back against the wall to block the button for the elevator. "It's big, yeah, but we won't be tripping over one another. The security is top of the line and no fans are getting past them. No attention, Haven. It's what you want. You won't have to worry about it here. If reporters ever find out we're in the building, they won't even get up to the front walkway before security is on them." He glanced at Kite as if for help.

Kite piped in. "You tell Ream you're looking to move out?"

I shook my head. "No." I had mentioned it at one point, but that was after I was done school and had a job.

"Then when the shit hits the fan, he may be a little more reasonable knowing you're safe here and it's close to school. Makes sense for you to move in."

Kite had a good point. It didn't solve the issue of the imagery plastered in my mind and screwing with my control.

"We move next week," Crisis said, shoving off the wall and turning to press the button.

"You bought it already?" I asked. And this was when I felt panic, because that meant he was leaving the farm. It meant I wouldn't see him every day. It meant I'd lose what we had.

"Yeah. So, tell your brother and start packing," Crisis said.

Oh. He sounded pissed off and I didn't like that I was the cause.

"Wow!" Dana stood frozen, staring at me. "We are so hanging at your place from now on."

The elevator doors opened and Crisis and Dana walked in. I went to follow when Kite snagged my arm, leaned in and in a low tone said, "He's been dying to show you this place for weeks."

My gaze darted to Crisis and I realized he'd been excited. He'd taken my hand and pulled me along like a kid in a candy store. And I was shooting him down at every opportunity when I had no right to. I'd ruined it for him.

This place made sense for me. Crisis had taken what I said to heart and found a place where I was close to school, a job and had the privacy and safety of security in place.

Shit. I was a bitch. I was okay with being a bitch to other people, people I didn't care about, but not to Crisis. He was good to me. No, it was more than that, much more. But what I was feeling would ease just like the memories of my past.

"Okay. I'll move in." Except, the memories hadn't faded and despite what I was trying to convince myself, I didn't think what I was feeling for Crisis would either.

"Okay?" Crisis repeated, beaming, and holding the door open with his forearm.

I walked into the elevator and sat on the loveseat. "Yeah. Okay."

"Yes!" Dana squealed.

"But both of you"—I looked from Kite to Crisis—"have to be with me when I tell Ream."

Two hours later, the boom of Ream's roar hit. "No fuckin' way! Out of the question. Jesus, what are you thinking, Haven? Live with these guys? Man-whore parading chicks in and out and Kite . . ." he glared at him. "You may not parade them, but you sure as hell have plenty of them, too. My sister is not living with you guys. Forget it."

He paced back and forth in the living room, shoulders tense, hands clenched into fists. Kite casually had one leg bent over the other as he sat on the couch and Crisis stood by the fireplace, looking rather relaxed considering my brother kept glancing at him with murderous eyes.

"It makes sense, pumpkin," Kat offered and smiled at me. She called my brother pumpkin? "Close to school and not stuck out here in the middle of nowhere."

Ream snorted. "Have you forgotten about the Crisis issue? The chick has written love letters on the internet to him." I stiffened. Love letters? "She's fine here with us. I can drive her anywhere she wants to go."

"She doesn't want that," Kat continued. "She wants independence. Away from her controlling bullheaded brother."

Did they forget I was standing right here?

"Jesus, I'm not trying to control her."

Everyone was silent and Ream stopped pacing then looked at each of us before his eyes landed on me. "Haven, you want your own place, I'll buy you an apartment. Or we can rent one, whatever you want. You can't live with them."

I hated the word can't. I didn't do well with the word can't. I pushed away from the wall and shook my head. "This is my decision. My choice." My tone hardened. "I get a choice now." Ream crossed his arms, but I saw the flicker of uncertainty in his eyes. "You of all people know what it's like not have a say in what happens to you. When you're forced to do things you don't want to do." Ream's jaw clenched, but his eyes softened, then closed briefly. "When other people make decisions for you."

"Haven . . ." Ream came toward me, but I held up my hand, stopping him.

"I don't want anyone's sympathy or pity. And I don't want to be told I can't do something. I had that. I hated it and I finally escaped it." I softened my tone. "Ream, I know you still see me as sixteen and weak, but I'm not."

"I don't see you as weak. I never did. Never. You were strong as hell, you still are. More than ever and I don't know how you've done that, but you have. I just want you to feel like you're safe. That you don't have to be so strong anymore."

"It's who I am now, Ream."

Kite casually played with his brow ring. "Security is top. Crisis had Luke check the place out, too." I averted my eyes to Crisis. I hadn't known that.

"And this Tammy chick? What about that?" Ream asked.

Crisis answered, "Luke is keeping an eye, but she's in Alberta and everything she does is on-line crap. No reason for her to come to Toronto when she never has before."

"She could." Ream was persistent and I realized he was a lot like me. He didn't give up easily and was stubborn.

"And if she does, we'll deal. Luke will deal. The police will deal," Crisis said. "We don't live like that, Ream." The two brothers locked eyes. It was kind of like an understanding between them with what Crisis said, and I wondered what it was. "Haven is travelling forty-five minutes to school and back. It doesn't make sense for her."

Ream stood silent for what seemed like five minutes, but was probably only a few seconds, then he nodded and his shoulders sagged. Kite got up and walked by me, placing his hand briefly on my hip while Kat reached for Ream and wrapped her arms around him, whispering something in his ear, which made him sag even more.

I approached them then reached out to him, putting my hand on his tatted forearm. "Living here with you and Kat on the farm . . . it's not the right place for me."

He nodded, pulled me into his arms and hugged me. "I love you so much, Angel," Ream whispered.

I love you, too.

Chapter Fifteen

Haven

"HAVEN, WAIT UP." I paused and looked over my shoulder at Dana, who jogged up beside me. "You want to go to karaoke tonight? Dillon booked a private room upstairs at this bar. There's eight of us going."

I opened the cafeteria door and the noise of dishes and boisterous voices drowned out my groan. "Not really my thing."

"I swear you won't have to sing if you don't want to. Just sit and laugh at me making a complete fool of myself." She placed a banana, water and bologna sandwich on her tray.

"Why do you want to do it, then?" My phone vibrated in my back pocket and tiny sparks flared across my skin. God, I was turned on by phone vibration.

"It's fun."

Dana talked about karaoke. I half-listened while thinking about the text, which I knew was from Crisis. I expected more texts since he hated when I didn't respond and he let me know it, but my phone remained quiet. Maybe it was my brother who texted; disappointment settled in.

We grabbed lunch then went and sat at the table by the window with Dana's crowd. Dillon's buddies were on the lacrosse team and they were pretty nice, not rowdy like the football team. Rebecca and Tanya hung with us, too, having gone to the same high school with a couple of the guys on the team.

"Hey, hon." Dillon slid over and Dana sat next to him.

"Haven, you coming to karaoke tonight?" Dillon's best friend was Lac, the guy from my Creative Writing class with Professor Neale. I found out his real name was Johnny, but everyone called him Lac because he was the captain of the lacrosse team.

Lac plopped down beside me and jerked his head to the right to flick his light brown bangs out of his eyes. "My shower singing skills will be revealed." He grinned.

I was starting to like Lac; he was polite and poised. There was a calmness about him, probably why he was the captain of his team. "I have studying to do."

Lac nodded. "Yeah, sure. Okay." Another reason I liked him, he never pushed me into joining them on their nights out.

"Oh, my God, Dillon." Dana smacked him on the arm and laughed. "Stop. Fine, I'll ask her." She turned to me. "Dillon wants you to ask Kite and Crisis to come tonight. I told him no way in hell."

Keeping a secret that I lived with two band members from Tear Asunder had been impossible, especially when Crisis showed up at school when he was bored. I didn't know how he ever got bored when he was in the recording studio most days, which often led into the nights.

He did attempt to keep a low profile, though, always wearing a baseball cap low over his face and head down and no Luke or his men.

We'd lived in the condo for three weeks and there were only two girls I'd seen, and both had their clothes on and were leaving when I was getting ready for school. I knew it was going to happen. God, I expected it. Still, it hurt, even though I had no idea if they'd been Kite's girls or Crisis.'

"Come on, Haven. It would be cool if they came." Kevin was on the lacrosse team, too, and was here on a scholarship. He wiggled his bushy brows then shovelled a handful of fries into his mouth. Funny, how a person changed their tune when suddenly the tables had turned. Kevin was acting as if he liked Crisis after calling him an asshole at the party.

I shook my head. Not a chance. I wasn't asking Crisis and Kite to be on display in front of my . . . I guess they could be called my friends. I hadn't experienced having any before, but we ate lunch together most days and I was invited to everything, although I rarely went.

Lac nudged me with his shoulder and smiled. "Not a big deal. I'm sure I can sing just as well as any of those Tear Asunder guys."

He was teasing and I half-smiled. It was getting easier to do, let others see my emotions. The normality was finally becoming reality. I was even going to start work at Georgie's coffee shop in two weeks. Crisis' doing. She was away with Deck, but her manager, Rylie, said I could work two nights a week.

"Hey, we should do dinner one night." Lac leaned into me and his hand settled on my lower back.

I stiffened at his touch. Was he asking me out? I liked him, he was definitely good looking, but I wasn't going to date him.

Dana interjected before I had a chance to respond, "So, will you come tonight?" She raised her brows and pouted.

I wanted to learn how to have fun, to socialize. This was why I'd moved downtown, why I went to school, to move on with my life. This was just another step toward doing that and this wasn't a party. Besides, I hadn't had any triggers lately. "Okay."

A hush slowly came over the group in a domino effect. I knew who it was before I looked, and my heart picked up and my skin tingled. When I did look, the tingles became sparks and my breath caught in my throat. He kept his head tilted down and didn't look at anyone, totally not Crisis' style, but I knew he did it for me. His long even strides were casual and confident with a swagger and so Crisis—that he couldn't hide.

I licked my lips and faced back around the other way.

"Oh, my God, I so have to get in his pants," Rebecca said. "That man is smoking hot. I can't even imagine what he'd do to a girl with that mouth." She giggled. "Actually, yes I can."

"Shut up, Becky." Dana threw a fry at her. "He's not interested in your hairy vagina. He likes Haven."

"We're just friends," I said. Except I wanted to kiss him and every time he was near me I had butterflies and distinct tightness between my legs that made my panties wet. It hadn't eased by living with him. It was worse, and worse was fucking with my control.

What I didn't like was thinking about Crisis taking Rebecca or Tanya home with him. Would he? If they put in a little effort . . . or no effort. Both of them were pretty and very willing.

I felt his presence come up behind me and my belly dropped. Jesus, it was as if my body went into an adrenaline rush and all I could think of was him coming up behind me and kissing my neck. Of the touch of his lips against my skin, his tongue flicking out to taste me. The nibble of his teeth on my ear that kind of hurt but didn't and he'd soothe it after with a gentle suckling.

Oh, God. I shifted uneasily in my seat as the heat rose in my body and the clench between my legs intensified.

Lac moved his hand from my back as Crisis moved in, which pretty much forced him to. His hard abdomen pressed into my back and he swept a finger across the nape of my neck, pushing my hair aside. Shivers darted across my skin and my breath stopped.

He leaned into me further and kissed the top of my head. I melted. I didn't think it was possible to melt from a simple gesture, but I did. It had become a habit of his and I loved that he did it. Being tall, I fit right underneath his chin and it was perfect for him to kiss the top of my head when I was standing, but he still did it when I was sitting.

The entire table stared at him and I looked back at my plate and grabbed a fry.

"Hey, baby." Crisis bent over me, snatched the fry I nearly had in my mouth, took a bite then put the other half to my mouth.

I opened and his finger grazed my upper lip as he slowly fed me. I locked eyes with him and expected a smirk, a smile, a grin, but instead,

I got that smoldering hot sexy look that had me wanting to say screw it and jump him.

Jump him. I hadn't wanted to jump a guy in my life. I quickly looked back at my plate, but he wasn't done yet and his hands came to rest on my upper arms. I stiffened when he slowly caressed up and down. Casual sex. Could I do casual sex? But there would be nothing casual about it. It would be heated and intense and . . . I sucked in air as his mouth came right next to my ear.

"I was hoping it was sloppy joe day. I'd love to see the juices around your mouth. I'd lick you clean this time, baby." And he had to go say shit like that. He knew. He had to know what I was feeling right now and was teasing me. "You mind shifting over, buddy?"

I glanced over at Lac who frowned but slid over anyway. Crisis stepped over the bench and sat beside me. "Introduce me to your friends, Ice."

"What are you doing here?" I whispered.

"I texted you to meet me outside. You didn't respond. I hate being ignored . . . you know that."

Yeah, I did and I still had my phone sitting in my back pocket. "How did you know I was here?"

"Your schedule has been posted in the library for weeks, babe." And he'd obviously read it. And he was obviously enjoying my discomfort because he made sure his thigh was against mine.

Becky piped up from across the table, her flirty smile full-blown. "I'm Rebecca."

Everyone introduced themselves, but it was Lac who Crisis paid attention to as he shook his hand. "You interested in dating Haven?"

Oh, my God. "Crisis."

But Lac didn't balk at Crisis' question; instead, he grinned. "Yeah. Haven is pretty special."

Dana interjected. "Crisis thinks so, too."

Lac didn't say anything.

Crisis stole another fry from my plate and ate it. "Yep. And she likes me . . . a lot."

I did. God, I did. I liked him a lot and he'd noticed. Excitement thrummed through me because I was thinking that casual sex was going to have to come into play here. And despite it being a bad idea, it was also a good idea because sex was something I'd never wanted. Now I did and I wanted to experience it with Crisis.

There were a few chuckles from everyone except Kevin, who got up and left. Maybe he was still pissed about his phone.

Rebecca leaned forward, her breasts accentuated as she pushed her chest out. "So, do you want to come out with us tonight?"

"What's tonight?" Crisis asked. He shifted his legs under the table, stretching them out and I felt the slow movement rub down the length of my thigh.

Rebecca started to tell him when Dana quickly interrupted and told him about karaoke. "Haven is coming if you want to join us. Maybe Kite, too? You guys can show us how it's done."

Crisis chuckled and Tanya and Rebecca sighed, their eyes having never left him. It was annoying and I had an odd tightening in my chest.

"He's busy," I said and went back to eating, although I could no longer taste the food.

"You going?" Crisis turned to Lac.

"Yeah, of course."

"I'm going," Becky chimed up.

"Me too," Tanya said and batted her eyelashes.

Dana snorted. "Don't be obvious at all. God, guys like a little challenge, not pussy thrown in their faces."

"Debatable," Dillon said laughing. "If it was Angelina—"

"Oh, shut up. You're a pig and don't count," Dana retorted.

Dillon laughed and kissed Dana on the cheek.

"Sure. Why not? Music. I'm in." Crisis cupped the back of my neck and leaned into me whispering in a low gravelled voice, "I can't wait to hear you sing, Ice."

What the hell was going on? Crisis was purposely trying to turn me on. He was flirting with me, not subtly like he did sometimes. This was bold, in-your-face flirting, and I liked it. No, I loved it and despite my hard limits to stay clear of attention—and Crisis was attention—I was faltering and I think Crisis was, too.

"I won't be singing." I'd never get up and sing. Not because I was scared of what others thought, because I didn't care; I just hated being watched.

Dillon asked about the band and what they were working on and the conversation stirred around Tear Asunder. Any personal questions, Crisis deflected but he was casual about it and easily handled the attention. He also never let go of the casual hold on my neck.

"Babe, I gotta go. Kite's waiting for me in the car."

"All this time?"

He shrugged, smiling. "He was talking to some chick and her friends. He's fine." Crisis climbed out of the bench seat. He nodded to everyone and I noticed his eyes avoided Becky and Tanya, who had yet to take their eyes off him. And that made the tightening in my chest disappear. It was hard not turning to watch Crisis walk away, because no matter what we were, he had a sexy-as-hell ass that deserved to be looked at as often as possible.

"See you tonight, Haven." Lac got up from the table. "Guys, we have practice in a half-hour."

As soon as he was out of earshot, Dana said, "Lac likes you. Like really likes you and Dillon said he talks about you all the time."

"He doesn't know me." I glanced over my shoulder at Lac and the boys as they left the cafeteria. Lac was tall, lean, and his arms were cut. Lac was a good guy and I liked him, but I couldn't imagine kissing him. I couldn't imagine kissing any guy except Crisis.

Dana nudged me. "That's what dating is for. Unless, of course, you're saving yourself for the playboy?"

I grabbed my water. "Crisis likes to flirt. He isn't into me like that."

"Bullshit. And you're hot for him."

My gaze darted to hers. Could she see it, too?

"You eating the rest of those?" Dana asked, letting it go.

I pushed my plate of fries toward her and then she asked me about my new job at Georgie's coffee shop, Perk Avenue, and the conversation steered away from Crisis.

My phone vibrated an hour later as I walked across campus to my last class.

So who's the guy?

What guy?

LOL. Cute. You know exactly who I'm talking about. He had his hand on your back.

He noticed that?

Shouldn't you be playing guitar or something?

Logan and Kite are arguing over lyrics. You going to date him?

No, I was considering casual sex.

I was kidding around because he'd really thrown me off today and deserved it. But the truth was, I was considering Crisis for casual sex. My phone started playing, "I'm too sexy," Crisis' idea of funny.

I hadn't even said hello when he said, "You serious? Or fucking with me?"

I was a little caught off-guard by his sudden phone call and the rough tone in his voice.

"You going to fuck that guy? Date him? What?"

"Crisis, I don't ask you about the girls who leave the condo in the morning."

"Then ask me," he shouted. He never shouted. "I want you to ask me because I'd tell you they aren't mine." I heard him take a deep breath. "I'm responsible for you and—"

I cut him off. "I don't want or need anyone being *responsible* for me." He felt responsible for me? God, that just stomped on any lingering desire I had. "I've had no one give a shit about me since I was sixteen. I don't need anyone now."

The phone muffled as if he was walking. "That's complete bullshit, Haven. We all need someone and whether you want it or not, you're part of the band, the family and we're responsible for one another. You know why? Because we care about one another."

151

My hand shook and tremors volleyed through me. "I don't want a family. I didn't sign up for a family." My only family had ever been Ream and he'd been torn away from me. Was that how Crisis saw me, just family? Like Kat or Emily? Had he been flirting with me today because of Lac? Because he felt responsible for me?

"Too fuckin' bad. You got one," he shot back then the line went dead.

I stared at my phone. What the hell just happened? Crisis was laid back and playful. I'd never heard him yell except when he stubbed his toe or something stupid like that. But, Crisis had been furious.

Well, at least he wouldn't go to karaoke.

Chapter Sixteen

Crisis

BY THE TIME we finished at the studio in Logan's house, it was after nine. Kite delayed us leaving with the bullshit over the lyrics not sounding right and despite the final decision he and Logan made, neither of them were happy with the outcome of the song. It was supposed to be a bit of a ballad, and they were right, it was missing something.

I hadn't talked to Haven since I hung up on her. Fuck, I hung up on her. What was I thinking? When I went to call her back five minutes after I'd cooled down, Logan and Kite had agreed and we were back to work.

It took forty-five minutes to drive back to the city. I jumped in the shower, changed and was ready to go in ten minutes.

Kite on the other hand dragged his ass. He wasn't impressed with going and wanted to go to Avalanche, Kat's brother's bar where we used to jam all the time. I made him a deal though, next time he wanted to go out, to wherever, I was there. No bitching.

Kite called down to Roman, one of Luke's guys telling him what we were doing and he brought a car around and took us to the bar.

Kite grabbed my arm before I opened the door to the private room the group was in upstairs. "Don't do anything stupid."

I shrugged his hand away. "What the hell are you talking about?"

"Haven. Don't screw it up for her. Maybe she likes this guy. And yeah, I heard you on the phone in the studio. You're lucky Ream didn't." I made a gruff sound in the back of my throat and Kite's brows rose. "You want to go there? I live with you. Known you since you were sixteen, lived on a tour bus with you. You can play it any way you like, but you like her more than you should."

My hand tightened on the doorknob. "What? There's a limit? Fuckin' news to me."

Kite hit me in the chest lightly. "That girl has some serious demons and the last thing she needs is your cock anywhere near her."

I slammed both my hands into Kite and he fell back a step. "I'd never do that. She's not some pussy. Jesus, Kite. She's my friend. Ream's sister and, yeah, she has fuckin' serious demons and no way in hell am I letting some lacrosse captain fuck with her."

Kite shook his head back and forth, grinning. "I knew it."

"What?"

He started laughing.

"What, asshole?"

"You have it bad for her. She's the one." What the hell was he talking about? And did he seriously just play me? "I'm so going to enjoy this." He shoved me out of the way and opened the door.

I trailed in after him, my eyes landing on Haven sitting on the L-shaped couch next to Mr. Lacrosse who had his arm across the back of it. He was leaning into her whispering something and the left corner of her mouth twitched upward in a smile. Well, as much as a smile as Haven gave. Except with me.

I could get a laugh, Mr. fuckin' Lacrosse.

Tanya and the guy, Kevin, sang and bobbed up and down when we entered. It was kind of funny and not half bad. I walked over to Haven and kissed the top of her head.

Fuck, she looked hot. Her cheeks had a slight pink hue and there was a sweetness to her tonight. As if she had let some of her guard down, or maybe it was due to the alcoholic fruity drink she was holding.

Kite and I were handed beers and we chatted, or rather I did. Kite went and sat on the couch, looking completely untouchable and I was betting that was his intent. I waited only twenty minutes before I was up scrolling through the songs until I found the one I wanted.

I was a stage junky; loved the thrill of being up in front of people when the music started. This was my thing. I craved it. Needed it. Didn't much care where it was or who was around me, if there was music, my body thrummed.

There was some risk in what I was about to do, but fuck it. Life was about risk and she was worth it. I stood when the guy, Jacob, finished singing a George Ezra song, and I tagged a spare microphone then strolled up front.

While everyone cheered, I leaned into Jacob and said, "Give your microphone to Haven."

His brows raised and he glanced in Haven's direction. I didn't. We were going to see how brave my chick was. I knew she hated being the center of attention, but it had nothing to do with her being shy or a lack of confidence. There was another reason she stayed out of the limelight. I just didn't know what that reason was—yet. Well, this wasn't limelight and she was among friends. I hoped she wouldn't back away from a challenge because that was what this was.

Fuck, it was more than that. I wanted her away from Lac and with me. I craved her attention. It was my drug. She was my drug and I wanted her to share with me the one thing I loved more than anything—music, and I didn't give a shit if she sang like a duck quacking. Okay, maybe I did a little, but I was pretty sure she wasn't completely tone deaf as her twin brother had a good voice.

I started the song and everyone laughed when they recognized it, "You're the One That I Want." Sung by John Travolta and Olivia Newton-John.

I kept my eyes on Haven as I sang my part, the music drumming through me as I belted out the words. Haven squirmed uncomfortably, the microphone Jacob handed her laying in her lap. She glared. I smiled as I sang in a raspy shout the last word to my part.

I swear I didn't think she'd do it. She sat there like stone until it was her turn and fuck if my cock didn't twitch when I heard the first words from her mouth.

My fingers curled around the microphone, watching her slowly glide to her feet, the words like honey from her throat. A slow stroll toward me, no smile but a slight sway to her hips that put my excitement for the stage to shame.

I was so stunned and completely taken that I nearly fucked up and forgot to sing my part, which was the tandem chorus. Our voices instantly entwined in perfect harmony and from the subtle eyes widening, I knew she was just as surprised as me.

The group faded into the background as we became the music, Haven completely playing the part as she sang over her shoulder to me while walking away. I trailed after until she swung around and came toward me, her hand on my chest and her voice a sexy melody. She edged in close and slid around me so her back was against my chest.

I played it up and trailed my hand across her abdomen then grinned when she spun and shoved me away like they'd done in the movie. When she wiggled her butt as she sauntered away, I fell to my knees.

Her body turned and our eyes locked as we sang the chorus together.

As the song neared the end, I jumped to my feet, snatched her around the waist, swung her around then dipped her. Girl didn't miss a beat.

Everyone stood and cheered. I didn't pay attention to them, my arm around Haven, my fingers grazing her bare skin between her blouse and jeans. My body refused to move as we stared at one another, her hand with the microphone on my chest. My heart raced, a combination of the exhilaration and having Haven so close.

Two favorite things.

No matter what we pretended to be, this was more. She had to feel it. There was no denying the spark that connected us. It was an inferno today in the cafeteria. But the chemistry wasn't enough. I wanted it all yet Haven didn't trust me. If she did, she'd have told me something. Fuckin' anything. Just a piece of why she had to protect herself all the time. That was all I needed to push this further.

I knew she was closing up before she moved. I saw the tiniest flicker of uncertainty in her eyes before she reacted and it was all over.

She moved away, but I snagged her hand before she could escape. "That voice . . . baby, that is something special. You sing before?"

I let her hand slide from mine when she pulled back. "Yeah. Some. By myself."

I was getting nothing more as that wall of ice slammed back into place and she walked back to the couch. I was at least thankful she chose to sit beside Dana instead of Lac, who was pissed judging by the scowl on his face.

Too fuckin' bad, buddy. She isn't going to ever be yours.

I played it cool for the next hour, chatted with everyone, had a few beers and even sang a couple more songs. Kite refused to get up and sing, but Dana did several times and she sounded like a cat in pain. She knew it too and laughed more than she sang.

Haven was actually looking like she was having a good time by the ease in her shoulders. What concerned me was the amount of alcohol she was consuming as Dana passed her another fruity drink.

Kite slapped me on the back. "She's fine."

"Yeah, I know."

"Then stop watching her."

Fuck, I was so screwed. I chugged back the rest of my beer and Becky plopped down beside me. "Want to sing with me?"

She was cute and I was pretty damn sure if I wanted to, I could fuck her tonight. And that was what was screwing with me. I hadn't fucked another chick in six months.

"No thanks, sugar. Vocal cords are on hiatus for the rest of the night."

She pouted and normally I'd take advantage and kiss a chick, maybe even drag her into the washroom and get her to suck me off. Fuck, that sounded so bad. Never thought that before—now I did.

Becky's hand came down on my thigh and squeezed. I should take her up on what she offered, but there wasn't a doubt in my mind that I was taken. I'd been taken for six months and nothing was going to change that any time soon.

"Not interested." I removed her hand from my leg. She stood, walked over to Kevin, and sat on his lap, to which he loudly slurred something unintelligible, and wrapped his arms around her.

Haven had a slight glow to her cheeks and her eyes filled with laughter as she watched Dillon sing the last verse to a Maroon 5 song.

The moment Haven came to her feet, my heart thumped and my eyes locked on her. She swayed a bit to the right and Lac jumped to his feet and reached over to steady her with his hands on her hips. There was a flicker of her brows lowering for a second then she took a deep breath as if she was shoving whatever she was thinking aside.

I was like my guitar strings, strung up too tight, as my gaze followed her every step of the way up to the front of the room in front of the big screen. She leaned into Dillon who had just finished singing and he smiled as he handed her the microphone.

"Woot, Haven," Dana screamed.

This so didn't seem like something she would do. I knew her. At least I thought I did. I'd pushed her to get up and sing before. This was on her own. She was reserved. Not in a soft, fearful sort of way, but definitely not a person who cared about standing up and singing in front of friends.

When the music began, I tensed because I knew . . . I fuckin' knew with that first stroke of the guitar on the speakers that it was one of our songs. No, it was *my* song. I wrote it, not that she'd know that.

Holy fuck. All the blood went straight from my head down to my cock and it hurt. I was so turned on that she'd sing one of our songs, it took everything in me to keep from jumping to my feet and slamming her against the wall and kissing her.

Shit, I wanted to kiss her so badly. I wanted her beneath me, to feel her writhe and hear her moan. I wanted to taste every inch of her skin, touch every part and then I wanted to sink inside her and make her come so hard she screamed. Because Haven screaming in ecstasy would be one kick-ass fantasy come true.

Kite was right; I liked Haven more than I should. We were friends, but it was a hell of a lot more than that. She'd quivered under my touch earlier and I'd heard her sharp inhale. I'd decided to take a chance and push her a little, and what I'd gotten was heat radiating from her. The reality was, I wanted Haven and no other chick would do it for me. Known it for a long time.

The moment she started singing, her glassy grey eyes found mine and she half-smiled. Yeah, she was drunk and was probably going to regret getting up in front of her friends and singing, but the girl had a voice.

One fuck of a beautiful voice. Her brother did, too. It was a slower song and I was accustomed to hearing Logan's gravelled voice that made the chicks go gaga, but if anyone heard Haven sing this version of it, we'd have a whole new crowd of fans—guy fans.

She moved easily to the beat, hips swaying side to side. She turned her back to us during the crescendo of Ream and my guitars, her slow sway erotic and sexy as hell.

"Jesus," I mumbled as I stared.

"She can sing," Kite said.

"Yeah." I couldn't take my eyes off her and I wanted to go up and join her, but I couldn't move. I was frozen. Mesmerized by her as her body moved to the beat, eyes closed, head tilted slightly to the side so her hair covered half her face like a silk curtain.

When the song ended, everyone clapped and complimented her. I didn't. I stared while my heart pounded wildly, hands shook, and with an overwhelming-as-fuck need to drag her out of here, take her home with me, kiss her until she melted in my arms and moaned my name with that sexy voice.

That image was sucked out of me like a high powered vacuum the moment Lac got up and strode over to her, his grin like a monkey getting handed a banana.

Yeah, well she was not getting his banana. Fuck that. And I was glad to see she failed to return the gesture of a smile. He didn't seem to care when he leaned in and kissed her. He fuckin' kissed her right on the mouth that had sung the words to my fuckin' song.

.ever given two shits about a chick. They used me just as as I used them. I had no misconception that they slept with me ᴄause of who I was. Even when we weren't famous, they slept with me because I was in a band and it was hot to fuck a guy with a guitar.

I played it up. And I kicked them out in the morning or better yet, right after. I didn't give a shit because they were just happy to tell their friends they'd fucked a rock star. I was cool with that. It never bothered me.

What bothered me was seeing another guy's mouth on Haven's. Kite's hand clamped down on my arm when I went to get up. "She's dealing with it."

I glanced back at Haven, and Lac was a few feet away from her and she looked pissed. She said something and I wished I could've heard, but by Lac's slight nod and his chagrinned expression, it was obvious she told him to back off.

"Chatted with him tonight," Kite said. "He's in the med. program. Is at U of T on a scholarship for lacrosse."

Great, he was smart and an athlete. Well, I'm a fuckin' rock star.

"Let's get out of here," I suggested as Lac sat beside Haven, his arm going around the back of the couch behind her, but she shifted away, thank fuck. Maybe she can look after herself. I was betting she had the gun in her purse, but I was a guy and the protective nature in me was strong. "Logan and Ream might still be at Avalanche." It was just after midnight, but I was betting they were still there. I quickly shot off a text to Logan.

Kite stood. "Yeah. I've had enough bad singing for the night. And now you owe me, twice."

My phone vibrated as Logan texted back. "They're still at Avalanche. Let's grab Haven and head over."

Kite scowled. "Haven? Man, she came with her friends."

I shoved my phone in my back pocket. "I'm not leaving her here, drunk with a guy who can't keep his hands to himself."

"His hands aren't touching her." Kite shook his head and ran his teeth over his tongue piercing. "I knew this shit would happen."

"What shit?"

"You. Her. Tonight. It's a shit storm about to happen."

"It's all good. Don't worry about it." I took a step toward Haven when Kite's hand shot out and grabbed my arm. "What?"

"Bad idea. Not tonight, man. She's drunk. You're high on her and it's going to end up in one of your bedrooms. Not cool. She'll hate you in the morning and you'll hate yourself. Not to mention what the hell Ream will do to you for fucking his sister. You need to deal with that first, before you make that move."

I shrugged out of his grip. "I can control myself, asshole. I have controlled myself for months."

Kite scowled. "Not tonight you can't. Hearing her sing . . . I saw your face." Yeah, well, she blew me away. "We'll take a cab to Avalanche and leave Roman here with the car and he'll make sure she gets back okay. Let her hang with her friends."

I ran my hand through my hair and shifted my feet. "Fuck." He was right. I had one shot with Haven and I wasn't blowing it. Her drunk was definitely not the time because after this afternoon, I was betting something would happen and I wanted her to come to me—sober. Because once we crossed that line, there was no going back, no running and no ice blocking me out.

"Fine, I'll tell her we're heading and if she wants a ride home or to come with us, then it's her choice." I pulled away and failed to bother excusing myself as I interrupted Lac saying something to Haven. Fuckin' rude and crass, but shit, I was hanging on by a thread seeing his fingers play with the few strands of her hair that fell over the back of the couch. I didn't think she even noticed him doing it, but I sure as fuck did.

"Need to talk a sec." I leaned over, entwined my fingers with hers and pulled her to her feet before she or Lac could object.

I ignored Kite's glower as I pulled her toward the door. Haven stumbled and I let go of her hand to hook my arm around her waist. "You okay?"

She nodded and it was nice to see she was smiling and didn't seem to care that I was being an ass. Shit, seeing that smile made my stomach do a leap in the air like I was jumping off a cliff—with her.

"I'll talk to Roman." Kite continued past us.

I settled her against the wall, a ways down from the room, then rested one hand above her head the other lightly on her hip. "We're headed to Avalanche. You want to come with us or we can drop you off at home?" Then I added, "Or stay here?"

"I swore to never drink, but they tasted good, not like the beer."

I half-smiled. She was cute tipsy with her cheeks flushed and her voice softer, sexier.

She reached up and touched me right between my eyes, the pad of her finger caressing back and forth. "The crease is there. You only get that when you're worried about something." My breath stalled. "And when you're angry, your voice gets all gravelly and deep." I closed my eyes a second and swallowed. Her finger trailed down my nose off the tip to my lips and it took everything, I mean everything, I had to not draw her finger into my mouth. "I love it when you sing. I can't figure out which is better, when you sing or laugh. Because when you laugh, it makes my chest all warm and tingly. It's nice."

She rested her head against the wall, arm lowering to her side. Oh, fuck. I was putty, fuckin' melted putty that was a puddle on the floor at her feet.

"You flirted with me today. At school."

It took me a second to answer because fuck if she wasn't the most stunning woman I'd ever seen and I was crawling back up from the puddle. "Yeah."

"Why?"

I couldn't very well tell her because I wanted to fuck her so badly my cock hurt. So instead, I said, "Things need to change between us."

By her frown, she didn't get what I was saying and probably wouldn't remember any of this in the morning.

"We're friends."

"Yeah, baby."

"I like when you call me that." She sighed then bit her lip. "I probably shouldn't say that. It's safer as friends."

Fuck no. No, it wasn't safer. Safer would be making her mine and kissing her, then scooping her up in my arms, taking her home and putting her in my bed, and then waking up to her in the morning. Kite was right. If we went home together, I'd fuck her if she'd let me. "Yeah. Whatever you want, Haven."

Because that was what it came down to. What she wanted.

I'd been good. Fuck, I'd been an angel, but the angel was losing its fight against the devil who wanted to kiss her. Take her. Make her mine. But I was determined that she had to come to me. Her past was too screwed up to have it any other way. She may not have told me what happened, but we all knew it was really fuckin' bad.

She was looking at me with parted lips, eyes a little droopy and if I pressed in a little closer, our lips would touch. Her warm breath drifted across my face like a sweet caress and I automatically leaned in closer.

Her breath hitched.

I felt it. Heard it.

"What's your real name?"

"Vincent."

"Are you going to kiss me, Vincent?" she whispered.

Holy fuckin' Christ. Her saying my name, my real name, was the hottest thing I'd ever heard. No chick I'd been with knew my real name. Never gave it to them and they never asked because they liked knowing they were fucking Crisis from Tear Asunder. "Do you want me to?"

"Haven?" And of course, Mr. fuckin' Lacrosse has to come out the door looking dapper in his dark snug blue jeans and pale pink dress shirt. "You ready to go home? I can call a cab."

Keep your mouth shut. But I had a mouth that liked to run even when I knew it was a bad idea. "You're not welcome back at our place tonight."

Lac held up his hands. "Crisis, man, I'm not like that. It's not like that. She already told me she doesn't want to date."

And he had to be a good guy unlike me who took pussy whenever I could get it up, until Haven walked into my life. Jesus. I shoved away from the wall.

"Hi, Lac," Haven said, as if just noticing him.

"Hey, sweetie. Just came to make sure you're okay. You had a few."

Sweetie? What the fuck was that? Since when did she become sweetie? "You think I wouldn't look after her?" I exploded.

Lac paled. "No! I wasn't saying that."

"Crisis." Kite's tone was abrupt. "Roman will wait downstairs for Haven." He briefly touched her arm. "You hear me? Roman is downstairs. Take the car home."

"Okay." She nodded.

I hated leaving her here. I hated leaving her drunk with Mr. Fuckin'-Ass-Kisser who was calling my girl sweetie. But I had no choice. Well, I could throw her over my shoulder and take her home. Kite, would kick my ass or at least try to, and Haven . . . yeah, I wasn't pushing her tonight and ruining our chances.

"Make sure she gets to the car," I said and stepped back, my stomach churning like a rusted propeller.

Lac nodded and put his hand on the small of her back.

I knew it was to steady her because she was drunk, but the roar inside was detonating. Kite saw it and put his hand on my shoulder. "What the fuck is wrong with me?" I asked Kite as I watched her walk away.

"Same thing that's wrong with Logan and Ream."

Yeah, I loved her. But I couldn't do anything about it until she made a move and it was killing me.

Haven was half-way down the hall when she spun around and walked back to me, swaying a bit, but not bad enough to warrant me insisting on taking her home. My breath locked down in my chest as she moved into me and placed her palms on my chest.

"Thanks. For coming tonight." She paused and her brow furrowed. "Not just for tonight . . . for everything." She paused then dragged her teeth over her bottom lip. "You were right. I do like you . . . A lot."

I closed my eyes and kissed the top of her head. "Yeah." That was the only word I could get out.

Her hand slipped away and I watched her walk down the hall until she disappeared behind the door. It was as if a fist slammed into my ribcage and broke through, yanking out my heart then stomping on it with both feet until it burst and became a pancake.

There was something between us that was special as hell, but it had to be her letting me in, not me letting myself in. And the only way I could push her to make a move was to step back.

Kite slapped me on the back. "Let's go to Avalanche."

Chapter Seventeen

Haven

I RAN TO THE washroom, fell to my knees and hung my head over the toilet. It was two in the morning. I'd been home for an hour and this was my third rush to the bathroom. My head was a time bomb with a constant tapping that refused to go away.

After dry heaving, because after three times there was nothing left to throw up, I crawled to my feet, grabbed my toothbrush and piled on the minty fresh toothpaste for the fourth time. I never drank. I'd seen enough drunken assholes to never want to lose control of myself that way and yet tonight I did.

But I was trying to erase him—Crisis. I felt like I was standing on the edge of a building, tipped forward about to lose my balance. With the slightest breeze, I was going to fall and never be able to come back from that.

My stomach rolled and I fell to my knees, head over the toilet again.

I was spitting into the porcelain bowl when a hand reached across and flushed. I jerked and looked up to see Crisis standing beside me.

He scooped my hair back, his fingers trailing over the back of my neck. He held out a glass of water. I gratefully took it and sloshed it around in my mouth then spit again.

He took it from me and set it on the counter.

I moaned. "Remind me not to drink again."

"There's a trick to it. Water between drinks and try to stay clear of the pop in the mixed drinks."

"Good to know. But never again." He held out his hand and helped me to my feet. "When did you get back?"

"Just now."

I moved to the sink and stuck my toothbrush back in my mouth while he turned on the taps. I watched him in the mirror as he went and flushed the toilet again, grabbed a facecloth from the basket, dampened it then passed it to me.

I wiped my mouth before saying, "I sang with you."

He half-smiled. "Yeah. And you rocked it."

"And by myself."

"You rocked that even better."

I hesitated then blurted out. "Lac kissed me." His smile vanished and he casually leaned against the counter, arms crossed to match his ankles. He was also no longer looking at me. "I didn't want him to. I pulled away and told him not to do it again."

"I saw," he replied.

"I don't like him . . . not like that."

"Okay."

I expected more than that. This was not my territory. I was confused and my head hurt like hell. I also didn't know what he wanted and he wasn't helping me here. God, I didn't know what I wanted. Well, I did. I just had been so determined to find normal. Subtle. Quiet. Of keeping my past in the past and suddenly I wanted to take a chance. "I don't know what to do."

"You need to figure that out, Haven." He pushed away. Whoa, what was that? "Advil's in the kitchen in the top drawer. Take two."

I snagged his arm before he had the chance to walk out and the muscles tensed under my grip. Warmth throbbed beneath my palm trickling into me.

It was the same thrill of electricity every time he was near, except this time, it was threaded with tension. Because I was breathing hard and so was he as we stared at one another. I knew this was bad. I knew I should let it go, but I didn't want to. I saw the hurt in his eyes when I mentioned Lac.

He threatened to release all the emotions I kept buried as they lifted into my chest and wanted to release. But the complete contradiction was that he was my rock. I needed him. I trusted him.

God, I trusted him. It hit me hard and I didn't know what to do with it. I'd never felt this way about anyone. I wanted to tell him everything, hand him my demons and trust him with them.

"This . . . confuses me," I finally said.

He kept his eyes on me as he gently pried my fingers off his arm and I hadn't realized I'd been holding onto him that hard. "I'll sum it up for you. I want you, and I think you know that. No, I know you know that. But you won't trust me and I won't be with you if you don't. So this is what's going to happen. I'm backing off. You clear up that confusion . . . then let me know."

It was like a hammer the size of a house crashed down on me. He knew I liked him? He was backing off? But he hadn't even really pursued me, had he? I mean we hung out and . . . and he was always there for me. It was him who I curled into when I broke. It was him who made me smile and laugh again. And I did trust him, just . . . I didn't trust him enough with my past. Or maybe it was I was scared I'd lose him if he knew.

"Crisis? I like you . . . and I do trust you."

"No, you don't. Not with the important parts. And I need more. From you, I need more because I want all of you, not just slices of what you think is safe to give me." He quietly walked out, shutting the bathroom door behind him.

I didn't know what to do with that. I was too hungover to do anything except lay on the cool bathroom floor.

I woke still lying on the ceramic tiles, still in the clothes from last night and still not feeling well. My mouth felt as if it had a layer of flour on my tongue. I swished my mouth out with peppermint mouthwash and carefully walked—carefully because my head thumped with every step—and changed into my linen white pajamas.

I had one knee on the bed ready to crawl under the covers and disappear for the day when my phone buzzed. I leaned over and grabbed the jeans I'd just taken off and pulled the offending phone from my back pocket.

We'll be there in five.

I sat up. *Fuck.* My brother. He and Kat were coming by to have breakfast. I threw my phone aside and quickly dove for the shower. Smelling like vomit and alcohol was not going to be a raving point for my living here.

I shampooed my hair, using the suds to douse my body then rinsed and was out of the shower within minutes. I dried myself off, wrapped a towel around and darted out of the bathroom, slamming right into a rock-hard chest.

"Ugh," Crisis grunted, falling back a step from my momentum. "Guess I know why you're in a hurry? Big brother is coming up the elevator."

"Shit." I paused as I realized what he'd said. "How did you know he was first born?"

He shrugged. "Didn't. Now, I do."

"How much did you know about me? I mean when he came to live with you."

"Nothing. I saw a picture of you once. You looked about six or seven, maybe. He had his arm around you and it looked like the water was behind you." The lake. It was the one time my mother took us to a lake, but it was more because the guy she was dating took us. "He kept it on him all the time, until mom washed his jeans and it got ruined. That was when he went and had 'Angel' tattooed on his arm. Didn't know why at the time."

"Do you know what happened to us? What I did." Please say no. The thought of Crisis knowing I was raped and on drugs . . . it made me feel weak and I'd fought a long time to get over that feeling.

"Nope." He nodded to the stairs. "And you better get changed, the elevator dinged."

I scrambled past him and dug into my drawer for clothes.

"Coffee's made. Kite's on the bacon," Crisis called as he left.

I came out into the kitchen just as Kite was finishing the bacon.

"If I could put horses out back, I'd move in," Kat said, then noticed me, came over and hugged me. She then pulled back and whispered in my ear. "Rum?"

Damn it.

"Don't worry. He was drunk off his ass at Avalanche last night. He won't know if it's him or you." She squeezed my arm.

I kissed Ream on the cheek, keeping my contact as brief and quick as possible. It wasn't unusual for me, so he didn't notice. "Hey."

"You doing okay?" Ream asked. "You still like it here? Living with these assholes?"

Ream had checked the penthouse and security out twice before he was okay with me living here. Well, he still wasn't okay with it, but he somewhat conceded. "Yeah. It's been good and close to school."

Kat grinned at me then called Ream over to the balcony. "Come here and see this view."

"I've seen the view before," he said.

"Not with me, baby."

I breathed a sigh of relief as Ream went outside. I rested my forehead against the cool fridge. "Never again." The smell of bacon had my stomach reeling again and I swallowed several times.

"Here." Crisis passed me a coffee. "Helps the head. Not much I can do about your smell."

I gasped. "Oh, my God, you can smell me, too?"

He chuckled. "No, bab . . ." He stopped. "No, but I heard Kat tell you."

I swear he was about to call me baby. Why did he catch himself? He'd always called me baby, even in our texts. I liked it.

I took out the egg carton from the fridge and Crisis held out his hand. "I'll do it. You're liable to throw up all over the stove and set off a ricochet of events none of us want this morning. Set the table."

I smiled. "Thanks."

"Yep."

I stared at him a minute as he reached up and grabbed a frying pan from the hook above the island. He was tense and . . . different. I didn't like it. Was this what he meant by backing off?

I set the table while Ream and Kat came back inside and talked about the chick Matt was eyeing at Avalanche last night. She was a dancer in one of the plays in town for a few months. A number of the cast members had been there and had sat with the band.

"The band?" I asked.

Kat nodded. "Crisis and Kite showed up late."

God, right. They told me they were going to Avalanche. I had a vague memory of standing against the wall, Crisis in close and I'd been thinking he was going to kiss me, but Lac showed up. Or maybe he hadn't been thinking about that at all.

My breath caught in my throat. I told him I liked him calling me "baby." I asked him if he was going to kiss me.

Ream laughed. "And the chick . . . what was her name, Crisis? The one who did a private dance for you on the table and ended up knocking over all the drinks? And there was a brunette . . . she was quiet, but she had her eyes on you, too." My gaze darted to Crisis, whose back was turned, and I heard the scrape of spatula on the pan. "You bring her home last night? Lena. That's her name. She still here?"

Crisis turned around, eyes murderous. "Fuck you, man."

Ream's brows rose. "What? Why are you bitching?"

I dropped the cutlery on the table causing a loud clang. I didn't need time for clarity . . . I wanted him for myself but giving him parts of me I'd shared with no one . . . that was where I faltered. I felt the heat in my cheeks and my stomach heaved as the smell of bacon and eggs hit me all at once. I put my hand over my mouth and ran for my bathroom.

But I had nothing to throw up. Kat found me sitting on the floor cradling my head. She held out her hand. "Come on. I moved everything out onto the patio. We'll eat out there in the fresh air." I took her hand and she pulled me to my feet. "You like him." It was a statement.

I deflated, sighing. "Yeah, but we're just friends."

She laughed. "Ream and I tried that, too. Didn't last. Better not to fight it, makes life a lot easier."

I shook my head. "Another guy kissed me last night and I didn't like it. All I thought about was Crisis." Vincent—he told me last night his real name was Vincent.

"I hope Crisis saw it." She shrugged when my eyes widened. "Sweetie, he's been a dog for years. He deserves to have to work for a woman instead of having them fall at his feet with their legs open." Kat smoothed back my hair.

"I have so much inside me that is bad. I don't want to put that on anyone."

"Haven, I know what happened to Ream as a kid and I also witnessed what Alexa did to him. I know what she was capable of, and I'm suspecting Olaf was like that, too. So whatever you're harboring, it's horrific." I'd brought Kat water when she'd been held captive in Alexa's basement. "When Ream and I were in a bad place, I saw a part of Crisis many don't get to see. He looked after me, protected me . . . Crisis may have girl issues, but behind all the crap he shoots off, I guarantee he's something special." Her voice softened, matching the look in her eyes. "He came to love your brother regardless of his demons. You can trust him with yours."

"Girls, let's eat," Ream said knocking on the door.

Kat yanked it open, took a couple steps toward him then leapt. Her legs curled around his waist and her arms around his neck. His hands came under her ass as he staggered, caught off-balance.

"Fuck, Kitkat."

She kissed him hard on the mouth then leaned back so all her weight was on Ream as she looked at me upside down. "Give him a chance to prove himself."

"He already has," I whispered more to myself.

"Who?" Ream asked.

"Nothing. Feed me. I'm starved, pumpkin." Ream carried her away and I quickly washed my face and brushed my teeth then joined them out on the terrace.

I managed to eat a couple pieces of dry toast and nibbled on the scrambled eggs. Crisis sat beside me, and even though there was a good foot between us, I felt as if he was against me. I kept glancing between us with the sense that he'd moved closer, but he hadn't.

"Sis?"

I jerked my gaze to my brother. "Yeah?"

"What did you do last night? I tried calling to see if you wanted to join us at Avalanche."

I pushed my plate forward and sat back in my chair. "Went to a karaoke bar with friends."

"Really?" he replied, his brows lowering. "The same karaoke bar you guys went to?" Ream looked from Crisis and Kite.

I jumped in even though the question was pointed at Crisis and Kite. "Yeah. Crisis came to my school at lunch and my friends convinced him to come along."

"You went to her school?" Ream asked Crisis, but he wasn't paying attention. He was looking at his phone scowling.

"Well, Kite, too." I added. "We were going for lunch." He was still looking at Crisis, who completely ignored the entire conversation as he scrolled on his cell. "Ream, what's the big deal? We live together, remember. Crisis is right. You're like the Terminator."

Kite choked on his coffee and Kat winced.

God, this was ridiculous. He had this thing about Crisis. I didn't get it. "And then after the bar we came back here and the three of us fucked all night. We woke up when you texted me, still on the floor naked, not even knowing whose legs were whose because we were still shit-faced."

Kat coughed, hiding her smile behind her hand, and put her other one on Ream's, which was curled into a fist next to his plate.

"Do you hear how ridiculous that is? If I want to fuck Crisis, I will, and if I choose not to, I'm capable of telling him to keep his hands off." Shit, I carried a gun with me and at night slept with it in the drawer of my nightstand. I picked up my plate and stood. "And by the way, I drank until I could barely stand, sang twice, and I don't remember how I got home. I also woke up on the bathroom floor."

Ream's jaw clenched and he didn't say anything, but what surprised me the most was that Crisis hadn't said anything and was still on his phone. I shoved away from the table and Crisis raised his head—finally.

"Where you going?"

I grabbed my plate and walked inside. I put the dishes in the sink and leaned my palms on the counter, hanging my head and closing my eyes.

"I'm sorry." Ream's voice was soft as he came and leaned against the counter beside me. "This isn't easy for me. I lost you, Haven. Christ, I thought you were dead and then I get you back and I feel like . . . you're not really here."

I raised my head and looked at him. His eyes were filled with pain, expression drawn and haggard. "I'm here." But he was right. I wasn't here. Not who he expected anyway.

Ream sighed. "No. You're not. Not my angel. Not the sister I grew up with. She's gone. I miss her and I'm fighting to find her, but you won't let me. You push me away and I'm trying to find a way back in, and my only way is to protect you. To make sure no one hurts you again." He shifted and crossed his arms. "I want my sister."

I didn't want to hurt him. God, I'd do anything not to, but if he kept searching for that girl, it would be forever, because she didn't exist. I became someone else and he'd have to learn to let go of who I once was.

"That sister, the one you loved, she's dead, Ream. I can't give you her. You can love me for who I am now or . . . not."

"Jesus, I do love you. I always will," he said quietly. "But, I have no idea who you are anymore."

No, he didn't. I didn't. And telling him that I danced naked with men's hands all over me, about Charlie, about the backrooms, it wouldn't make him understand me. All it would do was hurt him. I realized I was slowly running my finger back and forth over the brand on my wrist and he noticed.

The tension sprung from him and I even heard the slight sharp inhale. He put his hand over the brand. "We can get a tattoo artist to—"

I yanked away. "No. I want to be reminded that I survived. I survived and so did you, Ream. We both had horrible, disgusting things done to us. But I'm not the girl you sang to at night. The girl who Gerard raped and fed drugs to." He flinched and paled. "Do you get that? Because if you don't, then we'll never repair. We'll always be broken."

"Fuck, Haven." Ream grabbed me and pulled me into a hug. "I'm sorry. It's not easy to stop protecting you. I finally have you back and it would destroy me to see you hurt again. And Crisis . . . I love him, but I know what he's like and it worries me that you guys spend so much time together. Shit, he has some chick obsessed with him. It's just bad news."

"You're wrong." He tensed, drawing back. "He's better than that and if you step back, I think you'll see it."

Ream had been my protector all my life. It was his role and I knew this was hard for him to let go of. "Nothing will stop me from loving you." He stroked my hair and pulled back, bending a bit so our eyes were level. "I'll always love you, Haven."

It was enough—for now. We were both a little lost in how to find our way back to one another as brother and sister.

Kat and Ream left after we cleaned up and I went back to bed. It was my phone buzzing on my mattress that woke me hours later and I pried my eyes open and searched under the duvet for the phone where I'd tossed it this morning.

I looked at the screen—Dana.

How are you feeling?

Better . . . now. Rough morning.

LOL. You were wasted. So, meet in an hour?

What? I wanted to talk to Crisis. Well, want was the wrong word because I did, but didn't. It was important, though. I was confused, but one thing was clear—I wanted him, too.

For what?

Dinner then we're watching a movie at your place. You said last night.

I had a faded recollection of saying something like that.

I don't know if that's a good idea.

Come on, you promised. It's Saturday night.

My fingers hovered over the phone as I thought about it.

Fine, but just something to eat.

Cool. I'll tell the guys.

What? What guys?

LOL, you really don't remember anything. I crashed at Dillon's last night. Seven at Joe's. Meet you there.

Shit. I wanted normality and I was getting it.

It took me an hour to get ready moving in slow motion. The head throbbing was now a dull ache, but I suspected once I ate, I'd feel better. I grabbed my purse and came out of my room at the same time as Crisis emerged from the room across the hall—the gym.

I stopped and stared. I couldn't help myself. He was in loose workout shorts which were hanging off his hips, no shirt and a towel slung over his left shoulder.

And his skin . . . it was glistening with sweat. Every muscle accentuated the ink molding over his arms and shoulders vibrant and dark. His abdomen was an eight pack . . . an eight pack of hard delectable muscle.

"You going out?"

My eyes darted to his. Shit, I had been staring at his abdomen and was breathing hard. His brows rose and I realized I hadn't responded yet.

"Yeah."

"Haven?" Kite shouted from downstairs. "Lac's here. I buzzed him up."

Lac? Why was Lac here? I was meeting them at Joe's.

"You need Roman with you."

I frowned. "Why?"

"Because I said so." Whoa, what the hell? Crisis took the towel from his shoulder and wiped his face, then down his chest. "I'll call and tell him." He continued down the hall and disappeared into his bedroom.

I stared after him, unable to move even after I heard his door click closed. No teasing. No baby. No sexy smirk. It bothered me—a lot.

I straightened my shoulders and avoided looking at Crisis' door, although my step faltered as I passed it. I walked down the stairs and when I saw Lac, I was a little pissed off at him for showing up.

He was talking to Kite in the living room, where tennis was on the TV. They stood side by side, Kite a bit taller than him, but they had a similar build, lean and agile. That was where the similarities ended. Kite was tatted and pierced wearing ripped jeans, although he had a dress shirt on. Lac, wore straight off-the-shelf pressed jeans and a preppy-collared, long-sleeved, pale blue shirt.

When he noticed me, he looked nervous as he offered a half-crooked smiled. "Hey, Dana and Dillon are downstairs. It's not just me. I wanted to apologize to Crisis so I came up."

"Oh. Why?" Was I forgetting something that happened last night?

Kite crossed his arms, a subtle twitch at the corner of his mouth as he listened.

"Kind of a guy thing." He looked at Kite and he shrugged. "So, is he here?"

"Yeah, but in the shower." And really in a bad mood. "Maybe another time. We should go."

Kite chin-lifted to me. "You look better. Have fun, kids." I knew he was referring to my look this morning, skin green, eyes red with black circles underneath. He slapped Lac on the back of the shoulder. "Expect an early night."

He was teasing and it was rare coming from Kite. Lac didn't know that though and nodded. "Yeah, of course."

"He's teasing."

"Oh."

"Crisis and I are going to Avalanche later. He owes me after last night," Kite said. "Probably be late."

"Okay."

Lac walked over to me and put his hand at the small of my back, guiding me to the elevator. Just before the doors closed, I looked up and saw Crisis standing at the top of the stairs, hands curled around the railing, his skin still glistening with sweat and a towel wrapped around his waist.

Our eyes locked. Then the doors closed and broke us apart.

Chapter Eighteen

Haven

ROMAN STAYED CLOSE, walked behind us all the way to the pub then came inside and sat at the bar, always watching. Didn't know what he was watching for, but for some reason, Crisis insisted on it. Roman was cool like Luke, though. He didn't say anything and was inconspicuous, except he drew attention with his tatted neck that peeked out from under his dress shirt and the fact that he was tall and seriously built.

After wings and fries at the pub, which I decided was a great hangover food, I told everyone I was going to go home to bed. Dana pouted but she didn't push it. Going out two nights in a row was a record for me and she knew it.

Roman walked me back, beside me though, instead of behind, and never said a word until we were safely inside the condo building. "You going out again?"

"No." He had a rough voice, almost as if his vocal cords had at one time been damaged.

"You do, you call me." I had Luke's number programed in my

phone; that was Ream's doing before they went on tour. "It's on your phone."

It was?

Roman strode away and I went up to the penthouse. I didn't go to bed, though; no way could I sleep when I was still thinking about what Crisis had said to me that morning. I wanted to see him. I wanted to talk to him. Somewhere along the way, he'd become my best friend and I'd never had a best friend. I'd never had friends for most of my life. But Crisis, Vincent, had also raised something in me, an awareness of my body. A body I'd numbed out to feeling anything for years. But now I felt, and I liked what I felt.

He wanted me to give him something of me, but I was dirty. My past was dirty and Charlie . . . Oh, God . . . I swallowed back the memory.

I curled up on the couch with a blanket and watched *The Fast and Furious*. My past whirled around in my head as I tried to find something I could tell Crisis. Give him a piece of me. I knew that was what he wanted. For me to trust him with my bad parts. But I shut down when Charlie kept surfacing and I started to shake.

Instead, I focused on the movie, burying the memory again. I was completely engrossed in the ending when the elevator dinged. I sat up looking over the back of the couch, my heart pounding as I thought of seeing Crisis.

A girl with bright red shoulder-length hair with tats down her arms came prancing out of the elevator. She swung around as Crisis walked out and threw her arms around his neck and whispered something to him. He kept walking, his hands on her forearms as if trying to peel her away, but she was like cling wrap and refused to budge. Kite came out of the elevator, holding the hand of a short brunette, who was stunning with stark bold features, large breasts and a tiny waist. Miss Cling Wrap finally let Crisis go with his persistent urging and she strutted into the kitchen like she owned the place.

I uncurled from the couch and stood.

"Oh." The redhead said, her heavily made-up eyes roamed over me sitting on the couch. "You must be the girl he's been talking about.

And you are pretty. Maybe you'll join us." She laughed and it sounded husky—sexy.

My heart dropped. No, it rather fell into the pit of my stomach and burned in a bubbling pool of acid.

"Shut it, Lena," Kite said. He opened the fridge and grabbed a couple of beers, passing one to each of the girls. The brunette stared at me and when I stood, her eyes roamed the length of me then narrowed. She raised her chin and a slight smirk rose which contradicted her sweet appearance.

I walked over. I was not going to be the bitch here, but the real reason was I wanted them to know I was unaffected by them, which wasn't true. "I'm Haven." I held out my hand to the brunette.

She glanced at my hand a second before she took it. "Lily."

"Oh, my God, Haven? Like safe-haven?" The redhead danced over to me and lifted her butt up onto the island.

"No. Like Haven Dust—cocaine," I corrected and she stared at me for a second before she burst out laughing.

"Wow, cool. I'm Lena." She held out her hand and I shook it, squeezing a little harder than necessary. It was immature, but I knew exactly why she was here and I didn't like it. Crisis really was backing off. He was backing off so quick and far that he brought a chick home.

It hurt. No, it ripped me open and gutted me hurt, but it pissed me off, too, because this wasn't a chick wanting Crisis for the guy he was, but a chick who wanted the bragging rights of fucking a Tear Asunder band member. Crisis was better than that. He deserved better. And to add to my pissed off, he let a girl use him. But he probably saw it as he was using her and maybe that was what he wanted.

Lena. Lena was the name of the girl from Avalanche the night before. Ream had mentioned her. No wonder her body was toned and looking like it was sculpted from clay; she was a dancer. I glanced at Crisis who remained in the foyer by the elevator and a wave of heat passed over me.

Kite quietly came up beside me. "You good with this, Haven?"

Was I? No. I wasn't good with it at all. But I never thought I'd feel this way about it. I didn't want to feel this way about it, but I wasn't going to deny the fact that I did. Just not in front of these girls. "It's your place. You can do whatever you want."

"It's our place. We all live here," Kite corrected. He moved away and calmly stroked the side of Lily's face. She tilted her head so his palm cupped her cheek and her eyes flickered up, met mine. I looked away because despite it being a sweet gesture, Kite didn't have an adoring look. It was intense—serious. "Lena," Kite said.

"Baby, let me look after you," Lena said. I didn't bother looking behind me because I honestly had no desire to see her wrapped around Crisis.

But from the corner of my eye, I saw Lena snag Crisis with her legs around his hips and draw him up against the counter, her hand fisted in his shirt. She said something too low for me to hear, but he scowled and his hands pushed at her legs.

"Come on, sexy. It'll be fun," Lena purred.

I didn't want to see this. I started for the stairs, my stomach rolling with disappointment. But I put that there. This was my fault.

"Not happening—ever," Crisis said. "Kite, man. Come on. I fuckin' told you. Keep your chicks off me."

She wasn't with him?

I stopped, my heart pounding. I was facing the stairs, away from them when he came up behind me and rested his hands on my hips. I didn't have to look. I knew his touch, I knew his smell, and I wanted more.

"The chicks leave if you're uncomfortable with them here. Kite can go jerk off," Crisis' graveled voice whispered next to my ear. "Neither girl is with me, okay? I wouldn't do that. I'd never do that."

I did know that. He may have backed off, but he wasn't leaving me. He'd always be there for me. And I wanted to be there for him.

"You want to join us, Haven? Maybe then Crisis will, too, and I excel at licking pussy," Lena said. I heard the click of her heels as she jumped off the counter onto the marble floor. "I'm down for a little girl-on-girl-on-girl. Right, Lily? Didn't you say you liked girls?"

I flinched.

"Maybe Kite can tie us all up and fuck us one by one. Or is she the reason you won't touch me or Lily, Crisis? You get this one pregnant or something? Is that why she lives with you? You knock her up?"

"Shut the fuck up, Lena," Crisis threw over his shoulder.

"Well, she's not fat yet. So, I'm still game. Just met Lily last night, too, but she told me she wanted to come here and fuck you both."

"Lena. Stop," Kite ordered.

Maybe it was her mentioning me being pregnant that was the trigger. Maybe it was her voice. Maybe it was the fact that I was feeling vulnerable after contemplating all night what I was going to share with Crisis. It didn't matter what caused it, but I knew it was going to hit me before it did.

The coldness sunk into me. It was like I stepped from the center of the tornado and into the churning winds, its monstrous arms taking hold of me and squeezing so hard that I couldn't breathe.

"Haven?" Crisis pulled me around to face him. "What's wrong? Why are you shaking? Fuck, Haven?"

The image I'd buried surfaced like the tornado unearthed it.

I was lying on the bed, Alexa holding my shoulders down as I screamed and screamed. The pain excruciating as my body tore apart from hours of pushing. Olaf stood to the side, his hand on my bent knee, the doctor with his hands between my legs.

Hours of pain. Sweat dripped down my face, my hair plastered to my cheeks. And then . . .

It stopped. The pain stopped and a new pain began. One so crushing that I knew I'd never repair from it.

The silence. No wail of my baby's first breath.

Charlie.

My baby.

One I'd cradled inside me for six months. I wanted to hold him, see him. But I never saw his face. I never held him.

The doctor passed him to Olaf who looked at me briefly as he held him.

Then I begged.

I'd never begged. I fought. I screamed. But I never once begged until now.

I knew he was dead, but I just wanted once to hold him in my arms.

My cries were ignored as Olaf turned away with my baby.

The memory imploded.

I imploded as the pain of losing Charlie broke through the ice and shattered me.

I crashed.

"Get away. Get away from me." I shoved Crisis hard in the chest and he hit the wall with a loud bang.

My knees shook so violently I was afraid I wouldn't be able to make it to my room, but I ran anyway. My mind screamed as my body careened down into an abyss that I feared I'd never crawl out of again.

This was why I blocked it all out. *This. This. This.*

Everything in me roared and trembled, and threatened to give way. I was at the top of a tower and free falling, and any minute, I'd land and collapse, and never get up again.

I made it up two stairs before an arm snagged me around the waist and I was picked up off my feet. "Haven." Whose voice was that? Olaf? He was dead, though.

I had to reach Charlie. "Haven, baby. Breathe." I kicked my legs, frantic to get away.

"No. No. No."

"Damn, what a crazy bitch." It was a girl's voice, but I was having trouble deciphering where I was and who was with me as reality and my past clashed together.

"Get the fuck out of here." Crisis. That was Crisis and he was next to me. "Now. Out. Kite, man, get them out of here."

The arm tightened around my waist and I screamed wildly. My vision was blinded by tears and all I pictured was Alexa and the white coat of the doctor.

"No. Please. Let me hold him once." It was Olaf holding me down now, preventing me from escape as I screamed so loud my voice broke. "It's all my fault." Charlie was dead because of me.

"Jesus. Crisis, take her to my room. It's sound-proof at least."

Kite? Was it Kite talking? Sound-proofed? Were they locking me away? Was Alexa going to lock me up again? Would she put me in the cage?

I felt movement as I was carried up the stairs. All I saw was what my mind was telling me. Olaf, Charlie, Alexa and the doctor.

I screamed. "Noooo, I'm sorry, Charlie. I'm sorry." It was my fault he was dead. I killed him.

The images surfaced again like pellets shooting into me over and over again. "Nooooo."

"Baby. Please. Jesus. Calm down."

I knew it was Crisis' voice and yet I couldn't stop what was happening. I'd held everything in for so long that now that it leaked out of me, I had no control. I was in the tornado going around and around without an end. Spinning out of control.

I felt something soft beneath me. The bed. The bed. "Nooooo." It was months too early. I couldn't have him now. But the pain . . . it wouldn't stop.

I screamed over and over again as I was held down on the bed. I sobbed, my breath choked by the tears as they relentlessly fell for the first time since that night I lost my baby.

The hold on my wrists released and I punched as hard as I could, hitting something solid but unmoving. "Get off me. Get off."

It was Gerard on top of me and I was suffocating. His zipper, his hands between my legs and then the pain. Oh, God, the tearing pain as he entered me. The tearing pain of giving birth.

"Open your eyes. Damn it! Open your eyes."

Hands cupped my head and his breath swept across my face. I sucked in gulps of air.

"It's me, Haven. Please, I need you to look at me."

My fists stopped punching as Crisis' voice slipped between the cracks of my breaking mind and found me.

"That's it. Deep breaths. Now open your eyes."

I was afraid. I was terrified that it wasn't Crisis' voice I heard and one of the men from the club was on top of me. I couldn't go through that again. I squeezed my eyes closed tighter and screamed, the sound matching the ones so long ago when they carried my dead child away.

"No. No."

"You're safe, Haven."

No, I wasn't. I'd never be safe again.

Chapter Nineteen

Crisis

"WHAT THE FUCK do I do?" I asked Kite.

She wouldn't stop fighting me and refused to open her eyes. Her body trembled violently underneath me while her head rocked back and forth on the pillow as she repeated, 'No,' over and over again.

Kite stood beside the bed. "Maybe if you let her go, she'll calm down."

"Yeah. Fuck, yeah, okay." I had no clue what set her off or what the hell was happening. But it was scaring the crap out of me. I'd never seen anyone break like this and I knew it had to do with whatever horror she'd lived through, but this was more than Kite and I knew how to handle.

I slowly released her arms and lifted off the bed. I took a deep breath as she lay completely still and silent for a second.

Her eyes flashed open and she scrambled off the bed on the opposite side of Kite and me. She fell to her knees, but was up and running for the door faster than I could jump across the bed, and my hand just missed her arm.

Kite went to intercept her at the door and caught her around the waist. He lifted her off her feet as she kicked and yelled, tears streaming down her cheeks. Fuck, I'd never seen her cry. Even when she broke before, she hadn't cried.

"We need to call someone. She needs a sedative or something," Kite said.

Haven went wild. Her fists pounded his arm which was locked around her waist as she screamed. Kite didn't even seem fazed as he calmly carried her back to the bed.

From the glassy look in her grey eyes, she wasn't really seeing what was right in front of her. It was like she wasn't here; she was somewhere else, locked in a nightmare.

Kite gently laid her down, but the second his hands let her go, she tried to get up and go for the door again. This time I was ready and pulled her body up against mine as we went down on the bed together.

"Call Ream." I pulled us up to the headboard and leaned against it, Haven secured in my arms. My hand soothingly stroked her hair and I had no idea how I could do anything calmly when inside I was freaking out. But she needed me calm, despite the blood rushing through my veins like a river with a broken dam; I had to give that to her.

Her chest rose and fell in deep breaths, but she stopped screaming and mumbling, 'No,' over and over again. "Kite—call Ream."

Kite took out his cell. "It'll take him a half-hour to get here."

Her chest was up against my side and she clawed at my shirt, the material ripping under her distress. I kissed the top of her head. "Shh, baby. You're going to be okay."

My heart thudded violently and I felt as if I was shaking just as hard as she was. Fuck, she was cold, but I was afraid to move her under the blankets and have her freak out again.

"Maybe we should call an ambulance?" Kite suggested. "Shit, we might have the cops here if anyone in the building heard her screaming before you got her in here."

He was right. And then this would look really bad, me holding down a chick in a sound-proof room with . . . I looked at the rope on the bed posts . . . yeah, it wouldn't look good.

"Please, bring him back." She clawed at my neck, her fingernails digging deep enough to have blood rise to the surface of my skin.

"Ream," Kite said into his phone. "Yeah, man, you need to get here. Now."

I tried to keep her quiet by using my chest to muffle her moans, not wanting Ream to completely freak out hearing his sister.

"She's in a bad way. I think a hospital . . . yeah, okay. We won't. You have any sedatives or anything? . . . Okay." Kite hung up and looked at me. "He's coming, but no hospital. She'll freak."

Fuck, right. It was the last place Ream had seen her when she was taken away by the fuckers who'd had her prisoner since she was sixteen.

The frantic beat of her heart slowed and her grip on me weakened. I kept rhythmically stroking her hair and rocking back and forth with her curled up against me. She was calming, but I was sure it was more from exhaustion than anything.

"I'm sorry. So sorry." Her voice crackled.

My chest hurt and it wasn't from the torn skin, it was seeing her like this. Haven, the strong fierce chick who met me head-on. "It's bad," I said more to myself than to Kite.

"Yeah." The floor creaked as Kite walked to the door. "I need to make sure lobby security isn't buzzing or anything."

The door clicked closed behind him and it was then I let the tear that was teetering on the edge, slip from its confines. "Ah, fuck, baby. I don't know what to do. I don't know how to make it better."

She no longer fought me, but her breathing was harsh and she wouldn't stop shaking. No matter how close I had her against me, the shaking wouldn't ease.

Seeing her like this . . . it broke me. It was like she crawled inside me and was slashing at my insides.

It felt like hours before Ream burst through the door. I briefly caught a glimpse of Kat in the doorway with Kite talking to her, but neither came in.

Ream's expression said more than any words could—devastation.

His eyes glassy with tears, brows creased together, and his skin color-less. Our eyes met and he nodded.

It was a thank you. And I suspected as he looked at his sister trembling in my arms that he needed a moment before he could speak.

He sat on the edge of the bed and I went to move to let him take over, but he shook his head. "No. Don't move her." He ran his hand back and forth over his head. "How bad?"

"Bad, man."

He nodded and closed his eyes. "Kat has something like valium for when her symptoms act up. It's safe."

Kite opened the door. "Security had two complaints about a girl screaming and police are on their way."

"Shit," I said. "They see her. The blood . . . Ream . . ."

"Yeah, I know. I know." He got up, reached into his pocket and passed me a pill. "Put it under her tongue. I'll call Luke and see if he can do anything about the cops."

"Already done," Kite said. "Luke is on his way." He walked over to the dresser and grabbed a t-shirt from a top drawer. "Put this on." He passed it to me then helped me out of my ripped bloodstained one without shifting Haven around too much. She complained a bit, but she was pretty much half-asleep now.

Ream took my shirt and tossed it into the closet. "Okay." He glanced at me and then at Kite. "Let's deal with this. No one takes her out of here. You get me?"

Kite and I both nodded and I knew what he was saying. Do every-thing and anything to make certain Haven was kept clear of this. Ream would never risk her being taken away again. To him and his sister, a hospital was what had destroyed them.

Not that we could stop the police if they insisted on a hospital, but we'd lie and use our influence any way we could to make sure it didn't happen. They'd need a warrant to search the place and there was no question Ream would insist on that. "Take the rope off, for fuck's sake," I told Kite before he had a chance to leave.

"Fuck." He quickly untied the ropes on the bedposts and tucked them away in a drawer.

Then they both walked out to handle the situation.

It was only ten minutes later when the door opened again. I expected Ream or Kite, not Logan. "Hey."

And this was what we were—family.

There would've been no question Kite or Ream would've called him. I would've, too, if I was thinking straight. I was pretty sure Emily was here, too.

He strode over to the bed and looked at Haven sleeping in my arms. He put his hand on her head and lightly stroked. "Shit," he whispered, his voice breaking as he met my eyes. "You okay?"

"I'm not sure. But I have to be for her." Whatever was fucking with my head was being put in a jar and sealed tight, because Haven needed me to be her strength.

"You up for this?" Logan asked.

If it involved Haven, I was up for it. "Yeah."

He pulled his hand away. "Ream's going to want to shelter her. He isn't thinking straight. He lost her once and he won't lose his sister again."

Yeah, he was going to want her back at the farm. I had no clue about this stuff, but hiding her away was not the way to go. "I'm not letting her go."

Logan half-smiled. "No, I suspect not. I'm behind you and so is Kite. Ream is just scared, but he also saw you with her. I think it's hit him that she trusts you."

I glanced down at the vulnerable girl in my arms. Yeah, she did. And for Haven, I knew that was huge. "Logan." I had to tell him. "Bad timing, but that chick texted me. At least I think it's her."

"Luke know?"

"I told Roman tonight." And he would tell Luke, so I was sure they were already trying to locate her. She'd managed to get my cell number and that meant this was escalating. Fuck, not good. It was never a good time, but I didn't worry about shit like that. Now I did because I didn't want Haven affected by my shit.

"I'll talk to him. See what he's found out." He nodded to Haven. "You look after her. The police are gone. Kite told them it was the girl,

Lena, screaming because you kicked her out and she'd made one hell of a show leaving the building. Luke had the lobby security video and verified. The police didn't file a report. Just a disturbance." Logan had this God-like aura about him, part of the reason why he rocked the stage so well; he owned it. He was steady and confident, and the only time he lost his cool was when he was fighting to get his girl, Emily, back.

I called out to him before he walked out the door, "She's going to be okay, right?" Logan knew about bad. His mother had been a sex slave to Logan's father in Mexico.

Logan frowned, his hand on the doorknob. "I don't know. Depends on her." He nodded to me. "You're good for her. And Ream knows it, too. He's just ignored it until tonight."

After Logan left, I watched Haven sleep for a long time, until I finally drifted off.

I woke with my arms cramped and tingling from being in the same position underneath her shoulders for hours. I gently lifted Haven from my arms and she didn't wake, which I was guessing was partially due to the pill. Careful not to disturb her, I crawled out of bed, grabbed a grey throw blanket up on the shelf of the closet and laid it on top of her. I leaned over and kissed her temple then quietly left the room.

I had a piss, brushed my teeth, then walked downstairs. Logan, Kite, and Ream were sitting out on the terrace, their heads together, obviously trying to be quiet. I guessed the girls were in bed in the guest room.

I glanced at the time on the oven—three in the morning. We were used to the late nights though and seeing the guys still awake was nothing unusual. I grabbed a bottle of water and walked out to join them.

"How is she?" Ream asked before I even had the screen door slid all the way across. It was cold out, but the glass partitions on the balcony blocked some of the wind.

"Sleeping. Don't think she'll wake for a while." I sat beside Logan, stretched out my legs and cracked the seal of the bottle.

"I'll take her back to the farm tomorrow." Ream was pretty calm as he said it.

Logan said, "That's her choice."

Kite nodded.

"She's been fine at the farm. She lives here one month and look what's happened."

I remained quiet because there was nothing to talk about. I'd support Haven's choice, not anyone else's.

Kite put his beer down on the glass table a little hard and the sound clanged. "Because she hid there. Do you want her to do that the rest of her life? Because that's what's going to happen. Something triggered what happened tonight and this isn't the first time."

Ream stilled. "What?"

Shit. He was going to tell him. "Kite," I warned.

"No, he needs to know." Kite flicked his teeth over the stud in the tip of his tongue. "Nothing this serious, but it's happened. At the farm the day before you came home and again at the party we went to." Ream's face tightened. "We have no idea what has gone down while we were on tour. She runs too much and we all know why."

Ream quietly turned his beer bottle, something he regularly did when he was upset. "I know that, but she won't talk about it." Ream looked at me as if he was assessing me and then his shoulders sagged. I saw it in his face, the half-lidded eyes and the bottle stopped turning, and he was giving in to the possibility that Haven and I were close. "Has she talked to you?"

"No, but if she did, I wouldn't be telling her shit to you. Even if you are her brother."

Ream tensed and glared, super pissed-off, then he let it go and nodded because he knew I was right. "Yeah." He got it. I may not protect Haven the way he did, but I'd protect her my way, and there was no chance I'd break the trust we'd built. "But you can tell me what happened tonight."

I picked at the label of my water. Yeah, I could give him that. "It was like a grenade went off inside her." I crumbled part of the label between my thumb and finger into a ball and tossed it. "I was talking to her, but she didn't hear me or see me. Her eyes glazed over and . . . fuck, she just started screaming."

Ream swore beneath his breath.

My stomach cramped as I thought about her kicking and screaming in my arms, and nothing I did or said got through to her. "She wasn't here. You know? Like she was somewhere else and she had to get away or something." She'd begged and pleaded. I tapped my hand on the side of table thinking. "She said it was her fault. Do you know who Charlie is?"

"No." Ream held his head in his hands, his fingers digging into his scalp then dragging through his hair until he placed his palms flat on the table. When he spoke, it was muffled by the emotion ripping through him. "I'm telling you this because I think you need to know. After tonight . . . it's important you know why I want her with me back at the farm. Why she needs help. And this, I'm guessing, is only part of what she's suffered.

"She pretends to be strong. No, she *is* strong as hell, but she can't be alone in this any longer." Ream looked at each of us. "She was raped. Sixteen years old. Fuck, it was more than that . . . violated over and over again and I didn't see it." He kicked the table leg.

"The guy Gerard shot her up with heroine . . . that's how she got addicted." My heart thudded and tension gripped my insides. "He gave it to her and then . . ." When Ream looked up, our eyes met and there was so much anguish there that it was haunting. He never told me any of this and now I saw why. "I don't even know how long it was happening for. But she lost weight, withdrew, skipped school." He hesitated. "One night it all went down. She was fucked up on heroin and I saw the marks on her arm and freaked." Ream slowly shook his head back and forth. "He was in her room and I killed him. Took a marble statue and slammed it into his head until there was nothing left but blood and shards of bone."

I shoved my chair away, and stood, walking over to the railing. My hands curled around the metal bar. The roar rushing through me was like a tsunami churning the raging molecules into volcanic pellets of destruction.

"That's when we left. Lived on the streets a while, then in that old lady Urma's shed. The one who left us the cottage in her will. But Haven . . ." His voice cracked. " . . . she was too far gone. Lost. Broken. I didn't know how to help her. We were sixteen with no money and her addiction pushed her over the edge.

"Don't know where she got the drugs from, probably some pimp who was going to make her one of his girls once she was indebted to him. She overdosed a number of times and I had to take her to the hospital. We'd get out as quickly as possible before children's services were called. But the last time . . . a doctor came out and told me she'd died."

It wasn't long after that Ream came to live with us and he was seriously screwed up for a while.

"She needs professional help," Kite said.

"I know that, but she won't go. She won't talk about it," Ream said.

I heard the scrape of a chair and turned as Ream got up. He looked at me for a second then did something I never expected. "I don't know what it is between you two, but I know it's something. She trusts you." He took a deep breath and I knew this was hard for him. He knew my past, and my track record with chicks sucked. But there was resignation in his eyes and maybe he was getting that to me, Haven wasn't just a chick. She'd become my friend and I cared about her. No, it was more than that. I loved her, but that was not something Ream needed to hear right now.

Ream strode over to me and put his hand on my shoulder. "I love her," he said.

"I know."

"Thanks. For what you did tonight."

"I'd do anything for her."

Ream paused a second, then nodded and went inside.

Logan had obviously waited until Ream left before he said, "We have another issue."

Kite shifted and his chair scraped the cement floor. "What's up?"

"Received a few messages," I said.

Kite's brows rose. "That Tammy girl?"

I shrugged. "Don't know for sure. At breakfast with Ream and Kat, I had the first one. Some rambling about sex. Another one before we went to Avalanche about me liking to fuck whores." I shut my phone off when Kite and I were at Avalanche, but when I checked, there were three more, all explicitly sexual.

"Your mom or dad give it out?" Kite asked.

I shook my head. But fuck, you couldn't keep anything private anymore.

Logan tagged his water bottle. "Bad timing."

I nodded. "This crap with Tammy cannot touch Haven."

"It won't," Kite said. "Go, be with her. We'll worry about the rest."

"Thanks." I squeezed him on the shoulder as I walked by.

I went back upstairs and carried Haven to her bedroom, not wanting her to wake up in Kite's bed, then lay beside her and fell asleep with my arms wrapped around her.

Chapter Twenty

Haven

I WOKE SMOTHERED in weighted heat. My eyes flew open with panic thinking I was back at the club, but I immediately recognized the tatted arms curled around me. His breath lightly caressed the nape of my neck with each exhale while his heart beat against my back, steady and rhythmic.

Soothing.

Comforting.

Why was Crisis sleeping in my bed—?

I sucked in a lung full of air as it slammed into me. I choked back the strangled cry, tears filling my eyes. Last night. Oh, God, last night I broke. The buried particles of me broke through.

Crisis and Kite saw it happen.

My throat was raw and I knew what it was from—screaming.

A tear slid down my cheek and landed on Crisis' arm, darkening the ink as it soaked in.

I stiffened when his hand reached for mine and linked our fingers together. He rested them on my abdomen and gently squeezed. I was desperate to crawl away, to run and hide, find a place to build up my shield so I could forget and be strong again. That was my strength when I was held captive, to shield myself from what was happening—numbness. But now . . . I knew where I'd find strength. Letting those I cared about in.

"It's going to be okay," Crisis whispered, his voice vibrating against my neck. He kissed the back of my head, and for a few seconds, I took in his words and believed them. Reality was there was a chance I'd never repair.

"What if it's not?" Losing Charlie lived inside me like a rusted chunk of metal ready to slice me open if I took a wrong step.

He was quiet and Crisis rarely had nothing to say. His leg shifted and brushed against mine and I should've wanted to get away, but with Crisis I didn't. There was something deeper in him that I trusted. And right now, I needed that.

"We find a way."

He said "we" and it was as if a thousand pounds lifted off my shoulders. I wasn't alone. I never had been, but I'd made it that way. Crisis had been there all along, building something I didn't even realize, but it was brick by brick until I stood within his encompassing strength and trust.

"Okay." With that one word, I gave him me.

There was a comforting silence as we laid together, and it was us letting one another in. Trusting. Accepting and giving at the same time. Woven hands interlocked us.

It was going to be okay.

I sighed and, in response, he kissed me on the head again.

"My brother."

"Yeah, he's here. He's worried."

Shit, that was the last thing I wanted. This was what I'd been trying to protect him from.

"He's worried about you, but he's okay, Haven. He's even accepted this. I think he just wants to know that you're safe."

I shifted around so I lay on my back and Crisis moved up on his elbow, so he could look down at me. "Meaning?"

With his teeth, he played with his lower lip, his eyes on our hands that were still linked, fingers lightly stroking. "He's okay with me being here with you. He knows we're friends and I think he's realized that."

Oh. That was good.

He fell back against the pillow and let my hand go as he put his arm across his eyes. "Jesus, I was scared, Haven."

And maybe this was why I connected with Crisis. He was real. There was no pretending that he was okay with what happened. That it hadn't freaked him out.

I wanted to say 'me too,' but admitting I was terrified was too hard to say aloud yet.

I was swimming in an ocean of black, unable to find my way back to shore. I didn't know whether I'd sink to the bottom or if I'd have enough strength to tread water until shore found its way to me. But I had a life jacket. I had Crisis. And if I sank to the bottom, I knew I'd lift back up—to him.

I took a deep breath and when I exhaled, my chest quivered. The memories I'd compartmentalized in parts of my mind, where I'd locked them up, had escaped. But there was always a trigger. A key that could open up the compartments and set them free. Maybe it was time I gave the key to someone.

"I don't know where to start."

"Wherever you can, baby." He lay on his side, his head on his arm above me, fingers gently caressing my hair.

I swallowed. "I don't want to lose you. Or my brother. He's suffered so much. I can't do that to him again."

"Haven. You'll never lose him—ever. Your brother loves you more than anything."

"But when he hears—"

"Shsh." He kissed the top of my head like he always did. "No matter what happened or what happens, he will never stop loving you. And yeah, it's going to hurt him, but it's not your fault. You have to get that out of your head. I see the guilt in your eyes right now."

"I didn't fight Gerard."

He stiffened against me and his voice took on a harder tone. "Ream, told us last night about him. About the drugs. The rape. It wasn't your fault, baby. Jesus. You're here. You're alive and you survived. That's fighting."

I had no words. He knew about Gerard and the drugs. When I was at my weakest, scared and lost. "He killed him for me."

"Yeah, he told us that, too. Gerard deserved it."

He waited. I waited. And then I opened my hand and gave him my pieces. "The gun . . . I carry it because it ended the nightmare. It's what I used to kill Alexa and—" I stopped, thinking about it, trying to put my thoughts together. "It's my safety. My truth of what I did and what I'm capable of. It's a reminder of who I've become. A symbol I guess."

"Who do you think you've become?"

I didn't know. Not in words. I'd killed. I didn't let anyone in. I was cold. I hid behind a wall. But I did things, things I hated. "I don't know."

His rhythmic touch on my head calmed me and I closed my eyes as I spoke. "Alexa . . . in some fucked-up way I was her connection to Ream. She was obsessed with him when we were kids. Then when he was gone, it was like she took it out on me, but tried to love me at the same time. Just a wrong kind of love." I took a few deep breaths before I told him about the cage she used to put me in. I felt him stiffen and he swore beneath his breath. "Alexa told Olaf I was the one who killed Gerard so he wouldn't go after Ream and kill him."

"He wouldn't kill you?"

"No. I was money to him. Ream was dangerous being with us as he got older."

"Too protective."

I nodded. "Olaf knew it was Ream all along. There was no chance I could've lifted that statue. But it was easier for him to let Ream live knowing he had something over me while Ream thought I was dead."

"He'd go after Ream."

I nodded. "So, I didn't fight Olaf. I survived."

"Jesus, baby." He closed his eyes a second and I saw the pain in his expression. "He's gone. Deck's men killed him."

I nodded. "Yeah. But they needed information out of him first." Crisis's hand stilled on my hair. "About a club."

He leaned toward me and pressed a light kiss on my forehead.

"Vic found it and called me. That's when I went running for three hours and Luke called you." I inhaled a quivering breath. "Every Saturday night, I was blindfolded and taken there. There were other girls at the club, but I never spoke to them, wasn't allowed to. I was put in a room alone." I swallowed as my throat tightened. "I danced. Stripped. And after . . . I was taken back to my room and waited. They'd . . . the men would bid on the girls at the end of the night."

I know he was trying to stay calm and relaxed, but Crisis tensed around me and his heart rate picked up. But I had to keep going. He needed everything and I was beginning to realize this was for me, not him.

"Highest bidder got us for an hour. Olaf told me I always went for the most. I was known as an exclusive, meaning Saturday nights only. It drew higher bids plus . . . the men got to know I fought. I always fought when I had the chance. I couldn't help myself. No matter how long it happened, I couldn't stop."

"Oh, fuck, baby. No."

"After the first couple months, I got a reprieve from the club because . . . because I was pregnant." Crisis' fingers didn't even flinch as he continued to play with my hair and I was thankful for his steady reaction. "It was Gerard's. He's the only one I'd ever been with before Olaf put me on birth control pills. And the timing was right."

I closed my eyes and dragged in a shaky breath. A tear escaped the confines of my eyelid and trailed a path down my cheek. Crisis tilted his head and kissed it before it fell from the cusp of my jaw.

"God, I didn't even know I was pregnant until four months along. And when I was sick, I thought it was due to the drugs. All I cared about at the time was my next fix, so I could disappear.

"Olaf locked me up in a room when the doctor confirmed my pregnancy. And that was . . . well, getting off heroine was the second worst experience in my life. Withdrawal hit and it was all I could do to get out of bed. I vomited and shook. My legs and stomach cramped so badly I cried, but the sound of my sobs was worse. Any noise amplified like loud speakers blaring in my head.

"But what made it easier was knowing I had a baby growing inside me. It was all I had and I didn't care that it was Gerard's. It was mine and . . . it was a piece of joy that I didn't have." I choked on the sob, my throat tight and chest aching as the memory of that moment pushed through. "The drugs . . . I'd been taking the drugs not knowing I was pregnant. I miscarried at six months." I raised my head to look at Crisis. "They wouldn't let me hold him. Not even for a second. All I knew was that he'd been a boy.

"I never heard him cry . . . I never saw his face." Another tear slipped down my cheek and Crisis leaned into me and kissed it.

"Charlie?"

I nodded. I kept my eyes averted from him, afraid of what I'd see—disgust. Pity. Horror that I killed my own child. But when I finally did meet his eyes, there was none of that. He had that fierce crease between his glassy eyes filled with concern. I wanted to kiss the worry away. Ease the pain I saw in his eyes that matched my own.

"I freaked out after that and they kept me sedated for weeks. When I finally stopped crying, that was when something changed in me. I knew pain. I knew the loss of my brother and then my baby. That was my fault."

"Jesus, Haven. None of it was your fault." He moved and it was so he could look down at me and cup the sides of my face and make sure I was looking at him. "It's not your fault. You have to know that."

"I did the drugs."

"Gerard forced you to. He raped you. You were kept high and addicted to that shit. Did you have a choice? Baby, did you have a choice? Because if you didn't then you have to take it in that none of this is your fault."

It was a while before I answered. "No. But I craved the drugs for a long time even if I never wanted to touch them again." I separated our hands and ran my finger over the brand on my wrist. "This . . . this was a reminder that I was a possession. That I was no longer a person, but an object."

His thumb wiped away another stray tear underneath my eye. "He branded you because he saw your strength. He was trying to break you, prove that you were nothing. You didn't break, Haven. Your pieces may have scattered, but they didn't break."

I glanced over at him and saw the familiar quiet and calm steadiness within the depths of his eyes.

I reached up and he remained completely still as I traced my finger across his lower lip, the slight dampness from his tongue clinging to my skin. He never moved. It felt good to touch someone willingly, to know that it was my choice instead of the men who forced themselves on me.

"My brother . . ." I was his angel; this would crush him.

"He needs to know. He can't move on and repair from the loss of the last twelve years without you."

I'd asked him to accept me for who I was, but Crisis was right. How could I ask Ream to if he didn't know who I was? "Yeah."

We lay for a long time in one another's arms, no words. Him processing all that I'd told him and me going through the loss again, but this time, it was with acceptance for what happened.

A buzzing sounded on the nightstand and I pulled away, glancing over at my phone, but I didn't bother looking at the text. "How long has it been?"

"Eighteen hours." Oh, God. "Dana called. She was concerned when you didn't show up at school or answer her texts."

"What did you tell her?"

"You had the flu."

I nodded.

Crisis moved his arm away and sat up, swinging his legs over the side of the bed. His back was to me and even though he had a shirt on, I could still see his muscles flexing. The mattress squeaked as he rose. "I'll get you something to eat."

But I didn't feel like eating. "I want to go for a run."

I expected him to say forget it, but he nodded. "Okay, I'll go with you. Let me have a quick cold shower to wake up and call Luke." He opened the door.

I didn't know why security had to come with us, but I was just glad to go running. Running was my time alone; a way to find my steady again, but there was relief with his words. I wanted him with me. "Crisis?"

He half-turned toward me.

"Thank you . . . for not leaving me." He smiled and I loved that smile. It warmed me up from my toes up to the top of my head. "The deal in the stable? Why did you do it? Luke could've told you what was happening with me. I didn't have to text you."

"It was a way to get you to talk to your brother. He needed that, so did you. The texting . . ." He dropped his head forward and I could see him chewing on his bottom lip. I grew a little nervous when he hesitated, then he straightened and our eyes locked. "I was cocky enough to believe I could make you fall madly in love with me over text." I expected a wink or a grin; Crisis did neither. He turned and left.

My heart pumped wildly and a rush of heat soared through my body like a firecracker was set off inside me. The door clicked closed and I laid back closing my eyes as his words repeated over and over in my head.

He was serious. The deal wasn't so he could make sure I was okay, because that was Luke's job. The deal was to help my brother and I get back some of what we lost. And . . . and so I'd talk to Crisis. He'd known back then what was between us was more. He wanted me to fall in love with him?

He stayed with me.

He held me.

And now he knew my dirty secrets and he wanted me to love him.

I crushed the pillow to my chest. He never pushed me; he simply became the person I needed.

I climbed out of bed, went to the bathroom, brushed my teeth then changed to get ready to go for a run. I knew the running would be for a different reason this time. It wouldn't be to bury the memories; it was to let them in and accept them.

I sat on the end of my bed to put on my running shoes when there was a soft knock on my door before it creaked open.

"Can I come in?"

I didn't recognize the voice and tensed. Suddenly, I wished Crisis was still with me. He was like a buffer between me and everyone else.

The door slowly opened and an older woman dressed in black slacks, low black pumps and a white blouse with a red and gold silk scarf tied around her neck stood there. She looked classy and so not what I was expecting to be showing up in my room. My first thought was a psychologist or doctor or something.

"I'm on my way for a run." I met her eyes, refusing to buckle under the overwhelming pressure to cave and fall into an abyss of tears of self-pity.

She smiled and it was warm and kind. I knew I should feel bad for being rude, but I didn't. "I'll only be a minute." She approached me. "I'm Sophia Wesson."

"Oh." Crisis' mother and the woman who had fostered Ream. Some of the tension evaporated.

"Do you mind?" She gestured to the bed and when I didn't say anything she sat beside me, although at a distance.

My emotions were currently a circus of fucked up and I was uncertain about how I felt about meeting her.

"Both my sons are being evasive as to what happened." Sons . . . she called Ream her son. "But Ream has always been . . . reserved and . . . stubborn." Well, that was all true and he was reserved because of what he'd gone through. Trust was something both of us had a hard time doing. "But he called me. It's the first time he's ever called me for help. It was the first time he sounded scared."

Shit, he'd called her—scared.

"I won't pretend to have any idea of what has happened to you because I don't. I've had a pretty comfortable life with nothing too traumatic other than the loss of my cat." She shifted, crossing her legs. "My boys mean the world to me and seeing them worried and afraid, that breaks a mother's heart."

The word mother hit me hard. And maybe it was why some of the tension in me faded because she was a mother and good mothers did anything for their children. I may have never held my child, or known him, but it didn't matter. Charlie was part of me, always would be.

"I'm just a mother, Haven. But I'm a good one and I love my children no matter when or how they came into my life. You're part of our family now. I won't ever abandon or judge you and when you're ready, I'm here for you."

I realized I'd been holding my breath and slowly exhaled.

"Really, Mom?"

I jerked my eyes to the door to see Crisis standing with a towel wrapped around his waist, hair dripping wet. He must have seen the open door and glanced in.

"What the fuck? Why are you here?" He glanced at me then frowned at his mom. "She doesn't want you mothering her."

Sophia stood and walked toward him. Her back was to me, but I saw Crisis' frown drop away pretty quickly. "Go put some clothes on," she ordered. "I taught you better than that. Haven doesn't need to see you parading around half-naked. And when on earth did you get that tattoo on your side?" She made a tsking sound. "I don't know why you and Ream need to mark up your skin. You have beautiful bodies without all that ink staining it."

Crisis didn't bother moving like his mother wanted him to; instead, he raised his arms and held the top of the doorframe, which showed off his muscled abdomen.

"Fuck, Mom, give it up about the ink."

She smacked his arm. "Where did that mouth come from? God, what Haven must think of you? No wonder you never have a girlfriend."

He winked at me and my stomach flipped over. No matter what was screwing with me, Crisis could plow through it and make me feel better. It wasn't something I'd expected. It just happened, slowly, over time.

He never gave up on me. It was as if he crawled inside me and made himself at home. The thing was he never busted down the door. He knocked and it was I who opened it.

Sophia glanced over her shoulder at me and smiled then ducked under Crisis' arms. "Vincent, close the door. Give the girl some privacy. Put some clothes on and I'll make everyone something to eat."

"We're going running," Crisis said.

"I sure hope not like that." Sophia scowled. "And why would you shower before you run?" She made an exaggerated sigh while shaking her head. "I have no idea what goes on inside that head of yours."

"And a fuck of a good thing," Crisis said then chuckled.

I bit my lip to keep from smiling. It was cute. They had an ease between them. And Sophia's words resonated. No matter what Crisis had done or did, his mother would always love him.

Sophia reached up and kissed him on the cheek. "Behave yourself."

She left but Crisis stayed in the doorway, leaning forward, his weight on his arms gripping the top of the doorframe. "Give me two minutes, babe."

I nodded then said, "She's . . . nice."

"She's special as hell. There is no de-momming that woman." He smirked and his arms dropped to his sides. I loved that he was letting all that I'd told him go and was back to himself. I'm sure it was spinning inside his head, but I needed him to be Crisis and he was giving me that. "You're not a pissy-ass jogger are you? I like to run."

I smiled. "I can run." My eyes trailed over his damp skin and the low-slung towel sitting on his hips. I knew he worked out a lot and I was betting he was going to push me.

"Two minutes." Crisis disappeared.

I sat on the end of the bed to wait for him, knowing it wouldn't be two minutes, more like ten. My finger sliding back and forth over the brand. It was the first time I touched it and it didn't hurt so badly.

Chapter Twenty-One

Haven

3 weeks later

EVERY MORNING I ran with Crisis and Roman, the latter had become my personal bodyguard when I left the condo. Three weeks ago, after my breakdown, I'd asked Crisis while we were running why the extra security. He told me it was precautionary.

"Against what?" We were running hard and I slowed the pace.

"Baby, can I not tell you and pretend I did?"

I stopped, glancing behind me at Roman who also stopped and was watching the people around us. "It's that girl, isn't it?"

"She's texting me. Like I said—precautionary. I don't want you to worry."

"Anything else I should know?"

He nodded. "She's called my parents' house. Don't know for sure, but Luke is going back through all the records and seeing if any calls came from Alberta." I waited because I knew there was more with the way he shifted his weight and frowned. Nothing casual about him at that moment. "Maybe the farm would be better for you to stay at for a while. Lay low until we figure this out."

I put my hands on my hips, my chest still heaving from our run. "Are you suggesting? Or has this been decided?"

He moved in and I liked when he did that. But I was pissed because I had exams and I'd worked hard. I wasn't screwing up the parts of my life I rebuilt because of some chick who was obsessed with him.

"Luke suggested it. Just easier for them to watch us there. I also think we should tell Luke about your past. He's protecting you, too, and it's important he's informed."

I nodded. He was right. Luke had to know. Crisis placed his hands on my hips; I really liked that, too. Tingles sparked through me and despite all the shit that surfaced, it was stronger than ever. The compartments were opened and there was nothing left to hide.

I wanted him to kiss me, but my confidence around kissing and sex was fucked up, so I didn't make a move. He didn't either except for his light touches and holding me in bed.

Yeah, I had that, too. Every night since I'd freaked out, he slipped into my bed at night and wrapped his arms around me. I'd feel his light kiss on my head then he'd whisper, "Night, baby."

It was sweet and comforting and I'd never slept better than when I was enfolded within his embrace, listening to his steady heartbeat.

"I have school. Exams are soon, then Christmas break."

"Then you'll go after exams?"

"What about you?" If I wasn't out of breath, I'd be holding it as I waited for his answer, because I couldn't imagine waking up without his arms around me.

He grinned and my chest warmed. "You want me, cupcake?"

I raised my brows at the endearment. "Cupcake?"

"Answer the question."

"Yeah, I do. I want to wake up with you."

"Good, because I was coming with you anyway."

After that, things were sweet. He stayed in most evenings with me and we watched movies and had dinner together, often with Kite. There was an ease between us. It had always been there, just polluted by my demons.

Ream and Kat stayed at her brother Matt's place downtown for a few days after my breakdown so Ream could be close by. He came by every day and we talked about school and his music. I also told him I wanted to help kids like us. Kids who had no parents, who were like Ream and me. I knew I had a long way to go with repairing myself first, but I was determined to get there.

I knew I'd be good at it. I knew how to read people and I excelled at hiding and not talking. And I also knew how damaging it was to not talk.

That was when I told Ream about the club and Charlie. We were alone at the condo and sitting out on the patio, the wind cool against my skin, but not scary.

He took it pretty well for Ream and remained semi-calm. I sensed a part of my brother had changed over the last few days. Maybe what I'd been doing by hiding what happened had been hurting him, instead of protecting him.

In a way, what happened freed me. I always felt trapped in my need to be strong by burying everything that happened. I finally agreed to see a therapist, but talking about it with Ream and Crisis had helped.

Now, I had one more day of classes then a week of exams before I was off until the New Year. Roman stayed in the guest room since he was here all the time and he was already up with coffee made when I went downstairs.

Crisis was still in my bed and normally he woke when I slipped out of his arms, but he'd been up really late, not crawling into bed with me until almost four in the morning. I knew because I woke when he came in behind me and glanced at the clock. Then he linked our hands and rested them on my abdomen. I fell back asleep.

It was just after nine and I was in my sociology class listening to the drone of Professor Eric's lecture when my phone vibrated.

WTF. You left without waking me.

I never wake you. You wake up when I do and this morning you didn't. You were up late.

Roman with you?

Do you need to ask?

I waited but my phone didn't vibrate for a minute then,

I'm coming.

?

Where are you?

School.

Funny, babe. Which class?

Oh no, you don't.

You know I have access to your schedule. I'll text Roman and tell him I'm coming.

Crisis, no.

See you in ten, babe.

I turned around in my seat to the back corner of the room where Roman stood. He'd spoken to each of my professors when he'd first started coming to classes to inform them his purpose for being there.

Roman reached for his phone. *Shit.* I saw him type something back scowling. Well, he had already been scowling. Roman was like Luke, a permanent scowler, probably a prerequisite for the job.

Then twenty minutes later, the door opened and my heart stopped. Crisis.

Professor Eric stopped talking and raised his brows. "Can I help you?"

Crisis looked around the room until his eyes spotted me, then he smiled at the professor. "Nope. I'm good." He was wearing a baseball cap low over his face and had on a long sleeve shirt, probably to hide his tats that were a dead giveaway as to who he was to any diehard fan.

"Are you in this class?" the Professor asked.

211

"Nope. But my girl is and she forgot to kiss me when she left this morning."

My mouth dropped open. I never kissed him.

There were a few giggles and whispers as Crisis bounded up the stairs. My heart pattered a tribal dance as I sat in my seat, all eyes on me. Crisis stopped to say hey to Dillon and Kevin, who were taking the class for an easy elective, then strode over to me. I glanced at the Professor, who looked a little uncertain what to do. So, instead of making a production out of it, he went back to the chalkboard and continued his lesson, although, most of the students were twisted around in their seats and looking at Crisis, who was now standing beside me.

"Hey, you mind, buddy?" He nodded to the guy beside me.

"Umm, yeah, sure."

I didn't know how he got away with it, maybe his disarming smile, but the guy got up and moved to another seat. Before Crisis sat, he leaned over and kissed me on the lips. It was a quick and light, but my belly still whirled along with everything else.

It was the first time he kissed me on the mouth and my entire body reacted to it. It was different from the light kisses on the head, although it was still a peck. I had imagined Crisis kissing me—really kissing me—many times, and as I stared at him, my cheeks heated because this was the barrier I'd had trouble breaking for the past few weeks, and with his light kiss on the lips, he gave me the confidence I needed.

"Don't leave our bed again without waking me. I didn't like waking up and you were gone."

He called it our bed. "You kissed me."

He slipped into the seat, looking too tall and overwhelming for the chair. He pushed his legs out to the side, crossing his ankles. "You've been wanting me to all week. You're tough as nails, Haven. But the affection shit . . . babe, you suck at it. Luckily for you, I'm good at it."

"Are you here to learn or chat with your boyfriend, Haven?" Professor Eric asked. "Exams are next week, in case you've forgotten, and I seem to recall you being absent a few classes this semester."

"Sorry," I muttered.

Crisis chuckled and leaned back in his seat.

It was the longest class ever. I felt Kevin's eyes on me and looked over; he quickly looked away. Crisis listened and appeared to be enjoying the class. I didn't hear a single word the Professor said because all I could think about was him sitting next to me.

"Okay," Eric said. "The exam is next Tuesday. See you then." I leaned over and slipped my books back into my bag.

Crisis hopped up, took my hand and pulled me to my feet. "Let's go grab breakfast at that café down the street. Roman looks starved." He pulled me down the steps toward the door.

I glanced at Roman, who was coming down the auditorium stairs toward us. "He's not starving." The guy could live off his muscles for a year. "And I have classes."

He put his arm around me to get me walking again. Dillon was behind us, and from the tilt of his head, he was listening.

"I can't skip anymore. Exams are next week."

Crisis opened the door and let a few people pass; a couple of girls eyed him up and down and I waited for his smirk, but instead, he kept his eyes on me. "Your confusion gone?"

"What?"

"That confusion, Ice. Is it cleared up?"

There was no question it was. "Yeah."

"And what do you want?"

Jesus, he wasn't making this easy. Roman approached and Crisis slapped him on the back. "Give me five?"

Roman nodded and stepped past us, walked down the hall and leaned against the brick wall, arms crossed. Kevin walked by him, then was going out the door when a girl joined him and they left together.

"Need to hear you say it." Crisis pinned me against the doorframe, the door perched open.

My heart did a jiggly dance and my stomach somersaulted. I had the urge to blurt out that I was in love with him. God, I was. I was in love with him. I didn't know when it happened and maybe it had been buried along with everything else, but it was soaring through me like the wind. A strong encompassing wind that swept me up and carried me in its protective arms.

There was no fear. No need to sing to fade out the cries of the wind as it whistled through windows threatening to take me away. Because it was safe.

Crisis moved in so I was pressed against his chest, his hands resting on my hips. "Whenever you're ready, Haven. I'm not going anywhere." He tightened his hold and I met his eyes. "I'm not going anywhere," he repeated.

"Yes, you are. You're leaving my class," Professor Eric said as he walked toward us. "And next time I see you, it better be on stage and not interrupting my class."

My eyes widened, gaze darting to my professor. Professor Eric knew Tear Asunder?

Crisis laughed. "Yeah. Sure. Sorry, sir." He held out his hand and my Professor shook it. "Won't happen again . . . unless, of course, my girl leaves without a kiss."

"Nice to see you've settled down, young man."

"Pretty fuckin' easy to do when it's a chick like Haven. She's my forever girl."

My breath hitched and the professor smiled at me, then walked back into his classroom and started writing on the blackboard.

Crisis half grinned and cupped the back of my neck. "How long are you going to make me wait? Just give a time frame here so I can tell my cock?"

I laughed then licked my lips and he groaned, looking away. "Not long."

"Like an hour?" I laughed again and his fingers tightened on my neck. "Fuck, I love to see you laugh."

I smiled. "How is five seconds?"

He leaned in closer and I felt his warm minty breath on my cheek. "Five." He drawled in my ear.

I shivered, knees weak and my heart thumped against my ribcage. "I've wanted to kiss you since the lawnmower."

"Babe, not before that?"

I shook my head.

"Three." His fingers weaved into the back of my hair. "There's no going back after my mouth is on yours."

"Don't want to go back, Vincent. I want to go forward, always. With you."

"One," he said.

His mouth came down on mine and I expected soft and gentle, Crisis being careful with me, but he was just the opposite. It was hard and unrelenting. Our lips taking, claiming, tasting what we both craved.

The need.

The urgency.

The ache building inside catapulted me into a whirling pool of heat. The taste of him was minty like his breath. As his tongue danced with mine, it guided me as our mouths linked in a frenzy of passion. There was no give in him and I didn't want him to. I loved that he was taking and I was giving. He groaned into my mouth and my heart raced faster. God, this wasn't enough. I wanted his hands all over me, touching me. I never thought I'd want that. But what I'd escaped from had nothing to do with this.

This was about beauty and desire, and the giving of one another.

"We going to have an issue here, Mr. Wesson."

I pulled away and saw my Professor looking at us. He didn't look exactly mad, but rather annoyed that we were making out next to his door.

"Damn, you know my last name?" Crisis said, not even for a second uncomfortable that he'd been caught locking his mouth with mine.

"I'm a fan of Tear Asunder, not a fan of students making out in my hallway."

"But look at her, sir, she' fuckin' gorgeous and irresistible."

"Mmm," he mumbled, frowning.

"Tickets help? Next concert in T.O.?"

Professor Eric rolled his eyes. "Get out of here." Crisis grinned and pulled me behind him heading down the hall. "Leave them in my box," he called after us.

Crisis laughed. He pushed open the doors and strode outside, me in tow. "Fuck, I have to kiss you again."

He headed in the opposite direction of my next class. I glanced over my shoulder and Roman was following us, but keeping his distance. I was close enough to notice the slight twitch at the corner of his mouth. "I'm going to be late."

"Hmm." He stopped in the middle of the grassy area where students sat on benches and studied while others ran for their classes. He backed me against the tree. "I'm never on time, baby. You know that. Get used to it."

He lowered his mouth to mine.

Chapter Twenty-Two

Crisis

I HADN'T PLANNED ON kissing her. I wanted to. Fuck, I'd wanted to since the day I'd picked her up in my arms and jumped off the cliff into the water. I'd been suffering a perpetual hard-on for months. But it was more than that. I'd wanted to kiss her because I'd been falling in love with her.

It was all worthwhile kissing her now. Shit, if I'd tasted her mouth before, I'd have waited years just to get this again. Her past fucked with my unwavering steadiness. I didn't know what the hell I was doing, except I knew I wasn't letting Haven go.

Her demons weren't black shadows. They were fuckin' monsters and the road ahead was one that was going to test every part of me and her. But for some reason, it didn't scare me. Because as long as she was in my arms, we'd be okay.

As her lips submitted to mine, her body sagged against me and her mouth became pliable. I groaned, one hand on her hip the other at the back of her head so it protected her from the rough bark of the tree. "Fuck, baby. Your lips are like your voice—honey."

She nipped my bottom lip and my fingers tightened on her hip as my cock strained against my jeans. "I have to get to class."

Fuck yeah. Haven may have monsters, but her drive to get her life back was stronger. Despite not wanting to stop kissing her, I loved that part of her.

I lifted her up, so her ass was sitting in my hands and most chicks would've squealed and giggled, but not Haven. She grabbed hold of my neck, hooked her ankles behind me, her expression serious as she looked at me. Then she surprised me and leaned forward, lowering her mouth to mine.

It was soft and hesitant at first until I couldn't stop myself and deepened it, my mouth roaming, tongue skimming over her teeth then darting inside to sink into the velvet warmth.

"Class," she mumbled beneath my kiss.

I sighed, drawing back. "Tell me it's sex ed."

She smiled. "This isn't high school and it's an elective, Women and Gender studies. Roman hates it."

"Fuck." I let her slide down my body to her feet, then snagged her hand. "You tell any of the guys I'm sitting in some women's lib class, I'll get up in front of Professor Eric's class and sing to you." She missed a step and I smiled. I knew she wouldn't like that. "Let's get this over with."

I sat through listening to the history of feminism with two hundred women and me and Roman, then Haven told me the good news that her next class was her elective—Greek mythology. I couldn't even begin to pronounce half the gods' names the professor talked about.

Halfway through class, I nudged her leg with mine and leaned over. "You understand what he's talking about?"

She nodded, then went right back to listening to the Professor's voice drone on like a rusted factory machine. I couldn't take my eyes off Haven though. Fuck, but she was cute. The most I'd ever paid attention in high school were to chicks, except during music class. I became an exemplary student rocking it out with the band; it was too bad half of them sucked.

It was when Ream, Kite, Logan and I got together in my garage that shit really happened. It was like the stars aligning. The sound came alive in that garage, and I think we all knew what it was between us. It was something fuckin' special.

That was what it felt like with Haven, and that was something you held onto with both hands. I'd been a man-whore ever since high school. Fuck, Ream and I covered for one another when we brought chicks home and had to sneak them out the second-story window before our parents got home from some charity gig.

One chick got her top caught on the tree branch and ripped it right off. Chick went home in her bra and Ream and I watched her run down the street holding her breasts. We never laughed so hard, rolling around on the floor afterward, clutching our cramping bellies.

A pen tapped me on my forearm and I snapped my head up. "Shh, stop chuckling," Haven whispered.

I hadn't realized I was laughing. When I glanced around, students were turned in their seats and looking at me. The only one who didn't notice was the Professor, who was writing shit on the blackboard, her voice sounding like the dead. No wonder she taught mythology.

I smirked at the class and reached across the space between Haven and me, snatching her hand before she could object and pulled her chair closer to me. It scraped across the floor, making a loud echoing sound on the linoleum. We were in the last row, no one beside us and I grabbed her book bag and placed it on my desk as a sort of shield. No one could see what I was about to do. Well, maybe Roman, but he'd look away.

"Crisis? Stop."

"I'm bored as fuck," I complained. And, I'd been laughing by myself about some crap that happened when I was seventeen.

"I'm not your amusement park."

I had her close enough so I could put my hand on her thigh. Damn, she had rock hard thighs that were going to feel incredible around my naked ass. I knew it might be a while before we got to that point, but I'd wait forever . . . well, a few weeks, anyway. My cock might have something to say about that, but jerking off to thoughts of Haven would have to do until she was ready.

I ran my hand up her leg, fingers trailing along the inner seam of her jeans right up to where her pelvis met her thigh. I didn't want to push it so I stopped there. "Oh, you have no idea how wrong you are. Your body is my roller coaster, baby."

She snorted and put her hand on top of mine. I thought she was going to push it off, but instead, she pushed my hand up further until my baby finger grazed over her pussy. My cock jerked along with my body as every muscle tensed.

She kept her hand on top of mine, fingers lightly caressing my skin. I swallowed then flicked my finger over her pussy. Her breath hitched and her back straightened. I did it again. Her legs parted further and I took full advantage, placing my palm over her and applying pressure.

She now gripped the edge of her desk with both hands and her head tilted back slightly, eyes closed.

Jesus. The expression on her face . . . Haven with desire sparkling in her eyes, cheeks flushed . . . it was so fuckin' special because she was letting me in and letting go all at the same time.

I slipped my hand away, down her inner thigh again then back up until my fingers tap-danced across her pussy again. This time I applied some pressure, not too much, just enough to make sure she could feel every flick of my finger through her jeans over her clit. And I knew she did because she pushed back in her chair, and latched onto my wrist to stop me.

I refused. I was nice, but not when it came to playing. She started this and like I'd told her, there was no going back.

"Vincent," she hissed as she tried desperately to move away from my hand but couldn't without getting out of her desk.

I moved my fingers faster over her jeans. I swear I could feel the heat between her legs and I was betting my fuckin' car that she was soaking wet.

"Please. Stop." She panted and her grip was so tight on my wrist, I was sure to have bruises.

"Shh, baby," I whispered. "You need to be quiet."

And that was when she gave in to it. Right there in the back of the classroom with the teacher going on about some Greek God. It was also when Roman moved up to the front of the class and started coughing, taking any potential attention away from Haven. *Thank you, Roman.*

"Oh, God," Haven whispered as her legs quivered and shook, body tensing as she came against my hand.

She released my wrist, but I didn't move my hand away. Fuck, no. If I had to finish sitting through this class with a rock hard cock, I was keeping my hand right where it was.

And it was the longest class I'd ever sat through. Pure torture. As soon as the Professor dropped the piece of chalk on the ledge of the board and shut her book, I was on my feet. I grabbed Haven's books off her desk, shoved them under my arm and snagged her knapsack, hitching it over my shoulder.

Haven's teeth dragged over her lower lip and her eyes held a dazzling sexiness that smoldered with desire. "Are we in a hurry?" And that voice . . . fuck it was laced with graveled innocence.

I groaned, then held out my hand and she took it. Fuck, that was nice. "Yeah." A hurry to kiss her again. A hurry to have her against me. A hurry not be under the watchful eye of students, a professor and a bodyguard.

I tugged her out of there so fast, although tugging may have been an exaggeration because once Haven was on her feet, she followed beside me with just as much urgency and that right there was a huge turn on.

Haven was fuckin' mine.

Haven gave herself to me.

I made it through the building, outside to the stairs and around the corner before I pushed her against the brick wall, my thigh parting her legs so I could stand between them, hand at the nape of her neck, the other on her hip.

There were no words as we both panted and stared at one another before our mouths crashed together. And it was a crash. It was teeth hitting, and noses getting in the way and lips crushed.

My head tilted as I eased up for a second, our mouths finding their way against one another and molding into a passionate urgency that put all other kisses to shame.

This was what it was about. The feeling as if your heart beat right out of your chest and into theirs. Like you couldn't take another breath without them. As if everything inside united and there were no questions. No uncertainties.

It was nature finding its path and we were on it.

"Baby." I groaned as she gave in to my bruising kiss. There was no holding back with her and I'd always thought I'd have to be gentle and slow, but Haven's need was as strong as mine.

Her hand wrapped in my hair at the back of my head and kept me locked to her lips, not that I was going anywhere. Her other hand was pressed into my lower back and then slid down to my ass.

Holy fuck.

I grabbed her arm and pulled her hand away, but I felt her smile beneath my lips as she moved it back the moment I let her arm go and she squeezed my ass.

"Fuck." I tore from her arms, staggering back. My cock hurt so fuckin' badly that it was a grenade with the pin pulled and I was not going to be some tool who came in his jeans.

When I looked at her with red lips, eyes flaming with heat, the messed up hair, it didn't help. "Damn it. We have to stop."

She smiled and yeah, that didn't do much for my aching cock because Haven smiling was like being handed her soul in the palm of her hand.

Then she held out that hand.

I hesitated.

"My room or yours?" she asked.

"Huh?"

She raised her brows. "I want to feel *all* of you, Vincent."

Holy Jesus. I came a little bit and thanked fuck I wasn't going commando. "Haven, this is all new and maybe we should take it slowly." Not really, but I wasn't doing anything to fuck this up and this was what girls wanted, right? Go slow. Date. Kiss. Fool around. Long-term building shit.

She walked toward me, hand still outstretched. "We've been going slowly for months." She linked her fingers with mine and stepped into me. Her breasts pressed against my chest and I swear her nipples were hard and aching just like my cock. "I told you my darkest secrets. You're still here."

"I'd never leave you," I said a little annoyed.

She lightly kissed me and our lips stuck for a second as she drew back again. But she wasn't done and stood on her tiptoes and kissed the crease right between my eyes. "I'm going to call you Vincent when we have sex."

My breath left me. Sucked right from my lungs and vanished. I'd fucked a lot of chicks, too many to count; shit, half of them I couldn't even remember fucking. But none . . . none ever had called me Vincent. Because they were fucking the guitarist, the rock star, the band member, and even in high school I was Crisis. But no chick I'd fucked called me 'Vincent' and I finally knew why.

Vincent had been saved for her.

Chapter Twenty-Three

Haven

WE FELL ONTO his bed, me beneath him, our mouths locked, hands all over one another, desperate and unrestrained desire feeding us both.

There was nothing said on the way back to the condo, but our hands remained linked, even while he shifted gears. The power vibrating in the engine, the sound of his harsh breath and the movement of his arm flexing, all of it dispersed every destructive thought associated with sex and replaced them with new ones—with him.

Vincent.

"Vincent," I repeated his name aloud as his hands pulled my shirt off then slid slowly down my sides, shivers sparking all across my inflamed skin.

His mouth stole his name from passing my lips again. The velvet touch of his tongue swept into my mouth. Every particle in my body blazed in a heated inferno of desire, blood rushing through my veins, legs quivering on either side of him as he lay settled between my legs.

His cock pressed between my legs and the pulse in my clit throbbed faster with the pressure against it. It vibrated right through me like an echo of a drum and I squirmed beneath him, trying to move. Arch into it. I never thought I'd want that. Sex had always been cruel and vile and hurt like hell.

But none of this was like that.

"Baby." He shifted to the side and the pressure was gone.

It was a relief and a disappointment. I sucked in gasps of air, trying to settle the urgency that was driving my body.

"You still good with this?" He sat up on his knees and my hands drifted from his chest to his thighs. "I don't want to rush this—us."

"Yeah," I whispered. "Yeah," I said again to make certain he heard me.

"You need me to stop. Don't ride it out. Tell me."

"Will you make me have that again?"

His brows lowered questioningly. "What?"

"In the classroom. I want that again."

He grinned then yanked off his shirt and threw it aside. My eyes trailed down his muscled chest and abdomen. I'd seen it before but now . . . now I got to touch it and my eyes flicked to his before I placed my palms on his chest. In a slow tantalizing glide, I traced the tips of my fingers over every hard contour.

When I reached the cusp of his jeans, I glanced back up at him. His eyes were closed and his head tilted slightly back. He inhaled deep ragged breaths matching my own.

"You're beautiful," I said.

He met my eyes and there was a deep intense look to them as if he'd just realized something, but I didn't know what. Whatever it was, I knew it was good because he slowly smiled then grabbed my wrist, the one with the brand, and lifted it to his mouth.

His tongue darted out and he traced the scar. Our eyes never left one another as he did it. My heart pounded so hard that it hurt and I swear the pieces of me that had been scattered after Gerard, were sliding back into me.

It was like a magnetic pull as he trailed kisses up my arm, then leaned forward and continued along my neck, collarbone, between my breasts then down my abdomen to my jeans. His fingers undid the buttons and they popped open. He kept kissing me, the heat from his breath sending waves of pleasure through me.

"Fuck, I can't wait to taste you. Lift up." I raised my butt and he dragged my jeans off and tossed them on the floor. His hands slid up over my calves. "The best fuckin' legs." He caressed and stroked with his hands, then shuffled down the bed and lowered. "Going to give you what you want now, baby. Bend your knees."

I did. And he lowered his head between my legs. I'd never had a guy go down on me. At the club, the men fucked me, shoved their fingers inside me, pinched my nipples, but this had nothing to do with that.

I arched as his tongue flicked over me like his finger had, but softer, warmer—wet.

"Oh, God."

His heated breath was enough to make me moan. I was so sensitive, probably from the months of wanting him. From denying this.

"Vincent. Please." His tongue played, his mouth suckled and then his finger . . . oh, God, his finger trailed through my slick wetness up to my clit where he tapped over the sensitive nub that relentlessly throbbed.

His voice vibrated against me and I swear it was why he spoke. "Please won't work this time, Ice. Melting is a slow process."

I gasped as his finger pushed inside me at the same time as his mouth sucked on my clit. My butt left the bed as I pushed upward, the sheets clenched in my fists on either side of me. God, I never knew. I'd gotten myself off a few times, but it was always a struggle, and frustrating because as soon as the buried emotions began to surface, I stopped.

But now. Now, that everything had surfaced, it was like it didn't have to be a part of me anymore. I could push it away instead of letting it hold onto me.

"Fuck, you're wet."

"I've been wet for months."

He lifted his head and grinned. "Yeah?"

I nodded.

"Good. I've been hard for months." He pushed his finger into me slowly and I suspected he knew that was what I needed. I closed my eyes and moaned, legs clenching around him. "You good?"

And he was sweet. "I'm good."

He pushed in and out of me slowly and gently while his tongue and mouth danced across my pulsing sex.

"Oh, God. Oh, God," I cried, trying to keep myself from moving and yet wanting to get closer to him. I grabbed his hair and pulled, he groaned.

The pressure increased on my sex. Faster. Harder.

"Vincent," I screamed as it hit me and my body tensed then quivered under his fingers and tongue.

His fingers withdrew and his tongue licked every part of my sex before he climbed up on top of me. His hands slid up my arms and latched onto my wrists. Then he kissed me and I tasted myself on his lips, his tongue.

"Puddle."

"Hmmm?" he murmured against my lips. It was as if he didn't want to stop kissing me, so instead, he mumbled as he continued to roam my mouth.

"I'm melted."

That drew him away from kissing me, but it was only so he could meet my eyes. "I love your ice, too, Haven."

He leaned forward and kissed the top of my head before he climbed off the bed. My eyes widened and I sat up holding the sheet to my chest.

"Where are you going?"

"Shower." He walked toward the bathroom.

"Shower? Now?" Then I realized he wasn't going to have sex with me. "You're worried."

He paused, hand on the light switch. It clicked on, along with the fan making a low rumbling sound as it started up.

"Vincent." He didn't turn, but he also didn't disappear into the bathroom. "Vincent," I repeated. God, he was stubborn when he wanted to be. "I've had sex. I'm not scared of it and I'm not worried."

He abruptly turned, the familiar crease between his eyes. "You were raped, you mean. For years."

"Does that disgust you? Is that why you don't want to sleep with me?" Oh, that pissed him off. Vincent rarely got pissed, but he was now, with his hands curled into fists at his side and his jaw clenched.

"No. Fuck, no. Jesus, I want to be the one to erase all that. I want to be the one to give you what you deserve." He ran his trembling hand through his hair and lowered his head. "I couldn't bear it if I hurt you. If I saw that look in your eyes like when you screamed . . . Fuck, that would kill me."

I unfolded from the bed, let the sheet go and walked across the room toward him. "I'm not scared and I'm not worried. Vincent, you've already been inside me for months emotionally." I placed my hands on his chest, his heartbeat steady and strong beneath my palm. "Now, I want you inside me physically."

He reached for me, his arm around my waist, dragging me up against him before his mouth crushed mine. It was hard and yet warm and lazy at the same time. As if he was trying to be gentle, but parts of him refused to bend to that need.

My tongue slipped inside his mouth and I tasted him, the sweetness that I had craved. The love I'd been denied for most of my life. I finally felt it with everything there was between us.

He kissed my neck and I moaned, tilting my head back. Not long ago, I'd imagined him doing this. It was safe. I never felt that in my life until Vincent gave it to me.

"Okay?" I asked as he continued to kiss along the base of my neck.

"Okay." He drew back. "I haven't been with anyone and I'm clean, been checked. You're not on anything?"

I shook my head. I hadn't been since I escaped. "I was checked, too." Kat had taken me after I'd escaped.

"Get in bed." I did and he walked into the bathroom where I heard a drawer open and close. He came back out with a square package between his teeth, which he ripped open.

I watched as he undid his jeans and dragged them down his hard muscled thighs that had a spattering of fine hairs, just enough to be manly. I thought he was going slowly on purpose because Crisis had experience, lots of experience and there was no way it would normally take him this long to take off his pants and roll on a condom. He was either doing it for me so I had time to change my mind and run or it was the simple fact that Crisis was a stage junky and he liked attention. And right at that moment, he was getting it. I stared at him handling his cock in his one hand as it jutted out from his body. He jerked on it once and my breath caught in my throat.

His head was down; watching what he was doing, but I noticed a tiny smirk on his lips. He ran his hand up and down his cock several times before he slowly rolled on the condom.

By then, I was throbbing and ready for him again. Shit, I was ready for him again right after my first orgasm.

He stalked toward me then put one knee on the mattress and the springs squeaked. He straddled my waist, his hands sliding around to my back where he unhooked my bra and slipped it off.

"Lie back, sweetie."

I did. Pain was always associated with a cock. Pain and humiliation. But I also never gave those men my submission. They never had me; maybe physically, but I numbed out to them. They became the objects.

But Vincent was real and I wanted to feel him—every part of him. I reached between us wanting to feel the one thing that I'd always hated. I was a little disappointed he'd already put the condom on, but still it exuded power. And soon pleasure. I knew it. There was nothing in our way anymore.

My fingers touched the spattering of hairs that led down to his cock and he tensed above me, his mouth hovering above my right nipple. And then at the same time as my hand wrapped around him, he latched onto my nipple.

He swore beneath his breath with my breast in his hand, my nipple between his teeth, while I moaned at the swell of him in my palm. It jerked and I tightened my grip.

"Fuck, baby." He cupped my chin and kissed me, his other hand teasing my erect nipple, from pinching to caressing to a light-feathered touch. "Jesus. Never been like this. Never."

I slid my hand down further until I cupped his balls in my hand. I gently rolled them, my thumb caressing the delicate surface.

"Fuck. Stop." Crisis jerked upwards. "I'm going to come and I want to do it inside you."

I smiled and he reached between us, pulled my hand away. He grabbed his cock and settled it between my legs. "Going to ask one more time."

I lifted my hips toward him and looped my arm around his neck and dragged his mouth back to mine where I murmured. "Fuck me, Vincent."

His kiss deepened and then there was a slight pressure as the tip of his cock pressed into me. I closed my eyes, tilted my head back and relaxed my legs while he trickled kisses down the length of my neck. He pushed a little deeper before he stopped.

"Open your eyes." I did. "I want you looking at me the first time I sink inside you. I want you to know it's me."

"Okay," I whispered.

His hands weaved with mine above my head, him partially inside me and not moving. Our eyes locked on to one another. It was a moment of shifting pieces, like they were moving around inside both of us and we were waiting until they connected and found one another.

My lips parted. So did his.

Then he thrust and sank deeply, the pieces fitting together perfectly.

"Vincent."

"Say it again."

"Vincent."

He pulled out then pressed into me slowly, ground his hips and repeated. My legs wrapped around his hips and he sank further into me on his next thrust.

"Fuck, baby. I can't last long. I've waited so long for this." His face contorted as if he was concentrating and maybe in pain. I reached up, curved my arm around his neck and pulled him down, so his weight was on top of me.

"Harder," I said into his ear. "Faster."

He groaned as he moved up onto his hands on either side of me, then shoved harder, faster and his body kept hitting my sex when he thrust, sending waves of pleasure through me.

"Faster," I urged.

"Anything you want. Anything."

And that was it. All control vanished as our bodies slapped together time and again. The noise of our naked heated skin echoed through the room. He grabbed my hair and yanked to the side, before his mouth crashed into mine and that was what did it.

I came hard, again. My body stiffening and legs clenched around him.

He growled into my mouth as he came with me, his kiss bruising as he shoved one last time into me then stilled.

His cock throbbed inside me and our chests heaved, mouths still connected but barely moving. It was both of us unable to find the words to decipher what just happened between us.

He pushed stray strands of hair back from my face with the tip of his fingers. "You good?"

His brows were low over his eyes as if he was worried. "Perfect."

The crease disappeared and he grinned. "I lost it. I couldn't hold back and . . . I never want to hurt you, Haven."

No, Vincent had proven that to me that time and again, right from the day he found me in the rain storm. He built an *us,* whether either of us even knew it was happening. The monsters in the wind whirled around me, but they no longer had a threatening hold. It wouldn't be easy, but one day, they'd have no hold.

Crisis kissed me then stood, went into the bathroom and threw out the condom.

He came back and I watched him walk across the room. The ink covering both arms and up over his shoulders. He had one design down his side that I'd seen before weave into a large one on his lower back. Of course, he had the one on his butt that his mother had seen.

"Scoot," he said as he lifted one corner of the duvet.

I lifted up and he pulled the cover back. We crawled beneath and he reached for me right away, pulling me back against his chest. My butt pressed into his cock and I felt it jerk and harden.

"It's been cursing at me for months." He nibbled on my ear and shivers trickled across my skin like tiny firecrackers. "Probably laughing, too."

I secretly smiled because it was nice to know Crisis hadn't been with another woman all this time. "What's it saying now?"

His arms tightened around me, fingers splayed on my abdomen. "It's in love." I stiffened and he kissed the side of my neck. "I'm in love, baby. You're my best friend and I love every part of you."

Tears welled. Tears. I was annoyed that they did, but it was so powerful hearing those words from him, I had no control over my reaction. I swallowed. My throat was tight and I knew he had to feel my heart racing and pounding.

I shifted around because I wanted to look at him. I had to look at him when I said it. I faced him and his one hand settled on my hip, his leg thrown over top of mine.

I reached up and traced his lips and they parted before he sucked on one, making my sex clench. I slowly pulled my finger out of the heated wetness and replaced it with my mouth.

This time is was a seductive roaming of our mouths. No rush. A sweet ache being satisfied as we tasted what had been left behind from our urgency earlier.

I pulled back just enough so I could look at him. "I love you, too, Vincent."

Seeing the brilliant blue in his eyes fill with love for me was all I wanted, and then I kissed him again, but not just on the mouth—everywhere.

And it was a night of exploring one another as we left behind all the bad that had ended up bringing us together.

Chapter Twenty-Four

Crisis

I WOKE EXPECTING to find Haven's luscious body up against me. What I got was a pillow and cold sheets where she was supposed to be lying. I didn't like it. At all. It kind of pissed me off that she'd disappear after all that went down between us.

I heard the toilet flush then the tap turn on. She was still here. She hadn't run.

Fuck, I was being a girl.

I wasn't sure with the light of day what she'd do. But I should've known better. Haven was straightforward when she meant something. She may have buried shit, but not once had she ever bullshitted. Anything that passed her lips had been real.

And she fuckin' told me she loved me—Vincent Wesson.

I rolled over and stretched, the duvet slipping down to my waist. I rested one hand beneath my head and with the other lifted the duvet. "You hear that? She fuckin' loves us."

"Is this going to be a habit of yours? Talking to your cock," Haven asked from the bathroom doorway, the light still on and shining behind

233

her. God, she was a fuckin' angel.

I grinned and threw back the cover, so she could get a good look at it as it lengthened. I bent one leg then stroked my hand down the hardened shaft. "I'd prefer it if *you* talked to it. Maybe a lecture on . . . snow blowers."

Her brows rose. "Snow blowers?"

I tugged on my cock and her eyes darted to it. Okay, she looked interested, not scared. No matter what she said, there had to be parts of her that were damaged from what she experienced. "We could lie in bed all day and watch lectures on snow blowing."

"Lectures? What kind of lectures do they have on snow blowers?"

I was so hard that I had to stop playing with myself or I'd come in my hand. "You know on the internet. I'm sure we could find a tutorial."

She strolled toward the end of the bed and crawled between my legs. She wasn't smiling, but she did have a twinkle in her eyes which I fuckin' loved.

"I'm kind of a hands-on type of learner."

Christ, I loved this chick.

She fisted my cock and I groaned, closing my eyes, hand tightening around the edge of the pillow. "That's if you don't mind a few mistakes."

My eyes flashed open as her heated breath swept across the tip. "Fuck, no." I growled. "I'm all about learning from your mistakes. And practice makes perfect."

"Good," she murmured before her mouth closed around my cock.

"Jesus." She sucked, taking the length of me deep in her throat. I couldn't help it and jerked my hips and she gagged, but didn't withdraw.

I weaved my fingers through her hair and held tightly, helping her as she slid up and down, her hand on the base holding me firm and steady. My cock popped from her mouth and she looked up at me, her eyes glazed over with pleasure and her lips wet and glistening from my pre-cum.

"Any pointers?" Her hand started jerking me up and down like she'd seen me do.

I grunted, legs shaking as I tried to hold off longer. "Fuck no." My chest rose and fell in quick concessions as she continued to jerk me off while her other hand went beneath my balls and lifted.

"Do men like their balls played with?"

I didn't know about other men and I didn't want to know. All I knew was that I did. I liked Haven's hand on my balls handling them like precious jewels while her other hand fisted my cock like it was a bat.

"Baby, please."

She smiled then her mouth covered my cock and she did with her mouth what her hand was doing until I was thrusting my hips upward to meet her rhythm.

"Oh fuck. Fuck. Baby, I'm coming."

She didn't stop and I shot down her throat over and over again as she sucked every inch of me. When she raised her head, there were remnants of me on her chin and she wiped it with her finger then placed her finger in her mouth.

"Damn, that's hot. All of it. You're hot." I released her hair and stroked the side of her face with my knuckles. "You're made for me."

"I love you." She crawled up my body until she was snuggled into me, her head fitting in the crook of my arm, so I could kiss the top of her head. "I love you both."

"Huh?" I frowned. "You're talking about your brother while in bed with me after a blow job? Let's make it a rule. Ream stays out of bedroom."

She reached down between my legs and stroked my cock. "I'm talking about this. Since you talk to it like it's another person, I'm proclaiming my love for both of you."

I chuckled. "Yeah, we'd have an issue if you only loved one of us."

We lay around for another half-hour talking about nothing important, after I returned the favor with my tongue on her clit. Then our bliss was interrupted by Kite's knock on the door.

"You see Haven at all? She's not in her room and it doesn't look like she slept at home last night."

I kept my voice low. "I don't want to hide us, Haven, but I want to know you're ready for everyone to know."

Instead of answering me, she called out, "I'm fine, Kite."

"Good to hear," he replied without a second's hesitation. Fucker knew we were together. "Crisis, get your ass out of bed. We're going to Logan and Eme's in ten."

"Not going," I shouted.

"Like hell," Kite yelled back. "I show up without you, Logan will kick your ass."

"Yeah, right."

"You want to test him right now? He's already strung tight over the wedding."

I chuckled because this was a point of contention every time I saw Logan. He was constantly on the phone with contractors trying to get the house and stables finished because their wedding date was supposed to be in February at what I liked to call their 'fuck-nest' farm. If it wasn't done, no wedding.

"It's okay. I need to study for exams."

I'd never spent this much time with a single chick in my bed and I didn't want to leave. Fuck, the thought of leaving her for the day . . . well, I didn't like it. "Come with me."

She pulled back and perched on one elbow. "Everyone will be there."

"Yeah." I tucked a strand of hair behind her ear. "And it's not like we haven't known one another for a while, and shit, we already live together." I sat up and leaned over her until she collapsed back on the bed.

I was expecting a fight; her wanting to stay here and avoid the social scene like she'd always done. "Okay."

"You can study while we're recording," I continued.

"Okay."

"And if you need quiet, I'm sure Emily has a room you . . . you say okay?"

"Vincent,"—Fuck I loved when she said my name—"my brother—"

I kissed her forehead. "He's an overprotective stubborn dickhead, but he has his reasons and I get that. Maybe, he'll be happy I'm in your pants and watching out for you."

She snorted and it was adorable coming from Haven.

"What I was going to say was that my brother may not accept us being together. He's my twin and I love him more than anything, and he's my blood, my only family I have left, but I'll fight for us if I have to."

"Good to know because I wasn't planning on letting you go, anyway." I caressed her hair. "But blood doesn't define family, Haven. My parents are my family, yet there isn't a drop of their blood in me."

"You were adopted?"

"Yeah, when I was two." I rhythmically stroked her back. "My parents waited five years for a baby to come available. Don't know my real parents and . . . I don't care if I ever do. I have the best parents in the fuckin' world. Shit, you met my mom; you saw that. That's real, baby. That's family."

Her palm rested on my chest. "But what if your mother wanted you and—"

"My parents went through the right channels and my mother willingly gave me up. I'm okay with that. Known about it since I was old enough to understand and they've always been and always will be my mom and dad. Ream's my family and so is Logan, Kite, Kat, Emily, Matt, Deck, Georgie and you. There's no question what we'd do for one another—Anything. That's family and you need to realize that you're part of that now. Not just Ream, but all of us."

Kite's voice shouted through the door, "Two minutes."

I kissed Haven then tugged her out of bed. "Come on, we'll shower together to save time."

We didn't save time. I couldn't stop touching her glistening wet body. I ended up on my knees and we were a no-show.

But that wasn't why we were a no-show. It was because my phone vibrated with a text and there on the screen was a picture of Haven in her running outfit with a message below it.

She is a fucking whore.

Chapter Twenty-Five

Haven

I CAME OUT OF the washroom, toweling my hair, my sex still throbbing and heated from Vincent's mouth. He was dressed, pacing back and forth talking on his phone. And that crease between the eyes, it was there.

I picked up my clothes and opened the door to go back to my room when he grabbed me around the waist and dragged me back against him.

"We need to talk," he said, voice threaded with tension to match the stiffness in his body. He gently turned me around and put his finger under my chin, his thumb lightly stroking back and forth. It was calm, but what stormed in his eyes was not.

The shield of ice slammed down over me. "What's wrong?"

He saw it. He knew me too well to not see it, but he also didn't say anything about it. Which probably meant whatever he was worried about was not good.

"Got a text message." I knew where this was going. It was that girl. "It's a picture of you jogging."

SHATTERED BY YOU

Okay, that wasn't bad. Having a picture surface from the club would be bad. "Did I look okay?"

He didn't smirk. *Shit.*

"Could be a reporter got the shot of you and posted it online. With Roman jogging with us lately, it might have gained attention and they want to know who you are." His hand slid away from my chin and he sighed.

"You think that Tammy girl saw it and texted it to you."

He nodded. "That's best case scenario." Worst case was this chick was in Toronto now and took a picture of me jogging. "I forwarded it to Luke, and he's on his way here. Babe,"—his fingers tightened on my waist—"you should go to the farm."

I stiffened. "No."

"Babe."

"No. I've worked too hard for this. I never had this chance. I swore I'd do something with my life if I ever escaped. Now, I am. I can't walk away from it now because of some girl who thinks she's in love with you."

He stepped away from me and turned, running his hand through his hair. "Fuck. I know. I know." He paced back and forth then stopped, came to me and cupped my cheek. "I'm sorry. I thought it would just go away after a while. You don't need this."

I half-smiled. "No. But neither do you."

A loud knock sounded on the door. "Luke's here," Kite said. "Downstairs."

"Yeah, okay." Vincent kissed me sweetly and gently, before he opened the door. "Go get changed then meet us downstairs."

And I loved that about him. He wasn't going to keep me in the dark and give me tidbits of what he wanted or thought was safe for me to know. Vincent let me in just as much as I let him in.

Crisis

He had a steaming cup of coffee on the counter beside him that looked untouched. "We do nothing."

Luke wanted us to go about what we normally did. Roman stood with his arms crossed, leaning against the wall next to the TV. Kite was the only one who appeared relaxed as he waited for toast to pop up from the toaster. Usually, that was me; instead, I was reeling because this was the last thing Haven needed, some psycho bitch I'd fucked over a year ago being a pain in the ass.

Luke continued, "Haven goes to school. You work on the album. Everything stays the same except we have men on all of you."

"I'll go to school with her." No way was I leaving her.

"No." Luke shook his head. "You stay clear of Haven in public. If it's this Tammy girl and she's watching her, then seeing you with her will only make it worse." Fuck, he was right. "We need a hand on this. The police won't do anything. The picture and message wasn't a threat." He paused. "It doesn't fit. The messages on your phone are crude and sexual, her posts online are not. Don't think it's just about protecting anymore; we need someone to look into this more."

"Deck's men."

Luke gave an abrupt nod. "Can't get Deck, but got hold of Vic. He's flying in. He needs three days, though. He has the resources to deal with this while we do our job." Shield Security was just that, security.

The toast popped and I heard the creak of the stairs and saw Haven on her way down. I didn't hesitate as I walked over and slipped my hand in hers as soon as she reached the last stair, then we walked into the kitchen and I told her what was happening.

"Right now, she isn't much of a threat. But we need to be on top of it. We don't change your phone number. Let's see if she keeps texting and what." Luke picked up his mug and walked over to us. "You do not leave this condo without me." It was a direct order to Haven.

Her spine stiffened and she met Luke's fierce stare without flinching. She didn't like being ordered to do anything and I understood the reason why, and I hated the reason, but I loved that she was strong and didn't crumble under Luke.

"I want bullets for my gun."

My mouth dropped open. What the hell? There were no bullets in her gun? All this fuckin' time.

The corner of Luke's mouth twitched. "No." He took a sip of coffee and made a quiet snort as he looked over my shoulder to Roman. "Get her pepper spray."

Then he and Roman disappeared into the library.

I cupped the back of her neck and turned her toward me. "No bullets?"

She shrugged.

I laughed and she smiled. Then I dragged her—well, there wasn't much dragging because she was willing—upstairs and took her clothes off again. We had slow, lazy sex with her riding me until I flipped her over and made her wait. Once the hardness in her gray eyes slipped away again, I let her come around me. And it was sweet as fuckin' hell.

Haven

Crisis reached for my hand as we walked up the cobblestone path to Logan and Emily's house. Their German Shepherd, Tear, bounded toward us, his tail wagging as he woofed and greeted us one by one with his nose in butts and crotches.

Luke and Roman were with us, and, despite two more texts, both one words in capital letters BITCH and TEASE, which Vincent had shown me as we lay in bed the previous night, we decided it best to get out of the condo and the city for the day. I had studying to do, and the band had an album to produce. Ream also wanted to see me, so I went with them, making it the time to tell Ream about us.

The farm was stunning, a paved tree-lined driveway with paddocks for the horses on either side as far as the eye could see. The stone house was massive, with a wraparound porch and a gorgeous balcony that overlooked the property from the third floor. There were several work vans in front of a four-car garage, and I heard hammering coming from the back of the property.

Kite knocked on the door and before it opened, I felt Crisis' hand slip in mine.

I heard footsteps on the other side of the door and straightened my shoulders. Crisis and I were together and I'd protect that. My brother had accepted our friendship, but this was on another level, especially when there was the issue of the girl, Tammy, hovering.

Kite half-turned to me. "This,"—he nodded to Vincent and my hands linked—"I support and I know Logan will, too. Ream will"—he quirked the pierced brow—"after his initial shock."

Tear barreled past us as soon as the door opened. He grabbed a black motorcycle boot off a mat then skidded across the stone floors and disappeared around the corner. "Tear!" Logan shouted. But the dog was gone with Logan's boot.

It took all of a second before he registered Crisis' hand in mine. He shifted to the side, hand on the frame of the door, eyes widening for a brief second before a small grin emerged as he met my eyes.

"Good to see you, Haven." I was thankful he didn't say anything about the obvious change in Crisis and mine's relationship. "You want to watch us record? Or Emily's out in the barn overseeing the workmen." He chuckled. "You might be safer with us. She is on a rampage about the windows in the barn being put in wrong." He looked to Luke. "Don't worry, Darryl is with her." I was guessing Darryl was another of Shield Security.

"I'd like to watch the band," I replied. I'd never seen them live and I was a little excited to see Crisis and my brother rock their guitars.

He smiled. "Good."

We walked through the house to a staircase which led downstairs. "I think the song needs to slow down," Kite was saying to Logan as we walked through what I'd consider a guy's playroom with pool and foosball tables. "Sounds off, like we're rushing it."

Logan nodded as he opened a door. "Okay."

Crisis put his hand on the small of my back to guide me into the room. "I was thinking the first few chords should be no instruments. Like a ballad."

"Yeah. Let's try that," Kite agreed.

I stopped when I saw my brother leaned over, hand resting on the recording table, talking to some guy I didn't know. He glanced up and smiled at me, but it was soon lost to lowered brows when he saw my hand in Vincent's.

"Give us a minute, Dan," Ream said to the other guy.

The guy nodded and walked out a door on the other side of the room.

Logan and Kite remained on either side of us, neither saying anything, but ready for Ream's reaction.

"Vincent and I are together." Ream's eyes cut to Crisis, who remained quiet and still. I knew he'd speak up if I needed him to, but he was giving this to me. "I want you to be okay with this." I took a deep breath and Ream's gaze came back to me. "I need you to be," I corrected.

Ream's shoulders were tense and he'd crossed his arms over his chest, legs braced. I saw the uncertainty flicker across his face as he took in what I was telling him. Ream knew Crisis' history with girls and his overprotective nature was going to make it hard for him to accept this. He may have accepted us being friends, hanging out, even living together, but having a relationship was different.

What made this worse was the issue with Tammy, so Ream was not going to like this happening, especially right now.

His glare was directed at Crisis. "You're putting my sister in danger."

I stepped forward and put my hand on Ream's chest. His heart raced beneath my palm and it took him a second before he dragged his gaze from Crisis to look at me.

I took a deep breath before I spoke. I knew how to be strong. I'd done it for years, but that was a different strength. One where I had to do things in order to survive. Things I wasn't built to do, but forced to. Now, it was about finding my strength within my vulnerability and Ream needed to understand that no matter what stood in front of me, I wasn't running. I was living.

"Do you remember when we were kids and I was in the closet, scared the wind would take me away?" He sighed, then nodded. "It did Ream. It took me away from you and I lived in its hold for years."

His expression was pained as his lips pursed together.

I let my hand drop from his chest. "I've run from it ever since I escaped. It's been chasing me and I was scared of it catching me." Crisis moved even closer to me, his hands on my hips. He understood. "But now I don't have to run. I'm not scared of the wind or trying to fight against it. I let it in."

"But this chick—"

I interrupted him. "Yeah. It's bad timing. But I've lived with fear then numbness all my life. Now, I don't have to. Ream,"—the hardness in his face eased as I said his name—"I swore to never waste a second of my freedom. To live. To find some sort of normal."

"A stalker after your *boyfriend* isn't normal." Ream's eyes shot to Crisis.

"And neither is having a brother in a famous band. This is the normal we get and it could happen to you just as easily. From what I read, before Kat, you had your share of women, too."

Five seconds it took before it was like an overfilled balloon deflating as all the tension left him and he lowered his head, briefly closing his eyes. "I saw it," he said. "I was trying to ignore it." He looked at Crisis. "You're my brother and I love you. I also know the shit you've done." His arms dropped to his sides and he inhaled. "And that you like her—a lot."

"Love," Crisis corrected.

Ream stiffened. "Yeah. Maybe I saw that, too." He looked back at me. "And you?"

I leaned back into Crisis and his one arm curled around my waist. I loved that he was giving me this. He didn't fight with Ream or get angry; he stayed quiet and relaxed and let me have this. "I broke and he slid inside and found me. But he didn't take me. He waited until I took him." Crisis leaned over and kissed the top of my head. "So yeah, I love him."

Silence.

I knew the moment Ream let it go when his hands at his sides uncurled, and when he looked at Crisis there was acceptance. "You better fuckin' marry her."

"Ream," I scolded.

There was a look between the two men I loved as my eyes darted from my brother to Crisis. It was an understanding as both of them nodded.

"Okay, now that it's settled and no one is killing one another, let's get some work done." Logan slapped Crisis on the back.

We settled in. Well, the boys did as they went on the other side of the glass, and the guy Dan came out of what looked like an office and started sliding colorful levers up and down. Crisis sat me at a small table along the far wall, kissed me then said, "Study, babe. You need anything, tell Dan and he'll get me."

But I didn't study. I couldn't, not when they were playing the most heart-wrenching song I'd ever heard. It was almost haunting as Logan sang in his deep graveled voice, holding the microphone in his hand, eyes closed and the words filled with so much emotion.

On the chorus, they all sang, except Kite, and their voices came together in a perfect string of melody. It had been a long time since I heard my brother sing, but I easily picked his out amongst the others.

And Crisis . . . there was no question he was hot playing the guitar and singing. The energy in him filtered out through his fingers and vocal chords.

"Hold up, guys," Dan said.

The music dwindled to a stop. Crisis winked at me through the glass and I smiled back.

"It's too harsh," Kite said, turning to Logan. "It needs a softer sound for that part."

Logan nodded. I didn't hear anything more as the sound from the room cut off.

Crisis turned his back to the window and strode over to the drums.

I saw Kite's eyes dart to me then he pursed his lips together as if contemplating. Then all the guys were gathered around the drums talking.

Ream turned abruptly and stared at me. I had no idea what was going on until Dan turned on the sound again. "Yeah. Haunting. It's perfect," Crisis said. "Let me ask her." He lifted the guitar strap over his head and passed it off to Ream then came through the door.

"What's going on?" Dan asked.

"We'd like to change it up. Go talk to Logan for a sec."

I knew it was a hint to get out while Crisis talked to me. He strode the few feet toward me and it was a sexy swagger. He was thrumming with excitement and there was a sparkling glitter in his bright blue eyes as they locked on me.

"What?"

He didn't hesitate as he picked me up in his arms. I looped my arms around his neck and my ankles on the cusp of his lower back. He lowered his head and claimed my mouth, and it was claiming. Crisis was taking parts of me I didn't know existed.

He groaned underneath the hard kiss and his hands gripped my butt. I noticed he gradually moved us over to the side of the room where the guys couldn't see us from where they were standing. He pressed my back up against the wall as he continued to explore my lips with an intense need.

"Jesus. I'm addicted to you. Having you watch me while I play . . . it's like being handed the best fuckin' Christmas present ever." He smoothed back my hair and I slowly slid down his body until I was standing. "I didn't see any books open."

I frowned. "You're a distraction."

"I love that," he murmured as he kissed me again. "Since you're not studying, want to join us?"

My heartbeat picked up. "Meaning?"

"You trust me?" His hand cupped the back of my neck, thumb gently stroking back and forth. I nodded. "The song needs a softer tone behind Logan's. Not the whole song, but in parts." He leaned into me, his hard cock pressed into my abdomen. "Your brother being around is a pain in the ass. I want to drag you upstairs and fuck you so badly right now."

And now it was a lot more than my heartbeat racing. It was my blood rushing through my veins and the throbbing between my legs. The door opened and Crisis glanced over his shoulder at Dan, who shook his head grinning at us.

"You in, baby?"

Sing with Tear Asunder? Sing with my brother. And Crisis. "I don't know the words."

"Shit, neither does Logan. It's a new song Kite wrote. Don't worry about it. You'll learn it." He ran a finger over my red just-kissed lips. "I saw you that night, Haven. When you sang, there was a thrill inside you."

Because I was taken away to another place, the words flowing through me. Singing had always taken me away to another place. "Okay."

He growled, picked me up again and twirled me around. "Fuck yeah. My girl is going to sing." He slid me down his body, snagged my hand and slapped Dan on the shoulder as we walked by. "Wait until you hear her voice. Man, you're going to get hard." Then he scowled. "Fuck, that. You get hard for my girl, I'm kicking your ass."

There was no response or I didn't hear one because the door shut behind us. It all went down so fast and the guys took it seriously as they went over the song with me. It didn't take long to figure out my parts as I sat on a stool while Logan stood beside me. He looked completely non-threatening and at ease as he sang his part while mine drifted in and out as a soft undertone to his deep huskiness.

It was Emily walking into the studio several hours later that finally broke us up. When she saw me, her eyes widened then she smiled. She leaned over next to Dan and her voice echoed into the room. "Hi, Haven, boys, it's after nine. I ordered Thai and Tear is licking his chops so you might want to move it if you want to eat."

It was really cute the way Emily eyed Logan and he stared at her through the glass as if he was going to leap through the window and fuck her right in front of Dan. She winked at him, then left.

Logan reached for me, took my hand and squeezed. "That was

incredible. Thank you."

Crisis came up behind me, his hands on my hips, breath a warm breeze just below my ear. "Guess I need to feed my girl before I take her home and eat her out," he whispered.

"Shut the hell up. Seriously, she's my twin sister." Ream had just been walking by us with his guitar. He cuffed Crisis on the head. "I may accept this, but I'm not listening to your filthy mouth talk to her that way."

"Fuck, right—twins. Does that mean it's like I'm fucking you, too? Cause that's just—"

Ream shoved him in the shoulder and his hands left me as he staggered back. Crisis laughed and Ream grunted, shaking his head.

I laughed and Ream's eyes cut to me. Then he moved in and pulled me off the stool into a hug. I was stiff for a second before I let go and wrapped my arms around my brother like I used to.

"I've been waiting to hear that sound since you were four years old," he whispered. What? "That was the last time I heard you laugh." He hesitated. "Thank you." But it wasn't me he thanked; it was Crisis who came up beside us.

Chapter Twenty-Six

Crisis

I TOSSED MY PHONE aside but wanted to throw it against the wall, but I couldn't because Haven was with me and I needed to be cool, not pissed right the fuck off.

I grabbed Haven around the waist as she sat on the end of the bed putting her socks on. I pulled her backwards on top of me and kissed her neck.

She didn't squeal or struggle, which was fuckin' nice; instead, she curled her hand around my neck and brought her lips to mine and kissed me.

"Who was on the phone?" she asked.

I hated to tell her. It had been two days since Logan's and it had been quiet and sweet. We didn't go out jogging in the mornings; instead, she ran on the treadmill and I worked the weights, and yeah I couldn't keep my hands off her after seeing her panting and sweating. Both days we ended up on the bench naked.

"Don't know for sure."

She sat up. "But you think it was Tammy?" There was a hesitation with a lowering of her brows as if she was contemplating something. Then she did. "What did she say?"

I'd hung up on her and the most I said was hello. "She missed seeing us jogging." She'd been about to say something else and I did the exact opposite as to what Luke asked and hung up. But fuck, I didn't want to hear her voice. I didn't recognize it, but the reality was there hadn't been much talking when I'd fucked Tammy.

She reached up and cupped the back of my neck, her fingers weaving in my hair. Jesus, I wanted to taste her again, slip inside her and have her ride me. The thought of her on top of me, her breasts in my hands, her eyes closed, head tilted back, lips slightly parted . . . fuck, I hated that she had exams to go write.

"I'll be fine. Luke is with me." She tugged on my neck and I leaned down and kissed her. It was slow and hard. Feeling her tongue slip into my mouth was fuckin' heaven. "I'm worried about you."

Ah, fuck that was cute. She was concerned about me and that right there was what made her fuckin' special. She'd been through hell, lost her child, nothing in the world worse than that, yet she was worried about me. Roman and I were meeting up with Vic at the Unyielding Riot office. He was starting an investigation on Tammy and needed everything I could remember about her.

"Love you, Ice." I kissed her again and she melted beneath me, her mouth pliable and sweet. I groaned, pulling back. "Have to get ready. But babe,"—I slipped my hand under her chin—"be careful today."

Fuck, I didn't want to leave her. She was strong and tough as hell, but parts of her had cracked and I was afraid of her building up that shield of ice again.

She ran her finger over the crease between my eyes. "I have pepper spray, a bodyguard and a gun."

"With no bullets." She knew how to look after herself. Jesus, I was becoming Ream, worrying about leaving her. I kissed her one last time then hopped into the shower.

When I came out, Haven was gone. I went downstairs and Kite was sipping his coffee, leaning against the counter.

"You want me to come?"

"No." He hadn't met Tammy and I felt better knowing he was around if I wasn't back by the time Haven finished her exam. I snagged his coffee and took a sip. Kite didn't say anything; I'd been doing it for years. "After her exams, I want to take her away. Somewhere hot."

Kite's pierced brow rose. "You aren't sneaking off to get married, are you?"

"No. Jesus, Kite. It's been a week."

"No, it's been months. You guys may not have been fucking, but you were together long before you whipped out your cock."

He was right. I was Haven's a long time ago. "Then maybe she'll marry me sooner rather than later. I was thinking . . ." Kite huffed, but I ignored him. "Vegas. None of this bullshit Logan is going through."

Kite burst out laughing. "Yeah, you try and do that, Kat and Emily will be all over you and not in a good way. Not to mention how pissed Ream would be for doing a Vegas wedding with his sister like some drunken mistake. And your mom . . ." Yeah, fuck, my mom, " . . . she'd be worse than all of them put together."

"Haven wouldn't want a big wedding. She's not like that and I'm good with whatever she wants." I was even a little surprised at myself because a big event like me getting married would be a huge media draw and, normally, I'd be all over that, but I had no intention of sharing a special day with strangers. Shit, I was thinking about getting married. No, not thinking. I was damn sure I was. I just needed to get Haven on the same page.

Kite grinned and raised his mug. "Morning, Haven."

I swung around and saw her standing by the library door, Luke behind her. And from her frown, she'd heard at least part of our conversation. I stalked toward her and it was a stalk because I wouldn't allow her to escape even if she wanted to.

I looped my arm around her waist and kissed her neck. "I thought you left."

"Luke wanted to go over a couple things."

"So, you heard?"

"Most."

"Good." I was pushing my luck here because Haven had yet to wrap her arms around me. I pulled back so I could look at her. "Can't wait to call you my wife while tasting your pussy." A flicker of a smile and her hand rested on my hip. I lowered my voice and came in closer so my lips just grazed her ear. "And, baby, tonight, we are having a ceremony for my cock and your pussy."

"Do I get to dress him in a tux? Maybe with chocolate and vanilla ice cream"

Jesus, it was fuckin' nice she played along with me. "Sure. As long as I can put yours in pink cotton candy."

She stood on her tiptoes and kissed me.

The buzzer went off on the intercom and the doorman announced that Roman had arrived. I kissed her one more time then went to meet Vic and end this shit.

Chapter Twenty-Seven

Haven

I WALKED OUT OF my Sociology 101 exam, Luke beside me. We passed two girls in the hall who looked at me with a sort of sneer, then giggled to themselves. I stiffened, frowning as I walked by. I looked over my shoulder at them and they laughed again.

Luke's hand settled on the small of my back. "You know them?"

"No."

He stiffened, moving in closer to me while he put his phone to his ear.

"Haven," Dillon called as he came out of the classroom, Kevin with him. "Hey." He nodded to Luke who didn't nod back. It was nothing unusual for me to be with a bodyguard as Roman had been with me last week, but as far as everyone knew, it was just because of me being Ream's sister. "Easy exam." I nodded. "So, I guess everyone knows now. Maybe they can come to the party Friday night. That would be wicked."

I glanced at him. "Knows?"

He shrugged. "Yeah, that Ream has a twin sister. And the other crap, hey no judgement here."

My breath locked in my throat and I stopped walking. "Judgement?"

"Yeah, that you stripped." Bile rose in my throat and I swallowed several times.

Dillon took out his phone and typed something, then scrolled. He held it out to me, but Luke intercepted and took the phone while he already had his cell to his ear, although he wasn't saying anything.

"Let me see, Luke."

"No," Luke said abruptly while he scanned it quickly. "We need to leave."

"I have another exam."

"And you can take a make-up." He passed the phone back to Dillon who was looking from me to Luke. I snatched his phone before he put it away and peered at the words.

And there it was in big bold letters. 'TWIN SISTER OF TEAR ASUNDER'S, REAM DEDRICK, STRIPPED IN A CLUB RECENTLY SHUT DOWN FOR UNDERAGE PROSTITUTION.'

Oh, God.

It was as if a cold wave crashed into me and I was being dragged across the bottom, the sand scratching my skin as I struggled to breathe. But I wasn't struggling. I froze and let the ocean of emotions take me and do what they wanted.

"Haven." A hand latched onto my arm, but I barely noticed as I stared at the screen. "We need to leave. Now." I wanted to throw up. How? Who knew that?

Oh, God, Ream was going to be dragged through the mud along with me. And Vincent . . . I knew he'd accepted my past, but to have it publicised was another matter. This was what I'd dreaded, what I'd tried to protect them from.

I had to find my numbness. I needed that back.

"Haven. Move it," Luke ordered and it was then I noticed he was tugging on my arm. Dillon grabbed his phone from me.

Kevin reached for Luke but before he touched him Luke spun around. It took nothing more than a look and Kevin let him go. "Listen, ummm . . . well, you should know . . ."

"Spit it the fuck out before I rip it from your throat," Luke shouted. A few students passing-by gasped and darted away.

"This hot chick was asking about Haven."

Luke's entire body stiffened and if he wasn't already scary, he was now and Kevin paled. "What? When?"

"She came up to me coming out of sociology." He looked at me. "Crisis was . . . well, that was when he came to class." And kissed me outside of the class. "She waited until I left the building then asked me when our exam was scheduled for." Probably because Roman had been with us.

"And you didn't think that was odd?" Luke barely had control over his tone.

Kevin glanced at me. "Well, she said she was an old friend and had a surprise for you after the exam."

"Jesus Christ. Stupid." Luke grabbed my arm. "Next time some strange chick asks about a friend of yours, use your brains and not your cock."

Luke ushered me out of the building and into what was this crazy girl's surprise—a fray of reporters. "Fuck." He moved his arm to go around my shoulders and pushed through the horde of people shoving microphones in my face while cameras flashed.

How did this happen? Who would do this? Why? Luke kept me close, his hand on my head, keeping it hidden from the camera as we ran to where he always left the car. Kite was there, and as soon as Luke pressed the unlock button, Kite opened the door and while Luke ran around to the front, Kite shielded me from the reporters as I jumped in then dove in after me.

"How the hell did they know where you were?" Luke shouted as he took off. I noticed he didn't go too fast to draw attention to us, but he wasn't following the speed limit either.

"Jolie sent all of us the article ten minutes ago. I tried calling, but your phones were off."

"In her exam," Luke stated.

"Crisis, Roman and Vic are meeting us at the condo."

"No. Call them back. We head to the farm."

Kite got on the phone and I sat looking out the window as Luke navigated traffic toward the highway.

I glanced up and met Luke's eyes in the rear-view mirror; they were hard and unflinching.

"Tammy doesn't fit any of this," he said. "How did she find the story on you? No one knows you're Ream's sister except your friends and us." And my friends didn't know anything about the club. "Even if she did get that out of Kevin. Tammy may have seen you with Crisis and this is escalating, but the story about you stripping . . . that doesn't add up. Not a chance she can know about that."

Kite held out his phone to me. "Crisis."

I took it and noticed my hand trembled. Shit.

"Baby? You okay?"

I loved hearing his voice. It was like being handed a warm wool blanket to curl up with in front of a crackling fire. "Oh, God, I'm sorry—" I was cut off by Luke's shout.

"What the hell?" Luke slammed on the brakes and the tires squealed just before a loud bang as a large truck plowed into the side of the car, sending us spinning out of control.

"Haven!" I heard Crisis shout as I screamed, dropping the phone.

Chapter Twenty-Eight

Haven

VIOLENTLY ROLLING AGAIN and again, my head whipped from side to side making the seatbelt cut into my shoulder and waist. All I heard was metal being crushed under the impact until finally the car stopped rolling.

I moaned, my hand going to my temple where I touched the warm blood. My body felt as if it had been hit with a baseball bat and my neck muscles were strained from the whiplash.

Kite. Luke.

I opened my eyes and it took a second before I was able to focus and saw Kite with his head hanging forward, blood trailing down his forehead over his silver piercing then into his eye.

"Kite," I shouted.

His belt held him in place, but his eyes were closed. I heard a tire still spinning as it rumbled around and around and a loud swoosh like—

Water.

I looked out the window next to me. Water rushed by us, splashing the side windows that weren't yet submerged.

Oh, my God. We were in the Don River. I couldn't swim.

I didn't know how deep it was, but water leaked in through the cracked rear window that was completely submerged. We were at an angle, the front of the car above water, but I didn't know for how long.

I unsnapped my seatbelt after several tries then crawled through bent wreckage toward Kite.

Fuck. "Kite," I yelled, grabbing his arms that hung limply over his head. "Kite, we have to get out of here." Blood dribbled from the corner of his mouth and there was more on the side of his head.

"Oh, God, Kite. Kite." I shook his shoulders. "Damn it." I leveraged myself against the seat then kicked at the side window that was half-above water level. That was our way out. If I could get us on top of the car maybe we'd have a chance until help came.

I kicked and kicked at it, but it was like kicking a cement wall. Nothing. *Shit. Shit.*

There was no way I'd be able to open the doors with the water.

The only way was to pull Kite between the front seats, through the front crumpled windshield and onto the hood of the car. But if I kicked out the rest of the windshield, the spray of water might flood us. And even if I could get us all out, I couldn't swim to shore. I couldn't save any of us.

"Luke." His airbag had deployed and was covering half of him. "Luke." I crawled to him and put my hand on his throat. A pulse. I pushed the air bag out of the way and undid his seatbelt. His body slumped forward onto the steering wheel.

"Damn it, Luke. I need your help." I smacked his face and it wasn't gentle. "We have to get out. Wake up." He moaned and I saw his eyes move behind his lids.

A low moan again, but this time, it was the car as it started to slide. The river was going to push us downstream. The car had to be stuck on something; that was why we weren't completely submerged.

Every crackle and sound of metal crinkling made my heart jump, knowing that any second, we could all drown in a flooded car. I looked back at Kite. He was on his side on the backseat, a fountain of muddy water leaking at a fast rate through the back window onto his face. .

"No." I scrambled back to him and pulled him forward between the seats so his head rested on my thighs. "Come on, damn it." I put my arms beneath his shoulders and started pulling him to the front. The roof was caved in, making the process more difficult, but I slid back inch by inch, the water sloshing all around us.

I heard a loud cracking sound and water that had been splashing up onto the hood of the car now filtered in through the front windshield faster. I pulled harder on Kite. It wasn't good enough.

Water hit my face as I managed to get his shoulders past the two front seats. I spit and shook my head, trying to see through the constant spray.

"What happ . . ." Luke's eyes flicked open.

"Luke." I was crouched on the seat with Kite's upper body at an angle laying on my lap, my arm around his chest as I used my other hand to pull us closer to the front.

"Shit." He squeezed his eyes shut and shook his head, water sprinkling from his wet hair. "Where the fuck?" I saw the moment all of it came flooding back to him and he reacted. He pushed the airbag out of the way, and did a quick assessment of the car and the situation.

"Car is perched on a rock. Only reason the front isn't under water. The moment we let the water in, it will throw the weight off and we're going under."

I nodded, knowing what that meant. We had seconds.

"We get onto the hood of the car and jump clear of it. I got Kite. Don't stop. You hear me. Swim to shore. We'll be right behind you."

I heard sirens in the distance, but it would take them too long to get down the ravine to reach us. Luke heard them, too, as he raised his head, and our eyes met. We both knew we didn't have time to wait for a rescue. We got out ourselves, or died trying.

"I can't swim."

He paused a second then nodded. "Okay." He looked down at himself then undid his belt and yanked it through the loops. "Hold onto this. You climb out first, I'll follow then grab Kite. Don't let go of the belt. Ready?" he asked.

"Yeah." I had to be. We had no choice and I wasn't dying in a filthy river. I wasn't dying, period. None of us were.

I slipped out from under Kite and Luke wrapped the opposite end of the belt around his hand. "On three," Luke said and braced his foot against the windshield. I glanced at Kite then lifted so my feet reached the front windshield.

Luke gave an abrupt nod. "Two. Three."

We both kicked and the windshield crumpled. I felt the car's weight shifting as the spray of water rushed in and began to pool at the back of the car.

I climbed out onto the hood, having to let go of the belt for a second as it wasn't long enough. I turned around on my stomach and grabbed the belt again.

Luke climbed out then reached back inside for Kite. I did the same and we both pulled Kite onto the hood with us.

The car began to slide down the rock.

"Whatever you do, don't let go of the belt."

The car creaked and groaned, the sound a screeching as metal scraped rock. We crawled off the side of the car into the freezing cold water and the pressure of the river tried to pull me away from Luke and I started to sink.

Just before my head went beneath the surface, I saw the car slide the rest of the way off the rock then disappear beneath the surface.

I flailed my arms as I slipped into the darkness of the water. My grasp on the belt was slipping as I tried to keep from going under. My hand hit something and I let go of the belt to make a grab for it, thinking it was Luke's shirt, but whatever it was sank with me.

I realized it wasn't Luke, it was my bag. Fingers latched onto my arm and with a hard yank, I was pulled like a slingshot to the surface, the strap of my bag around the crook of my arm.

"I told you. Don't let go of the fuckin' belt," Luke shouted. "Hold onto my neck."

I did.

Then on his side and using one arm, he swam us to shore.

There were shouts and sirens, and people traversing down the ravine toward us. A fireman lifted me out and another went for Kite. Luke got out himself then made the few steps toward me. The fireman took his coat off and placed it over the top of my shoulders as I sat on the back of my heels shivering and breathing hard.

"Kite." I tried to get up but the fireman put his hand on my shoulder.

"Miss. You need to stay still. Paramedics are on their way."

Luke brushed my soaking wet hair back from my face and looked at the graze on my temple. After his gentle assessment, his eyes hardened. "Next time, I tell you to do something, you need to do it. No matter what."

I met his eyes unflinching, but I couldn't stop my bottom lip from quivering from the cold.

He stared at me for a minute, but it was so intense that it felt like two days. I didn't falter as I stared back. Then I saw it . . . the softness and concern. He'd been worried when I let go of the belt. The river could've swept me away and I'd have drowned.

"Okay."

He nodded then we both went to Kite, who was being lifted onto a stretcher.

As I stood shivering beside Luke, Kite unconscious with paramedics around him, I realized Crisis was right; we were family and we looked out for one another. I'd never had anyone since I was sixteen, but now I'd do anything for them.

And right then, I knew who I was.

Chapter Twenty-Nine

Haven

I SAT IN the waiting room in a hospital gown, my bag at my feet, a bandage on my temple, and my head pounding as I waited for news about Kite. I hated it here. I hated hospitals, but I wasn't scared. I was more concerned about Kite.

The ambulance had taken him from the scene of the crash and despite telling them I was fine, just cold, they insisted I go in an ambulance, too. And Luke refused to leave my side, so he went with me.

A nurse cleaned me up and once I was out of my wet clothes, the shivering stopped. Luke waited outside my door for me, but the second the nurse left, he came into my room and I was grateful for that. I didn't ever want to be alone in a hospital again.

"Kite?"

"Don't know anything yet. Taking him for an MRI. Still unconscious."

I swallowed and nodded, but everything in me was shutting down. I felt the compartments slamming shut one by one. "Crisis? Did you tell him? My brother?"

"On their way."

I stood. I hated these rooms. It was where Olaf had found me. I'd been all alone in a room just like this and so out of it, I could do nothing about it. Now I had Luke and still my gun. It may not have bullets, but it was my protection. "Can we stay in the waiting room?"

Luke walked to the door and opened it. "Will piss off the nurses." He shrugged. "But yeah, fine with me."

Two uniformed cops were in the waiting room. "Go sit. I need to talk to them."

I didn't sit; instead, I walked over to the window and parted the curtain. I was still reeling from what happened. The truck hit us out of nowhere. I didn't even see it coming and, suddenly, everything was out of control.

I looked over at Luke who shook hands with the cops like they were friends. He talked to them while they took notes and a few times, they glanced over at me. I stared back out the window, the sun sinking fast behind the buildings.

Luke came up beside me and I glanced at him, still in soaking wet clothes, yet it was as if he didn't even notice. They'd given him a towel when he refused to leave me and his hair was almost dry now. He'd taken off his jacket and was in a black dress shirt.

He didn't look at me as he spoke. "You kept your shit together. I'm standing here because you did. Kite's alive because you did." He gave a nod. I knew it was his way of saying thank you.

"The accident. Was it an accident?"

"Don't know that yet."

"But you saw it." I placed my hands on the window sill.

"Yeah, I saw it before it hit." He tagged my arm. "Go sit. You look like crap."

He wasn't going to tell me and I knew he was right. I had to look like hell, because I felt like hell, but I couldn't sit right now. Every breath hurt from where the seatbelt dug into my chest, but it was nothing compared to what Kite was going through.

Luke hesitated a second while he contemplated something, and my guess was whether to make me sit down. He decided against it as he walked to the nurses' station and used their phone.

I closed my eyes and rested my forehead against the cool glass window. That was when I felt him. I didn't have to open my eyes to know he was here. It was a magnetic feeling in my body knowing his eyes were on me.

My heart raced, blood rushed through my veins and my skin heated. I wanted to keep the cold all around me so it hurt less, but I couldn't. Not with him.

I straightened and opened my tear-filled eyes.

Then I turned and he was a few feet away from me, that worried crease accentuated between his eyes. "Jesus, babe." His voice caught on the word babe as he reached for me, then wrapped his heat and strength around me. He kissed the top of my head, lips lingering longer than usual as if he needed to reinforce that I was there. That he was holding me.

And damn it, the ice melted and I sagged against him, letting the tears fall.

It was several minutes before he pulled back, his eyes taking in the bandage on my temple and my hospital gown. "Fuck." He wiped the tears away with the pad of his thumb. "Never been so scared in my life."

"I'm doing that a lot to you."

He huffed and pulled me in close again so my cheek was pressed against his chest. "I heard you scream . . . fuck. We didn't know what happened. Where you were . . . we stopped the car and kept calling all your cells until Luke finally called Roman from the hospital."

"Kite . . . he hit his head pretty badly. The doctor says there's swelling."

"Yeah. I heard." He cupped my chin then leaned forward and kissed me. Lowering his voice, he said, "I nearly lost you." His voice broke and he held me tighter. It hurt like hell, but I didn't complain. Not as long as it was his arms around me.

Ream, Kat, Emily and Logan arrived ten minutes later. My brother strode in like a furious bull, but the second he saw me, it was like all the tension disintegrated and his shoulders sagged as he rushed toward me. It was the first time he wasn't cautious about touching me as he dragged me from Crisis and pulled me into a hug.

"Fuck. I got the call from Luke . . . if anything happened to you again . . ." His voice trailed off like he couldn't even say the words.

"I'm sorry."

His mouth dropped open and eyes widened. "Sorry? For what?"

"The story. What I did . . . it will be all over the media and it will look bad—"

"Stop." He cupped my cheek, his eyes softening, and for a second, I let that little girl that I used to be in, as her brother sang to her in the closet. "I don't give a shit what anyone says. None of us do." He looked at Crisis who remained with his hand in mine. "We've been together this long because no matter what happens, we stick together."

"What if they find out about Gerard—"

"Haven. We were sixteen living with a drug dealer who is dead because of the shit he did. That isn't touching you or me. We defended ourselves. We survived. And whatever happens with this story and what is dug up on you and me, we'll deal with it." I closed my eyes and took a deep breath. I felt like I'd been holding it since Dillon showed me the article. "We have amazing fans, sis. They support us. And they'll support you and see the truth no matter how the media spins it."

Emily and Kat came over and hugged me. Kat passed me a pair of jeans and a sweater. "We heard your clothes were wet." Logan came over and kissed my forehead and Roman squeezed my shoulder.

Kat and Emily went with me to the washroom so I could put on the clothes. Clothes, that still had the tags on them and were two sizes too big, but much better than a hospital gown, and I was able to take my gun out of the bag and put it in the pocket of the hooded sweatshirt. I was trying to be strong, but there were parts of me that were scared, that needed the safety of the gun which ended the nightmare for me.

When we came out, a doctor approached the group of us.

"Killian Kane's family?"

We all turned toward the doctor standing with a file in his hand looking at us.

"Yes." Logan, Ream and Crisis said.

Chapter Thirty

Haven

ILLIAN KANE? I hadn't known his real name, no one ever
mentioned it—ever. When I looked at Emily and Kat, both of
them had raised brows and wide eyes. I didn't expect to know
his last name or his real first name, but I thought Emily and Kat would
have. Obviously, they hadn't.

"The swelling has eased," the doctor said in a low voice. "Vitals
are good and we don't expect any complications."

"When can we see him?" Logan asked.

He frowned as he looked at the group of us. "Family only."

"We're all family," Logan said.

"And we all want to see him," Kat said, standing in front of Ream
while his hands rested on her hips.

The doctor pursed his lips together then gave an abrupt nod. "I can
allow one of you for now. And briefly." He didn't wait for us to decide
who should be the one to go and started down the hall.

I thought it would be Crisis, but there was no discussion as Logan
stepped forward and followed the doctor. Crisis pulled me over to a

chair, sat, then tugged me onto his lap. His brows rose when his arm touched the hard metal in my pocket.

"It didn't drown?"

I bit my lower lip. "Nearly." I knew he didn't like that I had it, but he also now knew that it was harmless. In a way, my gun was like a kid refusing to be parted from her teddy bear. The gun was my badass teddy bear.

"Why Logan?" I asked.

"When Logan moved here, Kite and him became friends. Some piss-ants in high school from Kite's old band went to beat him up. Logan stepped up and the two of them took them down. Been close ever since." Crisis lowered his voice. "Kite was the only one who knew Logan's real name for a while. Shit, and Deck, he fuckin' knew no doubt." Before I could say anything, he said, "Yeah, he knows Ream's past too and most of yours, I suspect."

Yeah, he did. He knew about Olaf and the club. What I hoped was that they found the girls, at least the ones who wanted to be helped. "I want to know."

"About?" Crisis ran his finger across the back of my neck and gently pushed my hair over my right shoulder.

"I want to know if they found the girls. I told Vic a while ago not to call me again about the club, but now . . . I want to know if they helped them."

"Olaf wouldn't be dead if Vic hadn't gotten what he needed from him. It might take time, but he'll find the girls."

"And the men, too?" The men who had fucked me; had their hands on me.

"They'd leave some of that to the police, but yeah."

Some of the tension eased from my body and I settled back against him, soaking in his comforting warmth.

He clasped his hand in mine and kissed my cheek. "Babe?" I tilted my head, which was resting on his shoulder to look up at him and he leaned forward and kissed me. It was a deep, intense kiss and I melted into him, my hands slipping into his hair as I angled my head and moaned under his mouth.

Fifteen minutes later, Logan returned and we all gathered around him. His voice said it all. It broke when he told us about Kite. He was trying to keep it together for the rest of us and I imagined it would've been devastating seeing his best friend with tubes and machines hooked up to him.

"He'll pull through," Logan finally said with a nod. He sounded as if he was trying to convince himself by saying it aloud. His eyes went past us toward the entrance of the waiting room.

Every one of us turned and I heard Kat and Emily both whisper, "Vic."

Vic I'd never met and he wasn't just a guy. He was a tall, built machine who currently wore a fierce scowl with narrowed dark eyes that matched his dark skin. He wore black cargo pants with combat boots and a vest. I knew what was hidden in all the pockets and behind the vest, weapons. I suspected if a cop took a look at him, they'd know, too, but I was betting they wouldn't touch him. Not only was the guy super intimidating, but there was no question he was one of Deck's men. And Deck's men weren't touched by the cops.

This was the guy who'd killed Olaf. Who extracted information before he'd killed him. And I knew whatever he did to Olaf wasn't a friendly chat.

Luke and Roman walked over to him and spoke, but Vic's eyes were on me. I stiffened. Crisis did, too. Luke was still talking, and scary new guy didn't even look like he was paying attention as he stared at me.

I put my hand on the cold hard metal of my gun sitting in my pocket. When they made their way toward us, I raised my chin because no matter how I looked or felt, I wanted to appear unaffected.

Crisis stood with his arm around my waist.

"Haven." He didn't offer his hand, which wasn't really surprising. I realized now that he was closer that he had beautiful russet-color skin and defined features with thick plush lips.

Vic held up the picture. "Luke said a Kevin Delaney spoke to a girl about you."

I nodded.

"Fuck," Crisis muttered next to my ear.

Vic put the photo back into his vest pocket. His tone hardened. "He's in custody."

Ream was beside us, as was everyone else.

Logan questioned, "It's not illegal for him to spill info to some chick."

Vic kept his eyes on me. "Not police. He's in my custody."

Oh, shit.

"He saw whoever did this. Whoever spread the story about you and informed the reporters." And I suspected he'd get them anyway he could.

Crisis' fingers dug into my hip, his body was tense. When I glanced up at him, I saw the muscles in his jaw throbbing and his eyes lost that easy casual laughter. They were hard and narrowed.

I knew he wouldn't explode or go on a rampage. He was angry that Kevin, a guy who had gone to karaoke with us, who ate lunch with me, had sold information about me. But, the steadiness in Crisis was still there and he'd be the rock I needed him to be just like when I'd told him all the bad shit that had happened to me.

"Police are still investigating the crash, but the truck that hit you didn't stay at the scene and several witnesses claimed there was no license plate, and they saw one person in the car. Disguised, but three people swear it was a woman."

"It's that fuckin' chick," Ream shouted.

Vic shifted his weight and a dried clump of mud fell off the bottom of one of his combat boots. "We'll start with Kevin. We'll know within the hour if it was Tammy."

Crisis spoke, "And if it's not?"

"Don't think it is. I reviewed her profile and everything you've given me. Her posts online and the text messages don't match. She's infatuated, but nonthreatening. The texts are crude and are directed toward Haven. Jealousy. Revenge."

"But there is nothing to be jealous of," I said.

"You're beautiful and dating a rock star," Vic stated.

"That's not enough to . . ." I shut up because Vic wasn't done and despite my ability to encase myself in ice, he was a guy who could flick his baby finger and make it shatter.

It was the first time I saw Vic's expression change. The corners of his mouth drew down to match his lowered brows as he met my eyes, then he moved in and completely surprised me as he ran his hand over the top of my head. It was a brief show of affection before he turned his attention back to Luke. "They can wait here until Kite's condition improves, then lock down at the farm."

Luke nodded then Vic turned and left. There was no good-bye or nod, nothing. He just strode out the hospital doors.

Chapter Thirty-One

Haven

THE DOCTOR GAVE us a report two hours later. Kite was awake and going to be okay. Crisis, Ream and Logan went to see him with Luke accompanying them. Roman stayed with Emily, Kat and me in the waiting room.

When I looked out the window this time, there were hundreds of people outside. Bouquets of flowers littered the area with lit candles, their flames dancing in the light breeze. I stared, stunned at the sight.

"Fans," Emily said, coming up beside me. "News of an accident travels fast when you're in a popular rock band."

God, my brother was right. They had good fans, people who cared. It was heart-warming to know they were here showing their support for Kite. For the band.

"Jolie's on her way." The publicist who Crisis had talked about. "Logan will make a statement. Let them know how Kite's doing."

"And about me," I said it more to myself than to her because they would have to say something about the story.

"Don't know," Emily said, then put her hand on my arm. "I know you must feel . . . invaded, especially after everything you've been through. But these men, *our* men, they will do anything to protect us." I met her eyes and there was no pity, instead a solid strength and resolve. "Anything."

"Are any of you Haven?" a nurse called from the nursing station, holding up a phone as she looked at Kat, Emily and I. "Phone call."

Roman straightened, pushing away from the wall he'd been leaning against and went to the nurse and held his hand out for the phone. She didn't want to give it to him at first, but quickly gave in when he whispered something to her and her face blanched.

I walked over and stood beside him.

Roman wasn't nice as he said abruptly, "Who is it?" He paused, listened then handed the phone to me. "Dana, she says she saw the news about Kite and has been trying your cell. Found out they brought Kite here."

My cell had fallen out of my back jeans pocket and was most likely at the bottom of the Don River. I took the phone and Roman walked back to stand by the door.

"Dana? How did you know I was here?"

"Actually, it's Lily."

Lily? Who the hell was . . . my grip tightened on the phone. The girl at the condo with Lena? The brunette? The night I broke down.

"Don't do or say anything. Keep your eyes forward and smile nicely at the nurse. I know you can smile now, Haven. I've seen you smile at him while jogging." A cold wave descended on me hearing the venom in her tone. Jogging. She'd seen me running with Crisis. This was the girl who'd been sending messages to Crisis. Not Tammy.

"How did you get his cell number?"

She laughed. "Lena put on a nice show on the table at the bar." Avalanche. "She also knocked over numerous drinks. Pretty easy to snag a phone for a second when she has everyone's attention. Stupid bitch got us kicked out of your condo. This would've been much easier if she hadn't."

I pressed my weight onto the counter then slipped my hand into my pocket and curled my hand around the gun. "Who are you? How do you know me?" It wasn't fear I felt it was the drum of anger pulsing through me.

"Shut up. No more talking. Listen clearly to my instructions. You didn't do that very well before, fighting them all the time." What did she mean? I didn't even know who the hell she was. "That bodyguard is watching. Smile at him for me." I jerked, looking around as I realized she could see me. "Smile, bitch, or I press 'send' on my phone and pictures of you naked from the club go viral. And I have to say, none of them are flattering."

"What?" My stomach flipped. That was impossible.

"Shut up," she yelled. "You're going to complain of severe head pain to the nurse in front of you. Tell her you need to lie down. If you do anything other than what I tell you, I press 'send.'"

I could signal Roman, but Lily obviously had eyes on me. Would she do it? Yes. There was nothing for her to lose and everything for me. But I didn't care about me; I cared what pictures of me would do to Ream, Crisis, and the band. She had to be lying. How could she find pictures of me? I'd never seen her at the club.

"The car accident? It was you."

"You were supposed to overdose on heroin that night at the condo, but you had to go freak out and get me kicked out. Over what? Poor Haven. Precious Haven. The girl every man wanted at the club."

"I don't even know you."

"No, of course you don't. You were like a fucking queen. You had the wealthiest men, made the most money, had a private room away from all the other girls. Olaf's girl."

"I was raped," I seethed.

The nurse at the desk looked up at me and frowned. The anger pulsed through me. She was jealous. Jealous? I was raped every Saturday night for years.

I searched the nurses walking around, trying to see if any of them were Lily. Where the hell was she? She had to have a phone and she could see me.

"Enough. Do what I tell you."

Like hell. I needed to keep her talking while I tried to find her.

"How did you find me?"

She laughed and I quickly looked around the room trying to find someone laughing. I saw Roman frowned when he caught my expression, but I gave a tentative smile. If he came over now, she'd post the picture then escape before we even had a chance to stop her. I had to get eyes on her first.

"Why do you think you were kept separate from everyone else? Twin sister of the famous Ream from Tear Asunder." They knew? Everyone at the club knew and no one helped me? God, it was sickening. "Then you went and ruined everything. You couldn't just leave the club and let us be. I was the Saturday night girl after you left. Me. I went for the most money until that fucking guy came and shut it down . . . Now, I have nothing."

Vic. And he'd been trying to find all the girls. Lily had been one of them, but by the sounds of it, she'd been there willingly.

"Stupid bitch. Stop delaying and do what I told you." I heard her. She was somewhere to my left. "Now."

I curled my hand around my gun and took a deep breath as I placed the phone on the cradle. I straightened and put my hand to my temple. "Nurse, is there anywhere I can lie down? My vision is a little foggy and my head is throbbing."

She stood, her eyes widening as she rushed to her feet. "Yes. Of course."

I glanced to my left as the nurse came around the desk and took my arm. Roman was striding toward me from the other direction.

"Haven? You okay?" he called.

Then I saw her. I let the nurse guide me toward a room as Lily pushed a supply cart toward me.

The nurse had the door to the room open and was urging me inside. "Miss, you can lie down in here."

I didn't move.

Lily frowned and stopped with the cart. She reached into her upper pocket of her nurse's uniform and took out her cell phone and gestured with her head to the room she wanted me to go in.

I didn't do what she wanted. I'd never do anything I didn't want to again.

Fuck her.

I pulled my gun from my hoody and pointed it at her. Her eyes flickered to it and I heard the gasp of the nurse who held the room door open.

"Fuck, Haven?" Roman said from somewhere behind me. "What are you doing?"

People noticed I was holding a gun pointed at a nurse and screamed, diving for cover in rooms. Lily didn't. She stood unflinching, staring back at me.

I saw movement behind Lily as Luke came out of a room down the hall, gun drawn. He must have heard the screams. He moved closer while Crisis, Logan and Ream all came out of the room and stopped, looking from me to my gun, to the nurse I was aimed at.

She tossed her phone on the cart. She obviously didn't have any pictures.

Lily smiled and that's when I knew she wasn't too concerned about whether she lived or died. Her whole purpose was to make sure I didn't. According to her, she had nothing left. I'd ruined everything for her.

It happened so fast that I didn't even know what hit me as Lily pulled a gun from the cart. I heard movement from behind me then Crisis' agonizing shout as a searing pain went through me seconds before I crashed to the floor.

Chapter Thirty-Two

Crisis

"NOOO." I SHOUTED as I ran toward her, shock and horror ripping through me. Everything was in slow motion, my legs couldn't move fast enough, taking me what felt like hours to reach her, but knowing it was seconds.

Ream ran, too. Her name repeated over and over even as we both crashed to our knees beside her. Roman was still on top of her, his body a protective shield as several more shots rang out. I didn't know where they came from, who was shot, what happened. The only image was of Haven's body jerking back from the impact of the bullet then Roman throwing himself on top of her and both dropping to the floor.

"Fuck. Baby. Baby," I cried as I fell to my knees beside her. Roman rolled off her and my heart lodged in my throat like a boulder, strangling me. "No. Baby. No." There was blood all over her sweatshirt, the red slowly spreading like a spider's web.

"Get a doctor," Ream shouted. "Now."

My mind was a haze of agonizing fear as I reached for her. Her eyes were closed, hair a curtain lying across her mouth then down to her shoulder, the tips now laying over her wound and soaked with blood. When I picked her up in my arms, her head fell back, limp as if . . . No. No. She wasn't dead. She couldn't be dead.

"Baby. Baby. Please, baby." I ran with her to a gurney and placed her on it.

She wasn't moving. She wasn't fuckin' moving.

Was she breathing? I couldn't tell with her sweatshirt.

"Out of the way," a man shouted.

I knew there were people all around me, someone tried to push me aside and I grabbed for her hand. It lay cold and lifeless in mine and terror gripped me like a dark suffocating blanket.

"Let her go, sir. You need to let her go," a female said.

I was running alongside the gurney, latched onto Haven's hand. I didn't even know I was running. All I saw was Haven unmoving, her lips slightly parted, her grey eyes hidden.

"Both of you, please, you have to let her go."

A hand came own on my shoulder. "Let her go."

I couldn't tear my eyes away from her enough to look at him, but I knew it was Logan. "I can't." I was terrified if I did, I'd never see her again. "I fuckin' can't."

"Vincent," Ream said. He was on the other side of the gurney, his face as devastated as I was sure mine was. "They'll save her."

It was then I noticed a nurse beside him, her gloved hands covered in blood as she pressed on Haven's shoulder. She met my eyes and there was sympathy in their green depths. "I'll take care of her."

The gurney started moving again, and each of my fingers slid down her palm then off the tips of her fingers. I watched her disappear behind the swinging doors, Ream beside me.

Anguish and staggering disbelief collided. It was an explosion detonating with the numb cold silence of shock. I didn't know which to grab hold of. Which was safer.

But the reality was if I lost Haven, I'd shatter and my pieces would be lost.

Head bowed, I sat beside Ream, arms resting on my thighs, and hands clasped, hanging between my legs. I hadn't moved in an hour as I waited for someone to walk back out the double doors where Haven had disappeared through.

There were police officers everywhere, talking to Luke, Roman, and Vic, who showed up and took control of the scene. A perimeter was taped off so the police could investigate Lily's death and what had occurred. Statements were taken from witnesses and we'd given ours, but I couldn't even recall what I'd said.

A gurney passed by us with a body—Lily's body.

The girl who shot Haven. Luke had taken her down from behind.

My head dropped lower as my gut twisted at the thought. She'd been in our condo. She'd almost fucked Kite.

Jesus.

I'd been told who she was, but I couldn't even decipher who told me; my mind refused to take in anything beside the continuous replay of Haven getting shot and falling.

"You really love her," Ream said.

I continued to stare at the beige linoleum floor. "Yeah." It was barely a whisper.

"It's like it's happening all over again." I knew what he was talking about. When he was sixteen, he brought Haven to the hospital after overdosing, and she never came back through the doors. "I can't go through that again."

I saw movement from the corner of my eye and Kat was beside him, reaching for his hand and linking their fingers.

"She's strong," I said. And that was what I had to hold onto. Haven wouldn't give up. She'd fight. For years, she'd fought and never given up. She wouldn't now. She'd keep her promise to herself and find normal.

Our normal. Mine and hers.

Maybe it was the shift in air as the double doors swung open.

Maybe it was the creak of the orange plastic chairs as everyone tensed. Whatever it was, I knew it was the doctor, who had taken Haven away, who strode toward us. I looked up for the first time in an hour.

It was going to be devastation or relief the moment I saw his face. He wouldn't have to say anything and all of us would know.

There was silence as if all the commotion around us stalled for the moments between raising my head and seeing the doctor's expression.

Then a tear escaped to trail down my cheek as I locked eyes on him and saw his smile.

Chapter Thirty-Three

Haven

One month later

HE STALKED TOWARD me, the casual swagger lighting the spark of desire to a firestorm of heat. I ducked left, then went right, my feet splashing through the water as I took off running.

We were in Fiji on one of the islands, a private ten-acre resort that was surrounded by the lush tropics. There were sixteen villas, which were built into the vegetation, each overlooking the ocean. Crisis had booked the entire resort and then invited everyone to come with us.

The media frenzy had lasted a couple of weeks, but we'd gone to the farm and avoided most of it. Kite spoke to reporters when he came out of the hospital and the fans were more focused on him than the story of me.

Of course, there were reports about the shooting at the hospital, but our involvement was kept quiet. The story was spun that a girl, Lily Hendrik, went on a shooting spree in the hospital and I was shot.

My association with Lily remained concealed and I suspected it had to do with Vic.

The wet sand squished between my toes as I ran as hard and fast as I could. My heart raced and my body tingled with anticipation of him catching me. Because he would. I was fast and could run far, but he was faster with his long lean legs, which covered the ground quicker than mine.

I thought of when he'd chased me in the thunderstorm. It seemed so long ago and so much had changed. Now, I wanted him to catch me, but I was never one to make anything easy for him.

The tide washed up on shore and sloshed against my calves. I was already soaking wet after the two hours spent in the water with him. He'd insisted on teaching me how to swim, and it was frustrating because a half-naked Crisis was hard to resist. And he was serious and kept having to unwrap my arms from around his neck. Eventually, he threatened to put his cock on hiatus if I didn't follow instructions.

Empty threat. No way would he do that, but I knew he wanted me to learn to swim, so I let him teach me.

I heard his feet gaining on me and put more effort in as I headed to our villa. As I left the beach, the deeper sand slowed me down.

"Oh, baby, you like games? Because I excel at them and never lose."

I was breathing hard. It wasn't far, but running as fast as I could in the sand was hard. "Bullshit." I was saying Bullshit, the card game, because I beat him at that.

Hitting the sandy grass at the bottom of our villa that overlooked the beach, I scrambled up the wooden stairs. I heard him right behind me and started taking the stairs two at a time. He did too.

Just as my foot hit the deck, his arm hooked my waist and I was running, but not going anywhere, as he lifted me right off my feet. His breath was harsh and ragged as he breathed against my neck.

"I'm thinking I should have taken you somewhere cold, not the South Pacific. Watching you run in a bikini and chasing you, with my cock hard as fuck . . . painful." I stopped struggling then turned in his arms and slid down his wet hard body.

I stood on my tiptoes, my hand reaching around his neck to drag him down to my mouth. "I love that you brought me here." It was my Christmas present, but really it was his, too. It was ours.

Crisis walked me backwards until my ass pressed against the railing. "Going to fuck you now. That okay with you?"

I bit my lip and nodded. He liked to do that, ask me. It just became his thing and I think it was to give him assurance that I was good with it, because once I said yes, there was no stopping him.

He hitched me up on the railing and I curled my legs around him. "I hope your parents don't decide to stop by."

He chuckled while he undid the bikini strap at the nape of my neck and it fell forward. "Have they yet?" No, and we'd been here three days. "Mom knows better than that. The damage it would do to her to see me eating you out."

"Oh, my God." I didn't even want to imagine it.

He ran a finger down between my breasts and I shuddered. He leaned in and nuzzled my neck and my fingers curled into his hair as I tilted my head back. "Don't worry, baby. Our villa is off-limits. Why do you think Luke and Roman came with us?"

"I thought you wanted them to have a vacation. I mean, Roman did save my life and Luke killed Lily." The bullet hit my shoulder, but it could've easily been my chest if Roman hadn't dove on top of me. I'd been knocked unconscious by the impact as my head hit the tile, but unconscious was better than dead.

"Vacation?" Crisis laughed as he unsnapped the back of my bikini and tossed it to one of chaise lounges. "Fuck that. They're here to make sure no one comes near our villa while I'm fucking my girl."

He nipped my neck then trailed kisses up to my mouth. I moaned when his mouth crushed mine, both hands cupping either side of my head and he took what I'd given him. Me. Every part of me he knew, the bad, the good, the tainted, and there wasn't a moment I wondered if he accepted all of them.

He did.

"Fuck, Haven," he mumbled against my mouth. "I love you." He picked me up off the railing. Without taking his mouth from mine, he lowered me onto the lounge chair. He broke away for a second and ripped off his shorts. "Lift." He had his hands on my bikini bottoms and slowly slid them down.

That had been a point of contention. With the tickets for my Christmas present was the bikini, one that was bright pink and left little to the imagination.

Of course, I refused to wear it, and wanted to go pick out a one piece. He'd been too accommodating and I should've known. We went and picked out a black one piece that wasn't sexy, but simple. I liked it. He said it was fine for a nun, but he let me have it.

It never made it to the island. I dumped all my clothes from the suitcase the first day and it was gone. Crisis had been standing on the other side of the room with those dimples and brilliant blue eyes blazing with mischief. Then he pulled the pink one from his suitcase and tossed the two pieces to me.

"I want you to wear it." Then he strode over to me and crouched as I sat on the floor, clothes all around me. "Please. It's sexy as hell on you and this will be the only vacation that I don't have to worry about other men eyeing up my girl."

So, I gave him that because I loved him . . . well, and he'd said please, then made love to me on the floor.

I parted my legs as soon as the bikini bottoms slipped off my feet and he crawled up the lounge chair. Butterflies lifted, goose bumps sparked and between my legs clenched just before his mouth kissed my inner thigh.

My breath hitched as his tongue slid over me. "Jesus, you're wet."

"I was in the water."

He lifted his head and grinned, his finger replacing his tongue as he trailed it down between my lips. "Oh baby, I know you're wet for me. I know how you taste on the tip of my tongue. I know how you feel on my finger. And my cock . . ." He sat back and took hold of himself. It was throbbing and ready. "It sure as fuck knows."

I raised my brows. "And what does your cock say right now?"

He shimmied up closer, his weight on his arms on either side of my head. Then he lowered his weight on top of me and my hand went into his hair while the other went to his ass and squeezed.

He had the best ass and I took to touching it whenever I could. There were definitely no complaints from him except when he was trying to teach me how to swim.

The tip of his cock was between my legs and I lifted my hips to meet him. He groaned, and before I could get my legs around his waist, he was inside me and his mouth was against mine at the same time.

Then he made me his, like he always did. Not that I was anything but. It was a carnal connection that released when we came together. It was an inferno of desire that thrummed through both of us, but it was also the rare beauty of peace and tranquility.

He made love to me in the chaise lounge, then I made love to him until we saw the sun lower over the horizon.

He leapt to his feet. "Babe, we have to go." Grabbing my hand, he hauled me to my feet and pulled me into the bedroom that was open to the deck. Its sheer white curtains lightly swayed in the warm breeze.

I went into the bathroom, washed my face then put on mascara and lip gloss. I took my dress off the hanger on the back of the door and slipped it over my head, then did up the tiny buttons in the front. There wasn't much I could do about my hair, so I loosely put it back in a messy clip.

When I came out of the bathroom, he was already dressed in a pair of charcoal gray linen pants and a white short-sleeved shirt. His hair was untidy and exactly how I loved it. He looked sexy as hell and I was thinking about undressing him slowly.

His eyes roamed over my outfit from top to bottom. I noticed he lingered on my thighs, he loved my thighs. "Ice, you can't wear shit like that and seriously expect me to keep my cock in my pants."

Laughing, I walked up to him and put my arms around his neck. I was wearing a white sundress with spaghetti straps, and a tight bodice that flowed into a mid-thigh simple skirt. It wasn't revealing, but I was getting that any dress I wore, he thought was sexy as hell on me. Rarely did we make it to wherever we were going without the dress coming off me first, making us always late.

I leaned against him and his hard cock pressed into me. "Then don't," I whispered into his ear.

He groaned and put his hands under my ass. "Love you hair like that, baby."

I smiled. "Does it look like I just had sex?"

"Fuck yeah. But they all know that's what we've been doing since we arrived, so no point hiding it."

"Want to be late?" I urged.

"No," he growled. "For once in my life, I'm not being late. Not to this."

I didn't pout because . . . well, I didn't pout—ever, but I did run my fingers up through his hair and gave an exaggerated sigh. He got that annoyed crease between his eyes and I leaned forward and kissed it. "Okay. But know I'm really wet and it isn't from the water."

He growled. "Let's go."

He latched onto my hand. His determination was kind of cute; instead of him being the one to delay and not worrying about keeping others waiting, it was me. And I wasn't necessarily delaying. I was soaking up every moment in order to put into the compartments and be able to open and enjoy the memories anytime I wanted.

"The sun isn't going to wait for us," he said as he led me through the bedroom.

The warm breeze sifted through the open doors. It was filled with the warmth and love that surrounded me. Not just Vincent's, but his family's . . . my family's.

I stopped to peer into the mirror at the dresser.

"Haven. You're perfect. You're my perfect." He smirked. "And I'm yours."

I bent down to grab my sandals when he tugged, throwing me off balance so I landed in his arms. "Barefoot baby. And soon pregnant if I have any say about it."

My heart skipped a beat at the thought; we'd decided not to use condoms anymore, so that was a possibility, although I was clear that even if I did get pregnant, I was finishing school. He was good with that. He knew how important it was for me to get a degree.

Our argument had been over him wanting to buy out Kite so we could have the condo to ourselves. Of course, I was uncomfortable with him paying for everything and I had nothing to contribute.

I had a feeling though that Kite would move out soon anyway. I'd noticed he never brought chicks home anymore and I guessed it was because of what happened with Lily and me.

Crisis had proposed to me two days after I was shot in the hospital. I'd had years stolen from me and I wasn't wasting what I was gifted. And he was a gift. I loved him. He was my best friend and my lover.

I smiled, reaching up and cupping his cheek and he leaned toward me, his brilliant blue eyes dancing with playfulness. "Then we better go get married first."

"Fuck yeah."

Then he picked me up, threw me over his shoulder and jogged down to the beach where his parents, Ream and Kat, her brother Matt, Kite, Logan, Emily, Isabelle, Dana and Dillon, all waited. Luke and Roman stood on the outskirts, but I was glad they were there, too. The only two missing were Deck and Georgie, who, according to Vic, declined the invitation; they were on an extended vacation.

Crisis carried me to the altar, and I heard a few chuckles at our grand entrance. Then he slid me down his body to my feet, rested one hand on my hip, the other on my ass and kissed me. It wasn't a gentle kiss. It was deep, dirty and sexy and without a hint of concern that everyone was watching.

"Are we doing the ceremony backwards today, young man?" the officiant said.

We separated, although not by much. Our lips merely unlocked. Then Vincent 'Crisis' Wesson married me as the sun went down on the beach, barefoot with our family around us.

The End

To the readers,

Thank you for reading *'Shattered by You.'* I hope you enjoyed Crisis and Haven's story. I'd love to hear your thoughts and opinions, so please if you have a moment leave a review. Your feedback is very helpful and appreciated.

I'm humbled by the kindness readers have shown me since the beginning of this series. Thank you is never enough, but know that it means the world to me.

Hugs,

Nash XO

About the Author

Nashoda Rose is a New York Times and USA Today bestselling author who lives in Toronto with her assortment of pets. She writes contemporary romance with a splash of darkness, or maybe it's a tidal wave.

When she isn't writing, she can be found sitting in a field reading with her dogs at her side while her horses graze nearby. She loves interacting with her readers and chatting about her addiction—books.

Books by Nashoda Rose

Seven Sixes (2016)

Tear Asunder series
With You (free novella)
Torn from You
Overwhelmed by You
Shattered by You
Untitled (Kite's Story)

Unyielding Series
Perfect Chaos
Perfect Ruin (Fall/Winter 2015)
Perfect Rage (Date TBA)

Scars of the Wraith Series
Stygian
Take (standalone)

Where to find Nash:

Goodreads link:
https://www.goodreads.com/author/show/7246093.Nashoda_Rose

Facebook:
https://www.facebook.com/pages/Nashoda-Rose/564276203633318

Website: http://nashodarose.com/

Instagram : https://instagram.com/nashodarose/

Email: nashodarose@gmail.com

UNYIELDING BOOK 1

Georgie

I SMOOTHED OUT THE wrinkles on my bedspread then placed my stuffed brown bunny rabbit against the white-and-pink flowered throw pillow. At sixteen, I was a little old for stuffed animals, but it had been a gift from my brother the first time he went away to Afghanistan with the military.

I straightened, then saw the sheet hanging down in the right corner and quickly tucked it back into the mattress. Perfect. I liked . . . no, I was obsessed with being organized. Everything had its place, even me. I kept to the same bland, colorless clothes, the same schedule, and the same hair style. Why mess with what worked? My brother often teased me and said I should join the Canadian forces like him. I may like neat and tidy, but I hated fighting, blood, guns, and, unquestionably, any killing.

Connor knew that. He'd helped me bury my goldfish, Goldie, in the backyard when I was seven, then the hamster, Fiddlehead, when I was ten. To this day, there is a marked stone Connor had made for him near the back fence. I could see it whenever I looked out the kitchen

292

window.

I jerked as a car door slammed, which sounded as if it was in our driveway. The sun had just peeked over the horizon; six in the morning was too early for any visitors, plus it was Sunday and Dad had the rule he and Mom sleep in. I always rose early wanting to get ahead of the day, another reason Connor said I'd excel in the military. Although, we both knew he'd never allow me anywhere near danger, which I was very content with. Danger to me was if my shampoo was missing and I had to use my brother's instead.

But Connor wasn't due back for another month, so that meant . . . A sudden freeze hit my body, locking my limbs in place as I realized why someone might be in our driveway at six in the morning on a Sunday. My breath trapped in my throat as if clamped hands were strangling me.

No.

No. I shook my head back and forth. *Please, don't knock.*

It was the newspaper boy. Early. He was an hour early today. In a second, I'd hear the clang as the newspaper bundle hit the metal screen door.

Eyes squeezed tightly shut, I waited for the familiar sound.

Nothing. I sucked in large amounts of air for my starved lungs.

Not him. Please, not him.

Connor.

Connor.

My heart thumped harder and harder in its cage and tears pooled in my eyes. I couldn't hear his footsteps, but I knew his team leader's black combat boots were walking up the stone path toward the house.

I can't lose him. Please.

Run.

Run and it won't be true.

But I couldn't move. My legs were locked in place as I waited for the nightmare to begin.

Thump.

Thump.

Thump.

It was as if each knock was a punch to the stomach. No air. I couldn't breathe. I was silently screaming and nothing could stop the fear gripping my insides.

Please. No. I need him.

I heard my parents' bedroom door open and the shuffling of feet down the hallway on the hardwood floors. The distinct click as the lock turned and then the front door opened, followed by the screech of the screen door.

Then silence.

It felt like hours as I stood in the middle of my room, afraid to look out the window and see the car I didn't want to see. Afraid to run. Afraid to move. Hoping I was still asleep and this was all a dream.

Yes, it was a dream. I'd wake up any second. I'd call Connor today. I'd tell him how much I missed him and loved him. It had been weeks since we last spoke. I should've emailed him more often. Why hadn't I?

My mother's loud wail pierced the air, and my perfect world crashed to my feet. It was like I was being coiled in the death grip of an anaconda and dragged under the water.

I fell to my knees, my arms wrapped around myself, and I rocked back and forth as my mother's cries became muffled as if she was being held against something.

There were more footsteps. Not quiet and soft like my mom's. Not slow and lumbering like my dad's. Long, confident strides.

No. Go away. Just go away. It's not real.

The steps stopped outside my door, and I heard the click as the door handle turned. It was opening my soul and ripping out my heart.

I stopped rocking.

The door swung open.

I clamped my eyes shut, not wanting to see him. Unable to face him, face what he was here to tell me.

"Georgie."

Deck's gruff tone, I'd recognize anywhere. It scared me. *He* scared me but what scared me more was my body's reaction to him. The strange tingling between my legs, the warmth on my skin and the whirling in my stomach as if I was falling from the sky.

I sniffled as my nose dripped, and I felt the trickle of tears slip from the corners of my eyes.

"Look at me, Georgie." If I ignored him, it would all go away. "Georgie."

It was the hint of softness in his voice when he said my name which had me opening my eyes.

My gaze hit his legs first, the long, lean length covered in black cargo pants. There was a rip in the material just above his knee. Dirt. Smudges of dirt on his pants as if he'd come straight from whatever hell they'd been in.

They. In a second, the word *they* wouldn't exist anymore.

My gaze moved upward, hesitant, as if my brain was fighting every step. His hands were curled into fists at his sides, his knuckles strong notches which had felt the harshness of pounding into another man. It was odd because his hands were clean, and yet I saw the dirt on his tatted arms and the . . . blood? Was it his blood or—

"Georgie."

The loud, abrupt sound of my name made me lurch and my gaze flew to his.

His jaw was tense. Eyes hard and cold—unemotional. He looked directly at me, not an ounce of compassion in his unyielding stare. But I saw other things. There beneath his stoic solidity . . . the torment, the pain, the darkness which was soon going to become my own.

I started shaking violently, and my throat tightened against the sobs that racked my body. "No." It was the only word I could get out.

Please, no.

He stood and watched me tremble and cry on my knees in the middle of my room for several minutes before he said, "I couldn't save him."

His words cut into me with the finality of the truth, and my breath hitched as more tears pooled and slipped from the confines of my eyelids. I tightened my arms around my body as if that would help the pain ease.

It didn't.

Nothing would.

Connor.

He was gone.

I'd never hear his teasing. Feel the touch of his hand ruffling my hair. Hear his voice calling me 'Georgie Girl.'

He promised to come back.

Pain.

Hurt.

Devastation.

'Chaos.'

My head screamed with anarchy as Connor's image played across my mind. It was distorted and broken with bits of light being sucked apart by the darkness.

Destruction. I had to destroy. My perfect world was no longer. Nothing would ever be the same again. I'd never be the same again.

I scrambled to my feet, grabbed my duvet and tore it off the bed, the flowered throw pillow and bunny tossed to the floor. A strange sound emerged from my throat as I dove for my dresser and swept my arm across the shiny, neat surface—books, my jewelry box, and a vase crashed to the hardwood floor. I could hear glass shattering, and silver stud earrings, pearls, and rings scattered in every direction.

I didn't stop. I couldn't.

Destruction.

I grabbed my light off my nightstand and threw it across the room. The bulb made a loud pop as it hit the wall. I needed to destroy. Everything I'd made into a neat and tidy place was no longer. It was all gone. Nothing would be perfect again. My world had just burst open, and I was bleeding. It hurt. God, it hurt.

I tripped over my duvet as I went for the closet and fell to my knees. It didn't stop me . . . the physical pain was nothing, almost welcoming to the emotional pain taking me apart piece by piece. I got up, then staggered to the closet and threw open the doors.

I wrenched my clothes off the hangers—the pretty, soft-yellow dresses, white ones, black ones. Then the plain, button-down blouses and the black pants. The empty hangers swung back and forth on the metal bar as every single piece of clothing was thrown to the floor. When the closet was empty, I picked up whatever was in reach and began tearing. Buttons popped. Silk and nylon tore, sleeves ripped from the cores—like me. This was me being shredded apart.

Carelessly, I yanked and pulled at whatever my hands could get a hold of.

Rip.

Tear.

Ruin everything. Destroy.

I was breathing hard when I finished. Nothing was left alive. Just like me. I had nothing left except to run.

Run.

Run.

Run.

I ran for the door. I couldn't breathe. I had to get out of here. Away from this ruined perfect world. He was gone. Connor was gone.

My mind was whirling and frantic.

Escape.

I didn't even see him; my vision blurred from tears and anger and pain. He blocked the doorway, his broad frame preventing my path of escape.

I ran anyway, trying to dive past him.

He snagged me around the waist with one arm and my feet left the floor. I screamed and squirmed in his hold like a rag doll. He set me down directly in front of him, his hands latched onto my upper arms in a bruising grip.

"Georgie, look at me."

I kicked and yelled, trying to leave, but nothing would set me free. I knew I'd never be free again. My brother. My best friend. He was dead.

"Let me go. Let me go. Let me go."

Run. Get away.

"Look. At. Me."

This time his voice cut through my hysterical need to escape, and I stopped struggling, staring up at his unflinching eyes. How could he just stand there? He'd just destroyed my life, my family's life. And he was standing there looking at me without a trace of sympathy.

"I hate you."

"You going to stand still?"

Chest heaving and heart pounding, I realized Deck had watched me destroy everything in my room. He never did anything to stop it. The one thing I did know about this man was that he was unbending. Connor always said Deck was the best team leader, because no matter what shit went down, Deck would never yield to anyone. He'd stand by his word no matter what, and I guessed he wouldn't let me go until I bent to his will.

I stopped fighting.

He waited a second then released me. He reached into his back pocket and pulled out a small, leather-bound book with worn edges and a cracked spine. "He'd want you to have this."

I didn't move as I stared at what I knew was Connor's journal. Deck grabbed my wrist and shoved it in my hand, the hard surface abruptly hitting my palm.

Connor's name was written on the top in his familiar, messy hand-writing.

I nearly fell, and probably would've if Deck hadn't grabbed my arm. He guided me further into my room, and I didn't object. All I did was stare down at the bound book. The last piece of my brother. It wasn't enough. It would never be enough.

I felt the softness of the mattress as Deck made me sit, and then the floor creaked as he started to walk away.

I looked up at the retreating figure. "I wish it was you, not him."

He gave no reaction to my words, and really, I hadn't expected any. It just came out. And I did hate that Deck was here instead of Connor. I hated that he could walk back to his family and laugh and hold them and my brother couldn't.

He turned his head and met my eyes. For a second, I thought I witnessed remorse, but it was so quick I could've imagined it or maybe I hoped to see it from my brother's best friend.

"Yeah." His whispered tone was barely audible as the door shut, and I listened to his steady, booted steps walk away.

The front door opened, and the screen door screeched. Both shut.

I had no idea why I did it, but I walked over to the window, parted the white sheer curtains and watched as he walked down the path. The tension in his back. The stiffness of his stride.

He stopped at the side of the car and stood still for a second. I couldn't see his face or what he was doing until he slammed both fists into the roof of the car. Then his head dropped forward and his shoulders slouched.

My fingers curled around the delicate material of the curtains, and I didn't realize how hard until they ripped from the rod and fell to the floor, leaving the window bare.

As if he'd heard it—but I knew that was impossible—Deck turned. Our eyes locked. It felt like he could see right into me with that direct gaze. I felt naked and vulnerable, unable to look away, trapped. He gave me these wounds. Wounds that would never heal. Deck was now part of the darkness inside me I'd never escape from.

His nod was barely distinguishable before he broke the connection and opened the car door.

I watched his lean form curl into the driver's seat.

The engine came to life with a loud purr.

Life. Something Connor had lost.

I turned away just as I heard the squeal of the tires on the street.

My perfect world had just been thrown into destructive chaos.

With You (now free)

A New York Times and USA Today Bestseller.

Sculpt is an illegal fighter.
He's also the lead singer of a local rock band.
No one knows his real name.
And from the moment I met him, he made me forget mine.

In order to convince Sculpt to give me self-defense lessons, I had to follow his one rule—no complaining or he'd walk. I didn't think it would be a problem. I could handle a few bruises. What I hadn't anticipated was landing on my back with Sculpt on top of me and my entire body burning up for him.

I tried to ignore it.

I failed of course. And having a hot, tattooed badass on top of me week after week, acting completely immune to what he was doing to me—it was frustrating as hell, so I broke his rule—I complained.

Then he kissed me.

Warning: Please be aware, this novella leads into a very DARK Romance. 18+

Huge cliff-hanger. Like huge! However, "Torn from You" the novel is released.

*Due to sexual content and strong language not recommended for readers under 18.

Torn from You

USA Today Bestseller.

Love is like an avalanche. It hits hard, fast and without mercy.

At least it did for me when Sculpt, the lead singer of the rock band Tear Asunder knocked me off my feet. Literally, because he's also a fighter, illegally of course, and he taught me how to fight. He also taught me how to love and I fell hard for him. I mean the guy could do sweet, when he wasn't doing bossy, and I like sweet.

Then it all shattered.

Kidnapped.
Starved.
Beaten.
I was alone and fighting to survive.
When I heard Sculpt's voice, I thought he was there to save me.

I was wrong.

Overwhelmed by You
USA Today Bestseller

Love is ugly and secrets will destroy you.

KAT

I don't beg.
I don't cry.
And I don't give second chances.

Ream, the lead guitarist of the rock band Tear Asunder, deserves a gold medal for best dick move ever when he ran the moment he discovered my secret after two days of hot sex. Then he brings some chick to my coming home party from the hospital—after being shot.

I hate him.
Until . . .

Ream's six foot two frame unfolds out of the car after being gone on tour for eight months. I stared. And in my defense, any girl would stare. It would almost be rude not to because Ream was the type of guy who stood out. Not because he was loud and obnoxious. No, it was because he was the complete opposite. Subtle and dangerously quiet. If he spoke, you'd better hope he liked you because otherwise you'd be falling at his feet begging for mercy. Except me . . . I don't beg—ever.

But when our eyes locked, it was Ream's steady confidence that had my nerves shooting off like jet sprinklers.

Then . . .

Ream told me he didn't need a second chance because he was still working on his first.

REAM

Sex is ugly. It's using someone for your own narcissistic pleasure. I did it, but hated it—until her. She was unfuckinexpected. Then I had to wreck our beginning with my screwed up past. I don't deserve her, but I'm selfish and I'm taking her anyway. This is who I am and it's too late to change me.

Warning contains violence, sexual content, and coarse language. Some scenes may be triggers. Mature audiences 18+

Take (Scars of the Wraiths)

MAX

Feelings are a luxury I can't afford. Hidden behind a shield of quiet placidity, I keep my secret safe from those who'd use it against me. Until him—the tatted up, self-centered Scar assassin hired to protect me.

He takes pleasure in tormenting me, chipping away at my defenses as if I'm a toy to be played with. I hate that he continuously reminds me that I'm nothing more than a job. I hate that my body responds to his touch. **I hate him**.

JASPER

I'm not a good guy and I don't pretend to be. Condemn me if you want, I don't give a crap. You're nothing to me. No one is . . . except her—Max. She's my target. And I was hired to do a hell of a lot more than protect her . . . I was hired to kill her.

It should've been simple, but it was complicated as hell.

Full-length novel. Come meet the Scars.

Stygian (Scars of the Wraiths)

Danni

I remember nothing of my abduction two years ago. Sounds and scents trigger horrific flashes, but it's all a blur except for one man with brilliant green eyes. When the tatted six foot two Adonis shows up at my door, my knowledge of the world is shattered.

Bound to the immortal Scar by an ancient spell, we are on the run. Because Balen is the hunted.

And if he dies, so do I.

Balen: Scar

My code of honor was respected without question . . . until I consumed the blood of a vampire in exchange for a mortal woman's freedom.

The Scars want me imprisoned. The Wraiths want me dead.

But the woman I can't forget needs me. And I'll risk everything to protect her.

Even if it means killing her.

Because in order for her to live—first she must die.

Scars: Immortal warriors with capabilities derived from the senses: Trackers, Sounders, Healers, Tasters, Visionaries, and the rare Reflectors. They each have what is known as an Ink, a tattoo that can be called to life.

Made in the USA
Middletown, DE
08 October 2015